DRONE STRIKE

DAVID AUSTIN

Drone Strike is a work of fiction. Names, characters, places, and incidents are products of the author's imagination or are used fictitiously. Any resemblance to actual events, locales or persons, living or dead, is purely coincidental.

Copyright © 2020 by David Austin

All rights reserved

ISBN: 978-0-578-78913-2

ACKNOWLEDGEMENTS

I WANT TO start out by thanking my family for their never-ending encouragement. Writing is a time-consuming endeavor and they have never waned in their support for my desire to create these novels.

I also want to share my appreciation for Max and Claire Sutton, the two people who go over my manuscripts with a fine-toothed comb to correct my typos and ensure I'm not butchering the English language too badly. I've learned more about creative writing and grammar over the course of working with you on these two novels than I ever could in any classroom.

And last, but certainly not least, I want to thank all the readers out there. Your encouragement and interaction drive me forward. Without you, these characters and stories would be trapped in a document on my computer, never to see the light of day.

DRONE
STRIKE

CHAPTER 1

THE MUTED SOUNDS of gunfire, men yelling orders, and the severely wounded screaming in agony penetrated the consciousness of the man hanging upside down in the front passenger seat of the Toyota Hi-Lux pickup truck. A destroyed vehicle burned like an inferno no more than twenty meters away, causing a pleasant warmth to wash over the exposed skin of his head and arms as if he were sitting on a beach.

But even in his semi-conscious state, he knew that didn't make any sense. And as much as he would like to take the time to figure it out, something stirring deep within his psyche told him that was not an option. No, something wasn't right, and the fact that he couldn't put his finger on it unsettled him. Whatever it was, he had the sinking feeling he was supposed to be doing something about it. But that sure as hell wasn't going to happen while he sat there contemplating his situation.

"Come on! Wake the fuck up and get your shit together!" He wondered if the sound of his voice was in his head or if he had actually said the words out loud? At the end of the day, it didn't really matter. What did matter was that he followed his own advice and got off his ass.

As he willed himself awake, the world outside the truck's cab grew louder as his hearing began returning to normal. The intensity of the automatic weapons fire and the explosions of hand grenades and RPGs grew as if someone had turned the volume all the way up on the opening scene of Saving Private Ryan.

Desperate to get a handle on what was going on, he forced his eyes to open. At first, he couldn't see much of anything, his vision obscured by a cloud of dust, sand, and smoke floating through the interior of the cabin. A gentle breeze wafting through the truck's shattered windows cleared the haze and he was confused more than ever by what he saw. He closed his eyes and vigorously shook his head back and forth to try to clear his vision. It didn't do any good. When he reopened them, the scene unfolding around him seemed more bizarre than ever.

What the hell? he thought, as a pair of scuffed combat boots raced past his head. They passed so close that he could have reached out and touched them. *Why am I upside down?* Glancing around the interior of the over-turned vehicle, he felt utterly alone…until he heard someone behind him calling his name.

"Dammit, Joe!" the voice yelled. "Wake up! We've gotta get out of here!"

He tried to turn around to see who was there, but the seatbelt digging into his lap and left shoulder was doing its job and held him securely in place. Straining against the taut fabric, he was able to turn his head just enough to see a man's face staring back at him. The sight instantly cleared the fog and the reality of their predicament crystallized in his mind.

Under the cover of darkness, Joe Matthews and his team of paramilitary operations officers had driven a pair of Toyota Hi-Lux pickup trucks a hundred and fifty kilometers across the Jordanian desert. They had entered Syria's southern province of al-Suweida on a track that was little more than a goat path running through an uninhabited and unguarded stretch of the border.

His five-man team was in the middle of a sixty-day rotation on the CIA's Protective Resource Group, a unit whose primary mission was to protect Agency officers in high-risk locations around the world. Based out of the embassy in Amman, Jordan, tonight's mission involved supporting a case officer named Greg Jacobs on a cross-border operation into Syria. They were there to conduct a clandestine meeting with an asset who claimed to have information on the Syrian government's stockpile of chemical weapons.

Since the civil war began in 2011, the United Nations and the Organization for the Prohibition of Chemical Weapons had accused Syria's president of using sarin and chlorine gas against his own citizens and the rebels fighting to overthrow his regime. As a result, UN and OPCW inspectors had mounted an operation in 2013 to locate and destroy Syria's chemical arsenal. The effort was deemed a success at the time, but evidence emerged in the ensuing years that the regime had used the poison gas once again.

Renewed use of the banned weapons meant Syria had either re-started their production program or possessed stockpiles that had not been discovered during previous inspections. Russia, arguably Syria's most powerful ally in the conflict, had used its vote on the UN Security Council nearly a dozen times to veto resolutions that would have renewed investigations into the use of the illegal weapons.

The CIA was hoping tonight's mission would be a redemption of sorts after their mistaken analysis of Saddam Hussein's WMD capability. The invasion of Iraq and the mismanagement of the war's aftermath were behind much of the turmoil currently taking place throughout the Middle East.

Iraq's deterioration in the wake of Saddam's fall, along with the civil war that erupted in Syria when the regime refused to capitulate during the Arab Spring, forced a collision of secular Syrians, homegrown Islamic extremists, and foreign jihadis. The chaos that spread across the region led to the rise of the cult-like organization called the Islamic State in Iraq and Syria, or ISIS.

Led by a black-clad fanatic named Abu Bakr al-Baghdadi, the group's goal was to establish a caliphate across the Middle East and return the region to a rule of Islamic law reminiscent of the fourteenth century. And it nearly succeeded. ISIS captured and held large swaths of land and declared the city of Raqqa, Syria, as its de facto capital. Eventually, Iraqi military units and a loose coalition of militias in Syria backed by the United States and a few other Western countries had managed to defeat ISIS and retake the captured land from the militants. In the ensuing chaos, the remnants of the Islamic State scattered, escaping to Libya and other lawless regions in turmoil across north Africa.

Even though Joe and the members of his team understood the rationale for tonight's mission, it did little to ease their concerns about a covert penetration deep into Syrian territory. The government in Damascus was battling the remnants of ISIS and rebel forces attempting to break the president's ironclad grip on the country. Meanwhile, Turkey was conducting cross-border strikes against U.S. backed Kurdish forces and a variety of antigovernment rebel militias. Iran, with the help of Hezbollah, their proxy based in Lebanon, was assisting Syrian military units while simultaneously building up resources and capabilities on Israel's northern border. Throw in the Russians, who were supporting the regime in Damascus while advancing their own agenda with Turkey and Iran, and an argument could be made that Syria was perhaps one of the most unpredictable and complex battlefields in the history of warfare.

Operating under these conditions, it would not be difficult at all to get yourself killed, or worse, captured, by the absurd number of opposing groups fighting in such close proximity to one another.

CHAPTER 2

THEIR INSERTION HAD gone off without a hitch, and that should have been the first indicator that Murphy's Law – if something could go wrong, it would – was going to come into play sooner rather than later. A flat tire or vehicle breakdown, a loss of comms with the drone circling overhead, or running into a random patrol were all well within the realm of possibility when old Mr. Murphy was involved.

As they entered the town of Salkhad, the team drove a predetermined route through the city, looking for any indication they were being followed or monitored by hostile surveillance. With businesses shuttered for the evening, and most everyone asleep at this late hour, there were few people on the streets. Anyone attempting to follow the Americans would have stuck out like a sore thumb. When Joe was confident they were clean, he gave the command and the two-vehicle motorcade headed to the designated meeting site atop the highest point in the city.

Built into the crater of an extinct volcano during the Ayyubid dynasty in the thirteenth century, the Salkhad Citadel protected Damascus from the threat of a Crusader attack from Jerusalem. The fortification was the prominent centerpiece of Salkhad, and over the years the town had gradually expanded outward around it. The fort had been under military control for decades but the government had only recently relinquished its authority over the site and allowed it to be open to the public, serving as an attraction of sorts – not that there were many tourists visiting Syria's historic sites these days.

Two entrances, one from the north and the other from the south accessed a perimeter road that encircled the site. Joe had chosen the south entrance and the team made their way to the parking lot midway up the volcano's escarpment. Backing their trucks into a dark space between a set of long rectangular ruins, the small CIA team melted into the shadows.

Joe Matthews, the team's leader and former member of the Army's Special Missions Unit, better known as Delta, or the Unit, was in the right front seat of the lead truck. His best friend, and former Navy SEAL Chris Ryan was in his usual position behind the wheel, and Greg Jacobs, the case officer from Amman station, was in the back seat.

Mike McCredy drove the second Toyota. Originally from Poughkeepsie, New York, he had joined the CIA after an unsuccessful tryout as a line-backer with the Buffalo Bills. John Roberts, the team's communication specialist, sat up front next to McCredy to monitor the radios, and Kevin Chang, a defensive tactics instructor and accomplished skier and snow-boarder from Vermont, rounded out the team.

Joe hit the push-to-talk button on his MBITR multiband radio. "Warrior One Seven, this is Spartan, over."

Warrior One Seven was the call sign of the man piloting the MQ-9 Reaper supporting tonight's mission. Medically retired from the Air Force after losing his right leg while ejecting from a doomed F-15, Travis Mullin found that flying UAVs for the CIA gave him the same sense of service to his country, albeit without the exhilaration of going full afterburners in the cockpit of a multimillion-dollar fighter.

"Good evening, Spartan. Comm link is good and I'm reading you five by five."

"Are you on station?"

"Doing lazy circles twenty-thousand feet above you as we speak," the pilot replied.

"Roger, that. See anything out of the ordinary?"

"Not unless you consider a team of Agency operators hunkered down on a Syrian hilltop a little unusual."

With the Reaper orbiting above using its electro-optical, infra-red cameras to keep an eye out for trouble, Joe had his men dismount. After a quick check of the area, they assumed defensive positions around their vehicles.

The team had only been in place for ten minutes or so when the drone pilot's voice came through their earpieces. "I've got a single vehicle heading your way. It's about a kilometer from the north gate."

Joe acknowledged the call and ensured each member of the team had heard it as well. "Heads up, boys. It's showtime." Then, he leaned in next to the case officer, and asked, "How reliable is this asset, Greg?"

"Tariq? He's about as good as we've got in Syria. His reporting has been spot-on since the beginning of the war."

Colonel Tariq Kabbani was an officer in the Internal Security Division of Syria's General Intelligence Directorate, or GID. The unit's primary role was to monitor and suppress dissent and antigovernment activities inside Syria's borders. Countering the various militias involved in the civil war and the presence of the Islamic State had kept his department of the Syrian intelligence apparatus busy for the better part of a decade.

Jacobs continued. "He isn't a hard-liner like so many in the Syrian government. Tariq's a patriot, but he's also a realist. He cares about his country and its people, but that same loyalty doesn't necessarily extend to Assad or his family. And he despises ISIS for what their bastardized version of Islam did to his religion and his country." The case officer paused to take a sip from a bottle of water. "Tariq did his part for the cause, putting plenty of the black-clad fighters in the ground personally, but he was just as disgusted by his government's response to the rebels fighting the regime. Assad's use of chemical weapons on his own citizens was the seminal event that drove Tariq to come work for us. At this point, he wants Assad and his henchmen out of power as much as he wants ISIS out of his country."

Joe thought about what he would do if the roles were reversed, if he were in Kabbani's position. "The Syrian people have been dealt a pretty shitty hand. I can see how having to choose between ISIS and Assad would drive someone like Tariq to look for help from outside his own country."

The Mercedes sedan that entered the citadel's grounds was not the type of vehicle a casual observer would expect a high-ranking officer in the Syrian security forces to be driving. It was nearly as old as the men awaiting its arrival and had open holes in the bodywork where rust was winning the battle of attrition. But the car's age, along with the wear and tear on display, helped it blend in and didn't draw unwanted attention to the driver.

Kabbani followed the road around the western perimeter of the grounds, the mound of the volcano and the ruins of the citadel looming high above on his left. He continued along the access road, passing the southern entrance, then made a hard left onto a switchback that took him up to the parking area. Finding a spot in the shadow of the citadel, he brought the car to a stop and turned off the engine.

Before getting out, he pulled a burner cellphone from his pocket and thumbed in a text message. The phone vibrated a few seconds later, and he was relieved to see the appropriate response appear on the screen. The people he was here to meet had arrived and the area was secure. He exited the vehicle and, following the text message's instructions, walked toward a gap in the ruins.

The sudden appearance of two men emerging from the darkness startled Kabbani at first, but he relaxed when he saw one of them was Greg Jacobs. He didn't know the second man, who was tall and muscular with a chest rig and spare magazines partially concealed under a light-weight jacket. *Must be security,* he thought.

Jacobs embraced his asset, then put a hand on Kabbani's shoulder and guided him back into the shadows. "It's good to see you again, my friend. How's your family? Are they well?"

"They're fine. Thank you for asking. The conditions in Damascus are relatively normal, which is more than I can say for the rest of the country."

With the pleasantries out of the way, it was time to get down to business, so Joe headed back to his truck to give the men some privacy. He was reaching through the open window for the can of Red Bull in the center console's cup holder when he heard the drone pilot's voice come back over the net.

"Heads up, Spartan. You've got four vehicles approaching the north entrance. I can't tell if they're military, police, or one of the local militias, but the trucks at both ends of the convoy appear to be technicals." Mr. Murphy had just made his first appearance of the night.

"Son of a bitch." Joe cursed under his breath. He drew his pistol and stormed past the case officer, delivering a forearm shiver that pinned Kabbani against the ancient stone wall of the ruins. Startled by the unprovoked hostility, the Syrian recoiled and his hands instinctively came up to protect his head. Pressing the Glock 19's muzzle into his temple Joe snarled, "What have you done, Tariq?"

"I...I don't know what you're talking about," Kabbani stammered. "I've done nothing,"

Jacobs was just as stunned by Joe's actions and hissed, "What the hell are you doing? Have you lost your fucking mind?"

Without taking his eyes, or his pistol, off Kabbani, Joe said, "Four military-style vehicles just entered the grounds." Not one to believe in coincidences, he figured the Syrian had either set them up or got sloppy with his tradecraft and led the patrol right to them. "Did you set us up, Tariq?"

"N...no," the Syrian stuttered. His eyes darted from Joe to Jacobs looking for support. "Greg, you know me. After all you've done for my family, I would never betray you. Tell him!"

"Put the gun away, Joe. Tariq didn't turn on us."

Remaining laser focused on Kabbani, Joe asked, "How can you be so sure?"

"Because," Jacobs said, "a couple of years back, not long after Tariq had begun working with us, his wife had complications with her pregnancy. When we found out about her condition, I persuaded him to get her to Europe for a few weeks on a so-called vacation." He made air quotes with both hands as he said the word vacation. "I met them in Germany and got her admitted to the med center at Landstuhl."

Joe's gaze began to soften, and his eyes drifted to the case officer as he spoke.

"The doctors were able to treat his wife's condition during the two-week stay. Three months later, Rima gave birth to a healthy baby boy named Nabil. I have to admit, I'm still a little bummed they didn't name him Greg. But hey, there probably aren't a lot of Greg Kabbanis running around Damascus these days. Anyway, without the treatment at Landstuhl, there's a good chance neither the mother nor the child would have survived. That's how I'm so damn sure of Tariq's loyalty."

Holstering his pistol, Joe turned to Tariq and extended his hand. "I'm sorry for jumping to conclusions."

"Apology accepted. I probably would have thought the same had I been in your position."

"Now that we're friends again and ready to sing Kumbaya around the campfire, what's the plan?" Jacobs asked.

"I'm working on it," Joe replied as the headlights of the lead technical extended around the bend at the base of the hill. He keyed his radio and raised the drone pilot. "Are you seeing any other movement around our location?"

"Negative Spartan. Other than the four vehicles, everything's quiet."

Joe looked to Jacobs and Kabbani, who had only been privy to his end of the conversation since they didn't have radios or earpieces. "Tariq, are you coming with us if we have to bug out?"

In a thoughtful but firm tone, the Syrian said, "No. For many years the military was responsible for securing the citadel, and it was only recently that they relinquished that duty. I don't know why these men are here, perhaps they still do random patrols, but I should be able to talk my way out of this if we're not discovered together. My GID identification should be enough to intimidate even the most curious soldier."

"What do you think, Greg?"

Tariq cut his case officer off before he could answer. "If I leave with you, and my government finds out, my wife and son will pay a terrible price for my actions."

He knew exactly what horrors his family would endure because he had inflicted the same punishment on others in the name of suppressing dissent. He was also keenly aware that his friends and counterparts in the GID would not go lightly on his family because of their personal relationships. If anything, the fact that he was one of their own would make his family's torture exponentially worse. The thought of Rima and Nabil being subjected to that type of cruelty shook the hardened Syrian to his core. "No, I'd rather take my chances here than have my family endure such consequences."

"Maybe it won't be necessary," Jacobs said, his voice tinged with hope. "Let's hang here in the shadows for a minute and see what happens. Like Tariq said, it could be just a routine patrol. With any luck, they'll exit through the south entrance and go find a nice place to get some tea."

Joe and Tariq exchanged skeptical looks. Both men had seen their fair share of action and knew one thing for certain – hope was not a plan. One way or another, they would know for sure in the next few minutes. If the convoy turned right, it would be heading back into town. If it continued straight it would only be a matter of minutes before four truckloads of armed men would be working their way up the switchback to the citadel's parking area – and the Americans.

Come on, Joe thought, trying to work his best Jedi mind trick on the driver of the lead technical. *Make the right. Nothing to see here. These aren't the spooks you're looking for.*

CHAPTER 3

THE MEN LOOKED on as all four trucks bypassed the south gate and continued their methodical advance up the road.

Fuck! Joe was cursing himself for agreeing to the citadel as the location for tonight's meeting. While it was a secluded, out-of-the-way spot, it had one major drawback. With the single road leading up to the parking area, there was only one way in, and more importantly, only one way out.

The situation reminded him of a story he had heard about another Protective Resource Group team who had gotten themselves into a similar predicament outside Baghdad in the early days after the war. The case officer had set up a meet with an asset on the western outskirts of the city. He had chosen a u-shaped area in the desert that was surrounded on three sides by a tall berm.

After being searched for weapons by a member of the PRG team, the asset was escorted into the back of an armored Mercedes G-550 SUV to begin the debriefing with the case officer. The meeting had only just begun when two Iraqi police cars eased into the open end of the berm.

The PRG team leader didn't know if the asset was compromised or if he was just bad at his tradecraft and was followed by some curious cops. The one thing he did know was that they were surrounded on three sides by a wall of sand and that the only way out of this situation was straight ahead. While he didn't particularly want to get into a shootout with some local police officers, he wasn't about to let his team get arrested and hauled off to an Iraqi jail either.

Seeing the patrol cars blocking the entrance, the other members of the

PRG team exited their Nissan Patrol and took up positions on either side of the SUVs. The Iraqi officers came out of their cars with guns blazing, leading the team leader to believe they had aced the class in shoot first and ask questions later at the academy. He would never know whether they were corrupt cops looking to loot the Americans' dead bodies or diligent officers of the law investigating what they thought to be suspicious activity. As rounds from the officers' AK-47s snapped past their heads, the CIA protective team returned fire with a volley of their own and dropped the four Iraqi policemen like a bad habit.

Knowing the gunfire was sure to draw unwanted attention, the team leader made the decision to end the meeting. He flung the G-wagon's back door open, grabbed the asset by the shirt collar, and physically removed him from the truck. As he took his place in the right front seat of the Mercedes, he glanced down and noticed a hole in the unbuttoned plaid shirt he was wearing to conceal his gear. Pulling the shirt around he saw a matching hole in the back where a bullet had passed through the fabric. Had the policeman's aim been an inch or two to the left, the round would have entered the team leader's abdomen just below his trauma plate. *Sometimes it was better to be lucky than good,* he thought. Giving the order to move out, the two-vehicle convoy sped past the squad cars and headed for the safety of the Green Zone.

*

Joe ran through his options and determined they were all bad. He didn't see any way they were going to avoid getting into a gunfight, so he gathered the team around and laid out his plan for a hasty ambush. If they were going to fight their way off this hill, it would be on his terms.

The only person with a question was Jacobs. "And what about Tariq? He can't stay here and talk his way out of the situation if you engage and kill a bunch of these guys."

Looking at the Syrian, Joe said, "As I see it, you've got two choices. You can come with us and we'll figure out how to get you home once we're rid of these guys. Or, you can hide in the shadows and hope we draw them away as we make our escape. Either way, you need to decide quickly."

Time was running out. Once the convoy made the sharp left at the switchback, it would be only about five hundred meters or so from the

Americans' position in the ruins. With the help of the trucks' headlights, Joe could clearly see figures standing in the bed of the first and fourth trucks manning Russian designed DShK 12.7-millimeter heavy machine guns. Putting those two Dishkas out of commission immediately jumped to the top of his priority list.

Tariq considered his options for a few seconds, then said, "I will stay behind. My government has no reason to suspect me of conspiring against them. And I'm sure I practiced good tradecraft on my way here. I wasn't followed. There's a good chance this may be nothing more than a classic case of wrong place, wrong time."

"For your sake, I hope so." Joe said.

Reaching into his pocket, Tariq withdrew a small, black USB thumb drive. Handing it to Jacobs, he said, "The locations and security precautions in place around my government's chemical weapons facilities. Research and manufacturing laboratories, storage warehouses, and the command and control structure – it's all on the drive."

Jacobs eyed the slim plastic storage device in the palm of his hand. "Thank you for this. Any issues accessing the information?"

"None. I used the login credentials of a scientist we were questioning on an internal matter. He was already under suspicion for corruption and sharing confidential information, so this will only dig his hole a little deeper if the breach is discovered." Before turning to leave, Tariq paused, then said, "There's one more thing you need to know."

Intrigued, Jacobs asked, "What's that?"

"It's the Russians."

"What about them?"

"As you know, they've had a large presence in my country for several years. Their advisors are assisting our military, and Spetsnaz units are running operations in support of the regime. Russian air support has been the single biggest reason the tide of the civil war has turned in favor of my government."

Jacobs concurred, "Yeah, we know. They've been conducting operations out of the air base south of Latakia and the port in Tartus. We've been keeping pretty close tabs on them."

Tariq continued, "I've attended several briefings with members of the GRU, their military intelligence, and it appears Moscow is becoming less tolerant of your actions in the region. I don't know the details at this point, but I get the feeling that they are putting together an operation that will make meddling in your presidential election seem like child's play."

Jacobs let out a low whistle, and his imagination ran wild contemplating what the Russians might be planning. "Thank you for all you have done for us tonight." he said, stepping forward to embrace Tariq. "Safe travels, my friend."

"To you as well."

With the intelligence gathering portion of the mission complete, it was time for Joe to focus on the team's extraction. Tariq's information would be actionable only if they were able to get it back to the analysts at headquarters. And the first step in that process was getting off this damn hill without being torn to pieces by the convoy's heavy machine guns.

Joe reached through the pickup's open window and grabbed his Ops-Core helmet. He turned on the night vision goggles attached to the front mount before putting it on and securing the chinstrap. Shaking Tariq's hand, he said, "Find some cover and keep your head down. Once we open fire, all hell's going to break loose."

CHAPTER 4

THE AMBUSH HAD gone according to plan…right up to the point that it didn't. There's an old saying that a plan is only good until first contact, then the enemy gets a vote.

When the fourth and final vehicle in the convoy crested the hill, Joe gave the command, "Execute! Execute! Execute!"

Suppressed rounds from the team's HK416 rifles cracked through the air. Joe sent a couple of controlled pairs into the gunner manning the lead vehicle's Dishka. The first two bullets hit the man in the chest and were immediately followed by two more that snapped his head back as if he had been punched in the face by Mike Tyson.

Chris Ryan followed up, sending a stream of high-velocity rounds through the truck's windshield, killing the driver and the soldier sitting in the front seat. The truck drifted to the left and broke through a low retaining wall that ran along the edge of the parking area. Before the two men in the back realized what was happening, the driverless technical crested the edge of the escarpment and began to pick up speed as it descended the steep angle of the mountainside.

Any hope the trapped men might survive this crazy rollercoaster ride evaporated when the truck's headlights flashed across the scene below. They were rapidly approaching an area dotted with rocks the size of basketballs. Looking as if it had been rehearsed by a Hollywood stunt-coordinator, the front wheels hit one of the rocks and canted hard to the left, causing the back end of the truck to swing around. It was only a matter of seconds before the tires dug into the soil and the truck began a violent roll, throwing the men around the interior of the cab like a couple of kids who had crawled into their mom's dryer. Their misery ended forty meters later when the truck slammed into a boulder as big as a house.

Through the green hue of his NVGs, Joe watched as men poured out of the next two trucks in line, looking around in the darkness for the source of fire that had just killed their comrades. Aided by their night vision goggles and infra-red lasers mounted on the rail systems of their rifles, the American operators began picking off the confused and unorganized Syrians one at a time. It was like shooting fish in the proverbial barrel. *We may get off this hill in one piece after all,* he thought, almost feeling bad for the soldiers.

But the feeling quickly faded when he noticed four men calmly exit the technical at the rear of the convoy. There was something distinctive about them. They looked confident and sure of themselves, not scared or disorganized like the rest of the soldiers. The men wore uniforms, but even through the NVGs, Joe could see they weren't the same as the others. Their kit was different too. Unlike the ragged mag pouches and beat up AK-47s the Syrians had been issued, these guys wore top-of-the-line chest rigs and carried AK-74s and AK-12s outfitted with advanced optics slung across their chests. The kicker, though, was when the four men reached up to their helmets in unison and clicked their own night vision devices into place. *Shit. Russians.*

Rumors had been circulating through Western news organizations for quite some time that Russia was supplementing their forces and those of the Syrian military with mercenaries. Joe had read enough intelligence reports on the subject to corroborate the stories, but he hadn't planned on coming face-to-face with them on a mission.

Even though private military contractors, or PMCs were illegal in Russia, the law seemed to apply only to companies that weren't on the president's payroll. The most prominent PMC in Russia was Wagner Group. It had deployed mercenaries in support of the conflicts in Ukraine and Crimea and appeared to be at it once again, bolstering Russian forces fighting on behalf of the Syrian regime.

The use of Wagner's soldiers for hire benefited the Kremlin on two fronts. First, it allowed Russia to reduce the number of troops in theater. And second, the spin doctors in Red Square reported on casualty numbers only for official members of its armed forces. It didn't include the dead and injured contractors in its releases to the media, thereby minimizing the appearance of Russian casualties in the conflict. Stories of mass graves and the burning of mercenaries' bodies to hide evidence of their participation in the war were commonplace.

Joe didn't particularly want to mix it up with the Russians, but his job description didn't include worrying about diplomatic relations with guys who were trying to kill him. As far as he was concerned, a hostile was a hostile, regardless of where they were from. And he would not think twice about smoking a bunch of mercs if they were a threat to his team or his mission. Besides, Washington was overflowing with eggheads who were getting paid a lot of money to deal with those big-picture issues. His primary concern was getting his team and the man they were there to protect out of this firefight alive.

Whether these men were hired hitters from Wagner, or a Spetsnaz team was of little consequence right now. The Russians had taken charge of the situation and were barking orders in Arabic to the rag-tag group of Syrians. The effect was almost immediate, and the soldiers regained some semblance of a professional fighting force. Once the men were organized and taking advantage of available cover, the Russians used their night vision devices to direct the soldiers' fire on the Americans' positions.

One of the Russians pointed and yelled something at the soldier manning the Dishka on the last truck. The big gun came to life and bright flashes erupted from its muzzle, lighting up the night like a powerful strobe as the gunner sent rounds slamming into the ruins lining the parking lot. Rightly assuming the stone structures were providing cover for the ambush, he continued firing, punching holes the size of softballs in the centuries-old walls. The withering barrage sent the CIA operators and their case officer scrambling for more substantial cover.

Kevin Chang leaned around a corner and fired a quick burst at the gunner but missed as the heavy 12.7-millimeter rounds chewed up the wall he was using for protection. Forced to retreat, he called for covering fire, then turned and sprinted for the remnants of a small building ten yards away. He had covered about half the distance when something struck his left shoulder. Feeling as if he'd been hit with a baseball bat, the impact spun him around and he landed hard on his back. Ignoring the pain, he rolled over, scrambled to his feet, and stumbled the last five yards to the building.

Relatively safe, for the moment at least, Kevin leaned against the wall and slid down into a seated position. He glanced at his shoulder but couldn't get a good look at the wound through his NVGs. Knowing the devastating affect a 7.62-millimeter bullet had on the human body, he was thankful he couldn't see the extent of the damage.

Wincing as he tucked his left hand between his body armor and his chest to stabilize the useless arm, he pressed his radio's transit button with his good hand. "I'm hit."

Joe's reply came back instantly. "How bad?"

"Took a round in the shoulder," Kevin said, the pain evident in his voice. Through gritted teeth, he added, "It must've just missed my plate."

Joe flicked his head and without a word, Chris, who doubled as the team's combat medic, took off. "Hang in there, Kev," Joe said. "Chris is on the way."

Seeing a Syrian soldier sneaking a peek over the hood of one of the trucks, Joe took advantage of the young man's poor tactics and drilled two rounds through his forehead. As he searched for another target, Joe radioed instructions to his team. The first order of business was to put the remaining Dishka out of commission, then they would start picking off those fucking Russians. Without their leadership and direction, this fight would have been over a long time ago.

John Roberts opened the breech on the left side of his H&K grenade launcher and dropped a high explosive round into the chamber. Keeping low to stay under the barrage, he crawled to a spot that would provide him with a good angle on the truck, but he needed something, or someone, to distract the gunner.

John yelled into his mic to be heard over the clamor of the machine gun. "Mike! See if you can draw his fire."

Son of a bitch! Why do I get all the glamorous jobs? Mike McCredy thought as he broke cover and fired at the Dishka gunner. Sending controlled double-taps at the technical, he raced forward and approached a waist-high stone wall. Sliding to a stop, he took a knee to make himself a smaller target and continued firing.

Mike's incoming rounds startled the gunner and the man ducked behind the truck's cab to avoid the salvo as it spiderwebbed the windshield and punched holes in the bodywork. Maintaining his crouch behind the cab, the soldier reached up and grabbed the machine gun's twin handles. He swiveled the beast in the direction of his new attacker and thumbed the trigger.

The Dishka's assault disintegrated the wall Mike was using for cover with the destructive force of a massive jackhammer. The former linebacker dove to the ground, instinctively bringing his arms up to protect his head from the large chunks of stone knocked loose by the gun's massive rounds. As the remnants of his protection rained down around him, Mike felt his right leg jerk violently. The sensation reminded him of a game in college when an offensive lineman blindsided him on a block that buckled his knee. The illegal hit tore two ligaments and brought his season to a premature end. A fraction of a second later the thought evaporated from his mind as a pain he never thought possible radiated up his leg and registered in his brain. Mike heard someone screaming in agony. He just didn't realize it was the sound of his own voice.

Even with the noise of a firefight raging all around him, John heard the cries and knew instantly that they were coming from his best friend. He cradled the grenade launcher and low-crawled under the withering fire to Mike's position. Setting his weapon aside, John was about to perform a quick assessment to determine the extent of Mike's injuries, but his attention was immediately drawn to his friend's right leg, or what was left of it. Jagged fragments of bone entangled with tendrils of muscle and ligaments dangled out of the destroyed joint where one of the Dishka's rounds had struck Mike just below the knee.

Reaching for the combat application tourniquet attached to Mike's plate carrier, John reassured his friend. "It's alright brother. I'm here."

He then looped the tourniquet around Mike's injured leg and maneuvered it up to the top of his thigh. Mike screamed again as John cinched the strap tight, then began turning the windlass rod to add additional pressure in hopes of stemming the flow of blood streaming from the gruesome wound. When he couldn't crank the rod another spin, John secured it in the clip and pulled over the Velcro tab to keep it in place. With the bleeding staunched, at least for the time being, John reached for the grenade launcher and returned his attention to the Dishka gunner.

The deafening roar ceased as the heavy machine gun ran dry. In his haste to eliminate the attackers, the gunner had blown through the rounds in the ammo can and was scrambling to load a fresh belt.

Fueled by equal parts guilt for putting his friend in a position to be wounded and a fury at the man who inflicted the damage, John took advantage of the pause in the action and rose to a knee. He centered the grenade launcher's sights on the truck, disengaged the safety, and pressed the trigger. The audible thump and the weapon's recoil in his shoulder felt righteous as the 40-millimeter high-explosive round left the tube. The grenade's explosion blew the gunner off the back of the truck, killing him before he was able to complete the reloading process.

CHAPTER 5

With both heavy machine guns out of commission, it seemed to Joe like things were starting to look up – until he heard the radio traffic.

"Kev's wound is packed and sealed. The round broke his shoulder blade and may have nicked his collarbone. He's in a lot of pain but is mobile and can still fight."

When Chris was finished, John followed up with an update of his own. "Mike was hit in the leg and has lost a lot of blood. The tourniquet has stopped the bleeding but he's critical and needs immediate evac."

Hearing that two of his men were seriously wounded hit Joe like a sucker punch to the gut. Their safety and well-being were his responsibility. And right now, he was failing them miserably. Mike and Kevin weren't just a couple of guys. They were his teammates. His friends.

A searing pain snapped Joe's attention back to the task at hand. While he was mentally scolding himself for his men's injuries, an AK round took a chunk out of the wall he was using for cover. A piece of the bullet's jacket had broken off and opened a gash above Joe's right eye. Blood streamed along the edge of his eyebrow and ran down the side of his face. He didn't think the wound was serious, knowing cuts to the forehead tended to be shallow but bled a lot. It was a reminder, however, that there were still bad guys out there trying to kill them and one had almost succeeded.

He wiped his brow with his sleeve, then applied pressure on the gash with the palm of his hand. With his free hand, Joe activated his radio and ordered the team to consolidate on his position.

Chris and Kevin were the first to arrive. Kevin propped his rifle on a low wall and began sending rounds downrange toward their attackers. Chris pulled up on Joe's right and was about to begin firing as well when he noticed the blood coursing out of the wound above his team leader's eye. "You okay? Want me to take a look at it?"

In between trigger presses, Joe said, "It's just a scratch. Probably looks worse than it is."

John paused behind one of the ruins and shouted, "Blue! Blue! Blue!" to let the team know he was coming up behind them. Joe turned just in time to see his man round the corner with Mike in a fireman's carry across his shoulders, his gait somewhere between a fast walk and a slow jog. John's face glistened with sweat even though it was a cool night as he struggled under his muscular friend's weight. Joe helped him ease Mike to the ground, then the exhausted operator collapsed next to his team.

Kevin stole a glance at his wounded teammate while performing a one-handed reload of his rifle and recoiled at the grisly sight. "Dude! His leg... it's...gone."

"Yeah," was about all the response John could muster between gasps of air.

Joe looked at each member of his team. Mike and Kevin were the most severely injured but none of them had made it to this point unscathed. The rest of the guys, Joe included, were bleeding from at least one open wound somewhere on their bodies. They would be running low on ammo soon, and it was highly likely the Syrians, or the Russians, had called for reinforcements. If additional troops, or even worse, air support showed up, it would only be a matter of time until Joe and his small team of operators would be decimated. They had to get off this hill.

Joe raised the drone pilot. "Warrior One Seven, is your bird armed?"

The MQ-9 Reaper's seven external mounts allowed it to carry an assortment of Hellfire missiles, laser-guided bombs, and JDAMS. Joint Direct Attack Munitions were GPS-enabled guidance kits that could be attached to conventional bombs and used to direct them to designated targets.

"That's affirmative, Spartan. She's carrying four Hellfires and two GBU-12s." The Reaper's seventh mount was carrying an external fuel tank to extend its time over target.

Thank God. Joe thought. "Do you have authorization to engage if we're in hostile contact?"

"I do, but not at your current location. Orders from Langley say damaging or destroying a historical site is a no-go. My boss is on the horn with HQ as we speak trying to get the restriction lifted."

You've got to be fucking kidding me! We're getting shot to pieces and Langley is worried about damaging a crumbling pile of rocks? Joe's temper was raging on the inside, but he managed to remain professional on the radio. "Copy that. Do me a favor and ask him to be persuasive."

When Joe ended the transmission with the drone pilot, Chris channeled his inner Laurel and Hardy. "Well, this is another fine mess you've gotten us into."

Ignoring his friend's attempt at comedy, Joe eyed their trucks and said, "With the convoy blocking the road, we obviously can't get out of here the way we came in. And if our request for the Reaper is denied, that leaves us with only one option."

"Well?" Chris said. "Spit it out. The suspense is killing me."

"Think we can make it down the side of the hill in one of the trucks?"

Chris took a few seconds to consider the question before responding. "The slope looked pretty steep on the overhead shots we studied back in Amman. And it's so dark, I couldn't get a good sense of the angle when we drove in. But if I had to bet a significant amount of your money on the prospect, I'd wager we should be able to make it. The key will be to keep the truck from getting sideways. If that happens, we'll probably flip and roll all the way to the bottom."

Joe felt better about the idea after discussing it, so he gathered the team and laid out his plan. He and Jacobs would make a break for one of the Toyotas while Chris and John kept the soldiers busy. When he pulled the truck around, the two operators would help Kevin and Mike into the truck. Once everyone was loaded, they would go over the side and head down the hill. If they were pursued, Joe would find a lonely stretch of road where the drone pilot could fire his missiles without causing any collateral damage.

With everyone clear on the plan, Joe said, "Greg, on me!" and the two men sprinted in a crouch toward the nearest truck while the rest of the team provided covering fire. Jacobs climbed into the back seat and began rearranging gear to make room for the guys.

The key was pre-positioned in the ignition, so Joe turned it with his right hand as his left hit the transmit button on his radio. "Any update on the request for the fire mission?"

Before the pilot could respond, Joe heard someone call out, "RPG!" His head snapped to the left, just in time see the projectile scream by within a foot of the truck's hood. He was about to thank his lucky stars for the near-miss when it penetrated the driver's side door of Tariq's Mercedes beater and exploded. Joe hoped the Syrian had chosen someplace other than his car to hunker down just as the fuel in its tank ignited. The twin shockwaves of the back-to-back explosions slammed the side of the Toyota like a freight train, lifting it off the ground and flipping it onto its roof. Joe's head bounced off the door frame and his world went dark.

CHAPTER 6

ONE OF THE first things Joe noticed when his eyes finally opened was the faint light of the sun's rays cresting the eastern horizon. Even in his dazed and disoriented state, semiconscious and hanging upside down, he knew that was a bad sign. Ideally, the mission was to be carried out under the cover of darkness and the team would have been in and out before the sun came up, the citizens of Salkhad blissfully unaware that they had been visited in the night by a team of the CIA's best. But things obviously had not gone as planned.

Joe took a couple of deep breaths and forced himself to relax. The cobwebs began to clear, and as they did, the events of the last few hours came rushing back. The drive across the desert, the clandestine meeting near the summit of the Citadel, the firefight with the Syrian and Russian troops, his men being severely wounded, and the RPG blast that flipped his Toyota on its roof. He remembered it all.

"How long have I been out?" Joe asked.

"Not sure," Jacobs replied. "I only came around a minute ago myself."

Using his left arm, Joe pressed on the ceiling of the truck's cab to support his weight while he retrieved a folding knife from his pants pocket with his right hand. He flicked the spring-loaded blade open with his thumb, slipped it under the seatbelt, and began cutting himself free. "Are you injured?"

"My head hurts like hell where I banged it when the truck rolled. But other than that, I think I'm fine."

Joe held himself in place as the knife sliced through the last of the seatbelt's fabric. He collapsed the blade and returned it to his pocket, then he eased out of the seat, rotating his body until he was in a kneeling position on the ceiling of the overturned vehicle. Pausing a moment to regain his equilibrium as the blood drained from his head, he used the time to put together a quick mental checklist of the tasks he needed to accomplish in the next few seconds.

While he was checking items off his to-do list, multiple rounds impacted the side of the truck. Their metallic thuds sounded like someone was beating on the bodywork with a hammer. The enemy must have seen Joe's movement inside the truck and adjusted their fire to engage the new target. It was time to get the hell out.

Joe called out over the radio, "Give me a status update."

The first voice to come through his earpiece belonged to Chris. "Welcome back to the land of the living. You had me worried there for a minute." Then, with his sense of humor still intact, he continued, "If you and Greg are done with nap time, we've got a helluva gunfight going on out here. You're welcome to join us anytime."

"Yeah…sorry about that," Joe replied, annoyed that his plan to evacuate his men had been derailed by the RPG blast.

"It's about time to get off this fucking hill, boss. We're running real low on ammo."

"Greg and I are going to link up with you in a minute, then we'll move on to Plan B."

"Plan B? I'd say we've got to be down to about Plan E, F, or G, by now. But just for argument's sake, what exactly is Plan B?"

"I'm working on it," Joe replied before addressing Jacobs. "Look around and grab anything sensitive or that you might need to survive the next few minutes. Give me an up when you're ready and we'll move on my command."

Reaching up into the truck's inverted floor well, Joe grabbed his H&K rifle from where it was wedged between the seat and center console. He dropped the magazine to make sure it was full and to confirm there was a round chambered. Satisfied with the condition of his rifle, he slipped the sling over his head, then drew his Glock from the holster on his right hip and press-checked the handgun. Seeing the glint of brass through the ejection port, he holstered the pistol, then slid his arms through the shoulder straps of his ruck.

"About ready, Greg?"

Jacobs performed one last sweep of the cab to make sure they weren't leaving anything behind that could be exploited, then answered, "All set."

They crawled out the driver's side window and knelt by the front of the truck. Eying the open ground between their position and the Alamo-like structure the guys were defending, Joe chose the route he was going to take to rejoin his team. "Alright, Greg. Stay on my heels."

Jacobs took a couple of deep breaths, psyching himself up for the dash to safety, and said,

"Ready when you are."

Joe keyed his radio, "Moving!"

Chris replied, "Move!" and the increased volume of covering fire let Joe know it was time to go.

Rising to a position like a runner in the starting blocks, Joe said, "Now!"

The soldiers saw the movement and shifted their fire in the direction of the two Americans breaking from cover at a full sprint. As they ran, bullets snapped and whizzed by their heads while others kicked up rocks and chunks of packed dirt around their feet.

They had just passed the imaginary point of no return, that half-way point where it was faster to continue forward than turn back, when Jacobs let out a cry and Joe heard the sound of his body crashing to the ground. With lead flying in both directions, Joe slid to a stop, and ran back to the fallen case officer.

Jacobs screamed in agony as he cradled his injured leg, waiting for shock or a dump of adrenaline to set in and dull the pain. A horrified look, as if he was wearing a Halloween mask, spread across his face when he saw, then comprehended the extent of the damage. He had taken an AK round just above the ankle and the powerful bullet had splintered both bones in his lower leg. Held on only by a few strands of muscle and tendon, his foot dangled grotesquely in its boot.

Joe slowed his momentum then reached down and grabbed the drag handle on Jacobs' vest. He turned, and with the wounded case officer in tow, began running for the cover of the ruins. Rounds cracked past the men and kicked up debris as Joe summoned every ounce of strength and speed he could muster to get them out of the line of fire.

As he ran, Joe couldn't help but steal a quick glance toward the soldiers, sure a bullet with his name on it was on the way. Truth be told, he was a little surprised he hadn't been hit yet. Catching movement to his right he saw one of the Russians step out from behind a vehicle with an AK-74 tucked into his shoulder. The son of a bitch was tracking him through his optical sight.

Joe snapped his head to the ruins, doing a quick calculation of the distance he still had to cover, and his heart sank. It was too far. He was doomed. There was no way he was going to make it to cover before the bastard fired. Joe inwardly cringed, wondering if he would feel the impact or if everything would just go black as if a switch had been flipped. One second, you're there. The next, you're not.

With an almost morbid fascination, like being unable to look away from a car wreck as you drove by, Joe turned his head and looked the Russian in the eyes. If this was going to be the end, he wanted to face it head on, to see it coming. Even so, the word quit wasn't in his vocabulary and he continued dragging his thrashing protectee across the open ground.

In his quest to get Jacobs to safety, Joe thought he noticed a slight shift in the angle of the Russian's muzzle. *What the…?* Then it dawned on him. "NO!"

The soldier centered the optic's red dot on the side of Jacobs' head and pressed the trigger. The rifle cracked once and the world around Joe seemed as if it were moving in slow motion. He saw the flash spit from the barrel and the weapon rise as it bucked in the man's shoulder.

Jacobs' painful thrashing ceased, and his lifeless body went limp as the high-velocity round struck him above the left ear and blew out the right side of his skull. Joe heard the unmistakable sound of lead hitting flesh and bone and felt Jacobs go still and quiet, but he continued the quest to get him to safety. He glared at the Russian as he made it to the cover of the ruins. The man was aimed in, had him dead to rights, but didn't fire. Instead he lowered his weapon and gave Joe a respectful nod for his effort. Clearly pleased with his marksmanship, a big smile spread across his face.

CHAPTER 7

JOE BOLTED UPRIGHT in bed, breathing heavily and covered in a cold sweat. The sheets clung to his body as he looked around the room trying to get his bearings. Rays of sunlight streaming through the sheer curtains penetrated the darkness, and after a moment, his sleep-filled eyes recognized the familiar surroundings of the hotel room.

The recurring nightmare, along with the room's air-conditioning and the thin layer of moisture on his skin had chilled him to the bone. Tossing the sweat-soaked sheets aside, he slid his legs over the side of the bed and glanced at his watch on the nightstand. Eight thirty-four. *Damn, I must be getting old.* He couldn't remember the last time he'd slept past six thirty or seven, at the latest. But he was on vacation and decided he wouldn't beat himself up too bad for sleeping in.

Joe grabbed the bottle of water sitting next to his watch and downed it in one long swig. He screwed the cap back on, then threw the empty into a nearby trashcan. Raising his arms above his head, he leaned to the left, feeling the stretch in his right oblique muscles. He held the position for ten seconds, but before switching sides and repeating the motion to the right, he took a deep breath in anticipation of the pain he knew was coming.

Joe winced as he eased into the stretch and reached down with the fingers of his right hand to trace the outline of a scar that ran from the top of his hip to the bottom of his ribcage. The pink tissue, standing out in stark contrast against the rest of Joe's tanned body, resembled a cross or an elongated plus sign. It was a constant reminder of the ambush he and Chris had walked into during a Quds Force attack on Director Sloan in downtown

D.C. last year. They were pursuing the leader of the hit team through the backyards of a nearby neighborhood when the Iranian shot a propane tank attached to a grill. Chris was knocked unconscious in the resulting explosion and Joe had ended up with a jagged piece of shrapnel embedded in his side.

At one point, when neither he nor the Iranian assassin had a functioning weapon, the fight had devolved into hand-to-hand combat. The Quds man had taken advantage of the injury and grasped the shrapnel, working it back and forth as if he were trying to saw Joe in half. But the fight ended abruptly when Joe pulled the metal shard out of his side and jammed it through the man's right eye socket and into his brain.

The skin and scar tissue were still tight even though the injury had occurred nearly nine months ago, leaving Joe to wonder if the wound would ever heal to the point where it felt normal again. Or would he be one of those old men who could tell changes in the weather were on the way from the aches and pains in various parts of their bodies?

With his morning stretching routine complete, Joe pulled on a t-shirt and shorts, then stood and crossed the room. On the way to the balcony, he grabbed a fresh bottle of water from the counter, twisted off the cap, and arced it like a three-pointer into the trashcan. Parting the curtains, he slid the glass door open and was greeted by the warm tropical breeze coming off the dark blue waters of the Caribbean. The warmth of the sun felt good against his skin.

The hotel Joe had chosen for his vacation was on the seaward side of Cancun Island at the mid-point of the Zona Hotelera, or Tourist Zone, a fourteen-mile spit of sand lined with beachfront hotels and condominiums. Bracketed by the Ritz Carlton to the left and the JW Marriott on the right, it didn't offer the premium highlife of those two properties, but he wasn't slumming it by any stretch of the imagination.

Standing on the balcony, Joe took a pull on the water bottle and looked down at the early risers claiming their spots by the pool or one of the many lounges shaded by umbrellas along the beach. His gaze shifted to the gentle roll of the waves as thoughts about what to do next ran through his mind, thoughts not only about the day's activities, although that was certainly important, but regarding his career as well.

After returning home from the disastrous mission in Syria, Joe had isolated himself in the office, spending hours on end scouring intelligence reports and reviewing footage taken by the Reaper that had been overhead for the entirety of the operation. None of the countries with personnel involved in the firefight had acknowledged publicly that it had occurred, so media reporting on the incident was nonexistent. Instead, he focused his attention on the video, watching the recording of the firefight with the intensity of a football coach preparing for the Super Bowl.

Joe had lost count of how many times he had viewed the recording, probably somewhere in the neighborhood of a hundred or so, and sometimes it seemed as if it was running on a loop in his head. But no matter how many times he saw it, he still flinched involuntarily each time he watched one of his men get wounded, each time the RPG barely missed his truck and destroyed Tariq's Mercedes, each time Greg Jacobs' head snapped to the side from the impact of the Russian's bullet.

A black star would be engraved on the Agency's memorial wall in the lobby of the Original Headquarters Building to honor Jacobs' sacrifice. Though Joe couldn't help but feel responsible for that star after failing to protect Jacobs on the hilltop in southern Syria that night, he was thankful there would be only one added to the memorial. There could very easily have been four or five more stars engraved in the white marble if it had not been for the actions of the drone pilot.

*

Travis Mullin had been watching the firefight through the Reaper's electro-optical, infra-red cameras while his boss, the chief of air operations, was on a secure line lobbying Langley for permission to engage the hostile force. While the decision-makers back at headquarters were dragging their feet, Mullin was busy calculating the distance between the team and the main body of the attacking force. If he were to get permission to fire, he needed to make sure Joe and his men wouldn't be caught in the explosion's blast radius.

Langley finally came through, greenlighting the fire mission. As Mullin maneuvered the drone to line up the shot, he noticed four figures sprinting away from the group of soldiers. He watched with fascination as the men's images disappeared over the edge of the escarpment. *The Russians are bailing,* he thought, wondering if they had correctly assumed air support was inbound to save the American team, or if they had been alerted by a Beriev A-50U, Russia's version of America's AWACS or Airborne Warning and Control System. With its upgraded radar and communications systems, the plane's crew may have warned the Russians on the ground that the Reaper was preparing to fire.

Mullin's sensor operator confirmed the missile systems were in the green, and after receiving one last affirmation from the chief of air operations, Mullin keyed his mic, "Stand by, Spartan. Firing in…three…two… one. Missiles away."

Powered by their solid-fuel rockets, two AGM114-M Hellfire missiles left the Reaper's underwing pods and streaked through the night sky. The missiles' active tracking capability virtually eliminated any chance they might miss their targets. The Syrians on the ground were already dead, they just didn't know it.

Mullin flew watchful circles over the citadel, providing air cover while Joe and the uninjured members of his team loaded their dead and wounded in the remaining Toyota truck and evacuated the area. Having survived the firefight, Tariq Kabbani made his way down the mountain into the town of Salkhad. Finding a vehicle to hotwire, he contemplated the events of the past hour on the drive back to Damascus.

*

Needless to say, Joe's employer, the Central Intelligence Agency, had not been happy with the outcome of the mission. And losing one's principal was a black mark no protective agent wanted on his resume. But unlike in the movies, black-clad operatives would not be visiting him in the dead of night to eliminate or neutralize a loose end. Instead, they might assign him to a mundane desk job that would be so mind-numbingly boring, it would force him to resign. Or the more likely scenario was that they would yank his clearances and inform him the United States no longer required his services.

Thinking a couple of weeks of rest and relaxation would be just the thing to get his head right, Joe's bosses at Langley had ordered him to take some time off. Also, having him out of pocket for a while would give them the opportunity to evaluate his performance and determine what, if any, actions would be warranted. Joe wondered if they would really fire him, especially after all he and his team had done to track and kill the Iranian hit team that had been gunning for the director and his senior staff last year. Maybe he should beat them to the punch and resign to save everyone the trouble. Either way, if this ended up being the end of his government career, it was time to begin exploring his options for the future.

So, after being literally kicked off the headquarters compound for a couple of weeks, he'd headed south, to the sandy beaches of Cancun. Joe had never operated in Mexico so it was a place where he could remain anonymous, be just another Norte Americano tourist traveling south of the border to enjoy the sun and sand.

The laughter of some kids playing on the beach below refocused his attention on the beautiful scene laid out before him and he banished the thoughts of work. There was nothing to be gained by worrying about something that was out of his control. It was a waste of time and energy. *Besides, I'm on vacation,* he told himself. *Start acting like it.*

Looking down at the waves gently crashing onto the beach, Joe decided a long run would be just the thing to clear his head. Retreating into the hotel room, he laced up his running shoes before donning a faded Washington Nationals baseball cap. He grabbed his sunglasses, phone, and earbuds and let the door close behind him as he headed for the bank of elevators.

CHAPTER 8

JUST A STONE's throw across the Mediterranean Sea from the island nation of Cyprus lies the city of Tartus, Syria. The ancient city on Syria's west coast has been a center of trade dating back to the Phoenicians, and prior to the civil war, had been a main point of entry for imports on their way to Iraq to aid in the war-torn country's reconstruction.

Since the early 1970s, the Russian Navy has maintained a constant presence in Tartus, using the port as a repair and replenishment facility, what they designate as a Material-Technical Support Point, or MTSP. For ships' captains patrolling the Med, having the option to dock in Tartus meant they didn't have to sail all the way back to their home bases in the Black Sea. After a quick refit and a little shore-leave for the crew, a ship could put back to sea and resume its patrol schedule with minimal delay.

With the buildup of forces to support Syria in its civil war, an agreement was signed between the two countries that would allow Russia's navy to expand the size and scope of the naval base and have sovereign control over its port facilities. The Russian Air Force struck a similar deal with the Syrians for the use of Khmeimim Air Base, located fifty miles up the coast just south of Latakia.

Once the upgrades to the facilities in Tartus were complete, men and materiel began flooding into the country. Protected by two companies of Russian Marines, the port quickly became the primary entry point for troops, armaments, supplies, and other cargo necessary to support a large contingent of warfighters. The sheer amount of activity on the base, with people and machinery moving in every conceivable direction, made it relatively easy for a group of elite soldiers to blend in and go unnoticed.

A small compound surrounded by ten-foot walls sat near the port's northernmost breakwater. It contained two flat-roofed buildings that were arranged in an "L" shape. The two-story building facing the blue waters of the Med housed offices, the armory, and gear lockers. The other building was set up as a barracks, gym, and dining facility.

It was from this location that two teams from Spetsgruppa "A," or Alpha Group, stand-alone special forces units belonging to the FSB Special Purpose Center, ran operations throughout Syria. The unit was created by the chairman of the KGB, the FSB's predecessor, in 1974 to act as Russia's counterterrorism task force. Members of Alpha Group, or Alpha as it was commonly known, were cherry-picked from other Spetsnaz units, and were the best of the best.

Based largely on its success in resolving hostage rescue and hijacking situations throughout the Soviet Union, Alpha moved into counterintelligence operations, working as spy hunters against hostile foreign intelligence services. Over the years the unit continued to take on additional roles and responsibilities that were not included in its original charter, such as paramilitary and covert operations.

In the late seventies, Alpha began operating outside the borders of the Soviet Union. During Operation Storm-333 in 1979, Alpha was part of an assault force that conducted a surprise attack on Afghanistan's Tajbeg Palace, overthrowing the government in Kabul and subsequently installing a regime controlled by Moscow.

Alpha was deployed to an overseas location again in 1985 when four Soviet diplomats were kidnapped in Beirut, Lebanon. KGB operatives were able to identify each of the kidnappers, and in turn, the Alpha team systematically began taking members of their families hostage. Rumor had it that the KGB team killed one of the family members and sent a few of his mutilated body parts to the kidnappers as a warning – release the Russian hostages or there would be more grisly deliveries. One of the diplomatic staff died during his captivity, but the other three were released unharmed. In the years since, Alpha Group had continued its counterterror mission at home, most notably with the questionable resolutions to the hostage crises at a school in Beslan and a theater in Moscow, while operating in the conflicts in Chechnya, the North Caucasus, Crimea, and Ukraine.

*

Captain Gennady Kalugin knocked on the door three times and waited for permission to enter before opening it and stepping inside. Although the weather in Tartus was beautiful this time of year, sunny with temperatures in the mid-eighties, the dark interior of the office reminded him of a gloomy winter day back home.

Blackout curtains covered each window, creating an impenetrable barrier that prevented even the thinnest sliver of sunlight from entering the room. The only source of illumination was a solitary lamp sitting on the corner of a desk, its lone bulb revealing little about the rest of the office. But as one of Alpha's team leaders, Kalugin had been in the office enough times to have committed its layout to memory.

The desk was in the far-right corner of the room, away from the windows to prevent a sniper from having a direct line of sight on the person sitting behind it, not that Kalugin could remember a time when he had been in the office and the heavy curtains had been open. But just because you're paranoid, doesn't mean someone isn't out to get you.

The innermost corner of the office was occupied by an unused seating area with a small dust-covered coffee table. A massive conference table covered with oversized laminated maps of the region filled the remaining space. All in all, the room was a drab and depressing sight.

Kalugin closed the door behind him, and with a noticeable limp, hobbled to within a meter of the desk. He stopped, shifting most of his weight onto his good leg, and saluted. "You wanted to see me, sir?"

A blue cloud of smoke hovered above the desk as the man sitting behind it took a long drag on his cigarette. He nearly sucked it down to the filter before blowing the smoke upward, adding to the haze. Stubbing the butt out in an overflowing ashtray, he fished a fresh cancer stick out of the pack and lit it with a cheap butane lighter. Only after he had taken a long, satisfying pull and expelled the smoke did he look up from the files spread out before him.

Colonel Konstantin Gusarov was the commander of all Alpha Group units in Syria. He was a bear of a man, thick and barrel-chested, with close-cropped hair that was more gray than black these days. Having been awarded the title Hero of the Russian Federation for his actions in Chechnya, he was one of nine Alpha officers to earn the prestigious honor. Over half of the men had received the award posthumously, giving their lives in the line of duty, so he considered himself lucky to a part of the small group still drawing breath. That luck had almost run out on a mission outside Kiev when an improvised explosive device detonated under his vehicle. Gusarov survived the blast but lost both legs above the knees. From a physical standpoint, he had made a full recovery from his injuries and maintained an active lifestyle even though he smoked like a chimney. But the mental scars took longer to heal. While he was still bitter those fucking Ukrainians had robbed him of his ability to operate, he was thankful Moscow wanted to keep his knowledge and leadership in the unit by promoting him to the command position.

In a casual tone, more like two peers than commander and subordinate, Gusarov gestured at Kalugin's knee and asked, "How's the leg, Gennady?"

Kalugin cringed inwardly, hoping his commander hadn't noticed the limp when he had entered the office. Not wanting to risk being taken off operational status while it healed, he downplayed the severity of the injury. "Getting better every day, sir. Thank you for asking."

A blind man could see Kalugin was hurting more than he was letting on, but Gusarov would have responded to the question in the same manner. Hell, he had lost track of how many times throughout his career he had lied to his commanders about an injury to remain with his team. Gusarov pointed to a chair in front of his desk. "Why don't you sit down before you fall down."

Kalugin eased into the chair and unconsciously began messaging his knee. The pain served as a reminder of how fortunate he was to be sitting here in his commander's office. He and three members of his team had been on a routine patrol with the Syrian Arab Army when they entered the town of Salkhad. The townspeople had been complaining that members of ISIS had been using the citadel as a layover point as they attempted to flee the country. But upon reaching the summit, the patrol had come across a small group of Americans instead of the black-clad fighters. Kalugin had no idea why they were there, but a firefight ensued with both sides taking casualties. The battle ended abruptly when a drone fired two missiles into the soldiers' positions on the hilltop.

His team had been saved only by a last-second radio call when the crew of a Beriev A-50 early warning aircraft had noticed an American UAV maneuvering into firing position. Kalugin had ordered his team over the side of the escarpment to get below the blasts. Ensuring all his men were accounted for, he was the last in line when the shockwave propelled him over the three-foot retaining wall and sent him cartwheeling down the hill. While his knee, along with every other part of his body, was battered and bruised, he had managed to endure the tumble without sustaining any major injuries. Kalugin knew they were fortunate to survive the encounter, the warning from the plane circling above the only thing that had kept his men from having their remains scattered around that hilltop with the rest of the Syrian soldiers.

Gusarov opened a drawer on the right side of the desk and withdrew a bottle of vodka and two glasses. Pouring a couple of healthy portions, he handed a glass to his young captain, then raised his own. "Salut," he offered, before draining the contents in one shot.

CHAPTER 9

GUSAROV WAITED FOR the slow burn of the vodka to dissipate, then refilled the glasses. Returning the bottle to its place in the drawer, he said, "Only one more, Gennady. We have much to discuss and need our heads to be clear."

Having no desire to get fall-down-drunk in the middle of the day, Kalugin was relieved when his boss put the bottle away, even though the vodka making his aching knee feel a little better.

"As you experienced firsthand on the mission in Salkhad," Gusarov began, "our interactions with the Americans on the battlefield are becoming more frequent."

Kalugin felt a twinge of pain in his knee, as if he needed a reminder of the encounter.

"I don't know if it's part of some grand plan concocted by the generals and politicians in Moscow, or a result of both country's forces operating in a relatively small battlespace. But after your engagement, and the abortion of an attack on their Special Forces base in Deir al-Zour, I get the distinct feeling that Moscow is tiring of the proxy wars we've been fighting with America since the end of World War II. The Kremlin seems to have developed an appetite for more direct action against the United States."

That last sentence momentarily stunned Kalugin. Were they really going to begin targeting American forces? Like everyone else in Alpha Group, he often felt his talents and those of his men were being wasted on inferior opponents. Their current deployment to Syria was a prime example. Running operations against antigovernment rebels or ISIS fanatics who have little or no formal military training was a joke. While he was perfectly happy to kill every last one of the zealots, what Kalugin really wanted was to test his skills against the best the world had to offer. Whether it was against the British, the Germans, or in this case the Americans, he relished the opportunity. But like any professional soldier or intelligence operative, Kalugin knew it would have to be done in a manner that would not escalate into an all-out war with the West. And if the battle in Deir al-Zour was any indication, the planners in Moscow needed to seriously up their game before directly targeting American forces again.

The Deir al-Zour governate is an oil-rich region located in the northeast corner of Syria. Sandwiched between Turkey to the north and Iraq to the east, Kurdish forces maintained a base in the northernmost part of the region roughly fifty miles southwest of the town of Shaddadi. Wanting to reassert control over the area's oil fields, commanders in Damascus sent a substantial force of Syrian Arab Army soldiers backed by tanks, mobile artillery batteries, and Russian paramilitary contractors to clear out the Kurds. There was only one problem with the plan. A team of American special operations advisors were living on the base as well.

With the attack looming, the Kurdish commander had used a prearranged protocol to call a Russian liaison officer in hopes of avoiding the impending battle. The Russian denied any knowledge of an attack, so the Americans notified their command, who used a similar deconfliction protocol. Once again, the Russians assured the Pentagon that no U.S. or coalition forces in the area would be fired upon.

Thirty minutes later, supported by a barrage of tank and artillery fire, the Syrian and Russian units advanced on the Kurdish base. Fearing they would be overrun, the Special Forces team called in air support. The response was immediate, and deadly. An Air Force AC-130 gunship, supplemented by armed UAVs, laid waste to the battlefield. While death was raining from the sky, the Russian liaison officer who claimed to have no knowledge of an attack called the Kurdish commander to ask for a pause in the hostilities so they could collect the dead and treat the wounded.

Reports estimated that one hundred Syrian soldiers and Wagner contractors were killed, with two to three times that many wounded. In the aftermath of the attack, Russian officials claimed the forces were pursuing a group of ISIS fighters and that the battle was nothing more than a case of mistaken identity. The statement was ridiculous because it was common knowledge that the U.S. and its coalition had driven the radical group from the region. The whole episode was an embarrassment to the governments in Damascus and Moscow.

Having given Kalugin a moment to fully comprehend the severity of his last statement, Gusarov continued. "Our orders for this next operation are coming directly from the Kremlin. President Polovkin has decided that Russia will be the dominant outside influence in the Middle East from this point forward. And to make that happen, we have to remove the Americans from the equation."

President Yaroslav Polovkin had always been a shrewd operator, learning the old ways of the KGB as a young man, and he brought those same skills with him to the Kremlin when he was elected to the highest office in the land. Since Russia's entry into the conflict, the former KGB and FSB officer, was running its involvement in Syria's civil war as if it were an intelligence operation by sowing seeds of discontent across the region.

He had cut deals with the U.S. to establish de-escalation zones along the Syrian and Turkish borders, then allowed Assad's forces and the Iranians to shred the Kurds. He sat back and watched as Syria and Iran exchanged blows with Israel by flying drones across the border and shooting down an Israeli Air Force fighter on a sortie over Syrian territory. Russian and Syrian forces pounded U.S.-backed rebel positions east of Damascus, and then there was perhaps the boldest move of all, the attack on the Kurdish base east of Deir al-Zour, even though results had been disastrous.

The one common denominator bringing multiple countries into direct conflict with one another was Russia's not so invisible hand behind the scenes, orchestrating the chaos like a puppeteer manipulating a marionette. Polovkin was betting he could push the Americans out of the Middle East by helping the regime in Damascus remain in power, allowing Turkey to over-run the Kurds, and enabling Iran to dig in on Israel's northern border.

As an avid reader and student of history, and as a soldier with a direct role in the operations taking place throughout the region, Gennady Kalugin had a front row seat to what was possibly the most interesting show on the planet. A spike of adrenalin seeped into his system, and the dull pain in his knee temporarily faded to a distant memory as he contemplated what his commanding officer had in store for him. Kalugin found himself on the edge of his seat, literally and figuratively, as he awaited his orders.

Gusarov took a long drag off his cigarette and blew another toxic cloud toward the ceiling before taking another from the pack. He stubbed the old butt out in the ashtray only after using its glowing embers to light the new one. Gusarov opened a folder and studied its contents a moment before beginning. "As I'm sure you've noticed during your time in the unit, the Kremlin typically sees itself as a sledgehammer and deals with every problem as if it were a nail. But there must be some new blood in the planning shop because what has been proposed is quite creative. And if all goes to plan, there won't be a country in the region, excluding Israel, that will have anything to do with the United States."

"Then Russia, led by President Polovkin, will step in to fill the void?" Kalugin asked.

Gusarov took another pull off his cigarette before responding. "Precisely."

Kalugin was intrigued. "And how does Moscow plan on turning the sentiment of the entire Middle East against the Americans?"

"With the use of a single drone," Gusarov replied, as he flicked a length of ash from the end of the cigarette

A single drone? Kalugin couldn't see how the use of one drone could have such an effect over a region as large as the Middle East. He thought he had a decent grasp of his country's UAV capabilities, and they were not very impressive. The workhorses of Russia's drone program were the Forpost and Orlon-10 unmanned aerial vehicles. The Forpost was a licensed version of Israel's Searcher MK II, a medium-altitude, long-endurance class of UAV with a wingspan of twenty-eight feet. While the Forpost was a large drone with a dual-tail design, the Orlon-10 resembled a miniaturized, pilotless Cessna 150. Both drones were capable ISR or intelligence, surveillance, and reconnaissance platforms, but neither had the ability to carry any weapons.

"Forgive my skepticism, sir, but I find it hard to believe we can effect change of that magnitude with a single drone." Kalugin paused, gathering his thoughts as they took shape in his mind. Working through the problem, he continued, "Besides, we don't have any UAVs with an offensive capability. And if we used one of our platforms, it would quickly be identified as belonging to Russia. Everyone would know it wasn't the Americans."

"I agree, wholeheartedly, Gennady." Gusarov said as he leaned back in his chair and exhaled another lungful of smoke. "That's why we're going to steal one of theirs."

CHAPTER 10

JOE MATTHEWS SAT in the left lane on Route 123, listening to the tick, tick, tick of his turn signal as he waited for the light to change. Every time he made the drive into work at the CIA's headquarters compound and got caught at this traffic light, his thoughts drifted back to that deadly day in 1993 when a Pakistani national named Mir Amal Kasi exited his van and began shooting indiscriminately into the vehicles waiting to make the turn. Kasi killed two Agency officers, Frank Darling and Lansing Bennett, and wounded three others before fleeing the scene. He managed to get out of the United States and make his way back to Pakistan, where he hid out for the next four years.

Kasi was captured in 1997 and returned to Northern Virginia to stand trial. In a show of support for the families of those impacted by the attack, the wife of the Director of Central Intelligence attended much of the proceedings in the Fairfax County courtroom in person. Kasi was found guilty in 1998 and remained on death row until his execution in 2002.

Joe would have given anything to have been sitting in this very spot that day. He could have saved so many families the pain and anguish of losing a loved one by putting a couple of rounds in the Pakistani's head.

The light turned green and he made the left onto the quarter-mile access road that led to the CIA's main gate. Joe slowed his dark-green 2003 Land Rover Discovery and showed his identification to the uniformed member of the CIA's police force, the Security Protective Service. After having his ID checked, Joe was waved through the gate and continued to the right, staying on the compound's perimeter road until he found a vacant parking spot along the fence line.

Entering the Original Headquarters Building's main lobby, he walked across the seal inlaid in the granite floor, but a quick glance to his right stopped him in his tracks. Until recently, there had been one-hundred-twenty-nine black stars carved into the marble of the north wall, a solemn memorial to honor Agency officers who had given their lives in the line of duty. But a new star had been added in his absence, bringing the new total to one-thirty. The Book of Honor attached to the wall beneath the stars contained the names of ninety-one of the fallen officers. The additional thirty-nine are represented by only a star, their names and the nature of their sacrifice still classified. Even though the most recent addition to the book had no name, Joe knew it belonged to Greg Jacobs, the man he had failed to protect in Syria. Running his fingers through the grooves in the marble, Joe bowed his head and offered a silent prayer, ending it by apologizing to Greg for not bringing him home alive.

He acknowledged the SPS officer as he passed through the turnstiles and made an immediate left. Hidden in a small alcove was a private elevator that accessed the outer lobby of the director's seventh floor suite. Use of the elevator was restricted to the Agency's senior staff and members of the director's protective detail. Having done several rotations on the Director's Protective Staff, Joe and his team had access keys to the private lift.

As he waited for the elevator, he checked his appearance in the reflection of its metal doors. The last time he had been in the director's suite, he and the guys had been called off the firing range and hadn't had time to change out of their 511s and Salomon hiking boots. Today though, wearing a gray suit, a starched white shirt and navy-blue tie, and black Allen Edmonds Oxfords polished to a shine that would make the Sentinels at the Tomb of the Unknowns in Arlington National Cemetery proud, his attire was more appropriate for the seventh floor.

A chime sounded and a moment later, the doors slid open. Joe stepped in and hit the button on the panel for the seventh floor. Thirty seconds later the doors opened, and he entered the suite's lobby. He nodded to a member of the protective detail seated at a desk near the door. The guy looked vaguely familiar, but Joe couldn't put a name to the face. He passed the desk, then turned right and stuck his head through a door to say hello to Paula Hanson, the director's long-time executive assistant. Paula was happy to see him, but her poker face didn't give any indication if his career at the Agency would continue or if it was about to come to a screeching halt.

As he contemplated the fact that this could very well be his last day with the CIA, his mind wandered back to how he got here in the first place. At six feet, three inches tall and a chiseled 215 pounds, Joe looked as if he should be playing strong safety for the hometown Washington Redskins. And if not for the events on the morning of September 11, 2001, he very possibly might have had a career in the National Football League. At the time of the attacks he was a hard-hitting All-American defensive back at the University of Arkansas, and as a junior had led the Southeastern Conference in interceptions. Many NFL scouts were projecting him to be a late first, or early second-round draft pick.

But those plans changed when his world was turned upside down that infamous Tuesday morning. Joe's mom worked for a small financial firm and had traveled to New York to meet a client. The meeting was supposed to have been held at the firm's office on Wall Street, but the client had been running late and asked if she could come to their office in the World Trade Center instead. It was scheduled to begin at 9:00 am, but true to form, Joe's mom had arrived a little early. She was in the building at 8:45 when al-Qaeda terrorists hijacked American Airlines Flight 11 and flew it into the North Tower. His mother, along with nearly three thousand other innocents, died when the towers fell that day.

After taking time off to grieve with his family, Joe had walked off the campus and into the local Army recruiter's office. Instead of signing a lucrative NFL contract, the All-American enlisted with the guarantee of an opportunity to try out for the Army's elite Special Forces.

His father had tried to convince him to finish college, then serve his country by joining the CIA. Joe came from a long line of covert operatives, and the joke around the house was that the Central Intelligence Agency was really a cover for the family business. His grandfather began the Matthews' journey into the Intelligence Community during World War II as a member of the Office of Strategic Services, then had continued serving his country with the newly formed CIA. Joe's father had carried on the tradition, joining the Agency in the late sixties, determined to fight the

Communist aggression of the Soviet Union. Now he was on the brink of retirement after a long and distinguished career in the shadows. With the family's background and history with the Agency, Joe understood where his dad was coming from, but he wanted a more direct role fighting the nation's newest enemy. He was going to make those responsible for the attacks of 9/11 pay a hefty price for what they did to his family and his country.

After completing basic and advanced individual training at Fort Benning, Georgia, Joe managed to fall out of a perfectly good airplane enough times to graduate from Airborne School and receive his silver jump wings. With that out of the way, it was time to start preparing for Assessment and Selection and the fabled Special Forces Qualification Course.

Joe's father made the trip to North Carolina for the graduation ceremony at Fort Bragg, and the veteran intelligence officer swelled with pride as his son earned the iconic Green Beret. The CIA had begun its existence as the Office of Strategic Services during the Second World War under the command of General William "Wild Bill" Donovan. The missions carried out by the OSS set the groundwork for the creation of the modern-day special operations community. The Agency and the Special Forces enjoy a special relationship that began not long after the unit was created in the early 1950s. If Joe wasn't going to join the Agency, then serving in SF was the next best option. Besides, his dad knew the experience he would gain as a Green Beret would be invaluable to the Agency if he ever decided to leave the Army and take his place in the family business.

Joe began his military career with an assignment to the 1st Special Forces Group based at Fort Lewis, Washington. During multiple deployments to Afghanistan he saw firsthand the value of language skills and why the Special Forces put so much time and effort into teaching its soldiers a foreign language. Units who were able to speak to the Afghans in their native tongue earned their respect and were much more successful conducting missions against the Taliban and al-Qaeda. As a result, Joe volunteered for immersion courses in Arabic and Pashto between deployments.

After his tour with 1st Group, Joe could shoot, move, and communicate with the best the military had to offer. With a natural proficiency for picking up foreign languages, helped along by growing up overseas as his father had moved from assignment to assignment, Sergeant Matthews was quickly becoming a hot commodity in the special operations community. Not long after he had been promoted to the rank of Sergeant First Class, the secretive Delta Force, officially known as 1ˢᵗ Special Forces Operational Detachment – Delta, came calling. Once again, Joe successfully completed the assessment and selection process and headed east to his new home in a remote and highly classified section of Fort Bragg, North Carolina.

Between the unit's ridiculous operational tempo and continuous training cycles, the years seemed to go by in the blink of any eye. Joe's current enlistment was about up, and without giving it much thought, he figured he'd re-up for another four years with the Unit. He had enjoyed his time in the Army, twelve years at this point, and he could easily see himself sticking it out for a full twenty. Besides, what other job could be as satisfying as having your government pay you to kill bad guys? As far as he was concerned, it was good work if you could get it.

But before his reenlistment, he was farmed out to the CIA on a special assignment with a team from the Counterterrorism Center. It was an experience that, for the first time, made him seriously consider leaving the Army. The team he worked with was based in Kabul, and he quickly struck up a friendship with the chief of station. As his temporary assignment was winding down, the COS asked Joe if he had ever thought about applying to the Agency fulltime. The two men had several late-night discussions on the topic while consuming more than a few ice-cold beers in the Station's lounge, aptly named the Tali-Bar.

Valuing his dad's opinion, Joe had called the seasoned CIA officer to discuss the chief's offer and the possibility of a career at Langley. He had spent the last decade in direct action against the enemy, fulfilling the promise he had made to himself that morning when he walked into the recruiter's office. And he knew he would be perfectly happy continuing down that road, but the Agency offered a new way for him to use the skills he had honed on battlefields across the globe. The job sounded like the opportunity of a lifetime, and by the end of the week he had made his decision.

Joe left the Army and spent the better part of the next year living at the CIA's training facility, commonly referred to as the Farm. Instructors taught him the finer points of tradecraft, improved on his already decent

Arabic and Pashto, and even added passable Farsi to his repertoire. He spent hours on the firing range to maintain and improve the shooting skills he had developed in the Army. Joe felt like a kid in a candy store as he sent thousands of rounds through the barrels of the handguns, submachine guns, assault rifles and sniper rifles at his disposal on the various ranges throughout the wooded expanse of the facility.

But as good as he was with a weapon, Joe really excelled when the action was up close and personal. On more than one occasion he had gotten the better of a few of his instructors when they faced off on the mat in hand-to-hand combat. He was stunned at how far he had come since he first set foot on the Farm almost a year earlier. After his time in Special Forces and Delta, he thought he was pretty much an all-American badass, but after spending twelve months with the Agency's dark arts instructors, his skills had risen to a level he never thought possible.

Upon graduating from the Farm with what could only be described as a doctorate in counterterrorism, Joe was officially certified as a paramilitary operations officer in the CIA's Special Activities Division. In the years since, he had conducted covert missions all over the world, targeting terrorists for assassination, conducting snatch and grabs – officially known as extraordinary renditions – and performing reconnaissance and surveillance in hostile, nonpermissive, or denied locations. In other words, Joe Matthews had spent his post-football career playing offense, taking the fight to the enemy.

*

Turning left, he headed down the hallway. Passing the detail's command post, he rapped on the doorframe of the next office before entering. Doug Kelly, the chief of the Director's Protective Staff, stood and came around his desk to greet him. "Welcome back, stranger. You're looking tan. How was Mexico?"

The two men shook hands as Joe thought back to the view from his hotel room. "It was pretty damn good. You should take some time off and head down there for a little R&R yourself."

"I keep telling myself that, but you know how it is around here. Something always seems to come up. Do me a favor and hang here for a sec while I check to see if they're ready for you."

"Sure thing," Joe said. "I don't have anywhere else to be at the moment."

Kelly returned a minute later and escorted Joe down the hall to the director's conference room. He knocked twice, then paused a beat before opening the door. Under his breath, he whispered, "Good luck," as he moved to the side and allowed Joe to enter the room.

CHAPTER 11

A LARGE RENDERING of the CIA seal was centered on the wall at the far
end of the room, perfectly positioned to act as an impressive backdrop
for anyone using the secure videoconference system. Portraits of previous
directors lined the wall to Joe's right. The wall to his left was undecorated,
lined only by a row of additional chairs, and a door that led out to the seventh floor's main corridor.

The room's dominant feature was the long, polished oak table. Joe had
sat at the table on several occasions in the past and thought nothing of it,
but today it seemed almost ominous. Feeling as if he were walking to the
gallows and expected to bow his head before the executioner, he moved
deeper into the room. When he came to a stop near the table, he found
himself practically standing at attention. Even though he had left the military years ago, he was still presenting himself to his command structure,
and those old habits were hard to break.

Lawrence Sloan, the CIAs long-tenured director, sat at the head of the
table. To his right were Katherine Clark, the deputy director for operations
and Richard Cutler, the CIA's general counsel. It was never a good feeling
to have the Agency's chief lawyer sit in on a meeting, especially one where
your job performance was being analyzed and your future with the organization was at stake. To the director's left sat Joe's more immediate chain
of command, Carl Douglas, the chief of the special activities division, and
Stephen Murphy, a career officer who headed up the protective operations
division.

It was Director Sloan who broke the tense silence in the room. "Good morning, Joe. Thank you for coming in. Please, take a seat."

Choosing his place at the table, Joe left three chairs as a buffer from the assembled group. *Here we go,* he thought as he settled in.

"You know everyone in the room," Sloan continued, "so we'll dispense with the formal introductions." Then, he motioned to Cutler, and said, "Richard, why don't you get us started."

Richard Cutler was a no-nonsense lawyer who had begun his career as a prosecutor in Boston. With a string of high-profile convictions under his belt and a reputation for being incorruptible, he became one of the youngest district attorneys in the history of the city. After twenty successful years fighting crime in Boston, the Agency poached Cutler to fill its top legal spot. Unlike some of his predecessors, he was not afraid to roll up his sleeves and get down into the weeds of a problem to find a solution that met the CIA's operational needs while adhering to the laws of the land.

"As I'm sure you're aware, Mr. Matthews, my office provides legal advice and consultation to the director and others within the Agency, prior to the initiation of covert action programs or other operations." With that opening statement out of the way, Cutler's tone reverted to that of a Boston DA talking with a police officer over a cup of coffee. "Basically, we're here to make sure the director, and those of you out in the field conducting operations, don't get sideways with the law while you're doing your job protecting the country."

Joe had seen Cutler around the building and remembered him being on some movements with Director Sloan. He had always treated the men and women on the protective detail with respect, and Joe liked what he was seeing this morning. He just wished their interaction had been under different circumstances.

Cutler continued, "There are occasions though, say, when an operation goes bad, that we're asked to sit on a review board to conduct an after-action assessment. The mission in Syria that resulted in the death of Greg Jacobs and injuries to two of your men prompted the formation of one of these review boards. We're here this morning to inform you of the board's findings."

"Yes, sir," was about all Joe had to say at this point.

"The other thing I want to make clear is that this assessment was not conducted by a bunch of lawyers from an ivory tower here at Langley. Mr. Douglas and Mr. Murphy were intimately involved in the process. As were Mr. Kelly, the chief of the DPS, a Special Forces colonel attached to the Office of Military Affairs, and several instructors from the Farm. So, as you can see, this was not a review by a bunch of out-of-touch stuffed shirts sitting in a comfortable conference room a thousand miles from the battle-field. If anything, I would say it was more of a review by your peers and Agency officers with specific knowledge in your line of work."

Well, at least I've got that going for me, Joe thought. *Or is he softening me up before dropping the hammer?*

Cutler opened a folder and shuffled through several sheets of paper to refresh his memory on some details before continuing. "We reviewed the official after-action report and recordings of the UAV footage, along with the conversations between you and the pilot. Interviews were conducted with each member of your team, and we even managed to contact Tariq Kabbani, the Syrian asset, to get his version of the events that night."

Joe sat stone-faced as he took in every word of Cutler's presentation. While his external demeanor portrayed a quiet confidence, he was dying on the inside. He understood the need for the process but wished Cutler would just cut to the chase. Joe shifted in his chair but remained silent as the general counsel paused to take a sip of water.

Placing the glass on a coaster, so as not to mar the highly polished oak, Cutler referred to his notes once more before continuing. "Based on all of the available information and interviews with everyone involved…"

Joe braced himself. *Here it comes.*

"The review board has determined that, while the death of Greg Jacobs was tragic, and the wounds your men sustained were regrettable, you did everything within your power to complete the mission under nearly impossible circumstances. You found yourself up against a numerically superior force and we were unable to find fault with any of your decisions or actions." Cutler paused to give Joe a moment to absorb the full weight of what he had just said.

Joe bowed his head and let out a relieved sigh, expelling all the tension from his body. Feeling as if he hadn't taken a breath since he entered the room, he inhaled deeply. Looking up, he made eye contact with each person at the table. Settling on Director Sloan, Joe said, "So, is it safe to say, sir, that I can put those post-Agency career plans on hold for a few more years?"

The question drew a round of chuckles from the assembled group. "Indeed, it does, Joe," Sloan replied. "You and your team have been a credit to this Agency, and we hope to retain your services for quite some time." Directing the conversation back the review, he continued, "The panel did find some issues that need to be corrected. It took us too long to grant the Reaper pilot permission to provide you with close air support. A separate group is taking steps to streamline the process for the air crews when there are extenuating circumstances that conflict with their general orders. A prime example would be firing near a historical site when there is an imminent risk and lives are on the line."

"I'm just glad he fired when he did, sir. If he hadn't, we wouldn't be having this conversation. None of us would have made it off that hill alive. Speaking of the pilot, do you know where I can find him? I owe him a steak and a case of his favorite beer for what he did that night."

Sloan looked to Carl Douglas, who said, "I believe he's here going through a similar review. We can get you his name and contact information when we're done."

Turning back to Joe, the director asked, "Is there anything else we can do, or questions we can answer?"

"Just a couple, sir. First, how are the guys doing?

Stephen Murphy said, "Chris and John are fine. As you know, their injuries were minor, and they came through the firefight relatively unscathed."

Douglas picked it up from there. "The prognosis on the other two is good, but they have a long road to recovery ahead of them. The AK round Kevin took shattered his shoulder blade and broke his collarbone. If it had been a couple of inches to the left, it would have obliterated the joint and he might have lost the arm. The docs inserted a bunch of steel plates to stabilize the bones so they can heal properly. He'll have fun going through TSA checkpoints for a while, but he's expected to regain full use of his shoulder. Mike's injury, on the other hand, is another story altogether. That Dishka round took his leg off just below the knee. He's already endured several surgeries and just received his first prosthetic. His supervised rehab is taking place over at Walter Reed's MATC." The National Medical Center's Military Advanced Training Center, or MATC, was a state-of-the-art facility that used a sports medicine model and advanced prosthetics technology to help wounded service members overcome the daily challenges caused by the loss of a limb. "You know Mike's mentality and work ethic. It won't come as a surprise to hear that he's been spending all his free time in the gym downstairs. I guess he figures if some rehab is good, then more is better."

Joe knew firsthand that Mike was a maniac in the gym, no doubt a habit instilled by a lifetime of playing football. "That's good to hear. I'll swing by and check on him when we're done here." Talking about his guys, his friends, made him realize just how much he had missed them during his mandated vacation.

"What else can we do for you?" Murphy asked.

"You mentioned we've been in contact with Tariq. Did he have any insights on how we were compromised that night?" Joe needed to find out how the patrol knew they were in Salkhad, especially if it was because of something he did or overlooked in the operational planning. If it was his mistake, it was one he would own so he wouldn't make it again in the future.

"We have. He's a valuable asset and we're in the process of selecting another case officer to handle him. But to your point, it appears to have been nothing more than a bit of bad luck. Apparently, the locals have complained about remnants of ISIS units moving through the area and thought they might have been using the ruins for an overnight stop on their way out of the country. The patrol was probably going up there to see if the rumors were true, and if so, to clear out the radicals."

Bad luck, my ass, Joe thought. *That would have been a nice nugget of info to incorporate into our selection of a meeting site.* "Just before the attack, I overheard Tariq mention that he thought the Russians were planning something big. Have we been able to determine what he might have been talking about?"

Katherine Clark took the question. "We're still not exactly sure what they're up to. But from what Tariq has gathered from conversations with his GRU counterparts, it has something to do with the presence of a team from Alpha Group on the naval base in Tartus."

Alpha Group? Joe wondered if the Russians he had gone up against in Salkhad had been from the unit. He'd heard stories about Alpha and read numerous intelligence reports on their exploits. Even in the chaos of combat, he could tell the four men were well-trained and equipped. And they all appeared battle-hardened. None acted as if it were their first time in combat.

"Tariq is pressing his sources as hard as he can without drawing unwanted attention to himself," Clark continued. "And we've begun targeting what we believe to be the Alpha team's in-country headquarters for collection. But the Russians are excellent at compartmentalizing and protecting their sensitive information. I'm afraid they may act before we're able to gather enough intelligence to paint a picture of what they're planning."

"Anything else?" Sloan asked.

Joe thought a moment before speaking. "Last one, sir. How soon will I be put back on operational status?"

The question brought a slight smile to Sloan's face. He looked around the room and everyone agreed. "I don't see any reason why we can't make your reinstatement effective as soon as we adjourn this hearing."

"Thank you, sir. The time away was nice, but I'm ready to get back to work."

CHAPTER 12

TEN MINUTES AFTER the meeting had ended, Joe strode into the gym on the basement level of the headquarters building. Greeted by the familiar smell of sweat and workout equipment, he felt out of place in his suit. He saw the guys huddled around Mike, cheering him on as he bench-pressed what looked to be upwards of two hundred and fifty pounds with relative ease.

Finishing his last rep, Mike set the barbell on the rack, then sat up to catch his breath and stretch out his chest and shoulders. Sweat soaked the front of his t-shirt and shorts. John Roberts, Mike's closest friend on the team, stepped aside to grab him a towel. It was then that Joe got his first look at Mike's leg. A soft, sock-like material covered the stump and was stained with blood in a few spots. He figured there was some drainage or seepage from the wound still occurring but would not have been surprised to find out Mike had popped a couple of stitches while throwing the weights around. The sight sent a wave of guilt churning through Joe's body. He was about to approach the team when he heard an explosion of laughter from the group. Instead, he hung back and ducked behind a pillar, not wanting to interrupt the guys' moment.

"Did you get some new boots?" John asked, noticing his friend's fresh out-of-the-box Salomons.

Looking down at ehis foot, Mike said, "Yeah. No thanks to you."

"Me? What the hell have I got to do with you getting a new pair of boots?"

Without missing a beat, Mike deadpanned, "Because you lost one of my old ones."

Having no idea what Mike was talking about, John pressed forward. "Really? I lost one of your boots?"

"Yep," Mike said, trying to keep a straight face. "You left it on that hilltop in Syria."

"I left your boot on that hilltop in Syria?" John repeated, more confused than ever.

"That you did, my friend," Mike agreed, as Kevin Chang and Chris Ryan could barely contain their laughter. "When you threw me over your shoulders, a little roughly I might add, given the circumstances and nature of my injuries, and ran though that hail of bullets to carry me to safety, you left my leg with the boot on it behind."

The guys were laughing so hard that Kevin was doubled over, and Chris had tears streaming down his face.

Incredulous, John said, "So let me get this straight. I risk my life to come to your aid, put a tourniquet on your leg to keep you from bleeding out, destroy the technical and kill the gunner who shot you, then carry your muscle-bound ass through a wall of lead to cover, and you're upset because I didn't grab the remains of your leg before we left?"

"Pretty much," Mike said, pointing to his prosthetic leg. "I can't very well run around with a bare foot, can I? And the last time I checked companies only sell boots in pairs. You can't buy just one."

Stepping out into full view of the guys, Joe said, "He does have a point, John. I've never seen single boots for sale. Not even in the discount bin at Walmart."

The four men turned in unison toward the familiar voice of their team leader. Joe's best friend Chris was the first to speak. "Well, I'll be. Look who's back from the beach. You realize I'm the surfer, right? How is it you get sent on vacation to Mexico while I have to stay here and babysit our two wounded warriors?"

With as straight a face as he could manage, Joe said, "You should know by now that rank has its privileges. Otherwise they wouldn't get anyone to take the job."

Chris moved in and threw an arm around Joe's shoulders. "So, I guess things must have gone well upstairs since you're not being escorted off the compound by a squad of SPS officers."

"Yeah," Joe answered with an exhausted sigh, just now realizing how much the stress over this morning's hearing had been weighing on him. "As of now, I'm back on operational status."

"Thank God," Kevin said in his heavy New England accent. "It would have sucked if Sloan had ordered us to sneak up in the middle of the night and kill you." That sent another round of laughter through the team.

"You're right about that. How's the shoulder?"

"Still hurts like hell, and physical therapy is a bitch. But the docs say I'll be good as new in a few months, so don't even think about filling my spot on the team."

"Don't worry, Kev. Your spot's safe. Do you know how hard it is to find someone with an accent like yours? We'd have to keep you around just for sheer entertainment value."

"Fuck you, boss. And I mean that in the most respectful sense of the phrase."

Another round of laughter filled the gym, but when it died down, Joe asked the guys to give him a minute with Mike. When they had cleared out, Joe pulled a stool next to the bench and took a seat. He looked down at the sweat-stained floor before facing his friend. "Mike," he began, trying to find the words to express his sorrow and guilt for what had happened. But the best he could manage was a heartfelt, "I'm so sorry." As the team leader, it was Joe's responsibility to take care of his men. It was an obligation he felt he had failed, since two of them had been seriously wounded in Syria.

"It's okay, Joe." Mike interrupted, reaching out and putting a hand on his team leader's arm. "It wasn't your fault. Occasionally, shit happens, and that night, it happened to us. It's no different from getting injured in a game. You can go through the entire season without so much as a sprained ankle, then blow out your knee on the next play and be done for the year. At least that's how I'm looking at it. Don't waste time beating yourself up over something that was totally out of your control. Besides, you brought us home that night. We could have died on that hill. But we didn't, thanks to you. Yeah, Kevin and I were wounded, and it sucks. But you brought us home. And I'd rather be here, right now, having to deal with losing my leg than buried in a shallow grave in the desert or rotting away in a Syrian prison awaiting a grisly execution."

Seeing the break in the conversation, the rest of the guys wandered back over. Reaching up and giving Kevin a fist bump, Mike said, "Kev and I don't need a pity party. What we need is to work our asses off to get healthy, so we can get back to runnin' and gunnin' with the team. So, get your head out of your ass, stop feeling sorry for us, and more importantly, yourself, and let's get back in the game."

Joe looked up at the rest of the guys. He had come down to the gym to console his guys and cheer them up, but the opposite had happened. They had turned the tables and were taking care of him instead. The four men gathered around him were more than teammates or friends. He loved each one like a brother.

Now that Joe was back, the team was whole once again, and all was right in their world.

CHAPTER 13

THE NORTHEAST CORNER of Jordan, near its border with Iraq, is as desolate and unforgiving a place as there is on earth. The barren landscape, dotted with ruins from long abandoned villages, resembles the fictional planet Tatooine from the Star Wars movies. Crisscrossed by the occasional dirt track, the only noticeable sign of civilization is Highway 10, a solitary paved road that runs from the outskirts of Jordan's capital, Amman, into the heart of Iraq.

Uninhabited except for the occasional Bedouin, the Jordanian desert is a great place to hide something, which is why the CIA chose the location to build a clandestine UAV base. The United States, and the CIA, has had a longstanding relationship with the Hashemite kingdom's royal family since the early 1950s when Hussein bin Talal became king after his father's abdication. King Hussein ruled Jordan until his death in 1999 and that special relationship remained in place when his son, Abdullah, ascended to the throne.

Jordan's proximity to Lebanon, Syria, Iraq, and Iran, all target-rich environments, made this base one of the CIA's busiest. There was never a shortage of work for the pilots and the ground crews, given the sheer number of sites and individuals targeted for intelligence gathering or missile strikes. The workload required at least one Reaper to be in the air nearly twenty-four hours a day, and pilots often rotated through their shifts behind the controls, resuming their duties after mandatory rest periods without the Reaper ever returning to base.

The men and women flying the UAVs out of Jordan were racking up flight time and kills at an unprecedented pace. The operational tempo, combined with the short flight to Amman for a little rest and relaxation, made the base one of the Agency's most desired assignments. Even though the temperatures during the summer months felt like you were living on the face of the sun, Jordan still beat the hell out of the CIA's other UAV bases in Pakistan and Djibouti or deployments to Niger or Mauritania targeting al-Qaeda in the Islamic Maghreb across much of Mali and North Africa. The living conditions at those bases could only be described as primitive at best, and that was being kind.

The centerpiece of the base in Jordan was the smooth, nine-thousand-foot east-to-west concrete runway. Although the drones needed less than a third of that distance to take off and land, the extra length came in handy when an Air Force C-17 Globemaster came in on a monthly supply run. It also provided coalition pilots with a friendly place to land if they had mechanical problems or were damaged by ground fire flying sorties over hostile territory in the region.

At the easternmost end of the runway sat a square tarmac and three steel frame hangars. Each hangar was large enough to accommodate two MQ-9 Reapers apiece, although the third, slightly smaller building, was used for maintenance and storage of spare parts. To the left of the hangars was a fourth building, which served as the command center. The flat-roofed, cinderblock structure housed offices for the chief of air operations and his communications officer. Individual ground control stations, one for each of the Reapers, filled the remainder of the available space. The building also acted as the unofficial air traffic control center for the few aircraft with humans in the cockpit occasionally flying in and out of the base.

Directly across the runway from the command center and the hangars was a heavily fortified magazine surrounded by an electrified fence topped with razor wire that stored the Reapers' ordnance. Above-ground fuel tanks had been constructed at the west end of the runway, far away from the hangars and living quarters. Keeping the flammable liquids and things that go boom nine thousand feet apart seemed like a reasonable idea when the blueprints for the base were drawn up. It would have been more efficient to run underground fuel lines to the hangars, but that decision was scrapped in order to protect the personnel and UAVs in the event of a fire or explosion. Instead, the ground crew used an old Texaco truck, flown over in the cargo bay of a C-17 to fill the Reapers' tanks prior to take off.

The CIA's drone program was lethally effective, but it was a barebones operation when compared to its counterparts run by the Air Force. On average, there were usually no more than thirty people on the base at any given time. Only fourteen or fifteen were directly involved with the operation of the UAVs. The remainder of the base's inhabitants were contractors who provided perimeter security or logistical support.

Everyone lived together in the housing complex a hundred meters from the command post. Earth-filled HESCO barriers surrounded the compound, which included individual trailers, the dining facility, or DFAC, a fully equipped gym, and an equally well-stocked bar. Each of the trailers was air conditioned and contained one of the biggest perks on base, a private bathroom. High-speed Internet made keeping in touch with family easy and convenient, and flat screen TVs with hundreds of satellite channels helped the crews pass the time by staying current on their favorite TV shows and movies. Meals at the DFAC were better than most, probably because the staff was relatively small, and the cooks didn't have to prepare food in mass quantities like their counterparts on a typical military base.

The crew preparing for their upcoming mission wouldn't be having a cold one or binge-watching their favorite show anytime soon. The pilot had just settled into the cockpit of his ground control station and was going over the preflight checks for the mission. He glanced up at a monitor next to his heads-up display, which showed an overhead shot of a single MQ-9 Reaper, designated Romeo Three, on the tarmac. *God, she was beautiful.* He never tired of looking at the long, sleek lines of its wings or the V-shaped tail fins that extended upward from the fuselage on either side of the Honeywell turboprop engine. And he marveled at the capabilities of the technology encased in the Reaper's bulbous nose. The combination of cameras, multimode radar systems, and the ability to intercept signals made it an incredible intelligence, surveillance, and reconnaissance, or ISR, platform.

But unlike its predecessors which were surveillance platforms that had been transformed to kill terrorists, the Reaper was just the opposite. With its seven under-wing pods capable of carrying a variety of laser guided bombs and Hellfire missiles, it had been built from the ground up to be a hunter that could perform a variety of ISR missions. In fact, when the Reapers were airborne on a kill mission, their designations were changed from Romeo to Grim. As in Grim Reaper.

There was a flurry of activity around Romeo Three as the ground crew prepared it for takeoff. Even though the drones were flown remotely, it still took a considerable effort to get them mission capable for the long hours aloft. Each Reaper had its own mechanic to check the integrity of the airframe and maintain the engine. An electronic technician ensured the avionics, sensors, and communications equipment were online and running within limits. And three ordnance handlers were detailed over from the Marine Corps to care for and load the bombs and Hellfire missiles. The Marines, along with everyone else on base, often felt a tinge of sadness when a Reaper returned with its full complement of weapons. It was a visual reminder that an enemy combatant had not been taken off the battlefield that day.

The pilots and sensor operators sat next to one another at the ground control station. The GCS was a technological achievement in and of itself. It was basically a self-contained, plug and play, piloting, targeting, and ISR control system. By using the satellite communication, or satcom data link, the UAV could be flown by the pilot in the forward deployed area or, with the flip of a switch, by a counterpart sitting in a similar station back on the headquarters compound in Langley, Virginia. If that were the case, the pilot in theater primarily functioned in a launch and recovery capacity but could take over control at any time if necessary. The entire system, the ground control station, satcom, and the UAV were packable in their own storage containers and capable of being transported in the cargo bay of a C-130 Hercules to any point on the globe at a moment's notice.

The pilot adjusted the boom mic attached to his headset and asked, "How's it looking out there?"

"Ordnance is loaded, and the fuel tanks are topped off. If systems are green on your end, we're good to go for engine start and taxi," the mechanic replied, his voice coming through the pilot's headset and a speaker mounted on the wall of the command center.

The pilot looked over to the chief of air ops who had been monitoring the conversation and received a thumbs up. "Roger that. Good for engine start and taxi."

CHAPTER 14

ROMEO THREE'S TURBOPROP engine sprang to life and the pilot let it idle for a few minutes to warm up while the sensor operator checked the readings on her instruments. Getting a quick nod, he released the brakes and applied just enough thrust to ease the Reaper forward and get it rolling across the tarmac. Walking to the right of Romeo Three, the mechanic performed one last visual inspection. One of the Marines did the same on the UAV's left side. If either of them noticed anything out of the ordinary, they had the authority to abort the takeoff procedures until the issue could be sorted out.

The pilot brought the UAV to a stop at the edge of the tarmac even though he knew that Romeo Three was the only aircraft queued for takeoff. He checked with the chief of air ops for permission to proceed. The mechanic and the Marine did a quick check of the runway and the airspace around it, looking to their left and right as if they were crossing the street at a busy intersection. The men always felt a little silly performing the routine. After all, their base was literally in the middle of nowhere, and any incoming flights were usually scheduled days, if not weeks, in advance. But protocols were protocols and the chief insisted they were followed.

Seconds before he was going to clear the Reaper to proceed to the runway, the mechanic heard the faint thumps of helicopter rotors in the distance. He turned to the Marine. "You hear that?"

The ordnance loader lifted the headset off his ear and tilted his head to listen. "Yeah. Choppers. Sounds like at least three or four."

The mechanic pressed the transmit button on his radio. "Stand by ground control. Hold what you've got."

With a questioning look on his face, the pilot took his eyes off the monitors and glanced over at the sensor operator. She double-checked the instruments before answering. "Nothing wrong on my end. All of my indicators are green."

Concerned with the delay, the chief of air ops grabbed a radio out of a nearby charger. "What's the hold up, Al?"

"We're hearing rotors out here, boss. Probably multiple birds."

"Do you have a visual?

"Negative. But it definitely sounds like they're heading our way."

While the presence of unannounced aircraft was unusual, it was not unprecedented. The base was known to the Jordanians and a few of America's closest partners in the coalition operating in Syria. There had been a couple of occasions where an allied aircraft had suffered a mechanical issue or taken fire over Syria and had made an emergency landing on the smooth runway.

The base had also served as a launch point for raids into Syria and Lebanon. Operators from Tier One, Special Missions Units appreciated the Agency's hospitality, and the secluded location of the base allowed them to prep for missions away from prying eyes. But those missions were planned and coordinated with the military well in advance.

The CIA had its own substantial fleet of aircraft, both fixed-wing and helicopters, operating in the region, but the chief knew his counterpart in Amman Station would have notified him if any of them were making an unscheduled visit.

"Alright," the chief growled, unhappy with the delay. "Stand by all, while I try to get us some answers." He set the radio back in the charger, then moved to a desk two paces to his right and snatched the secure phone's handset from the cradle. Dialing the number from memory, he waited impatiently for his counterpart in Amman to answer.

The Marine on the tarmac was the first to see the helicopters. Flying low and fast, four specks on the horizon banked around the northern end of the mountain range that rose out of the desert between the base and Jordan's capital city. "There," he said, pointing to the spot.

Al followed the Marine's gaze until he saw them as well, their image obscured by the heat waves shimmering off the desert floor. "We've got eyes-on, boss. Four birds inbound from the north. They're still too far away for a visual ID."

The chief was growing more frustrated by the minute as he waited for his counterpart to come on the line. Sure. They'd had unplanned arrivals in the past but there had been some advance notice, even if it was only ten or fifteen minutes. For some reason, this felt different, felt…wrong.

Finally, the familiar voice come on the line. "How's life out in the desert? Have you turned into a full-fledged Bedouin yet?"

"Hey, Larry," the chief said. "I've got a slight issue out here. We were in the process of launching Romeo Three when Al and one of our Marines heard rotors. Four helos are approaching from the north but we don't have any incoming flights scheduled for today."

The jovial tone in Larry's voice turned serious. "That is odd. Nothing comes to mind but let me double check the flight schedule for the week. Gimme a sec while I pull it up on my computer."

"Thanks. Normally I wouldn't call with such urgency, but something doesn't seem right. I can't put my finger on it, just a feeling in the pit of my gut that these guys aren't supposed to be here."

Al's voice boomed over the radio's speaker. "They're making a bee-line for us, boss. Probably no more than ten minutes out."

Turning to his communications officer, the chief ordered, "Give the security guys a heads-up that we've got some uninvited company on the way. If those helos land, I want to make sure we have a fully armed welcoming party ready to greet them. Then get HQ on the horn and let them know what's going on."

Larry's voice came back on the line, refocusing the chief's attention. "You're right. I don't have anything scheduled until your regular supply run next week."

"That's what I was afraid of. Not to sound alarmist, but could you do me favor and see if we have anyone in the area that might be able to do a fly-by?" What he wouldn't give right now to have a pair of A-10 Warthogs on station to put the fear of God into the men in the helicopters. While he waited for Larry to check on his air assets, the chief raised Al on the radio for a status update on the mysterious flight of helicopters.

The chief relayed the information to his counterpart in Amman and said, "Our security team has been alerted and is taking up defensive positions around the airfield. I'll stay on the line with you until we get a handle on what the hell these guys are up to."

Al couldn't believe his eyes as the helicopters grew closer. *No fucking way,* he thought. *That looks like a Russian Hind.* The Mi-24 Hind was the helicopter gunship made famous in the Soviets' war in Afghanistan. He was about to radio the chief when a pair of rockets soared from the pods attached to wing-tip pylons on either side of the fuselage. Al and the Marine ducked instinctively as the rockets screamed overhead and took out the communications tower and satellite dishes with an ear-splitting boom.

The blast rocked the command center. Loose sand and dust particles floated through the air and the lights flickered intermittently, creating an effect like the fog machines and laser light shows at a dance club. With their communications down and a generator that was providing only sporadic power, the chief grabbed his Iridium satellite phone and sprinted for the back door. He powered up the device and cursed as he stared at the screen, pleading with the device to hurry up and make the connection with the satellites orbiting overhead. After what seemed like an eternity the screen confirmed the connection had been established, and he redialed Larry's number. But before he could utter a single word, another of the Hind's rockets landed twenty meters away and detonated next to the generator. White-hot shrapnel penetrated the fuel tank, setting off a secondary explosion that sent bits of machinery flying in every direction. The chief's mangled body lay motionless on the sandy ground with the satellite phone still clutched in his right hand. Larry's voice could be heard over the speaker, begging his friend to answer.

CHAPTER 15

Captain Gennady Kalugin led the airborne assault of the American base from his seat in the Ka-226 observation helicopter NATO designated as the Hoodlum. His knee injury had prevented him from leading the ground assault, but there was no way he was going to stay back in Tartus and miss a chance to take part in this operation. Colonel Gusarov had finally agreed to let him participate, but only in a command and control capacity from the helicopter. Kalugin wasn't sure if he had made a compelling argument to be on the mission or if the colonel was tired of arguing and just wanted him out of his office. Either way, he was here, and they were minutes away from conducting direct action against a facility belonging to the intelligence apparatus of the United States of America. He still couldn't believe Moscow had approved the mission.

As they neared the base, Kalugin had the crew chief slide the doors open on both sides of the boxy, twin-rotor helicopter so he could get a better view of the battlespace. Warm air flowed through the cabin as he ordered the pilot to pull out of the formation, gain some altitude, and fly a racetrack pattern around the airfield. Switching his radio to the mission's tactical channel, he made the call to initiate the attack.

Taking out the Americans' communications had to be the first order of battle, and he watched as the Hind's crew sent its first pair of rockets into the satellite dish and antennae array next to the command center. For good measure, they fired a second pair into the rubble, setting off a secondary explosion that sent a fireball roiling into the air.

Like a vicious bird of prey, the heavily armed gunship flew over the command center, its rotor wash and exhaust creating small vortexes in the smoke and dust filling the air from the explosion. As its pilot and gunner searched for other targets, Kalugin noticed two SUVs, probably full of security officers, racing up the runway. They would have to be dealt with, and he preferred it to be sooner rather than later. He directed the crew's attention to the speeding vehicles, then sat back and let the Hind do what its designers intended. Destroy the enemy.

The pilot swung the big helicopter around in an arc as the gunner lined up the lead vehicle in his sights. The twin-barreled cannon under the Hind's nose came to life, spewing a burst of 23-millimeter rounds into the SUV. The heavy projectiles pummeled the vehicle, ripping through its metal skin and the men inside. Kalugin looked on from the open cabin of his command helicopter as the SUV drifted off the pavement and came to a stop in the deep sand on the north side of the runway. He marveled at the crew's skill and accuracy and made a mental note to ensure these two were providing air support on his next mission. With the lead vehicle and its occupants out of commission, the gunner turned his attention and the twin barrels of his cannon on the second SUV. Caught in the open expanse of the runway, there was no place to run, nowhere to hide, and the gunner dispatched it and the men it was carrying with the same deadly efficiency as the first.

With the communication lines cut and the immediate threat of the responding security officers neutralized, it was time to initiate the ground assault phase of the operation. Kalugin adjusted his headset's boom mic, then ordered, "Begin phase two."

The second helicopter in the lineup, an Mi-17 troop transport, landed on the tarmac directly in front of the still-idling Reaper. Ten battle-hardened Alpha men poured out of the open cargo door and hit the ground running. The two soldiers leading the squad raised their AK-74s and opened fire. Al, the mechanic, caught two rounds in the chest and was dead before he hit the ground. The second soldier's aim was a little high and his bullets tore through the Marine's neck, sending a spray of bright red arterial blood across the Reaper's gray fuselage. He dropped to a knee before collapsing on the tarmac next to Al as blood pooled around their lifeless bodies.

The ten soldiers split into two five-man fireteams and moved in a tactical train toward the command center. The first team stacked up on the main entrance while the other worked its way to the rear of the building and prepared to assault through the back door. Gunfire echoed through the dry desert air as a second Mi-17 dropped another ten-man team at the airstrip's housing compound. Undistracted by their comrades' firefight across the runway, the men at the command center remained laser-focused on the entry they were about to undertake.

When both teams were in position, Kalugin gave the order to execute. At the front of the command center, the lead man in the stack pushed the door open, then stepped back as the soldier in the number-two position tossed a flashbang grenade through the opening. Simultaneously, the men at the rear of the building were going through the same process, and both teams entered on the heels of the exploding bangers. The ten heavily armed men cleared the small command center in a matter of seconds and converged in the open area where the ground control stations were located.

Shaking off the effects of the stun grenades, the pilot stood and turned to face the soldiers closest to him. "What the fuck…?"

A rifle butt to the side of his head cut off the question and he slumped back into his seat, bleeding from a gash across his temple. The soldier secured the pilot's hands, then dragged him across the room and left him leaning against the front wall. Three other soldiers checked the sensor operator, communications officer, and medic for weapons, and once they were secured, had them sit next to the semiconscious pilot.

"The command center is clear, and we have four prisoners, sir," the team leader broadcast over the radio.

"Very good," Kalugin replied. Moving forward in the cabin, he stuck his head in the cockpit and said, "Take us down."

The pilot banked the Ka-226 and flew fifty feet above the runway before bringing it to a hover and touching down on the tarmac. Kalugin removed his headset, placing it on a hook mounted in the cabin, unbuckled his safety harness, and stepped out of the helicopter. He was met by the team leader as he approached the command center. Putting a hand on the man's shoulder, he ordered, "Have a man bring that tanker truck over and begin refueling the helicopters. I want the Hind topped off first and back in the air in case the Americans were able to put out a call for help before we destroyed the communications tower."

Fuel was one of the main logistical issues he'd had to overcome when planning this operation. Due to the limited two-hundred-and-eighty-mile range of the Mi-24 Hind, the flight of helicopters was unable to make the round trip on a single tank of fuel. Kalugin could have stopped off in Damascus but decided to set up a hasty landing zone in the desert seventy-five miles east of the capital to avoid drawing unwanted attention to the mission. They would more than likely need to land again on the way back, but he wanted the helicopters' tanks full just the same. "And have two men find some way to tow that security vehicle out of the runway so the Antonov can land."

Kalugin entered the command center as the team leader went about fulfilling his orders. Looking to the soldier left in charge of the prisoners, Kalugin asked, "Was there any damage to the equipment?"

"No, sir. We were able to make entry and secure the building without firing a shot."

"And the prisoners?" Kalugin inquired, looking at the four Americans sitting against the wall.

"Only the one offered any resistance, but he was dealt with easily enough."

A nasty gash and a pounding headache were the man's rewards for his efforts. *Don't worry, my friend,* Kalugin thought. *Your head won't be bothering you much longer.*

CHAPTER 16

KALUGIN CHECKED THE running timer on his watch as the cargo doors on the Antonov An-12 closed and the pilots began to spin up the four turbo-prop engines. Two hours and six minutes had passed since the initiation of the attack. They were behind schedule, but not by much.

With the airfield secured, he had given the all-clear, and the cargo plane, which had been loitering on the Syrian side of the border, had come in low and fast, flying nap of the earth to avoid being picked up on Jordanian radar. On loan from the Russian Air Force, it carried a team of aerospace engineers and aircraft mechanics who disembarked and broke into four small teams. The first went to work disassembling Romeo Three while the others began checking items off their specific shopping lists. One team headed for the satellite communication system while another began disconnecting one of the ground control stations. The last team was busy at the weapons bunker packing ten Hellfire missiles for transport.

Freeing up half his men to help load the components into their storage and transport containers had sped up the process considerably. Truth be told, Kalugin was quite happy they were running only six minutes behind schedule. He had built a bit of cushion into the mission's timeline in case there were issues securing the base or packing and loading the UAV and its support equipment. But for the most part, the operation had gone off without a hitch. Still, Kalugin had the nagging feeling they'd overstayed their welcome and he was ready to get back across the border into Syrian territory.

That feeling was confirmed when an F-16 Fighting Falcon belonging to the Royal Jordanian Air Force made a pass down the length of the runway a mere five hundred feet off the ground. The fighter shot silently past the command center and the idling Antonov, followed a moment later by the shriek of its single Pratt and Whitney engine.

Kalugin's head snapped to the left, his eyes following the fighter's trajectory as it banked and began to climb, no doubt gaining altitude for another pass. He admired the plane's sleek lines, the sun glinting off its bulbous plexiglass canopy. *Yes. It is definitely time to go,* he thought. *But first, we've got to do something about that jet.*

While the Hind gunship was an excellent weapon against targets on the ground, and possibly even other helicopters, it was no match for a fighter with the F-16's capabilities. It would be a waste of a talented crew to have the Hind engage the jet, so Kalugin raised the pilots and had them reposition to the opposite side of the mountain range to the north. He hoped the rugged terrain would hide the Hind from the jet's pilot and radar systems. Next, he instructed the remaining helicopter crews to fire up the engines and prepare for immediate take off. Finally, he grabbed the two men nearest him, issued a short order, and watched as they sprinted to one of the Mi-17s idling on the tarmac.

By the time the men reached the helicopter, its crew chief had already positioned two olive-green crates in the cargo door. Taking great care, they set the crates on the ground and unhooked the latches. The first soldier knelt as he opened the lid to reveal a 9K333 Verba. The Man Portable Air Defense System, or MANPADS, was a shoulder-fired, ground-to-air missile. Designated the SA-25 by NATO forces, it was the fourth generation in a line of air defense weapons that had been in the Russian inventory for decades. With its upgraded seeker, adding a third sensor to the prior versions' two, the Verba was more accurate and less susceptible to an aircraft's countermeasures than its predecessors.

The second soldier unlocked his crate, and the men attached the battery packs and electronic sighting systems before standing in unison and hefting the launchers' long cylindrical tubes onto their shoulders. They jogged to a spot in the center of the runway, activated the battery packs and targeting sights, and waited for the F-16 to make another pass.

Catching the dark speck speeding across the sky toward the airfield, the more experienced soldier said, "Be patient. Don't rush the shot."

As the American-built fighter drew closer, the Verba's targeting system began emitting a solid tone indicating its seeker had acquired the target. The soldier took a quick glance to his rear to ensure his back-blast area was clear, then checked the sighting system one last time to confirm the lock-on. Confident his missile was tracking the jet, he pressed the firing mechanism. The missile leapt from the launch tube and seemed to hang, suspended in the air for a split second, before its solid-fuel rocket motor ignited and it sped off at nearly six hundred meters per second in pursuit of its prey.

The interior of the single-seat fighter lit up like a Christmas tree the moment the early warning system, or EWS, detected the missile. The pilot banked hard to the right and hit the afterburners to put the F-16 into a steep climb, attempting to get above the Verba's flight ceiling of sixteen thousand feet. He activated the jet's electronic countermeasures, then began popping chaff, deploying hundreds of tiny bits of foil and aluminum-coated glass fibers that formed an electromagnetic smoke screen designed to distract the incoming missile's radar.

With a calmness in his voice that belied the severity of the situation, the pilot pressed the transmit button on his yoke. "Command, this is Falcon One Three. I've been fired upon by unknown forces at the base and am taking evasive maneuvers." Next, he strained against the g-forces of his maneuver to activate an additional countermeasure. White-hot flares fired out from each side of the fuselage, leaving trails of smoke in the plane's wake. Burning at two thousand degrees Fahrenheit, a temperature hotter than the exhaust of an aircraft's engine, the flares were an effective counter to a missile's heat-seeking sensors and could buy a pilot the time he needed to survive this type of engagement. While the pilot's concentration was focused on avoiding the immediate threat closing in on his aircraft, the second solider sent his missile skyward.

The F-16's EWS registered the launch and the indicators in the cockpit lit up once more, alerting its pilot of the additional danger. "Command, I've got a second missile in the air. I repeat, two missiles on my tail."

"Good copy, Falcon One Three. We're scrambling additional air support." The controller didn't mention it over the radio, but he had put CSAR, or Combat Search and Rescue, on alert.

The Jordanian aviator's head darted back and forth, first to his left, then to the right, looking over his shoulder to get a visual on the missiles. Sweat dripped under his visor as he cursed into his oxygen mask, something about the rocketeer's mother and a camel as he realized his idea to outclimb the missiles wasn't going to work. They were closing too damn fast. Deciding it was time to change tactics, he threw the stick to the left and right, carving up the sky, before pointing the plane's nose toward the ground. He popped a second round of countermeasures, leaving a virtual wall of chaff and flares in his wake as he put the F-16 into a steep dive. Confused by the amount of debris and heat in the air, the first missile lost its lock on the fighter.

The pilot breathed a quick sigh of relief as he watched it continue flying in a straight line until it ran out of fuel and crashed harmlessly in the desert. That was the good news. The bad news was that the seeker in the nose of the second missile was not fooled so easily and maintained its lock on the fighter. Blasting through the remnants of chaff and smoldering remains of the flares, it homed in on the heat signature of the F-16's engine. As the pilot pulled out of the dive and banked to the right to regain some of the lost altitude, the Verba's three-pound warhead detonated, completely shearing off the fighter's tail section.

Without a rudder to help it fly in a straight line, the plane was knocked into a spin and skipped across the sky like a flat rock across a still pond. As the plane disintegrated around him, and the g-forces of the spin drained the blood from his brain, the pilot struggled to run through the steps necessary to eject. In a slurred voice, he said, "May...day. I've...been...." He blacked out before he could finish the sentence or abandon his doomed fighter.

Kalugin and his men watched from the tarmac as the F-16 plummeted to earth and exploded on the side of a mountain west of the airfield. He was about to give the order to evacuate when his second-in-command approached and asked, "Sir, what do you want to do with the Americans?"

His reply was cold, detached. "We only need one. Bring me the communications officer. And make sure he has his computer. Execute the rest, then have the men board the helicopters. We need to leave before reinforcements arrive."

Without blinking an eye at the thought of killing the inhabitants of the base in cold blood, the officer acknowledged the command and relayed the orders over his radio. A series of single gunshots rang out across the airfield as Kalugin strode toward the Ka-226 command helicopter. He was about to enter the cabin when another of his men approached, manhandling a terrified and confused communications officer clutching a computer bag.

Eyeing the bag, Kalugin switched to English and asked, "You have the encryption codes?"

"N…no," the man stammered, knowing that was not the answer the big soldier wanted to hear.

"And why is that? You're the communications officer, are you not?" The calmness in Kalugin's voice making him seem even more menacing.

Wincing, as if he was expecting to be struck as punishment for his answer, the communications officer said, "Once the base came under attack and we were in danger of being overrun, protocol dictates I destroy the crypto keys. I had just finished when your men stormed the building."

"That's most unfortunate," Kalugin said as he imagined his superiors' displeasure when he broke the news to them. Furious with the man for beating his commandos to the punch, Kalugin drew his pistol from the drop-holster strapped to his thigh. "If you don't have the crypto keys, then I have no use for you." The pistol barked once, and the bullet struck the communications officer in the forehead. He collapsed on the ground, still clutching the computer bag in his arms. Kalugin knelt next to the man, withdrew the laptop from the bag, and climbed aboard the helicopter.

CHAPTER 17

EVERYONE STOOD AS a Secret Service agent opened the door and President Brad Andrews entered the White House Situation Room. The emergency Principals Committee meeting had been called only a few hours after word of the attack on the CIA's drone base in Jordan had reached Langley's operations center.

The president addressed his national security team while moving to his customary place at the head of the mahogany conference table. "Good morning, everyone. Please, take your seats."

Julia Maxwell, the national security advisor, sat to the president's right. Next to her was Andrews' chief of staff, Paul Owens, then Keith Hultsman, the director of national intelligence and Lawrence Sloan, the director of the CIA. The remaining seats at the table were filled by the secretaries of state and defense, Claire Nichols and Hank Coleman.

Given the nature of the meeting, two of the principals had been permitted to bring a deputy or other subject-matter expert. The chief of staff of the Air Force, General Maria Rodriguez, and the CIA's deputy director of operations, Katherine Clark, were the additional attendees.

President Andrews took a sip from a steaming mug of coffee. "Alright," he began, "I know it's early, but what do we know so far?"

DNI Hultsman was the senior intelligence representative in the room but deflected the question to Lawrence Sloan. Perhaps the gesture was out of respect for the spymaster's experience and the fact that it was his agency that had been attacked. But Hultsman was more a political appointee than an intelligence officer and probably didn't want to be the target of any blowback from the president once he heard the bad news.

Lawrence Sloan began the briefing without referring to notes, having committed the details to memory. "Sir, four hours ago, our UAV base in the Jordanian desert was attacked by an unknown force. It appears, based on a phone call our chief of air operations in Amman had with his counterpart immediately preceding the attack, that an unscheduled flight of helicopters was approaching the airfield."

"Is that unusual?" asked Julia Maxwell. "I mean, how would anyone know the base was there in the first place?"

Undeterred by the interruption, Sloan continued, "While the base is clandestine in nature, it is not invisible. Given its proximity to Lebanon, Syria, and Iraq, its use by the Special Operations Command to launch missions throughout the Levant and scheduled resupply flights, it is one of the busiest UAV bases in our portfolio. Based on that amount of activity, it wouldn't be unreasonable to assume that other countries are aware of its existence."

As a captain in the Marine Corps and the commander of an infantry company during the first Gulf War, President Andrews had led men in battle. His first concern was for the well-being of the personnel on the base. "Did we take any casualties?"

"I'm afraid we did, sir." Sloan paused, and his shoulders dipped ever so slightly, weighed down by the deaths of so many of his people. "The attackers killed everyone on the base. There were no survivors." The statement hung over the room as everyone observed a moment of silence and said a personal prayer for the men and women who died serving their country.

Claire Nichols was the first to speak. She was already thinking a couple of steps ahead as to how to handle the diplomatic fallout that was bound to result from an incident of this nature, especially if the attack turned out to be state-sponsored. "I know it's only been a few hours, Lawrence, but do you have any thoughts as to a motive for the attack?"

Sloan preferred to deal in facts rather than hypotheticals, so he offered what he knew, not what he suspected. "At this early stage, it would be premature to speculate on the motive behind the attack."

"Then how about who was behind it?" the president asked.

"The use of helicopters to conduct the air assault most likely rules out a terrorist organization," Hank Coleman interjected. Taking a sip from his own mug of coffee, the secretary of defense continued, "It's possible it could have been a retaliatory strike by a country that felt our UAV operations had been violating their sovereignty."

Again, Sloan refused to offer speculation. His job was to provide the president with answers, not guesses. "Based on the evidence left behind at the scene, the weapons used were of Russian manufacture. Whether Russian forces actually conducted the attack, or armed the group that did, is something we are still trying to determine."

"What evidence?" the president pressed.

"Shell casings, sir, 5.45-millimeter, the caliber most commonly associated with the AK-74 assault rifle, and the much larger 23-millimeter variety fired by the GSh-23 twin-barreled-autocannon often found under the nose of a Hind gunship. In addition to the shell casings, fragments from what we believe to be air-to-ground rockets bore Cyrillic markings."

Thinking her role in this incident might have just become exponentially more difficult, the secretary of state said, "I know Russian forces have been indirectly involved in a few engagements with our troops in Syria as advisors attached to Assad's military, but do you seriously think President Polovkin would approve a direct attack on an American facility?"

President Andrews liked to be on his feet and moving around whenever he was confronted with a complex issue, so he stood and walked over to a small table set with a coffee service. "The attack was on a clandestine base in the middle of nowhere," he said, almost to himself as he worked through the problem while refilling his mug. "There wouldn't be any media coverage, and he knew we wouldn't acknowledge anything publicly, so very few people would even know the attack had taken place." As he returned to his seat at the head of the table, he wondered aloud, "What are you up to, Yaroslav?"

Paul Owens, the chief of staff entered the conversation. "There has to be some greater objective behind the attack. Polovkin wouldn't mount an operation against one of our most important intelligence bases in the region just to stick a thumb in our eye because he's upset about our involvement with the rebels and Kurds in Syria."

"You're right, Paul," DNI Hultsman said, taking a quick sip of water before continuing, "This was not a simple attack on one of our bases. It was a robbery."

CHAPTER 18

THE PRESIDENT'S HEAD snapped to his left and he stared in disbelief at his intelligence chief. "A robbery? What the hell are you talking about, Keith?"

Hultsman took a moment to gather his thoughts now that everyone's attention was focused on him. "Sir, as you know, the base in the Jordanian desert was designed and operated to conduct UAV reconnaissance, surveillance, and strike missions across the Levant. In order to cover such a large area and meet the demands of the operational tempo, we had forward-deployed four MQ-9 Reapers to the base."

Feeling a wave of dread descend over the room, the president asked the question even though the felt he already knew the answer. "Keith, what exactly, was stolen?"

Hultsman cleared his throat before responding. "Sir, they took one of the Reapers." The DNI leaned back in his chair, almost relieved to have finally uttered the words aloud.

The tension in the room was palpable as everyone attempted to process what the DNI had just said. With a look of disbelief, President Andrews seemed to be having a tough time comprehending what he had just heard. "Let me get this straight, and bear with me because I was just a grunt officer in the Marine Corps. But you're telling me that an unknown force attacked our base in broad daylight, killed everyone in sight, then made off with an unmanned aerial vehicle? How is that even possible?"

Lawrence Sloan interjected, attempting to redirect the president's incredulity away from the DNI. He knew the situation would be bad enough if it was in fact the Russians who stole the Reaper in order to tear it down, study its design and technology, then incorporate what they had learned to reverse-engineer a similar capability of their own. There was no doubt that scenario would occur on some level, but what he had to tell the president led him to believe that wasn't the attackers' primary motivation for the operation. "Sir, there's more."

From the tone in Sloan's voice President Andrews could tell things were about to go from bad to worse.

"The UAV was not the only item taken from the base. Also missing was the ground control station a pilot uses to fly the Reaper, and the satellite communications system that maintains the link between the GCS and the drone." Sloan paused before delivering the last item on the attackers shopping list. "And ten Hellfire missiles."

President Andrews was trying his best to wrap his head around the seeming absurdity of the situation. What he had heard in the last thirty minutes or so sounded like the plot of a *New York Times* best-selling espionage thriller. But this wasn't a work of fiction. It was real. "I'll reiterate my original question, Lawrence. How is that even possible? You said the assault was carried out by helicopters. There's no way everything could be transported on a helo."

Sloan looked to Coleman and the secretary of defense took the cue. "Mr. President, I believe it would be best to have General Rodriguez take over this part of the briefing. Prior to being appointed to her current position as chief of staff of the Air Force she was the commanding officer of the 432nd Operations Group. The 432nd operates Predators and Reapers out of Creech Air Force base outside Las Vegas. She is the Air Force's foremost expert in UAV operations."

All eyes in the room locked on the woman in the blue uniform. "Thank you for coming, General," Andrews said in a welcoming tone. "I'm hoping you can shed some light on how an operation of this nature was carried out."

Undaunted by her audience, she began. "Well, sir, there were a couple of conditions that, under normal circumstances, would be considered positives about our UAV operations that ended up working against us in this situation."

"Explain, please."

"As a former combat commander," she said, referring to the president's past service and building that instant bond of those who had served in uniform, "I'm sure you can appreciate the need for agile units capable of the rapid deployment of personnel and resources."

"I can," the president replied.

"Our UAVs, specifically the MQ-1B Predators and MQ-9 Reapers, were designed to be portable plug-and-play systems that could be packed up, transported anywhere in the world, and be operational in the shortest amount of time possible. In order to achieve that capability, the drones, their ground control stations, and satellite communications systems can be broken down into their individual components, packed into specially designed crates, and loaded onto something as small as a C-130 Hercules for transport anywhere in the world. Once in-theater, the components can be unloaded, reassembled, and ready to conduct operations in a matter of hours."

President Andrews nodded as she spoke, at once grasping the concept. "What was the other condition, General?"

Not wanting to sound like she was throwing the Agency under the bus, Rodriquez stole a quick glance at Lawrence Sloan, who indicated she should proceed. "It would be the remote location of the CIA's base in Jordan. And the same could perhaps be said of many of their other bases around the world. Although the remoteness keeps their operations away from prying eyes, it makes them difficult to defend. A small group of the Agency's security personnel, no matter how good, are no match for an attack by a determined, professional, military force."

"She's right," Katherine Clark, agreed. "In the early days of the Global War on Terror, we had military support to protect the airfields. Often, it was company-sized elements of the 82nd or 101st Airborne Divisions. But as the wars in Iraq and Afghanistan continued through the years, those soldiers were needed for warfighting, not force protection missions. As a result, we began relying on in-house security personnel or contractors to protect the bases."

"And I believe the attackers used that knowledge, coupled with the remote location of the base, to pull off the theft of the Agency's Reaper," Rodriquez added.

Accustomed to working and making decisions at the strategic level, President Andrews found himself enjoying getting back into the weeds of a tactical discussion. "How much time would the attackers need to breakdown the UAV and its equipment and load it onto some type of transport aircraft?"

Rodriquez thought for a moment while she did the calculations in her head. "In an evacuation type scenario, an experienced ground crew would be able to pull it off in just under an hour."

"So, the helos bring in the assault force," Andrews said. "Then, once the base is secured, they fly in a cargo plane, say an Antonov AN-12, or something similar, with a crew of technicians to handle the teardown and loading."

"Sounds about right to me, sir. And with the base under control, some of the assault force could be diverted to assist with the heavy lifting to help expedite the process."

Now that they had a working theory on how the attack took place, it was time to focus on the why and to find out who was responsible for one of the greatest heists of all time.

CHAPTER 19

IT WAS NOT beyond the realm of possibility that a nation-state without a viable UAV program might have stolen the Reaper to reverse-engineer its technology. In many cases it was easier, and more cost effective, for a country to steal technology than to spend the time and resources to develop its own. And then there was the strategic advantage of being in possession of another country's advanced weaponry. The weapon system could be studied to determine how best to defeat it if the pointy end of the spear ever ended up being aimed in your direction.

Claire Nichols was the first to voice what everyone else was thinking. "Forgive my lack of knowledge in this area, General, but if someone has the drone and all its components, would it be possible for them to actually fly it?"

"That's an excellent question, Madame Secretary. I'm not as familiar with how the Agency runs it's UAV program, but if it is in any way similar to what we do in the Air Force, I would have to say the odds are against the attackers being able to operate the Reaper."

"Why is that?" Julia Maxwell asked from across the table. "If they have the drone, the ground control station, and the satellite link, what's stopping them from firing everything up and taking it for a spin?"

The CIA's drone program fell under Katherine Clark's purview, so she answered the national security advisor's question. "Encryption, Julia. The satellite link between the UAV, the ground control station, and our pilots back on the headquarters compound at Langley, is encrypted. The crypto keys are changed daily, sent to the field, and then loaded into the systems before each day's missions. If they had time prior to or during the attack, the chief of air operations or the communications officer would have been responsible for destroying the crypto to keep it from falling into enemy hands. The document destruction protocols are similar to those used in our embassies and stations in hostile areas overseas. But as a precaution, we have already changed the encryption keys here at headquarters and sent an update to the field."

"So they might be able to connect the ground control station and communication system, but nothing would happen?"

"That's correct. Everything would turn on, but the GCS wouldn't be able to establish the link necessary to control the Reaper."

President Andrews jumped back into the conversation. "What would it take, or is it even feasible, to think they could override or break the encryption and make a connection of their own?"

In the early days of the program, the satellite link beaming video from the drones to commanders in the field had been unencrypted. As a result, the feeds were available to anyone using an inexpensive computer program designed to intercept shows and movies broadcast by satellite television providers. The military first became aware of the issue in the 1990s when drone footage was found on Serbian laptops during the air campaign in Bosnia. Because the unencrypted feeds were intercepted, the drone was not technically considered to have been "hacked" and the breach was undetectable. The problem persisted, unaddressed, as drone operations transitioned from Europe to the Middle East and Afghanistan because the leadership in the Pentagon did not believe their new adversaries had the technological chops to intercept the transmissions. They could not have been more wrong.

Saddam Hussein had a young relative with a master's degree in computer science working out of an office in the Baghdad Aerospace Research Center whose only job was to find ways to intercept the broadcasts from U.S. satellites. Then in 2009, Shia insurgents in Iraq, probably trained and funded by Iran's Quds Force, had been able to download video footage from drones using the movie-pirating software. Laptops seized in military raids on insurgent strongholds yielded hard drives full of captured video.

But as the government plugged one hole in its drone program by encrypting the video feeds, the Iranians were busy exploiting another. In

2011, an electronic warfare unit belonging to the Islamic Revolutionary Guard Corps was able to hijack an RQ-170 Sentinel drone by interrupting the signal it used to communicate with its ground control station. They were able to fool the drone's GPS system and reconfigure the coordinates to make its computers think it was landing at its home base, while it was, in fact, landing at an airfield of the Iranians' choosing.

The loss of the Sentinel was a wake-up call for the military and civilian leadership in Washington, and all UAVs were grounded until an unbreakable end-to-end encryption package could be loaded into their electronic brains and accompanying ground control stations. So far, thanks to the algorithm created by a computer scientist working for the National Security Agency, the embarrassing string of UAV misadventures appeared to have come to an end. Until now.

Clark said, "Sir, working with our counterparts in the military, we have red-teamed our UAV encryption protocols in every manner we could imagine." Red-teaming was a practice used by organizations or units to have individuals attempt to breach security in order to identify gaps in the systems. The CIA and the Pentagon had put a combined team of internal and external computer scientists and hackers together to try to break any of the encryption protocols a UAV would use during a mission. The mandate covered video feeds, GPS navigation, and satellite communications between the UAV, its ground control station, and the ultimate command and control authorities in the Washington, D.C. area. She continued, "And to this point, we haven't found any weaknesses in the encryption."

Feeling a little better about the fact that whoever stole the Reaper would most likely be unable to fly it, the focus of the conversation shifted to identifying who might have been responsible for the operation. The use of air assets and the technological savvy to disassemble a UAV and its support system probably eliminated foreign terrorist organizations like ISIS or any of the al-Qaeda affiliates operating in the region. Nation-states ranging from the Syrians to the Iranians were considered, but just as quickly dismissed.

"Mr. President," the sound of Lawrence Sloan's voice quieted the room. "As we said at the beginning of this meeting, the investigation is in its earliest stages, but I believe it was Russia who attacked our base."

President Andrews mulled over what his DCIA had just said before responding. "I realize we've had a few skirmishes and close calls with their troops and mercenaries over there, but I'm having a tough time accepting that President Polovkin would sanction a direct attack on a U.S. facility."

Sloan asked, "Sir, do you recall a briefing several weeks ago when I mentioned that a highly placed asset in the Syrian government reported the Russians were planning something big? Something that would make meddling in our election look like child's play?"

"Vaguely," Andrews replied, having sat in on so many briefings that they all tended to run together at some point. He looked to his national security advisor to refresh his memory.

Maxwell picked up where Sloan left off. "The asset reported he'd been in a meeting where a GRU officer had slipped up and made the comment in his presence."

Sloan continued. "President Polovkin has publicly stated his desire on numerous occasions to expand Russia's sphere of influence in the Middle East, and he's counting on using their bases in Syria to gain a permanent foothold in the region. We are his biggest obstacle to achieving that goal, and our presence must be diminished for him to step in and fill our shoes. The attack on our base in Jordan may very well be the first overt sign that his plan is in play."

President Andrews shook his head. In this job you just never knew what the day had in store when you woke up each morning. Paul Owens tapped his watch with his index finger, implying they needed to wrap it up to give the president a few minutes to prepare for his next meeting.

Feeling a little better about the situation than when he had walked in the door, Andrews stood and said, "Thanks everyone. Please keep me in the loop with any new developments. And do me a favor. Let's get a few more details on the UAV encryption protocols from the computer scientist who created the algorithm. The last thing we need is a rogue drone flying around loosing Hellfire missiles on unsuspecting targets."

If only he knew how prophetic his last sentence was.

CHAPTER 20

THE ARRIVALS HALL at Larnaca International Airport in Cyprus was busy this time of day. Incoming flights from Europe, North Africa, and the Middle East delivered a steady stream of tourists looking to enjoy the beaches and rich history of the tiny island nation. The country's third largest city, after Limassol and the capital, Nicosia, Larnaca was located on the eastern coast of the island and offered all the benefits of a moderate climate and the spectacular waters of the Mediterranean Sea.

Two men sat at a café, having chosen a table with a clear view of the entrance all arriving passengers passed through after clearing customs. Wearing khaki shorts, a navy-blue polo shirt, and Salomon hiking shoes, Joe Matthews looked like any other tourist as he sipped from a bottle of water while keeping an eye on the people milling around the terminal. The other man at the table was Scott Garrett, a veteran CIA officer and current chief of station in Jordan. They had known each other for years, and Joe had come to think of the older case officer as both a friend and a mentor.

Nearly a year had passed since they had seen each other, so both men appreciated the opportunity to reconnect on this operation. The last time they were together was when Joe and the guys were working in Iraq as Garrett's protective detail. The deployment had been eventful and culminated when an assassination team belonging to Iran's Quds Force ambushed their convoy on the highway between Baqubah and Baghdad. The fact that Scott and Joe were sitting at a café on a beautiful Mediterranean island and the Quds men were not testified to the outcome of the encounter. The attack didn't end well for the Iranians, but Joe's team had not come out of it unscathed either, losing a teammate to an RPG blast.

Garrett absent-mindedly stirred his coffee with a spoon while it cooled. He wasn't sure when or where he'd picked up the habit. He drank his coffee black so there was nothing in it to stir. But it gave him something to do while he waited and helped him blend in with the other customers. Joe, on the other hand, was blending in by focusing his attention on his encrypted smartphone. His thumbs were a blur as they tapped the screen's virtual keyboard, getting a status update through a group chat with Chris Ryan and John Roberts, to make sure they were in position.

The team, and Garrett, were in Cyprus to meet with Tariq Kabbani, the Syrian intelligence officer and CIA asset. Tariq was understandably a little skittish after the firefight that erupted at his last face-to-face. The encounter had claimed the life of the only case officer he'd ever known, so the Syrian had insisted on seeing a familiar face in Larnaca, and the face he wanted to see belonged to Joe Matthews. Even though their relationship had gotten off to a rocky start, the Syrian respected his professionalism and the way his team responded to an unbelievably tough situation.

And while it was a little unusual for a chief of station to be meeting with an asset, Scott Garrett was the CIA's most experienced and well-respected officer in the Middle East. In the wake of Greg Jacobs' death, Langley thought having Garrett handle Tariq would send a message to the Syrian about just how much the Agency valued him and the intelligence he provided.

Joe looked up from the phone to check the flight status on the arrivals board and glanced at his watch. The plane was on time and due to land in ten minutes.

"It's kind of nice getting to work someplace civilized for a change. Is this what it used to be like back in the old days when you were going up against the KGB during the Cold War? Cafés and cocktail parties? Surveillance and dead-drops?"

Garrett was taking the first sip of his coffee and almost spit it all over the table. "Cold War? Jesus, how old do you think I am?"

A thoughtful look crossed Joe's face. "Hmm. Let me see." He made a show of counting on his fingers, then deadpanned, "You don't look a day over sixty-five or seventy to me."

Garrett just shook his head before returning his attention to the coffee while his eyes constantly scanned the arrivals hall. "But the answer to your question is yes. Back when I was first starting out as a young case officer, the job was more about developing assets and gathering intelligence that would allow the administration back in Washington to make strategic foreign policy decisions." He paused for a sip of coffee, then set the cup back on the table. "Nowadays, as you are intimately aware, we're more focused on taking bad guys off the battlefield before they can conduct the next big strike at home. Don't get me wrong, I have absolutely no problem cleansing the earth of every shithead who wants to do us harm, but we need to strike a balance between counterterrorism and intelligence gathering. Those policy makers back in D.C. still rely on the information we provide, and it's up to Director Sloan to make sure they get it."

Joe couldn't argue with a word the man said. It was one of the reasons he loved working with Scott. The veteran spook was always willing to share his knowledge and experience with the younger generation of officers and Joe usually felt smarter after one of their conversations.

He checked his watch again, then looked up at the big board displaying the arrivals. The status on Tariq's flight had changed from On-Time to Landed. *Five minutes early.* He picked up his phone and messaged the guys to let them know the plane was on the ground. He finished the text by having everyone insert their earpieces and switch to voice comms through their phone's encrypted link.

The team was shorthanded with Kevin Chang and Mike McCredy sidelined, but Joe felt he had a good plan in place, nonetheless. After the fiasco in Syria, Joe and Scott had decided to run Tariq through a surveillance detection route. The SDR was designed in such a way that his movements and direction of travel would appear perfectly normal for a tourist who had come to the island for a couple of days of fun and sun. But by observing him along the way, the team would be able to determine if he was being watched or followed by anyone other than the team of CIA operators.

The doors separating customs and immigration from the main terminal parted and a group of passengers emerged, most wearing shorts and beach attire, their intentions for coming to the island obvious. Joe was the first to spot Tariq moving through the crowd but gave no indication he recognized the man. In his loose-fitting linen shirt, shorts, and sandals, the

Syrian intelligence officer looked like all the other passengers as he stopped at a kiosk to exchange some currency. With his transaction complete, he headed for a nearby counter to sign paperwork and pick up the keys for his rental vehicle.

As Tariq exited the terminal in search of his car, Scott stood and dropped a few Euros on the table. "Let's go."

Joe relayed, "We have the eye," letting the team know he and Scott had positively identified their asset and were on the move. He grabbed his well-worn GORUCK GR1 rucksack and slung it over his shoulder as they headed out into the Mediterranean sun.

CHAPTER 21

REACHING THE SHORT-TERM parking lot, Joe handed the ruck to Scott before sliding behind the wheel of their rented Nissan Qashqai, a crossover SUV like the Rogue model the Japanese automaker sold in the States. The engine purred to life as he pressed the start button on the dashboard, still shaking his head at the egghead who came up with the name Qashqai. *Must've been the brainchild of some marketing genius at corporate headquarters in Tokyo.* Wondering what the hell Qashqai meant, he had conducted a quick Internet search on his phone while filling out the paperwork for the rental company. The first result that popped up was from Wikipedia, so he knew it had to be true. The name Qashqai referred to the people living in the mountainous region of southwestern Iran. Joe couldn't believe his eyes. Those damn Iranians were everywhere. After his run-ins with the Quds Force hit squads, he almost refused the vehicle on the spot.

But that had been three days ago. And after seeing how many of the vehicles were on the roads around the island, he'd decided to hang onto it. Besides, other than the name and the fact that it was right-hand drive because the Cypriots drove on the left side of the road, he was starting to enjoy the mid-size SUV. Joe would have typically preferred a larger vehicle with more space for people and gear, but on the narrow, ancient streets of Larnaca, the Nissan's size was just right.

Scott eased into the passenger seat and placed the bag on the floorboard between his feet. He unzipped the compartment built into its back panel and withdrew a small tablet. Setting the device in his lap, he reached over his shoulder for the seatbelt and buckled himself in before flipping open the tablet's cover and tapping in the passcode. The screen unlocked, and he checked the settings to make sure it was connected to the cellular network. He then returned to the main screen and tapped an icon that opened a mapping program. Using his thumb and index finger to zoom in on the airport, Scott saw two dots on the satellite image. The first represented their SUV in the airport's short-term parking lot. The other, in the rental car lot, identified Tariq's silver Renault sedan.

Fred Jackson, a technical operations officer in the Directorate of Science and Technology, had hacked into the rental agency's system and preselected the car Tariq would be assigned. Ever the overachiever when it came to his government-sponsored hacking, Jackson had linked the Renault's internal GPS system to the tablet's mapping program. Adhering to the adage of two is one, and one is none, Chris Ryan had placed a tracking beacon under the sedan's bumper as a back-up, just in case.

Joe had worked hard to forge a relationship with Jackson ever since the hacker had proved his worth by locating the Iranian hit team's location just prior to their attack in Washington, D.C. last year. What he didn't know, and probably never would, was that Jackson had been the architect of an elaborate cyberattack on Iran's nuclear enrichment facility in Natanz. Joe had seen news stories of the incident and the virus computer security experts called Stuxnet, but he had no idea that the man he'd befriended was behind the attack. But what he had figured out was that the guy's skills with his keyboard might come in handy at some point down the road. And even though what Jackson had done on this mission was a simple task for a man of his considerable ability, it was exactly the type of operational support Joe had envisioned needing from the hacker.

The dot representing Tariq's rental began moving across the tablet's screen, so Scott pinched his thumb and index finger together to minimize the zoom and expand the map's field of view. As he did, two more dots appeared on the screen, revealing Chris and John's positions along the surveillance detection route. "He's on the move," Scott informed them, and both men acknowledged the call over their encrypted mobile phones.

Tariq turned left onto the access road that separated the rental lot from short-term parking, then entered the roundabout near the main terminal. He took the first right to leave the traffic circle and followed the road to the airport's exit.

Joe put the SUV in gear, backed out of the space, and left the short-term parking lot. They were second in line at the stop sign when Tariq's silver Renault passed by. The car in front of them made the left onto the access road and Joe eased up to the stop sign, the tracking beacon and GPS link affording him a bit of patience. Scott kept a watchful eye on the cars trailing behind the Syrian as Joe looked for an opening in the traffic. A gap appeared a moment later, and he merged into the flow of vehicles leaving the airport's grounds.

The route they had created for the SDR took them up the A3 past plots of farmland with dark, rich soil, to the Domolaxia Junction. They snaked their way around the junction's large traffic circle, taking the exit onto the B4. The terrain turned industrial as the highway led them back past the airport, paralleling the runways, cargo terminals, and a large flat tarmac that served as a parking lot where a mismatched variety of private and commercial aircraft baked in the sun.

As instructed, Tariq took the first opportunity to leave the highway and entered the Makenzie section of Larnaca. Located at the southern tip of the city, Makenzie was a popular tourist destination that offered a half-mile stretch of sandy beach dotted with umbrella-shaded lounge chairs and an ample supply of coffee shops, bars, and restaurants. Tariq had memorized the route before leaving Damascus but consulted the Renault's GPS to be sure, before turning off Piale Pasa and finding a spot in the large parking lot that ran the length of the strip.

Joe negotiated the traffic and found his own parking space in the lot just in time to see Tariq enter a small convenience store. The Syrian reappeared five minutes later with a plastic bag in hand. Containing several bottles of sparkling water and a tube of sunscreen, the items would seem completely innocuous and reinforce the appearance that he was just another tourist visiting the island for a couple of days. With his purchases made, this next leg of the SDR would be conducted on foot, so he headed for an alley between a nightclub and a restaurant.

Joe was out of the vehicle and on the move before Scott closed the tablet's cover and slid it back into the rucksack's zippered compartment. With the tablet stowed, Scott moved around the SUV and took Joe's place in the driver's seat. He would keep an eye on the Renault while Joe trailed Tariq at a discreet distance.

Exiting a similar alley two shops down, Joe turned left onto Mackenzie Beach's concrete-tiled promenade. Bars and restaurants offering sidewalk seating lined the left side of the spacious walkway while the right was dotted with umbrella covered tables interspersed among a lengthy line of palm trees to shade customers from the sun. Twenty yards past the tables and palms was the white sand of the beach and the blue waters of the Med. Joe thought the area would be a good spot for a vacation, although he had no idea when his next opportunity for some time off might come around.

He kept Tariq in his peripheral vision, using him as a reference point while observing the people around him, looking for threats or anyone paying any undue attention to the man on a casual stroll along the promenade. So far, so good. Nothing appeared out of the ordinary.

Playing his role as the tourist, Tariq would stop every now and then and pull out his phone to snap a photo, photos that, unlike those taken by most of the people on the promenade, would never be posted to Instagram or any other social media platform, for that matter. He placed the smartphone back in his pocket, then entered the next stop along the route.

The interior of the Caffé Nero looked less like a coffee shop and more like a reading room in a well-appointed library. Leather upholstered chairs and distressed wood coffee tables provided a warm, welcoming vibe that encouraged patrons to hang around, read a book, or surf the web on the shop's free WIFI all in the hopes that they would order a second or even third round of coffee while passing the time. Tariq approached the barista, placed his to-go order, then scrolled through the photos on his phone while he waited.

There was no need for Joe to enter the coffee shop to keep an eye on Tariq because Chris had it covered. The former SEAL had been inside for the past hour, seated against the back wall in a spot that afforded him a view of the entire shop. Wearing board shorts and a tank top from a local surf shop, his shaggy, sandy-blond hair and perpetual year-round tan did not fit anyone's image of what a highly trained American operative might look like. With his laptop out, and ear buds in, no one would ever imagine he was anything other than a surfer on a coffee break.

Glancing over the top of its screen, he watched as Tariq received his order from the barista and headed for the door. As he did, Chris made a show of speaking into the mic on his earbuds even though the communication was going out through his covert earpiece. "He's coming out. All clear in the coffee shop."

The SDR continued for another forty-five minutes, culminating with a visit to a dive shop where Tariq inquired about a scuba diving trip the following day. With his guided dive booked for ten o'clock the next morning, he meandered back to the parking lot and retrieved his rental car. Next stop, the hotel.

CHAPTER 22

CONTEMPORARY IN ITS design, the eight-story Sun Hall Hotel faced Phinikoudes Beach and offered guests a view of the Larnaca Marina. The hotel's prime location meant it was no more than a ten-minute walk from museums, the open-air market, or historical sites like the Church of Saint Lazarus or the Medieval Fort.

John Roberts closed the door that connected the two suites on the hotel's sixth floor. With the help of a logistics officer who had made the one-hour drive from the embassy in Nicosia with a technical-security-countermeasures package, John had swept both rooms for eavesdropping devices. Satisfied they were clean, he set up three covert wireless cameras that would allow the team to monitor the encrypted feeds of Scott and Tariq's discussion next door.

In addition to the TSCM gear, the logistics officer had brought the team a gift. John walked over to the coffee table and popped the latches on the black hard-sided case. What he saw when he lifted the lid brought a smile to his face. Four Glock 19 semi-automatic pistols, along with three magazines for each, rested in foam cut-outs. And as an added bonus, he found the logistics officer had included four suppressors. It was a nice touch, and John told the man so.

Using the suppressors to dampen the sound of gunfire was certainly effective, but they presented a unique set of challenges. First, the can, as the suppressor was called, became hot to the touch after the weapon was fired. That left the shooter with two options, either wear gloves or wait for it to cool before removing it. And second, with the suppressor attached, the pistol was absurdly long and difficult to conceal, not ideal when trying to move through a city without attracting any undue attention. However, if all went well, and at this point they had no reason to believe otherwise, the team wouldn't need to use the pistols or the suppressors. Still, John appreciated the gesture and felt it was always better to have a piece of equipment and not need it, rather than need it and not have it.

While they waited for Tariq and the rest of the team to arrive, John stripped down each weapon and performed a functions check. Approving of their condition, he went to work inspecting the ammunition and magazines. He began by thumbing the nine-millimeter, jacketed hollow-point rounds onto the bedspread, then disassembled the mags and inspected their springs before reassembling and reloading them.

"Looks like he's here," the logistics officer said as he monitored the laptop.

John finished with the weapons and placed three of them back into their respective cutouts inside the case. He tucked the fourth Glock into the rear waistband of his jeans before moving over to where the man was sitting. Leaning over his shoulder, John saw Tariq's image on the screen.

The sound of a keycard sliding into the locking mechanism on the outside of the room's door caught John's attention and he reached over to close the lid of the weapons case. If it was someone from housekeeping or the hotel's management team, he didn't want to have to explain why he had a small arsenal in the room. With the pistols concealed from view, John's right hand slid behind his back and his fingers wrapped around the Glock's familiar grip. The rest of the guys were supposed to be returning to the hotel any minute, but he wasn't taking any chances.

The lock clicked and he saw a sandaled foot push the door open. Recognizing the beat-up footwear, he relaxed, then walked over and grabbed the door handle, pulling it the rest of the way open. He was greeted by Chris Ryan's smiling face.

Looking like a beach bum in his tank-top and board shorts, Chris entered the room holding a carry-out tray of coffees in one hand and a white plastic bag filled with bottles of water in the other. "Thanks, man. For a minute there, I thought I was going to dump the whole damn tray in the hallway."

"Excellent!" the logistics officer said, a little too enthusiastic for either man's taste. "You brought coffee."

Chris gave the guy a strange look as he set the tray with four cups on the desk. "That I did, my friend." Confused, he glanced at John, then back at the man savoring the coffee as he monitored Tariq on the computer's screen. "If you don't mind my asking, who the hell are you?"

John made the introductions, then reached for one of the coffees and twisted it out of the cardboard tray. Approving of Chris's choice of blends, he pointed to the desk and said, "You only brought four? I know you joined the SEALs because the Navy recruiter told you there'd be no math, but including our new friend here," referring to the logistics officer, "there are five of us."

Ignoring the slight, Chris grabbed a bottle of water out of the plastic bag, spun the lid off, and downed half of it in one long pull. "Dude, I was in that coffee shop forever waiting on Tariq. Trust me, I am fully caffeinated." He finished off the bottle and tossed it into the recycle section of the divided trash can next to the desk. Spotting his North Face duffle sitting against the wall, he unzipped the top flap, and rummaged through it for a change of clothes. Time to swap the board shorts, tank top, and sandals for some jeans, an untucked shirt, and his favorite pair of Salomon X Ultra hiking boots.

John's phone chimed, and he read the text bubble that appeared on the screen. "Joe and Scott just entered the lobby. They're on the way up."

Five minutes later, the team was back together, going over the game plan for the meeting with Tariq when the secure video conferencing program on a second laptop began ringing. Joe took the computer off the desk and set it on top of the hard-sided case on the coffee table. Taking a seat on the couch, he checked to make sure the encrypted VPN was engaged, plugged in his earbuds, then hit the button to accept the video call.

While it was not at all unusual to get a call from Langley with status updates or changes to a mission's requirements, it was, however, odd for it to be coming in from the director's conference room. The image of Carl Douglas, Joe's boss, appeared on the screen, but his presence was overshadowed by the DDO, Katherine Clark, and Director Sloan himself.

Wondering what was going on, Joe said, "Good evening, sir."

Getting straight to the point, Director Sloan replied, "Is Scott there with you?"

"Yes, sir. He is."

"Please have him join you on screen."

Joe unplugged his earbuds and motioned Scott over to the laptop. "Sir, the rest of the guys are in the room, along with a logs officer from the station in Nicosia. Any problem with them hearing what you have to say?"

Sloan thought it over for a minute. "No. Let them stay. You and Scott would have to brief them after we spoke anyway, so this will save you the trouble."

Scott took a seat on the couch and slid next to Joe so both of their faces were visible on the video teleconference. He turned up the volume so the guys could hear the conversation.

"Have you had your meeting with Mr. Kabbani?" Sloan began.

"We were making the final preparations for it when you called," Scott answered.

"Good. There have been some developments, and I'm hoping he may be able to shed some light on them." Sloan spent the next ten minutes detailing the attack on the drone base and finished by summarizing the discussion in the White House Situation Room.

"So the consensus is that the Russians were responsible for the attack and launched the mission out of Syria?" Joe asked, mulling over the logistics of such an operation in his mind. It made sense. Their military bases in Tartus and Latakia would be a great jumping off point and provided all the infrastructure and support a unit would need to carry out such a mission. And if the Russians did have teams from Alpha Group in-country, they would have the training and expertise to take down an airfield, not to mention the ruthlessness necessary to kill everyone on the base.

"That's correct," Sloan agreed. "Ever since Russia's entry into the Syrian civil war, President Polovkin has been looking for a way to increase his influence in the Middle East. But to do that, he needs to undermine or marginalize our presence in the region. I'm sure he has a plan to do just that, but we're still working to figure out exactly what it is. Stealing the Reaper was not the ultimate goal of the mission, just his opening move. I'm afraid it's the beginning of something much larger, something more sinister."

A nightmare scenario was running through Joe's head, and from the looks on the other guys' faces, they were thinking along the same lines. "Sir, what's our level of confidence that the Russians won't be able to fly the drone? I mean, we've owned the skies on every battlefield for the last twenty years and our forces have been able to operate without worrying about airstrikes from our enemies. But if the Russians could get that Reaper operational, they could turn the tables on us, or worse, attack our partners in the region and make it look like we did it."

A slight smile spread across the DCIA's face. This was exactly the reason it was so important for him to have many of his best people in the field. There were plenty of smart people at headquarters who would be drafting analytical papers on what they believed to be the most likely scenarios. But Joe had just come up with perhaps the best explanation yet. It was an idea Sloan had been mulling over but hadn't shared with anyone up to this point.

"To answer your question, we don't think it's very likely." He went on to describe the briefing General Rodriguez had given the president, and that new encryption keys had been sent out to all stations and drone bases around the world. "That being said, the Russians have some exceptionally talented computer scientists and aerospace engineers. I wouldn't be surprised if they eventually figure out some workaround to get the Reaper airborne. But I think you hit the nail on the head with your second point. If they can get the UAV operational, it would open up the possibility of conducting aerial strikes with all the evidence pointing back to the United States."

"Scott," Katherine Clark said, "we need you to task Tariq with finding out everything he can about the attack and what the Russians did with the Reaper. And please impress upon him that time is of the essence. We need to get a handle on this situation before the Russians get our bird in the air."

The secure video call ended, and Joe closed the laptop. He looked at Scott sitting next to him on the couch. "Well, it looks like your meet and greet with your new asset just took on a whole new level of importance."

CHAPTER 23

BASSEL AL-ASSAD INTERNATIONAL Airport was located fifteen miles south of Latakia and shared runways and facilities with the Syrian Air Force's Khmeimim Air Base. Tariq Kabbani marveled at the hive of activity as his plane taxied to its parking spot. Under a mutual agreement similar to the one allowing the Navy to control significant portions of the port in Tartus, the Russian Air Force had set up its headquarters at Khmeimim. MiG and Sukhoi fighters and ground attack aircraft littered the tarmac, preparing to conduct strikes against the remnants of ISIS extremists and the myriad rebel groups attempting to overthrow the regime.

Ground crews refueled and rearmed the sleek jets, many with what Tariq recognized to be cluster bombs. The weapons, outlawed in 2008 under the Convention on Cluster Munitions, dispersed small bomblets or submunitions over a wide area. Although these types of bombs were an effective tool against ground forces, they caused just as much if not more damage to innocent civilians. Drawn to the shiny, unexploded ordnance, children were especially likely to be maimed or killed, as the bomblets would detonate when they were picked up. He knew his people would be paying for the use of the weapons long after the rebel groups had been eliminated from the battlefield.

It had been a week since Tariq had returned from Cyprus. The initial face-to-face with his new handler, Scott Garrett, had gone well, and he felt their relationship was off to a good start. Armed with a laundry list of taskings, most of which related to finding out more about the attack in Jordan, Tariq had flown up to Latakia under the auspices of conducting meetings at the local General Intelligence Directorate's office. But he was really in town to see what, if anything, he could find out about the Russians' involvement in the theft of the Reaper, and what was going on in the hangar complex across the runway.

Rumors were still swirling about the mysterious cargo plane and flight of helicopters that had landed on the far side of the base seven days ago. The plane, an Antonov An-12, had taxied to a spacious tarmac near the helicopter pads, where three large flat-bed trucks waited. Several boxy containers, followed by one that was long and slender, were loaded onto the trucks and transported a short distance to a heavily guarded hangar. The magnitude of the security around the building was so unusual that it only made the speculation grow. From his discussion with Garrett back in Larnaca, he thought he had a good handle on what was inside the containers and why the hangar was protected as if it were the presidential palace in Damascus.

Tariq crossed the tarmac and entered the main terminal building. Since the base was also a functioning commercial airport, passengers milled around waiting on their flights as soldiers from the Syrian and Russian militaries went about the daily process of prosecuting a war. Navigating his way through the passengers and soldiers, he shook his head at the absurdity of the scene and headed up a flight of stairs to the offices on the second floor. He reached the landing, which opened onto a long hallway that ran the entire length of the building.

Turning right, he walked up to a small desk manned by two Russian privates, who looked so young he thought they should be at home watching YouTube videos or gaming on their XBOX. Tariq removed his government credentials from the inside pocket of his sports coat and handed them to one of the soldiers. "I'm here to see Colonel Teplov."

Colonel Vadim Teplov was the commanding officer of all GRU units operating in the Syrian theater of operations. Answering only to the Minister of Defense, the GRU deployed more assets to international locations than Russia's Foreign Intelligence Service, the SVR. Aside from its size and scope of operations, the GRU was unique in that it had command and control authority over Spetsnaz special forces units. Meaning, it was not only an intelligence gathering organization but had a direct-action capability as well.

The soldier eyed Tariq's credentials, then checked them against an access list. Seeing his name, he handed the ID back and said, "Thank you, sir."

Tariq returned the credentials to his pocket and started down the hallway, but the other soldier blocked his path. The young man's body language exuded authority and confidence but he was betrayed by the tentative tone in his voice. "Excuse me, sir. Are you armed?" Protocol dictated that all non-Russian visitors check their weapons at the desk.

As an officer charged with suppressing dissent for his country's intelligence service Colonel Tariq Kabbani had made his fair share of enemies over the years. Granted, most of them were no longer living, but there were still plenty who were. So he always had at least one weapon, sometimes more, readily accessible. "Look around you, young man," he began. "You do realize that we are in the middle of a war? There are people out there who would be only too happy to cut your head off with a dull butter knife or set you on fire for no other reason than to listen to your screams." He paused a moment to give the image time to crystalize in the soldier's mind. "Of course, I'm armed." Flaunting his clout as he would with low-ranking soldiers of his own military, he brushed past the young man without another word.

Entering Teplov's office, Tariq saw the GRU colonel was finishing up with a very fit-looking man wearing the desert camouflaged battle dress uniform favored by Russia's special forces units. The man seemed annoyed at the intrusion, but if Teplov shared his feelings, he was better at hiding it. Teplov ended the meeting and dismissed the soldier. "Thank you, Captain Kalugin. That will be all." The captain shot the GRU colonel an annoyed look for using his name and rank in front of the Syrian, before saluting and excusing himself.

Tariq was stunned at having just come face to face with the man who had killed Greg Jacobs on the hilltop in Salkhad. Being in the same room with Greg's killer, he felt a rage begin to churn in his gut, and it took every ounce of his training and experience to maintain a neutral expression. At this moment, Tariq wanted nothing more than to draw his weapon and unload every round in its magazine into the soldier. But like so many of the insider attacks that had taken place against American troops in Iraq and Afghanistan, he knew there was no way he would survive the encounter. He was not suicidal. Besides, there was still so much work to do to end the civil war and hopefully change the regime in Damascus. And then there was his family. He couldn't leave Rima and Nabil with the burden of surviving these trying times on their own. He had too much to live for. Instead, Tariq made a mental note to have a conversation with Scott Garrett about how to make the Russian pay for his transgression.

Now that they were alone, Tariq pushed aside the thoughts of killing the soldier called Kalugin and got down to business. As he had expected, Teplov was tight-lipped when asked about the unusual activity at the hangar across the airfield, brushing off the question with a dismissive wave of his hand before changing the subject. The rest of the discussion had been fairly routine, with Tariq passing along some intelligence on rebels operating in the area and the Russian colonel offering support when and where he could.

Thirty minutes later Tariq was back downstairs on the tarmac taking in the fresh air and feeling the warmth of the sun on his face. Reaching into his pocket, he pulled out his phone, opened the web browser, and typed in a search for MQ-9 Reaper storage containers. The first link he chose took him to an article on the U.S. Air Force's webpage for Wright Patterson Air Force Base. The article described, in remarkable detail the containers used to store and transport the UAV. The Reaper could be broken down into four parts and each section, the fuselage, propeller, engine, and wings, had its own specifically designed container. Amazed at what the Americans would put on the Internet, he downloaded photos of each of the crates before navigating to another page describing a similar process for the ground control station and satellite communication system.

Armed with the album of digital ammunition, Tariq walked the airport's grounds in search of anyone who might recognize the items in the photos. He had been at it for about an hour without any luck, and frustration was beginning to set in. Either the Russians had done a great job of cloaking the unloading of the containers, or, as Teplov had said, the activity over at the hangar really was nothing of significance. Tariq decided he would give it another thirty minutes, then call it quits for the day.

When the half hour was up, a disappointed but not dejected Tariq Kabbani headed back toward the terminal. *This was the nature of intelligence work,* he told himself. There were days, like today, when it could be a grind. But he knew that he would keep grinding until he found the truth. Maybe it was time for a break, grab a bite to eat and figure out a new game plan. As he approached the VIP parking area where the local GID office had left a car for him, he noticed an old man pulling a hose around the corner of the building. Tariq stopped and watched as the man began watering the shrubs and flowers that welcomed passengers arriving in Latakia. *Why not?* he thought. *What have I got to lose?*

Putting his meal off for a few more minutes, Tariq walked over and greeted the man. "As-Salaam-Alaikum." Peace be upon you.

Startled that anyone would acknowledge his presence, the man looked up with a face that had been creased and weathered by a lifetime of toiling in the harsh Syrian elements. "Wa-Alaikum-Salaam." And unto you, peace.

Tariq asked, "How long have you worked at the airport, my friend?"

Tapping his fingers as he counted, the man said, "Twenty-seven years. I've done nearly every job around here at one time or another. I was a baggage handler when I was younger and stronger. But as the years continued to pass, I had to find other, less strenuous, jobs."

"Well," Tariq said, finding himself enjoying the conversation with the old man, "I'm sure you've seen quite a bit around here over the years."

"Oh, yes," the man replied. "We used to have flights coming in from all over the world, places like Europe, South America, and even the United States." The man looked a little melancholy as he recalled the old days. "But not so much lately. Since the war, it seems like the only people flying in and out of the airport are Russians."

Seeing his opportunity to manipulate the conversation toward the hangar, he motioned in its direction. "Speaking of the Russians, what do you think is going on over there?"

Glancing around to make sure they were alone, the man lowered his voice almost to a whisper and said, "They're guarding something very special."

"Really? What makes you say that?" Tariq inquired, suddenly interested in what the old man had to say.

"Because I saw it," he continued, excited to finally share his secret with someone.

"Tell me, sir. What exactly did you see?"

The man took one more look around, not wanting anyone to overhear their conversation. "About a week ago, one of their cargo planes landed and taxied over near the hangar. The odd thing was that after the engines shut down and the auxiliary power unit was connected, the crew remained onboard. No one came out and no other ground crew approached the plane. The whole procedure was very odd. That's why I noticed it."

"What happened next?"

"Nothing," the man said, pausing for dramatic affect. "Until the helicopters arrived."

Getting the feeling he was on to something, Tariq encouraged him to continue.

"There were four of them. One of the big attack helicopters, two transports, and one that was smaller than the rest. They landed about thirty minutes after the cargo plane."

"Then what happened?"

"Heavily armed men poured out of the transports and formed a circle around the plane. One of them began giving orders, then three flatbed trucks that had been idling nearby backed up to the rear of the plane and the crew began unloading their cargo."

Feeling his own excitement begin to rise, Tariq asked, "And what did this cargo look like?"

"It was a bunch of large gray crates. But one was different than the others."

"How so?"

"It was long and narrow."

Tariq fished his phone out of his pocket, opened the photos app, and moved next to the man so he could see the screen. "Did they look anything like this?"

The man scrolled through the photos with a gnarled finger, its skin resembling the texture of deeply tanned shoe leather. He looked up at the Syrian intelligence officer and said, "They looked exactly like that."

CHAPTER 24

INSIDE THE HEAVILY guarded hangar across the runways from the main terminal building, Vasily Zubkin walked around the reassembled MQ-9 Reaper. Trailing his right hand across its smooth, flat-gray surface, he marveled at the simple yet elegant design of the airframe that surrounded the state-of-the-art technology encased inside its fuselage. He had never seen anything so beautiful in his life and being in the presence of such a magnificent technological achievement made Zubkin realize just how far his country lagged behind the Americans in this arena.

Yes, Russia had been flying its own fleet of drones for years, but they were primarily variants purchased from countries like Israel, then modified to meet its own specific needs. They were small designs used primarily by on-the-ground commanders to conduct battlefield reconnaissance. While the Americans already had several newer generations of drones patrolling the skies, Russia had nothing even remotely close to this machine in its arsenal.

After graduating at the top of his class from the prestigious Moscow Aviation Institute, Zubkin had been offered his choice of assignments. Without hesitation, he chose his government's unmanned aerial vehicle program, believing UAVs were the wave of the aviation industry's future. Technology was advancing at a rate faster than the human body could adapt, and the g-forces pilots endured in the newest generations of fighter aircraft were making it more and more difficult to have an actual person in the cockpit.

Vitally aware of the gap between the two countries' programs, Russia's president had commissioned a top-secret initiative that would vault his military's UAV capabilities lightyears ahead of where it stood at the present. As one of Russia's brightest young minds, Zubkin was selected to be part of the team to design and build the drone his president had envisioned. Inspired by the bat-wing design of the American B-2 stealth bomber, the top-secret UAV would be jet-powered and have an internal weapons bay capable of holding a deadly payload. But it was probably still six months to a year away from leaving the ground on its maiden flight. And even though it was the most technologically advanced UAV Russia had ever designed, Zubkin had a nagging thought in the back of his head that their shiny new drone was not up to the standards set by this brilliant piece of machinery sitting on the hangar floor before him.

"Ah, there you are, Vasily," Colonel Teplov's voice echoed through the hangar. "I've been looking all over for you."

Snapped out of his trance-like reverie, Zubkin said, "Good afternoon, Colonel. What can I do for you?"

"I just stopped by to see how things were progressing. Moscow has selected our first target and would like to know when they can expect the attack to occur."

The aerospace engineer paused a moment, thinking of the best way to phrase his answer to emphasize the positives and minimize the negatives. "The Reaper has been reassembled and is airworthy. My technicians and the members of Alpha Group took the greatest of care loading the drone, and their attention to detail was well worth any additional time spent on the ground."

Teplov agreed. He had been impressed with the overall efficiency of the operation. "And what of the ground control station and satcom system?"

"The same," Zubkin continued. "All components are fully operational."

"Excellent!" Teplov exclaimed, slapping the engineer on the back. "So, when can I let Moscow know it will be ready to fly?"

Now came the hard part. "We still have two hurdles to overcome before we can conduct the first mission, colonel"

"Really, Vasily? And what would they be?"

"First, we would need to conduct several test flights in order to give the pilot an opportunity to become accustomed to the UAV's flight characteristics."

"I'm afraid that will be impossible," Teplov countered. "We can't risk having anyone see the drone."

"Sir, without the test flights, there's a much greater risk of a crash. And that would put an end to this operation before it even gets off the ground." The play on words was not lost on either man.

"And what of the pilot? Do you have so little faith in his ability to fly the Reaper?"

"It's not that I don't have confidence in our pilot, he's quite experienced from what I'm told. But please remember, we don't have a UAV in our entire inventory that is even remotely comparable to the Reaper. Asking him to conduct a successful mission his first time at the controls is an unreasonable expectation for even the most experienced pilot. Would we require a fighter pilot to fly a mission of such importance without ever being in the cockpit of our most advanced MiG? With only time in a training simulator? I think, not."

Teplov considered Zubkin's argument, weighing the risk of discovery against the very real need for the pilot to test-fly the Reaper. Knowing he would find himself in a Siberian work camp or with a bullet in the back of the head if the Reaper crashed on its maiden flight, he relented. "Alright, Vasily. I'll make the case to Moscow for at least one test flight."

Zubkin breathed a sigh of relief. "Thank you, sir."

"And the second hurdle you spoke about?"

Gesturing for Teplov to follow him, Zubkin led the way across the hangar and spoke as they walked. "The system's encryption."

They entered a room that had been fabricated to house the ground control station and serve as the operation's command center. The room was dark, the only illumination coming from the control panels of the GCS and the twin monitors on a desk next to the unit. A CAT-6 ethernet cable ran from the GCS to a desktop tower that would be the envy of any computer gamer. An odd-looking figure banged away at the ergonomic keyboard, sending what appeared to be random strings of letters, numbers, and symbols across the monitor to her right. Whenever she hit the enter key, she would shift her attention and watch the left screen for a corresponding response to the command she had just sent.

Taking advantage of the momentary break in the action, Zubkin said,

"Good morning, Anna." Motioning to his left, he continued, "You remember Colonel Teplov."

Seeing the men approach, Anna Kovaleski removed a pair of white earbuds and leaned back in her chair. Sporting a pink and purple mohawk with tattoos of AK-47s inked on the shaved sides of her head, she wore a leather biker's jacket, torn jeans, and thick-soled Doc Martens. Anna, or AK as she preferred to be called, looked like the poster child for the punk rock counterculture of the nineteen-eighties. She interlaced her fingers and raised her arms, palms to the ceiling. Stretching tired muscles, she yawned, "It's morning already?"

As a hacker of the first order, Anna Kovaleski was one of her government's most dangerous weapons in the clandestine cyberwar being conducted across the ether of the World Wide Web. Her talents were discovered almost by accident when she was arrested during a sting operation in St. Petersburg. Pressured by the international community to crackdown on the tidal wave of scams, malware, and ransomware attacks emanating from inside Russia's borders, the FSB had conducted raids across the country as a token effort to quiet some of the criticism.

Given the choice of a long, torturous jail sentence or living in relative freedom while doing the government's bidding online, Anna had chosen the latter. Spending time in a Russian prison would have been bad enough, but the thought of going years without access to the Internet was a fate she was not willing to endure. After agreeing to put her talents to work for the GRU, she was assigned to a cyberwarfare unit called APT28. It was just one of many such units belonging to Russia's military intelligence arm, but APT28 was the most well-known to the West for its targeting of the governments, infrastructure, and militaries of the Ukraine, the Republic of Georgia, and other states across Eastern Europe. Having been the team lead on many of those hacks had earned Anna the opportunity to crack the American drone's encryption.

Zubkin gestured at the monitors. "Making any progress?"

"It's slow going," AK said, rubbing her tired eyes. "Whoever wrote this code knew what they were doing." Her admiration for the other programmer's skills were obvious to the two men. "The encryption is so advanced that this process could take much longer than the timeline you've given me."

That was clearly not what Teplov wanted to hear. "Perhaps your skills are not as impressive as I was led to believe. Maybe I should bring in someone else, someone who can break the encryption in a timely manner."

Appearing bored with the conversation, the young hacker looked up at Teplov, "You have access to my file, no?"

Wondering where she was going with this, he said, "Of course."

"And you have read it?"

"I have."

"Then you have seen the operations I've led and should know there is no one better. If there was, you would have brought them here in the first place and they would be sitting in this chair instead of me. So quit wasting my time with insults and idle threats."

A sly smile spread across Zubkin's face and he turned his head slightly away from the GRU colonel to keep him from seeing it. He liked this girl and they got along well, so he tried a different approach. "Do you have any ideas as to how we could help speed up the process? Maybe come at the problem from another angle?"

It was AK's turn to smile, appreciating the aerospace engineer's analytical approach. If he were ten years younger, she might even find him attractive. Pushing the thought from her head, she said, "I like the way you think, Vasily." Then she looked up at Teplov. "You see, colonel, he's being helpful, trying to work the problem, instead of attempting to intimidate me."

Teplov rolled his eyes, knowing that with a single phone call, he could replace her at any point he felt she was not up to the task. As far as he was concerned, the hacking cells in Moscow were full of young talent who would jump at the chance to work on a project like this. But he decided to tolerate her insolence for the time being. "So, how exactly do you propose to, as you said, work the problem?"

AK swiveled on her chair and swiped a finger across a laptop's touchpad. As its screen came to life, Zubkin and Teplov leaned in to get a better look, but the multiple windows running strings of code were a foreign language that neither man could comprehend. Finally, Zubkin asked, "What are we looking at?"

She went on to explain that each window was running an exploit that attacked firewalls, servers, and computers' operating systems. Some of the software was of her own design, while other programs running on the laptop were created by the hacking cells in Moscow. She was even using a few tools that belonged to the NSA's Equation Group after they had been leaked online several years ago.

The target of all this black-hat computing prowess was an American company called General Atomics. Based in San Diego, California, it had been created in the 1950s as a division of General Dynamics. Specializing in nuclear fuel cycles, electromagnetic systems, and wireless and laser technologies, General Atomics was also the maker of some of the most successful and advanced remotely piloted aircraft flown by the CIA and the U.S. military. The MQ-9 Reaper, the UAV sitting several meters away on the polished floor of the expansive hangar, was one of General Atomics' products.

She clicked the touchpad, bringing up another window that had been minimized to the task bar and said, "I'm also running a phishing scam against a list of known email addresses within the company." She knew that some bonehead was bound to click on the link she had embedded in an authentic-looking corporate email. The link would activate a string of executable code that would give her access to the employee's computer. Once inside the system, either through the employee's machine or by using the more exotic exploits running in the background, she hoped to find something on the company's servers, a classified paper or technical blueprint that would allow her to bypass or reset the drone system's encryption.

Teplov was impressed. Perhaps Kovaleski had earned some leeway and deserved the benefit of the doubt after all. He had indeed read her file from cover to cover, and there was no denying the skill she had demonstrated on past cyber operations. He knew she was the most talented hacker in any of his government's cells, but he would never tell her that. Perhaps it was her appearance that rubbed him the wrong way. After thinking it over, he decided it was more likely her attitude. It reminded him of the rough spell he had gone through with his daughter during her teenage years, that rebellious period when it seemed that he was an idiot with no understanding of her or of what was happening in her world. Dealing with Kovaleski gave him that same feeling. And though he doubted he would ever totally understand the young hacker, he could appreciate someone who was an expert at their craft. And when it came to manipulating ones and zeroes, she was a craftsman of the highest caliber.

Teplov's phone vibrated in his pocket, snapping him out of his thoughts. Seeing the caller-ID on the screen, he excused himself and waited until he was back in the hangar to engage the call.

The voice on the other end of the line said, "He's here."

"You're sure?" Teplov asked, needing to be certain before he put the next part of the operation into motion.

"Positive, sir. His presence was advertised on an email circulated around NATO headquarters here in Brussels. It appears he will be in town only for a few days, so we must act or risk losing our window of opportunity."

Teplov thought it over for a minute. AK did seem to be making progress, but who knew how long it would take, or if she would be successful at all. No, better to have a contingency plan in place than to put all his eggs in one basket with the girl. His decision made, he said, "Keep an eye on him. But be discreet. I'll get the team on the way. Be prepared to receive them and provide any assistance the team leader requires."

He thumbed the red icon to end the call, then re-entered the room just as the laptop began emitting an audible alarm. He quickened his pace and joined the other two as a new window appeared on its screen displaying the view of a General Atomics employee's computer.

Slack-jawed, Zubkin pointed to the laptop. "Is that what I think it is?"

Someone had taken the bait and clicked the link. Allowing herself a subtle fist pump, AK leaned back in her chair and took a long sip of an energy drink, savoring its flavor as if it were the finest champagne on the planet. Swiveling her chair to face the men, she looked up at Teplov and said with a grin, "That, my good colonel, is how I work the problem."

CHAPTER 25

WITH THE OPERATION in Cyprus wrapped up, Joe's team had taken Scott Garrett to the general aviation terminal at Larnaca International Airport. There they handed him off to the crew of a Beechcraft King Air B-350 belonging to the CIA's Air Branch. With Garrett wheels up for the flight back to Amman, Joe and the team had been ordered to remain in Cyprus rather than head home right away. Headquarters wanted to keep them in the region in case something broke in the next few days.

So, with nothing better to do, the guys took advantage of their paid time off and acted like all the other tourists on the island. Joe made the two-hour drive in the rented SUV to the west and hiked the trails in the hills around Mt. Olympus, the highest point in Cyprus. Chris spent his time at the beach surfing and snorkeling while John explored Larnaca's historical sites, starting with the Church of Saint Lazarus, which dated to the ninth century, and the Medieval Fort, built in the twelfth century to protect the city's harbor.

At the end of each day the trio would meet for dinner before making their way to the promenade at Mackenzie Beach for a few beers. Joe thought it had been a pretty good couple of days. He just wished Kevin and Mike were there to enjoy the downtime with them. But at the rate the guys' rehab was going, he had no doubt they would be back with the team before long.

After spending a good deal of time and money in the local bars and restaurants, they decided to give the Irish-themed Bennigan's a shot. The three experienced travelers from the CIA could be away from home only so long before giving in to the cravings for a little Americana. Joe couldn't remember the last time he had been to one of the restaurants and wasn't even sure the chain was still open for business in the States. After a quick check of the company's website on his phone, it turned out there were still a few of the restaurants spread across the upper Midwest. But what really surprised him were the number of international locations. Apparently, the chain was a huge hit along the gulf coast of Mexico and had restaurants in Bahrain, Qatar, and Dubai as well. The big stunner, though, was that Cyprus had four of the eateries on the tiny island. Who knew the Cypriots were such fans?

Joe had just ordered the first round when his phone began vibrating. Flipping it face up on the table, he took a quick peek at the screen. Seeing the number, he wagered, "Ten bucks says our vacation on Uncle Sugar's dime just came to a screeching halt."

*

Eighteen hours later, Joe found himself sitting inside a sensitive compartmented information facility or SCIF, on the third floor of the U.S. Embassy in Brussels, while Chris and John were getting settled in a nearby hotel.

Three other people joined Joe at the table in the windowless, soundproof room designed to be impervious to electronic eavesdropping. Reed Ashton was a preppy Ivy Leaguer in his mid-forties who had graduated from Brown University before joining the CIA. He had worked his way up the ladder of the civilized intelligence community, never serving in a hardship post or war zone before being assigned as the chief of Brussels station. To Ashton's right was Vivian Vernon, the National Security Agency's representative to NATO. She wore a dark skirt with a matching blazer over a white blouse. Her neckline was accentuated with a gold necklace that looked like the letter W but was instead the two overlapping Vs of her initials.

Elijah Miller rounded out the group and was the reason Joe's team had been sent to Brussels. With advanced degrees in mathematics and computer science from Carnegie Mellon, he merged the two disciplines, using his knowledge of each to become one of the world's leading architects of algorithms used to protect everything from text messaging apps to banking transactions. Recruiters from tech firms like Google and Microsoft had made the trip to Pittsburgh singing the praises of their respective companies. They had offered everything from obscene compensation packages to enormous research and development budgets to entice him westward. While the offers were certainly generous, becoming another cog in the tech giants' machine or participating in Silicon Valley's digital snobbery was not what he wanted to do with the rest of his life.

Interestingly, it was a pitch from a fellow Carnegie Mellon alum who had gone to work for the U.S. government that intrigued Miller the most. Prior to the unexpected visit, he had never considered a career in Washington. His mental image of a federal job consisted of drone-like bureaucrats sitting behind gun-metal-gray GSA issued desks punching time clocks on their way to retirement and a taxpayer-funded pension. To Miller, it sounded like one of the nine circles of Hell depicted so vividly in Dante's Inferno.

But that all changed when the alum said he worked for one of the agencies in the intelligence community. Seeing that Miller's interest was piqued, the recruiter baited the hook by shifting the conversation to what they were doing in the areas of encryption protocols and code breaking, two subjects in Miller's wheelhouse. Intrigued by the seemingly unlimited resources of the national security apparatus, but more importantly, the work being described, Miller accepted the offer. Two months later, with graduation behind him and two advanced degrees in hand, he put Pittsburgh in his rearview mirror and migrated the two-hundred fifty miles south to Fort Meade, Maryland, home of the National Security Agency.

That had been five years ago. Now he found himself in Belgium, having given a talk earlier in the day at the NATO School's Joint Targeting Staff Course. The courses of instruction were normally held in Oberammergau, Germany, but that facility was being renovated, so Miller's presentation had been moved to NATO headquarters in Brussels. Designed to teach military officers the approved targeting cycle, the Joint Targeting Staff Course included instruction on target development, weapons systems capabilities, mission planning and execution, and combat assessment. Additionally, it dealt with the issues of collateral damage and time sensitive targeting, none of which had anything whatsoever to do with Elijah Miller's area of expertise. He had been invited there to talk about encryption and its role in securing the link between the UAVs, their ground control stations, and the satellites that allowed the three individual units to communicate in a secure manner.

Joe could see Miller was not in a good mood, and under similar circumstances, he probably wouldn't have been either. It was nearing the end of the business day and Miller had been looking forward to a couple of drinks at the hotel bar when he had received Vernon's text telling him to get over to the embassy. Now, instead of a relaxing evening before catching his flight home in the morning, he was sitting in the SCIF wondering what the hell was going on, and more importantly, what it had to do with him.

Reed Ashton looked at his watch, clearly annoyed with the late hour of the meeting. "So, what is it we can do for you, Mr. Matthews?"

Joe spent the next ten minutes giving the assembled group the Cliffs Notes version of the attack on the drone base in Jordan and the theories being thrown around about what the Russians planned to do with the stolen Reaper. Did they steal it to reverse engineer the technology, or was it a worst-case scenario, where they were trying to get the UAV operational? He was here to find out if the latter was even possible.

The room fell silent except for the ever-present hissing of the air conditioner as everyone took a minute to digest the magnitude of what they had just been told. Joe took a sip of the Starbucks he had bought on the way to the embassy, then turned to Miller. "Well, what do you think?"

He could almost see the gears spinning as the encryption specialist ran through the most likely scenarios in his head. Finally, Miller seemed as if he had completed his mental gymnastics and come to a conclusion. "You said during the briefing that the commo guy was able to destroy the crypto keys before the Russians gained control of the base. How confident are you in that assessment?"

"The commo shop in Amman got an email from him confirming the destruction protocols had been followed. The timestamp on the email indicates it was sent minutes before the control center was overrun."

"Good man," Miller said, appreciating the communicator's actions even more, knowing that he had been killed before the assault force left the base. "The Russians have some talented people over there, but without the crypto keys, there's no way they can break my encryption."

There was a fine line between confidence and arrogance. Joe had seen plenty of arrogant people overestimate their abilities and needed to find out what side of the line Miller was on. "You sound pretty sure of yourself."

"That's because I'm exceptionally good at what I do. Even with all the computing power we have at Meade, it would take the mainframes years to crack my algorithm. And truth be told, I'm not so sure they could even do it at all."

Feeling a little better about the situation, Joe continued, "So you're saying it's impossible for the Russians to get the Reaper operational?"

Sounding a little annoyed that the big redhead couldn't seem to keep up with the conversation, Miller shook his head. "What I said is that they can't break the encryption. They could, however, get in through a backdoor in the system if they could access General Atomics' servers."

"There's a backdoor? You've got to be shitting me?"

"Look, man," Miller explained. "Regardless of what the different agencies do with the drone, it's still just a flying computer. And at times, computers lock up. Ever had that happen with your machine at home?

"Sure."

"And what's the first thing tech support tells you to do? You either force it to reboot, or sometimes, in a worst-case scenario, you reinstall the operating system. Same concept applies here. If the UAV's computers lock up, and it does happen from time to time, then there has to be a way to reboot the system. Otherwise, what you have is an airframe that looks cool sitting on the tarmac or inside a hangar but is really nothing more than an expensive set of spare parts waiting to be scavenged for another drone. So in order to get it back online, the designers built in the backdoor."

Joe was afraid of the answer but had to ask the question. "And if the Russians can access this backdoor…"

Miller finished the sentence for him, "Then they can install their own encryption and the Reaper would never know the difference."

"And how many people know about this backdoor?"

"Officially?" Miller took a moment to think about his answer. "It's impossible to give you an accurate number, but it's probably way more than necessary. The backdoor is possibly the worst kept secret of the entire program. First, you have the programmers and employees at any of the companies who build the drones." He raised a finger as he counted off each one. "General Atomics. Lockheed Martin. Northrop Grumman. Then throw in all the Air Force and CIA maintenance techs who keep the drones airworthy." Miller shook his head. "It's a pretty big number, man."

Joe didn't like the direction this conversation was heading. "Think the Russians would know about this backdoor?"

"Probably. Like I said, they've got some smart people over there. And once they get a taste of my encryption, they'll know they can't break it. If the roles were reversed and I was the one looking for another way in, gaining access to the backdoor would be the first option I'd try."

Fuck. Joe needed to brief Langley, so he called for short break. As the others stood to leave the SCIF, he said, "Reed, why don't you stay for the video conference?" He knew it would stroke Ashton's ego to be included on the VTC. But Joe had an ulterior motive. He was going to ask for weapons from the station's stash and had the feeling the COS would balk at having an armed team he could not control running around on his turf. By having him onscreen in front of the heavyweights at headquarters, Joe hoped this would be one battle he would not have to fight. He was going to have enough on his plate in the next few hours and didn't want to waste time arguing with Ashton over the logistical support he would need to do his job.

CHAPTER 26

Now THAT HE had his answers and had reported the findings back to Langley, Joe's mission transitioned to a protective operation. He, along with Director Sloan and the rest of the CIA's leadership, had every reason to believe the Russians were aware of Elijah Miller's presence in Brussels. The GRU had penetrated several NATO members' militaries and would have had access to the school's curriculum and email distribution lists identifying the NSA encryption specialist as the keynote speaker at today's event. It was the consensus of the group that Russian intelligence was not above conducting a snatch and grab operation to bring the designer of the program in to help solve the problem if they were unable to crack the encryption themselves.

Joe called the guys, had them join him at the embassy, and reconvened the meeting once they arrived. With everyone back in the SCIF, he reiterated the director's concerns for those who weren't on the video conference and laid out his plan for getting Miller out of the country.

Vivian Vernon said, "Why isn't the NSA handling Elijah's extraction?"

Joe explained that while the NSA had a small protective detail that supported their director, it didn't have the larger, dedicated division on par with what the CIA had to offer. So, on occasion, members of the Agency's protective operations division, either from the Director's Protective Staff or the Protective Resource Group, would be detailed over to Ft. Meade to support specific requirements. This operation was a prime example of one of those occasions.

Eli sat there listening to the conversation, so far out of his element that the talk of a protective detail, a covert extraction, and Russians out to get him was enough to make his head spin. All he wanted to do at this point was to go back to the hotel, get a good night's sleep and fly home in the morning. "What makes you so sure it's not safe for me to stay at my hotel tonight?"

Pointing to the two other members of his team, Joe said, "Because if the roles were reversed, and we were the team conducting the rendition, we'd wait until you were tucked in and sound asleep before sneaking into your room and snatching you. If I had to guess, I'd say the Russians will have a similar plan."

The mention of the term rendition caused a visceral reaction from Miller, and Joe could see he was starting to freak out. Not that he could blame the guy. He was a computer nerd whose closest encounter with violence probably came in the form of a marathon session of Call of Duty on his XBOX One.

"This…this is bullshit," Eli's voice wavered, betraying the bravado he was trying to portray. "I came over here to give a talk at NATO. Now you're telling me I'm wrapped up in the middle of some international conspiracy and Russian spooks are here to snatch me? No way this is happening for real." He stood as if to leave. "I'm outta here. I'm going back to the hotel for a couple of beers, then catch my flight home in the morning. You guys enjoy your time in fantasy-land."

Chris pushed himself off the wall and blocked the exit. The sandy-haired operator said, "You're not leaving this building without the three of us, so why don't you sit your ass back down and let Joe finish briefing the plan."

From the look in the man's eyes and the tone of his voice, Eli got the distinct feeling it was an order, not a request. Without a word, he did an about face and returned to his seat. *Asshole.*

Joe always preferred to get along with the people he was protecting because it made the job easier on so many levels. He decided to come at Eli from a different angle. Speak a language he would understand. "Look," Joe began. "The GRU guys hunting you are the real deal, the boogeymen you wouldn't want to meet in your worst nightmare."

"If they're the boogeymen, then what does that make you?"

"You a gamer, Eli?"

"Yeah. What do you know about gaming?"

Joe said, "My call-sign is Spartan."

"Master Chief, huh?"

"HALO's my game, but I play some others as well. Ever tried World of Warcraft?"

Reed Ashton looked to Vivian Vernon who shrugged her shoulders, having no idea what the hell the muscular red head was talking about. It was like the two men were speaking some foreign language only they understood.

Eli said, "Sure. Everyone's taken a spin through the WoW universe at some point."

"So, you know what a Paladin is?"

"Yeah. The knight who fights for good."

"Who not only fights for good but is fully devoted to ridding the world of evil. A knight who, with a cause, is almost impossible to defeat in battle."

Thinking back to the character descriptions in the game, Eli said, "Yeah. Okay. But what's all this gaming talk got to do with the Russian boogeymen?"

Vernon and Ashton were wondering the same thing.

"Because," Joe said, pointing to the two members of his team. "We're those men charged with ridding the world of evil. We are the predators who kill the boogeymen. So, lose the attitude, follow our instructions to the letter, and everything will turn out fine."

Chris rolled his eyes. "If you two fourteen-year-olds are done with the nerd speak, can we please get the hell out of here and get on with the mission?"

*

After the video game discussion in the SCIF, Miller had seemed to be on board with the program, so Joe finished laying out his plan. About an hour southwest of Brussels, near the town of Chièvres, was a U.S. Air Force base that provided aerial and logistical support to NATO and SHAPE, the Supreme Headquarters Allied Powers Europe. In an odd turn of events that Joe could only explain by the conglomeration of units in the region, the airfield and its flight operations were run by the Air Force, but the overall maintenance and control of the base belonged to the U.S. Army.

Since the primary function of Chièvres Air Base was support, there were plenty of passenger transport aircraft standing by in case the brass needed to get around the theater. Joe's selection of the base for the extraction made the job of the Air Branch and Office of Military Affairs schedulers back at Langley that much easier. Within minutes of their request being processed, a crew was alerted and began pre-flighting a C-21A, the military version of the Learjet 35, for the quick hop to drop Joe, Miller, and the guys at Ramstein Air Force base in Germany. Once at Ramstein, the team would be met by one of the CIA's Gulfstream G650s for the leg back to Washington.

But first they had to swing by the hotel to pick up Miller's things, namely, the NSA issued laptop locked in his suitcase. Eli wouldn't leave without the computer, and they certainly didn't want it left behind for the Russians to exploit. Joe would have preferred to send Chris and John back to grab the bags, but Eli had insisted on going himself. The situation wasn't ideal, but Joe figured he'd give a little to get a little, hoping that by compromising with Miller on this, he'd be more willing to go along with something else when the time came.

They set off from the embassy with Chris, who dreamed of being a NASCAR driver in another life, behind the wheel. Joe was in the right front and Elijah Miller sat directly behind him. With the potential of having a group of Russian special forces operators in town looking for Miller, John had been sent ahead to advance the hotel. The last thing Joe wanted to do was walk the man he was charged with protecting into the waiting arms of a GRU or Alpha Group rendition team.

John sat in the modern, atrium-like lobby sipping a coffee. He had positioned himself so he could see the main entrance and reception area, but did so in a manner that didn't scream, "I'm a G-man on a surveillance operation." Like most others in the lobby, he had his tablet opened to a news site and pretended to swipe through articles as he kept an eye on the comings and goings of the hotel's patrons.

Activating the talk-around function on his encrypted phone, Joe let him know they were five minutes out.

Using a pair of generic earbuds as props to conceal his covert earpiece, John confirmed the call, sounding like every other businessman waiting on a colleague. "Sounds good. I'll see you in a few."

Joe didn't want to parade Elijah through the main lobby, preferring a discreet, low-profile approach, so he directed Chris to the hotel's side entrance.

Bringing the rented SUV to a stop, Chris said, "There's no parking on this street so I'm gonna have to move." He could only hang around for so long pretending to be waiting on someone before he would draw the attention of the local cops. "I'll make the block and pull into a spot across the street. Let me know when you're coming down and I'll meet you back here."

Finding a parking space with an unobstructed view of the hotel's main entrance, Chris took a minute to check out his surroundings. Called Place Jourdan, the rectangular parking lot separated two city blocks. Tree-lined sidewalks were packed with a variety of cafés, bars, and restaurants. On the hotel's west side, just across the Avenue du Maelbeek, was the Parc Leopold. Several government buildings and museums bordered the park. To the north was the House of European History, the state government offices, and the EU's European Committee of the Regions. The easternmost section of the park was dominated by the enormous home of the European Parliament, and to the south was the Museum of Natural Sciences. With a small lake and plenty of cobblestone and dirt paths, Chris thought the park would be great place for a run. Miller had chosen well, and Chris made a mental note to stay at the hotel if he ever came back to Brussels.

Using Eli's key card to access the side door, Joe and the NSA man entered the hotel. Being familiar with the building's layout, Eli led the way to the elevators. Before stepping in, Joe broadcast, "We're heading upstairs. Be down in a few." Both members of his team acknowledged the call as Eli hit the button for the third floor. Moments later a chime dinged, and the doors slid open. Before they exited, Joe asked, "Which way?"

"To the left. Room 312."

Stepping out of the elevator, Joe paused for a few seconds to glance up and down the hallway. *Clear.* Next, he scanned the area for security cameras and the locations of the stairwells. Satisfied he had a good feel for the floor's layout, he led the way to the room.

They stopped short of the door and Joe put a finger to his lips, indicating he wanted Eli to be quiet. Joe listened for a hushed conversation or sounds of movement while eyeing the door for any signs of tampering.

Seeing none, he gave a nod of his head, and Eli swiped his key card. The light on the sensor turned green and they heard the lock disengage.

Joe whispered, "Wait here," then entered the room, only drawing his weapon once he crossed the door's threshold and was out of the security camera's line of sight. The executive suite wasn't very large, and he cleared it in under fifteen seconds. Confident there weren't any Russian spooks hiding in the closet or under the bed, he summoned Miller inside.

CHAPTER 27

A WHITE PANEL van eased to a stop and double-parked along a line of cars across the street from the hotel's main lobby. The driver activated the van's hazard lights, implying that it was on some type of delivery and would only be there for a few minutes. From the design of the logo on the side of the van, it appeared to belong to some type of mom and pop furniture business. Chris guessed that made sense. Over time, furniture in the hotel was bound to get damaged or need repairs. And if the hotel staff didn't have the capability to do the work in-house, they would have to contract it out. He was about to dismiss the van as a concern when the side door slid open and three men stepped out. *Those are not Belgian furniture makers,* he thought.

*

"We're not operating in some backwater town in Syria," Captain Gennady Kalugin had reminded his men. "We're in the heart of Europe. Be discreet."

"He's a computer geek," one of his men said with an almost bored tone. "How hard could it be? What's he going to do, hit us over the head with his keyboard?"

The comment drew a few chuckles from the back of the van, but Kalugin stared daggers through the joker. "You should know by now that underestimating your opponent is a good way to get yourself killed in this business, Anton."

Given the target, Kalugin could understand the men's attitude toward the assignment. After being deployed to Syria for the better part of the last year, this assignment had to seem like a walk in the park. He knew the American target would be no match for his battle-hardened men. His bigger concern at this point was being compromised and having to deal with the authorities. Kalugin flicked his head toward the door. "Get moving."

*

Chris hailed the team. "You know those guys we were concerned about? Well, I think they just showed up. Three burly dudes heading your way, John. You should have eyes-on in about thirty seconds."

Looking up from the tablet, John keyed on the men immediately as he sipped his coffee. *Jesus,* he thought. *Could you be any more obvious?* "Got 'em. Dark suits and operator beards. Not very low-profile." He set the cup back on the saucer and watched as the men paused in the foyer, scanning the lobby with all the personality of three killer robots from the Terminator movies.

One of the men approached the concierge and John saw him point in the direction of the elevators. The trio cut through the gray-carpeted lounge, passing within three feet of his chair. They appeared uninterested in the people in the lobby, having dismissed them as possible threats. Apparently, John was doing an excellent job of blending in with the rest of the guests because none of the men gave him a second look.

When they were out of earshot, John relayed, "Get a move on, Joe. They're heading for the elevators." He downed the last sip of coffee, then slid the tablet into his rucksack. Moving with a purpose, he crossed the lobby to a stairwell and paused to glance at the elevator's floor indicator. Seeing where it stopped, he pushed through the door then sprinted upward, taking the stairs three at a time.

The elevator doors parted, and Anton stepped out onto the third floor. The other two followed, as he consulted the sign on the wall that denoted which set of rooms were to the left and right. Without a word, he turned left and strode down the carpeted hallway, eyeing the numbers on each door until he found the room he was looking for. The other two men took up positions on either side of the door, ensuring they were out of the peephole's field of view.

Anton knocked on the door three times and heard a voice asking who was there. Doing his best to soften his heavy Russian accent, he answered, "It's hotel management, Mr. Miller. I'm sorry for the inconvenience at this late hour, but may I have a word with you?"

The door opened, and with an annoyed tone in his voice, the room's occupant said, "What can I do for you?"

A confused look fell over Anton's face. The plan had been to positively identify the American, then the three operators would flood the room and subdue their target. But the man who answered the door didn't match the description he'd been given. Not even close. He was clearly American, but the man standing before him was no computer geek. This man had a hard look about him. And he was big. His hair was a dark shade of red and his skin was tanned from long hours spent out in the elements. It was a look Anton recognized in himself and the other members of the team who had spent long days in the harsh desert environments of the Middle East. But what stood out most were the man's eyes. Icy blue, they were the eyes of a predator. Something was terribly wrong. Anton reverted to his default solution for any problem and went for his weapon.

Joe took a step forward and used both hands to pin the man's right hand against his hip, his vise-like grip preventing the Russian from drawing the pistol. Even though he couldn't see them, Joe knew there were two other men nearby who would be joining the fray any minute. But rather than retreating into the room, or pushing out into the hall, he held his ground and used the big Russian to fill the door, making it harder for the other men to get into the fight. He would much rather take them on one at a time. Three on one would be a little much, even for a man of his considerable abilities.

With his right hand immobilized, Anton took a step back with his left foot, rotated his torso, and fired a left-handed jab at Joe's head. He would have preferred to wind up and throw a haymaker, ending the fight with one blow, but their struggle in the door and the room's narrow entryway made it feel like they were fighting in a phone booth.

Joe saw the move coming and ducked under the blow. As Anton cocked his arm for another attempt, Joe released his right hand's grip on the Russian's gun-hand but maintained the pressure with his left. Using the strength in his powerful thighs, Joe exploded upward, delivering a piston-like palm strike to the underside of Anton's chin. The blow shattered the Russian's teeth and broke his jaw. Teetering on the edge of unconsciousness, he sagged to the floor. On the way down, Joe grabbed Anton's head with both hands, pulled it forward, and delivered a knee strike to his face that flattened his nose and knocked him out cold.

As his limp body fell to the floor, the two men in the hall rushed through the door, stepping on and over their teammate on the way in. Joe began to retreat into the room but caught his foot on the unconscious man's arm and fell back, landing on his rear end. Using the momentum of the fall to his advantage, Joe rolled onto his back and brought his knees to his chest. As the first attacker lunged, Joe delivered a kick that caught the man in the shoulder. The blow spun him to the left and sent him crashing into the chest of drawers.

Before Joe could get his legs back up into a guard position, the second attacker was on him. With the skill of a professional MMA fighter, the man straddled his waist and sent a flurry of fists and elbows whirling around Joe's head. *Damn, this guy is fast,* he thought, bringing both arms up to absorb the blows. The thought had no sooner flashed in his mind when the tip of an elbow slipped through his defenses and caught him on the left side of the head. The skin above his eyebrow split open and blood flowed into his eye. With his vision obscured, Joe brought his left arm up to protect his blind side as the Russian feigned another strike to the bloody wound. The fake exposed his chin and the Alpha man took advantage of the opening, pounding it with a quick right cross instead, causing a galaxy of stars to erupt in Joe's head.

Wanting to get back into the fight, the man Joe had kicked into the dresser regained his footing and grabbed the forty-two-inch flat screen by each end. Ripping the TV from its mount on the wall, he raised it above his head, snapping the power cord and coaxial cable out of their ports, and waited for an opportunity to piledrive it into the American's bloody face.

Joe heard the man say something in Russian but had no idea what it meant. It wasn't until the operator on top of him leaned back that he was able to get a clear view of the man's partner with the TV held high. And vice versa. The beginnings of an evil grin tugged at the corners of the man's mouth as he prepared to bring the TV down for the deathblow.

Stepping over the unconscious body in the doorway, John entered the room and saw the man about to guillotine his team leader with a television. *You can't make this shit up,* he thought. *No one would believe it.* Clear of the cameras in the hallway, he raised his suppressed pistol, aligned the sights on the executioner's forehead, and pressed the trigger. The kinetic energy of a one-hundred-forty-seven-grain jacketed hollow point blew out the back of the man's head. He released his grip on the TV and crumpled in a heap next to Joe.

Stunned by the unexpected death of his teammate, the man straddling Joe turned to see where the shot had come from. He was greeted with a roundhouse kick to the face and his world went dark. John rolled the man to the side and offered Joe a hand, helping him to his feet. Still a little wobbly from the shot to the jaw, Joe eased himself down onto the corner of the bed to give the world a chance to stop spinning.

John moved to the bathroom door and knocked three times. "Eli, it's John."

The door cracked open and a single eye peered through the opening. "You sure it's safe to come out?"

Exasperated, John said, "Would I be standing here talking to you if it weren't?"

Thinking it over for a second, Miller agreed, "Point taken."

"Grab me a towel, then get your shit together. It's time to go."

He handed John a towel from the rack, then stepped out into the room to get his messenger bag and rolling duffle. But when he saw the carnage around the room and the brain splatter on the wall, he made an abrupt about face back into the bathroom and vomited into the sink.

Handing Joe the towel, John asked, "You good?"

Joe wiped the blood from his eye, then pressed the terrycloth against the gash to try and stop the bleeding. "Yeah. How's Eli?"

"He's puking his guts out. But other than that, he's fine."

Looking up to make eye contact, Joe said, "Thanks, John. I owe you."

"No sweat, man," John replied, as if it were just another day at the office. "You'd do the same for me. It's how we roll." Then he pointed to the trio of Russians on the floor. "What do you want to do about them?"

Joe thought it over for a second. "Leave 'em." He knew the Russians would have to spend a lot of time and energy explaining why one of their operatives was dead and two others were in jail. They were already behind the eight ball in the court of public opinion after the botched attempt to kill a defector and his daughter in the UK a few years ago. And the thought of heads exploding in the Kremlin over another international embarrassment brought a smile to his battered face.

After searching the Russians and collecting their pocket litter and cell phones, Joe led the way down the stairwell with Eli and John on his heels. They stopped on the ground floor landing and waited for Chris to give them the all-clear before bursting out of the side door and piling into the rental.

Chris looked his friend over in the illumination from the SUV's dome light. The left side of Joe's face was caked with blood and was beginning to swell. "Well, it looks like that went according to plan."

Wincing as he touched his battered face, Joe said, "You should see the other guys." The mere mention of the carnage in the hotel room caused Eli to dry heave in the back seat. "Let's beat feet before their friends come looking for them."

The drive to Chiévres was uneventful and Joe used the time to brief headquarters on the events of the last hour. While Director Sloan and the others on the call weren't thrilled about the contact with the Russians in a European capital, they understood the nature of such operations. The DCIA considered calling his counterpart in Belgium's State Security Service, but the organization was so dysfunctional he doubted it would do any good. Besides, the team had gotten out clean for the most part, and there were no recordings of the encounter with the Russians. The only footage on the hotel's DVR system would be of the team entering the hotel, transiting the hallway to Miller's room, and using the stairwell for their departure. Fred Jackson was already at work, hacking into the hotel's security system to delete the video.

The Air Force C-21A Learjet was waiting for Joe's team as promised. After a quick thirty-minute flight, the plane touched down on the runway at Ramstein Air Force Base in Germany and taxied to a pad at the far end of the runway. The pilots brought the small business jet to a stop next to a much larger Gulfstream G650, and Joe thanked them for their hospitality before stepping out into the cool night. He led Eli and the other members of the team across the tarmac and bounded up the air-stairs into the cabin of the Gulfstream.

Chuck Jamison, perhaps the most well-known and respected pilot Air Branch ever produced, stuck his head out of the cockpit to welcome his passengers aboard. Having worked with Joe and his team on a variety of operations from clandestine insertions to hot extractions, he said, "Jesus, Joe. Tell me you got the plate number?"

Falling for one of the oldest jokes in the book, Joe asked, "What plate number?"

The guys started cracking up, but Jamison somehow managed to keep a straight face as he delivered the punch line. "The license plate number of the Mack truck that ran over your face."

Joe would have joined in with the laughter, but his face hurt too damn much, so he dropped into a plush seat and grinned at the good-natured ribbing.

Barb, the flight safety attendant, was an experienced hand, having worked for the Agency's air operations wing for nearly twenty years. She was also a trained medical officer and had treated everything from food poisoning to gunshot wounds on her flights. Without batting an eye at Joe's battered face, she went to the galley, filled a zip-lock bag with ice, grabbed a beer from the fridge, and handed both to Joe.

Seeing the ice-cold beer, Chris asked, "Hey, Barb, can I get one of those?"

Not missing a beat, she said, "From the looks of things, Joe did all the work on this op. He earned his. You know where the fridge is. Grab it yourself."

This set off another round of laughter as Jamison's voice came over the jet's intercom. "We're cleared for take-off. Flight time home is about nine hours."

Joe looked across the aisle to his right where Eli sat, looking a little shell-shocked as he contemplated the events since he first set eyes on the red-headed operator in the SCIF earlier this evening. "Try and get some sleep. People at home are going to want to talk to us when land. It's going to be a long day."

But the NSA encryption specialist didn't think sleep would be coming anytime soon. He felt as if he had just lived through an action scene in a Jason Bourne movie, except Joe Matthews and his team were real. The Paladin analogy used back in the SCIF popped into his head, and he realized Joe was right. He had fought and bled, literally put his life on the line, to protect him from harm. Eli turned to thank the man sitting across from him, a gesture that didn't seem like nearly enough, given the magnitude of what he'd done for him over the past few hours, but Joe was already sound asleep as the Gulfstream's wheels left the ground.

CHAPTER 28

THE FINAL SHIMMERS of sunlight slipped below the horizon as night fell over the runways Bassel Al Assad International Airport shared with Khmeimim Air Base. Lights flickered to life around the airport's grounds, illuminating the main terminal building, hangars, and tarmacs acting as parking lots for the variety of Syrian and Russian military aircraft lined up in neat rows, awaiting the next day's sorties.

But one section of the airport remained shrouded in darkness. The heavily guarded hangar's doors slid open, and a three-man ground crew pushed the MQ-9 Reaper out onto the ramp. Having gone through the pre-flight procedures inside the structure, there was nothing left to do but arm the Hellfire missiles attached under the wings and give the pilot the all-clear for engine start. As it had on the test flights the previous two nights, the engine purred to life and the pilot taxied the UAV onto runway Three-Five Right. Using only a fraction of the runway's nine thousand feet, the Reaper lifted into the air, taking off to the north and gaining altitude before the pilot eased the joystick to the right and pointed the nose toward the Iraqi border.

After Anna Kovaleski had reeled in the victim of her phishing scam, it was only a matter of time before she found what she was looking for. It took a couple of days to sift through General Atomics' servers, but the instructions for accessing the backdoor to reboot the UAV's systems was there for the taking once you knew where to look. Armed with that knowledge, it was just a matter of following the steps in the maintenance guide to wipe the system's memory and install the encryption and communications protocols of her choosing. With the satcom link connecting to satellites under the control of the GRU, the stolen Reaper was flying its inaugural mission on behalf of the Russian Federation.

Three hours after taking off from the darkened runway, the Reaper was in a holding pattern above a mosque in the Al Tamim section of Ramadi, Iraq. Located in a neighborhood south of the Euphrates River, the call to prayer from the minaret towering above the Great Mosque of Badr echoed through the working-class development of high-rise apartment buildings three miles north of the University of Anbar. All vestiges of sunlight had faded from the western sky, and it was time for the Isha, the final prayer of the day.

Looking over the pilot's shoulder, Vasily Zubkin, the lead aerospace engineer, marveled at the clarity of the images displayed on the ground control station's monitors. He checked the console's altimeter and saw it read twenty thousand feet. Even at that altitude and in the darkness of the moonless night, the UAV's electro-optical infra-red camera system allowed the sensor operator to zoom in on individuals entering the mosque and read license plates on nearby parked cars. *Simply amazing,* Zubkin thought.

When it appeared that everyone was inside the mosque and the service had begun, Colonel Teplov tapped an entry in his phone's contact list. After identifying himself to the operator, he was put on a brief hold while the call was transferred.

Inside the Kremlin's version of the Oval Office, President Yaroslav Polovkin sat in a high-backed leather chair and stared into the flames crackling in the hearth of a massive stone fireplace. Two identical chairs were arranged on either side of him. Anton Shubovich, whose official title was Minister of Defense of the Russian Federation and General of the Army, sat to the president's right. He was a short man who, regardless of his mood, seemed to have a perpetual scowl on his face. His demeanor stood in stark contrast to the third man in the room. Vice Admiral Evgeny Mishkin, the head of the GRU, had the appearance of a doting grandfather. But behind that kind-looking countenance was a ruthless intelligence officer who would have been right at home in Stalin's NKVD during the Great Purge. A coffee table separated the men from the fireplace and held a tea service and the speakerphone.

Since the man on the other end of the line was under Vice Admiral

Mishkin's command, he initiated the conversation. "Good evening, Colonel. What news do you have for us?"

Hearing the head of the GRU's voice, Teplov felt himself snap to attention while still holding the phone to his ear. "Sir, the drone is in position and we are ready to initiate the attack."

Mishkin looked to President Polovkin, who gave his approval. "You are authorized to commence with your mission, Colonel. From this point forward, there is no need to call back for authorization. Prosecute the target packages at your discretion. We will contact you if there are to be any changes to the missions' profiles."

Teplov acknowledged his orders. "Yes, sir."

"And Colonel," Mishkin said, "any more fuck-ups like the debacle in Brussels and you and that embarrassment of an Alpha Group officer will be wishing for a quick death at the hands of those Islamic militants you're fighting in Syria."

Once they had regained consciousness, Anton and the other Alpha man had reported in. Captain Kalugin had managed to get them and the body of the third man out of the room, but there was no way to clean up the mess left behind. Local media was reporting on the mystery after a member of the hotel's housekeeping staff found the gore as she was going about her normal routine the following morning. But so far, there was nothing in the stories implicating any Russian involvement. Without any bodies or eyewitnesses, Belgian authorities were stumped.

Gritting his teeth at the failed operation to capture the NSA encryption specialist, Teplov vowed that if he was going down, he was going to take Captain Gennady Kalugin with him. "Understood, sir."

With that, Mishkin leaned forward to disengage the call on the speakerphone and retrieve his cup of tea. "Well, Mr. President, you are about to take the first step to driving the Americans out of the Middle East."

"Fitting that their own weapon will be the key to their undoing," General Shubovich added.

*

The executive dining room was just down an inner hallway from his office, but Lawrence Sloan preferred to have lunch in the first-floor cafeteria with the dedicated men and women under his command. He would often find a table occupied with one or more of his officers and ask to join them. Sloan enjoyed the informal discussions and thought they gave him a good feel for the pulse of the building. With the long hours and inherent stress of the job, keeping morale high was an important ingredient to the success of the organization.

Jeanne Emerson, an agent on the Director's Protective Staff, scanned the large room and spotted the boss sitting at a table near a window over-looking the inner courtyard between the two headquarters buildings. In between bites of salad, he was carrying on a conversation with two young officers. From the looks on their faces, Jeanne couldn't tell if they were excited or terrified to be having lunch with the veteran spymaster.

Sloan saw her heading his way and leaned in close to his dining part-ners. "Well, it looks like lunch has just come to an end. Thank you so much for sharing your table with me." He excused himself, then stood and dropped off his tray by the trash cans.

Five minutes later Sloan entered the conference room on the seventh floor. His senior staff had been rounded up by other members of the pro-tective detail and were arrayed around the highly polished table. Dana Criswell, an analyst from the Operations Center one floor below, stood at the front of the room waiting for permission to start the briefing. Sloan took his seat at the head of the table and asked her to begin.

"At approximately 8:50 pm local time," Criswell glanced at her watch and did the math in her head, "roughly one hour ago, the Great Mosque of Badr, in Ramadi, Iraq, was attacked." She pressed a button on the remote to activate the large screen on the wall behind her.

The images appeared the be a live feed from Al Jazeera. In typical form for the Qatar-based network, the video on the screen was horrific. Only a crater and burning piles of debris remained of what was once a place of worship. Unafraid of broadcasting grisly images that networks in the West would never air, the cameraman panned across the gaping hole in the ground showing battered and broken limbs protruding from the rubble. Spotlights illuminated the scene revealing torn bodies lying in pools of blood that appeared black in the artificial light. Large chunks of concrete had been turned into projectiles and damaged surrounding buildings. The force of the impacts had caused the police station next door to collapse, killing four officers and six prisoners who happened to be inside at the time.

"What do we know about the method of attack?" asked David Brewer, the deputy director for intelligence. As the CIA's top analyst, he was intimately familiar with conducting bomb damage assessments, or BDAs.

The chief of CTC, Harold Lee, was curious as well. "The blast pattern doesn't look like a car bomb, and there's no way a suicide bomber could carry in enough explosives to create that much damage."

"I agree," Brewer added. "It looks more like an airstrike to me."

"Yeah," Lee concurred. "I was thinking the same thing."

Criswell confirmed their suspicions. "Preliminary reports from people in the area said the attack did, in fact, come from the sky. Residents claimed to have seen two streaks of light emerge from the clouds. They were followed immediately by bright flashes and thundering booms seconds later." Activating the picture-in-picture function on the monitor, the live Al Jazeera footage shrunk to the bottom left corner of the screen. The larger portion now displayed three still images of what appeared to be fragments of a projectile. "As I'm sure you're aware, there are often pieces of the casings that are not destroyed when a bomb or missile detonates. These fragments were reportedly found at the scene."

Fearing this was the opening salvo in their worst-case scenario, DDO Katherine Clark asked, "Are those markings on the larger piece serial numbers?"

"Yes, ma'am. They are. We don't have the entire number, but the eight-digit string in this photo matches the lot of Hellfires that were stockpiled at the UAV base in Jordan."

A stunned silence fell over the room as everyone contemplated the ramifications of the analyst's statement. "My God…they've done it," Clark said, breaking the silence.

"It appears they have," Sloan agreed, fascinated as to how the Russians managed to bypass the encryption and get the Reaper in the air.

Lee was struggling with a question of his own, so he threw it out to the room. "What I don't understand is, if you have this newfound capability, a Reaper and its complement of missiles, why waste two of the weapons on some local mosque in the middle of Iraq? I mean, wouldn't you want to use them on a more significant target?"

"Maybe it was a test run," Brewer offered. "You'd want to get a few flights under your belt before going after your primary objective. But I agree with Harold. Why would you hit a mosque full of innocent people in the middle of nowhere?"

"That's a very good question, though it's only one of many we need to answer," Sloan said, addressing the group. "David, please get your analysts working on a list of potential targets based on the Reaper's operational range. And I would appreciate some ideas on the most likely scenarios they think the Russians may implement to try to reduce our standing in the region." Turning to the operational leads in the room, he continued, "We need to figure out a way to track the drone the next time it's in the air. If we can follow it back to its base, perhaps the Air Force can do us a favor and solve our problem with an airstrike of our own."

Everyone had their marching orders, so Director Sloan thanked Dana Criswell for the briefing and adjourned the meeting. On the short walk back to his office he stuck his head in the command post to let the protective detail know they would be heading to the White House in the next thirty minutes or so. President Andrews would not be happy with the news, but Sloan had never let that stop him from delivering it, and he wouldn't start today. The leader of the Free World needed information to make strategic decisions. And good, bad, or indifferent, it was Sloan's job to provide it.

After briefing the president, Sloan and Hank Coleman hung back as the other members of the national security team filed out of the Situation Room. Sloan waited until they were alone before running his idea of tracking the Reaper back to its base so the Air Force could carpet bomb the area by the SECDEF. Needing a subject matter expert's opinion, Coleman picked up a handset and asked the operator to get General Maria Rodriguez on the line. Two minutes later, her voice came over the speaker, and they filled her in on the dilemma.

"It would really help if we had a starting point to begin the search for the drone," Rodriguez began. "We have several AWACS forward deployed to the region, but I would need to know where to place them to have the best chance of picking up the Reaper." AWACS, or Airborne Warning and Control System were converted airliners with large, rotating radar dishes attached to the roof of the fuselage. Capable of scanning and tracking targets within a two-hundred-and-fifty-mile radius of the aircraft, the AWACS would serve as the early-warning eye in the sky. But first, they needed to know where to look.

I'll see what I can do to help narrow down the search field," Sloan offered. "In the meantime, I'll have our UAV teams pass along their flight schedules. We'll consider any Reaper appearing on the radar that doesn't match that schedule as hostile."

"Works for me, sir. I'll alert the crews but won't alter their current flight patterns until we hear back from you."

"Thanks, Maria. I'll fill you in on the rest when I get back over to the Pentagon," Coleman said before hanging up the call.

Both men exited the West Wing and were greeted by members of their respective protective details. Secured inside their armored motorcades, they buckled in for the short drive back to Virginia.

CHAPTER 29

Tariq Kabbani believed the elderly groundskeeper's story about what he had seen at the heavily guarded hangar, but like any good intelligence officer, he lived by the mantra, "Trust, but verify." And he needed to verify the old man's story before passing the intelligence along to his CIA handler, Scott Garrett. Tariq had seen the news story about the attack on the mosque in Ramadi and figured it had to have been conducted by the stolen drone. He knew the value Americans put on human life and the precautions they took to avoid collateral damage. As far as he was concerned, there was no way the U.S. would ever deliberately attack a location full of innocent civilians. But if for some reason they did, it would not have been in a manner that would point the finger directly at Washington.

Tariq fidgeted in the driver's seat of his rental car trying to get comfortable. He had parked on a seldom used dirt road on the far side of the airport with a clear view of the mysterious hangar. For the last three nights he had been in place shortly after sunset, hoping to get a glimpse of the drone, but all he had gotten for his efforts was a loss of sleep. He would give it another night or two, but at that point it would be time to reevaluate his plan and come up with a better idea.

On this fourth night, the lack of sleep was finally catching up with him, and Tariq began to doze off. Tired lids drooped like heavy blackout curtains over eyes that felt as if they were filled with sand. His muscles relaxed as he fell into the much-needed slumber and his head fell forward. Jolted awake by the sudden jerk, he snorted, then looked around in confusion, trying to get his bearings. He could feel sleep tugging at his eyelids once again when he noticed the hangar doors separating, spilling a sliver of light onto the ramp. Instantly awake, he was laser-focused on the task at hand, thoughts of sleep all but forgotten.

The massive doors continued to part, the light from inside the hangar illuminating the tarmac. From his vantage point he could see three men maneuvering what he knew from his research to be a General Atomics MQ-9 Reaper into position. *It's here! The old man was right after all.* Tariq looked on as the men moved around the pilotless aircraft performing their final inspections. With their checks complete, they backed away, and he could see the propeller mounted at the rear of the fuselage begin to turn.

Checking his watch, Tariq saw it was two thirty in the morning. Was it too late, or too early, depending on your point of view, to call Garrett? He knew he would want to know about the discovery of the drone sooner rather than later if the roles were reversed, so he retrieved a burner phone from the backpack sitting on the passenger seat and thumbed in the number he'd committed to memory.

Putting the phone to his ear, he listened as it rang, never taking his eyes off the UAV as it taxied onto the runway, then rolled down the smooth concrete until it gained enough speed and lifted into the air. The line on the other end rang four more times before a groggy voice answered, "Hello?" Tariq was so in the moment, so excited to find the drone, that he didn't notice the patrol approaching his car.

Two soldiers dismounted the vehicle and spread out, covering the car and its occupant with their weapons. With his men in position, the third soldier, a lieutenant in a starched khaki uniform, stepped out and approached Tariq's vehicle from the rear, being sure to stay in the driver's blind spot. The officer had a large metal flashlight in his left hand and held a pistol in his right. He lifted the flashlight to shoulder level and aimed it at the driver's face. Simultaneously, he pressed the light's button and rapped twice on the driver's side window with the barrel of his weapon.

The sudden bright light and noise on an otherwise dark and quiet night nearly sent Tariq through the roof. He dropped the phone and the call disconnected as the cheap handset bounced off the center console and disappeared into the floor well. Cursing himself for letting his guard down, Tariq looked to his left and put a hand up to shield his eyes from the flashlight's glare.

Using the barrel of his pistol, the soldier rapped on the window twice more and yelled in Arabic, "Who are you? What are you doing here?"

Tariq took a moment to size up the situation. In addition to the soldier yelling at him, he spotted a second, offset at an angle to the front of his car, weapon shouldered and aimed at his windshield. Glancing up at his rearview mirror, he saw the reflection of a third soldier positioned at a similar angle to the rear quarter panel. These guys knew what they were doing, covering him from the front and the rear while managing to stay out of each other's line of fire. There may have been more men deployed around his car, but it was impossible to tell through the blinding glare.

Keeping his right hand in plain sight on top of the steering wheel, Tariq moved his left in a slow, deliberate manner toward the armrest and pressed the button to lower the window. The officer seemed a little amped up, and Tariq wasn't sure if it was because he was nervous or just posturing for his men. Either way, he did not want to do anything that might escalate the situation, so he began the conversation with a tone of deference in his voice. "Good evening, Lieutenant. What seems to be the problem?"

"The problem," the Lieutenant began, "is that you are in a restricted area. Didn't you see the signs? This section of the airport is off limits."

Tariq feigned ignorance. "What signs? It's completely dark out here. I can't see any signs. Can you?"

Without thinking, the lieutenant actually took a second to look around for the signage he claimed was in place. If it weren't for the other soldiers providing cover, Tariq could have shot the man in the side of the head and gone about his business. But they were supposed to be on the same side, and he really didn't want to shoot one of his countrymen just for doing his job.

When the lieutenant couldn't pick out any of the signs in the darkness, he moved on to his next point. "It's past curfew. Why are you out here so late? Maybe a few nights in a military jail will teach you a new respect for the rule of law." He took two steps back and ordered Tariq out of the car.

Tariq's head drooped in frustration. He didn't have time for this and was done playing Mr. Nice Guy with the soldier. He opened the door and got out of the car. In a slow, deliberate motion, he opened the right side of his jacket with one hand and used the other to remove a worn leather folding case from an inner pocket. He held the case up and opened it with one hand, saying, "I'm here on an intelligence matter, Lieutenant. What I'm doing here is none of your concern."

The officer approached Tariq and snatched the folder from his hand, aiming the flashlight's powerful beam at the folder to read its contents. Seeing the words, General Intelligence Directorate – Internal Security Division, his eyes went wide. The bravado he had exuded minutes earlier evaporated into the cool night air, replaced with fear at coming across such a high-ranking member of the GID. "Lower your weapons!" he ordered, unable to get the words out of his mouth fast enough, afraid one of his men might have a negligent discharge and shoot the colonel by accident.

Extending his hand, Tariq gestured for the return of his credentials. "Well, Lieutenant, it looks like you've managed to compromise my position, so I believe my work here is done for the night. I guess I can thank you and your men for granting me a few extra hours of sleep."

"Sir," the lieutenant pleaded, "please accept my apologies. I had no idea…"

Tariq realized he had accomplished a significant part of his mission tonight, and it wouldn't be the end of the world if he took a few minutes to manage the situation with the soldiers. Softening his tone, he said, "Not to worry, Lieutenant. I can't fault you or your squad for doing your job. I commend your attentiveness and professionalism in carrying out your duties."

The young officer was visibly taken aback. Praise from superior officers in the Syrian Army was a rarity, especially under circumstances like these. Unsure of what else he could say or do, stammering "Th…thank you, sir," was about the best the lieutenant could muster.

"Now, you'd better continue with your patrol. I'll finish up here and be out of the area in a few minutes."

After throwing crisp salutes, the soldiers retreated to their vehicle and sped off, wanting to create some distance between themselves and the GID colonel before he changed his mind and decided to make their lives miserable.

With the taillights fading in the distance, Tariq returned to his car and rummaged through the floor well, searching for the burner. Forty-five seconds of groping later, he found it tucked behind the gas pedal, then hit the redial button.

Having been awakened from a deep sleep by the first call, Garrett sounded more alert when he answered this one on the second ring. "Hello?"

Using his designated codename to identify himself, Tariq said, "It's Bastion. I've found the drone."

Scott couldn't believe his ears. "Where?"

Tariq paused as movement to his left caught his attention. His eyes were still adjusting from the brightness of the soldier's flashlight, but he could make out six or seven shadows emerging from the darkness between the runway and his position. The silhouettes were large, too big to be Syrians, and were kitted out with night vision goggles attached to their helmets. The one in the center stopped a few feet from his car and raised the NVGs, locking them in the up position. With his face exposed, Tariq instantly recognized him as the man he had seen in Teplov's office. It was the Spetsnaz officer.

Captain Gennady Kalugin drew his rifle back and crashed its stock into the side of Tariq's head before he could utter another word to the person on the other end of the call. The Syrian intelligence officer collapsed in a heap next to his vehicle. Sand from the unpaved road clung to the blood seeping from a gash along his cheekbone. Kalugin knelt and picked up the phone. Holding it to his ear, he listened for a few seconds. Hearing nothing, he said, "Spokoinoi nochi – Good night," then dropped the cheap handset onto the dirt and crushed it with the heel of his boot.

CHAPTER 30

Scott Garrett threw his legs over the side of the bed and sat there, thinking about what he had just heard. He was quickly forming some conclusions, the only problem was that none of them were good, at least as far as Tariq was concerned. He pushed himself off the bed and headed for the shower.

Thirty minutes later he was walking through Post One of the massive U.S. Embassy on Al-Umawyeen street in the western section of Amman. The Marine Security Guard on duty, a corporal who looked young enough to be his son, greeted him. "Damn, Mr. Garrett. You're getting an early start this morning."

"That I am, Corporal Hall. I have a feeling it's going to be an extra pot of coffee kind of day," Garrett said as he crossed the lobby to the bank of elevators. Getting off on the fourth floor, he opened the vault door securing the CIA's office space and punched his code into the alarm panel. After flipping on the lights, his first order of business was the coffeemaker. He put a pot on, making it extra strong, then went to his office to jot down some notes while he waited on the brew.

With a steaming mug of coffee and his thoughts lined out, he reached for the secure phone's handset and hit the speed dial button for the DDO, Katherine Clark. With the time difference, it was a little past eight in the evening in Washington.

Katherine Clark collapsed on the couch next to her husband, looking forward to a quiet evening streaming a few episodes of their favorite show. He was about to hit play on the remote when they were interrupted by the unmistakable ring of the secure phone in the study. She leaned over and gave him a kiss on the cheek. "Sorry, hon. I'll try and make it quick."

Being married to the nation's top spook for over thirty years, he was accustomed to interruptions at all hours of the night. "No sweat," he said, flipping over to the Georgetown basketball game. "You know where to find me when you're done."

Clark closed the door to the study and walked over to her desk. She picked up the phone and waited for the digital readout on the small screen to read SECURE before answering. An officer in the Operations Center at Langley said, "Sorry to bother you at home, ma'am. I have Scott Garrett in Amman on the line for you."

She glanced at her watch and muttered, "It must be around three in the morning over there. This can't be good. Put him through."

Garrett spent the next ten minutes running her through the call with Tariq, the Russian coming on the line, and what he thought had happened. When he was done, he asked, "Can we get some of the DS&T whiz kids to try to track the last known location of Tariq's phone? That will give me a starting place to begin my search for him."

"Sure. Wait. What?" Clark said as that last sentence registered in her brain.

"I'm going in after him, Katherine. Tariq has been a great asset to the Agency over the years. He has more than held up his end of the bargain, and I can't just leave him there to be tortured and killed by the Russians. And you know as well as I do what the Syrians will do to his wife and kid when they find out he's been working with us. I can't have that on my conscience. Besides, he said he saw the Reaper. This will give us a shot to narrow down the location so we can call in an airstrike and level the place."

Realizing the quiet night on the couch with her husband had once again been hijacked by events, she reached for a pen, and a slid a legal pad across the desk. "First things first. What's Tariq's number?" She jotted it down, then opened her laptop and fired off an email to her counterpart in the directorate of science and technology, emphasizing the urgency of the request to geo-locate the phone's position. "Now, about you going to Syria," she began, "there's no way I'm authorizing you to go in on your own."

"C'mon, Katherine. You know we can't just leave Tariq swinging in the wind. First, it's simply the wrong thing to do. And second, who's gonna want to work with us in the future if word gets out, and you know it will, that we don't protect the people we recruit? There won't be a guy in the region we'll be able to pitch."

She knew he was right on both counts. There had to be that level of trust between an asset and their case officer, that if things went bad, the CIA would be there to take care of them. Finally, she said, "Hell, Scott. Even if I do give you approval to go into Syria, there's no guarantee the director will go for it."

Before getting on the call, Scott had thought over the possibility of going regardless of whether he had permission, but in the end decided against that course of action. He was completely comfortable working in the gray areas necessary to be effective at his job. He would gladly push any boundary, was willing to walk right up to the line, and maybe dip a toe over on occasion. But he couldn't bring himself to go rogue, to go off reservation on an unsanctioned op. Instead, he offered a compromise. "How about if I take a team to keep me out of trouble? Maybe Joe and his guys?"

The last mission she had approved into Syria could not have gone much worse. Visions of Greg Jacobs' funeral and the ceremony in the lobby of the Original Headquarters Building to add his star to the memorial wall flooded her mind. And with the injuries sustained by the members of Joe's team, she thanked her lucky stars there had been only one engraving added to the wall that day.

But this was not the time to be timid or risk averse. A second drone strike had taken place, this time on a historical mosque in Ankara, Turkey, and once again the evidence pointed to the United States as the culprit. Mass protests and demonstrations were beginning to occur in front of America's embassies and consulates in the region. Angry crowds burned flags and chanted "Death to America!" with a furor that had not been witnessed in years.

President Andrews was fielding calls daily from his counterparts in the Middle East, and the attacks were the only topic any reporter wanted to discuss at the press secretary's daily briefing. He was contemplating sending Secretary of State Claire Nichols on a tour of the region to reassure the leaders of the Arab world that America was not attacking their religious sites. She would emphasize that his government was doing everything humanly possible to identify the perpetrators and bring them to justice. Nichols had been burning up the phone lines at Foggy Bottom and thought the trip would be a good idea as well. The only problem was her safety. With the unrest on the streets of the major cities she would need to visit, not to mention the threat of a rogue drone patrolling the skies above the Middle East, the Diplomatic Security Service was concerned that they wouldn't be able to protect her under such extreme circumstances.

No, Clark thought, *if there was ever a time for bold action, this was it.* Finally, she said, "Let me run your idea by Lawrence first thing in the morning. I'll call you when I have his answer."

*

The DDO must have made a compelling argument for the mission, or maybe it was a case of desperate times calling for desperate measures, but Director Sloan sanctioned the mission, with the caveat that Joe's team would lead from start to finish. They were to have any and all resources at their disposal.

Joe left the DCIA's seventh-floor office with a spring in his step after receiving his marching orders in person from Director Sloan. Anxious to excise the demons of his last mission into Syria, he waved to the DPS agent and the executive assistant as he crossed the outer lobby of the director's suite and inserted his access key into the panel next to the private elevator. The doors parted and he stepped inside for the ride down to the garage level. Alone with his thoughts inside the descending car, the images and sounds of the firefight in Syria flashed through his mind, the memories as fresh as if they had occurred yesterday. He would not be able to live with himself if things went to shit again and it cost the lives of one or more of his guys. The experience left Joe more determined than ever to make sure things turned out differently this time, and that if there were casualties on this mission, the other side would suffer them.

A chime sounded inside the elevator, the doors slid open, and he stepped into the carpeted foyer that led to the underground parking garage. He paused for a moment, giving the combat reel running through his head a chance to clear. The area was a hive of activity as agents swarmed around two black Chevrolet Suburbans stowing long guns and checking comms and medical equipment in preparation for a movement with Director Sloan. Joe watched in silence as the men and women of the elite protective detail went about their duties with a quiet professionalism, prepared at a moment's notice to put themselves in harm's way to protect their principal.

He noticed a change in the agents' demeanor and knew that it meant they had received the call letting them know the director was in his way down in the elevator. An agent got behind the wheel of each SUV and started the engines. Two agents with long guns took their positions in the back seat of the follow car, while the shift leader, Jeanne Emerson, held the limo's back door open. She was already a highly respected member of the detail, and her reputation was further solidified when she took two rounds to the trauma plate of her body armor while shielding a wounded Katherine Clark during the Iranian Quds Force attack on Director Sloan and his senior staff. And as if that weren't enough, she then had the wherewithal to draw her weapon and take down the shooter. Jeanne Emerson was an operator Joe would be happy to work with anytime, anywhere.

The elevator chimed again, and Joe moved to the side of the hallway to make room for Director Sloan and his contingent as they headed for the Suburban's open doors. Doug Kelly, the chief of Sloan's detail, slapped Joe on the shoulder as he passed by. "Make your own luck. We'll go for beers when you get back."

"Sounds like a plan," Joe replied, as he watched Doug button up the director, then take his place in the right-front of the limo.

Jeanne gave him a quick smile then took her seat in the front of the follow car. He watched her raise the radio's microphone to her mouth, and even though he couldn't hear what she was saying, he knew from his own experience working the position that she was giving the limo driver the order to move out.

As the motorcade headed up the ramp to exit the garage, Joe crossed the hall, punched in the three-digit code on the door's lock, and entered the ready room. With Sloan's departure, and the deputy director out of town on a trip to South America, Joe and his guys had the place to themselves.

John and Kevin were in the lounge, sitting on the oversized couch with their feet up on the coffee table, flipping through the news channels. Chris was in the kitchen, manipulating the plunger on a French press coffee maker with a level of concentration that made Joe think he was disarming a nuclear bomb. But if history was any indication, he knew Chris's efforts would result in a world-class cup of coffee. The door at the end of the corridor opened, and a freshly showered Mike McCredy stepped out of the locker room.

Once the coffee was ready, Joe gathered the men in the lounge. "John, do me a favor and get the TV." John thumbed the power button on the remote and the room fell silent.

Joe said, "How's the shoulder, Kev?"

"Good as new, boss. Rehab's done and I've been killing my workouts. Why?"

Joe's gaze moved to Mike. "And your leg, big man?"

McCredy locked eyes with Joe and replied, "Good to go. So, don't even think about going on another mission without me."

A smile creased Joe's lips, proud of his guys' eagerness to get back to work. "I guess it's settled then. Consider yourselves back on operational status."

"Hot damn!" Kevin said, bounding off the couch and giving a high five to each man in the room. "The boy band is back together again! Where are we kicking off this reunion tour?"

Unsure how everyone would react, Joe said, "Would you believe, Syria?" The light-hearted mood in the room turned instantly serious at the mention of a return to the Arab nation. He filled the guys in on the morning's briefing on the seventh floor and laid out the parameters for the op.

After a tense couple of minutes, Chris said, "Well, at least this will give John a chance to redeem himself."

Confused, John asked, "Redeem myself? What the hell are you talking about?"

"I thought, if we had the time, that we could swing by that hilltop in Salkhad and you could look for Mike's missing boot"

The room erupted in laughter as Kevin began rapping his version of an old LL Cool J song, "We're going back to Syria, Syria, Syria. We're going back to Syria...hmm, I don't think so."

CHAPTER 31

MARKA SERVES AS Amman's main airport for charter and VIP flights. It also operates an aviation training center and is home to a sizable fleet of fixed wing and rotary aircraft belonging to the Central Intelligence Agency.

In a hangar halfway between the main administrative offices of the Royal Jordanian Air Academy and the southwest end of the runway, a ground crew was preflighting an unmarked Mi-17 helicopter. The big, Russian-built utility helicopters were a workhorse of an airframe that had been used by the CIA in harsh environments for the past twenty years. They tended to blend in, not drawing enemy fire like a Blackhawk or other American helo, and after refits of the engines and avionics, had become a favorite among the Agency's pilots.

Joe and Scott Garrett stood in front of a bulletin board in a far corner of the hangar studying a large satellite image of Syria's west coast. While they strategized about the insertion, the other members of the team were busy loading magazines, checking weapons and commo gear, and packing the kit they would need for the mission.

Taking a moment to observe his men, Joe looked for any sign that they weren't ready for a return to the country where they almost died. But he liked what he saw. The men were focused but relaxed as they went about their individual pre-deployment routines. Everyone dealt with the stress before this type of mission in his own way. For Joe, it was like the butter-flies he used to get before a big game. There was that nervous excitement during the pregame warmups, but it all faded away once the ball was kicked off and he delivered that first big hit. The same was true here. The nerves would burn off once his feet hit the ground and the mission was underway.

He returned his attention to the bulletin board and the overhead shot of Bassel Al-Assad International Airport. A clear overlay was pinned over the image, marking the location of each cell tower within a three-mile radius of the airport. Due to the limited number of towers in the area, it was the best the tech wizards at Langley had been able to do to identify the location of Tariq's call to Scott. Although it wasn't the pinpoint-accurate information they were hoping for, it did give them a place to start looking for the Syrian asset.

A man hopped out of the open door on the side of the Mi-17 and crossed the expanse of the hangar. Wearing a Detroit Tigers t-shirt, worn jeans, and a pair of beat-up canvas high-tops, Chuck Jamison looked more like an old college student and less like the most accomplished pilot ever to strap into the cockpit for the CIA. Famous within the small fraternity of pilots for conducting some of the most daring aerial missions no one would ever hear about, he was beloved by field officers and Tier One operators alike for his willingness to extract them from hot landing zones.

"The bird's prepped so we can take off whenever you're ready." Eyeing the satellite image, Jamison asked, "Figure out where you want me to drop you off yet?"

Pointing to a spot of open terrain ten miles east of the airport, Joe asked, "How about here?"

Jamison moved in to get a closer look at the imagery and examined the area. "That should work. The farther away from the airport the better, as far as I'm concerned. That way I don't have to worry about the air defenses protecting the base. But it's going to mean a longer hump for you guys to get to the target. You're not planning on walking all that way, are you?"

"No. There's a Ground Branch team operating in the area. They're going to meet us at the LZ with a couple of vehicles."

"Cool," Jamison said. "At least you'll have some friendlies in the AO. What do you say we try and avoid a repeat of that shit show the last time you were in country?"

Joe looked back over at his men, keenly aware of the inherent dangers of the operation they were about to undertake. "That's the plan, Chuck.

But the enemy does get a vote. So, I'm counting on you to come get us if things get hairy."

"Always, brother," Jamison replied, offering Joe a fist bump. Then, turning to head back to the helicopter, he said over his shoulder, "Just let me know when you're ready to go."

Joe was about to tell him they were waiting on one more person when a lone figure with a large rucksack on his back and a long, padded case in his left hand entered the hangar. The other members of the team noticed the newcomer as well and followed Joe over to greet the man. Extending a hand, he said, "Thanks for joining us on this one, Tim."

Tim Shannon was one of the finest long-distance shooters the SEAL teams had ever produced. After twenty years in the military he pulled a LeBron James and decided to take his talents to the Central Intelligence Agency. Since joining the outfit, he had worked in a number of roles, from training other snipers to investigating assassinations involving precision marksmen. But his preferred assignments, since the CIA didn't officially employ snipers of its own, were those that got him back in the field providing overwatch on high-risk missions for teams like Joe's.

Setting the rifle case gently on the hangar floor, he took the big red-head's hand. "When I heard about this hair-brained operation, I just knew it had to be one of yours. Don't you have any boring run-of-the-mill days on the job?"

"Where's the fun in that?" After giving the guys a minute to catch up with Tim, Joe asked, "Is there anything you need before we take off?"

"I'm good. Had a chance to study the op-order and look at images of the terrain on the flight over. Unless something has changed, I think I have a pretty good handle on the game plan."

"Great," Joe said, appreciating Tim's professionalism and the fact that he showed up ready to go to work. "John will get you set up with comms and we'll take off in about fifteen minutes."

*

Flying a northeasterly heading out of Amman, Jamison gave Damascus a wide berth and plotted a course that took them over the desert terrain of central Syria. He looped around to the east of Homs, a city that had been under siege for three years before being retaken by government forces. The sight of the bombed-out buildings reminded Jamison of the pictures and video of the German cities that fell victim to the allied air forces at the end of World War II. Through the green hue of the night vision goggles affixed to his flight helmet, the abandoned remains of the city took on an additional eerie quality as he watched it go by through the plexiglass cockpit's windows.

The rotors thumped the night air as the helicopter continued north, passing between Al-Salamiyah and Hama before Jamison changed course and banked to the west. Here the terrain changed to lush farmland, and the dark shapes of a mountain range loomed in the distance. It was there, in a small clearing on the other side of the mountains, that the Ground Branch team would be waiting at the landing zone.

Jamison hailed the paramilitary operations officers on the ground, and after going through a series of authentication codes, the Ground Branchers gave the all-clear and indicated they would mark the LZ with infrared strobes.

Ten minutes later, the Mi-17's thick rubber tires touched down on a rocky outcropping. It was on the ground just long enough for the seven men onboard to exit the chopper before Jamison had the big helicopter back in the air, the touch-and-go delivery taking no more than sixty seconds.

As the sound of their ride's rotors reverberated through the hills and valleys, Joe and the team linked up with their welcoming party.

A hulking African American man emerged from the shadows of the wood line surrounding the landing zone. He spit a stream of tobacco juice onto the rocky terrain as two other men silently retrieved the IR strobes. The man approached Joe, then wrapped him in a bear hug with arms the size of most men's thighs. "God damn, it's good to see you again."

The sound of Ron Foster's deep Texas drawl was comforting and reminded Joe of his roots back in Arkansas. "Good God, Ron. I didn't think it was possible for you to get any bigger. What the hell have they been feeding you? Raw meat?"

"Just livin' clean, bro. I've actually lost a few pounds since we've been in country."

Joe shook his head. "Damn sure wouldn't know it from looking at you."

Foster had been a team leader in the Protective Resource Group but decided to make the move and fill a similar billet as a paramilitary operations officer in Ground Branch. Motioning to his men, he made the introductions. "This here's Ivy," he said pointing to the shorter of the two. "And that's Abrams."

The two men could not have been more different. Ivy was a stocky, muscular former Green Beret with short dark hair that was graying at the temples. Abrams, on the other hand, stood about six feet five inches tall and the moonlight reflected off his shaved head. He was a former Marine who had spent most of his career in MARSOC, the Marine Corps' Special Operations Command.

Handshakes and fist bumps were offered all around, then Chris exaggerated craning his neck to look up at the tall operator. "Hey, Abrams. You hiding out in Syria to escape from the NBA?"

Abrams bent over and put his hands on his knees, so he was eye to eye with Chris. "Wanna know what the weather's like up here too, motherfucker?"

Chris burst out laughing and offered up another fist bump. "I think we're going to get along just fine, Lurch."

"Now that we've completed our Welcome Wagon duties, let's get moving," Foster said. "We've got a safe house about twenty klicks from here. You guys are welcome to crash with us and use it as a base of operations."

As the men piled into the vehicles, Kevin reminisced, "Huh. Syria seems a lot nicer than I remember it."

Mike lifted his prosthetic leg as he got into the back seat and closed the door. "That's because no one's shooting at you yet."

CHAPTER 32

WITH EACH SUCCESSIVE flight, the Russian drone pilot was becoming more and more comfortable at the controls of the Reaper. While the United States was still the enemy, he couldn't help but appreciate the technological development that had gone into creating such a fine machine. He was a patriot in every sense but spending so much time in the ground control station's cockpit, he was skeptical that his country could ever create anything comparable.

The sound of Vasily Zubkin's voice startled the pilot. The aerospace engineer had an annoying habit of creeping up behind him and standing there silently while he analyzed the information displayed on the station's monitors. "I trust tonight's flight is going well?"

For this third mission, the flight plan had taken the Reaper over the dark blue waters of the Mediterranean, avoiding major cities along the route to reduce the chances of it being detected. A weather front moving across the sea had delayed the mission for two days, but the storms finally pushed through and a half-moon illuminated a partly cloudy night. "We should be on-station in just under an hour."

The Reaper made landfall between Port Said and Damietta, two cities on the northern coast of Egypt. Lush farmland passed below the drone's sixty-six-foot wingspan as the Honeywell engine powered the UAV to the south. Fifty-three minutes later the pilot guided the hunter-killer down the Nile, as he flew the last five miles into the heart of Cairo.

As the pilot put the Reaper in a holding pattern twenty-thousand feet above the city, his sensor operator toggled the zoom on the powerful cameras and took in the night-time sights. Traffic was always bad in Cairo, and the streets were packed on this Friday night as people celebrated the end of the work week. Headlights from cars stuck in bumper-to-bumper traffic intermingled with streetlights and neon signs.

Even though Cairo was a metropolitan city, there were still plenty of devout Muslims heeding the evening's call to prayer. Many of those worshipers were heading to the Masjid Omar Makram mosque in the Garden City section of the capital. The mosque occupied a prime piece of real estate between two of the highest profile locations in Cairo, Tahrir Square, the site of the demonstrations during the Arab Spring, and the American Embassy. The pilot and sensor operator watched a stream of people dutifully enter the mosque, eager to fulfill their religious responsibilities before getting on with the weekend – a weekend that was about to be cut short.

The Muezzin finished the call to prayer from the tall, clocktower minaret, and the congregants completed their ablutions. When the men and women filled their respective sections, the Imam began the service. Prostrating themselves before Allah, the worshipers knelt, touching their foreheads, noses and palms to the ground, blissfully unaware of the destructive force circling above them.

Rising to the kneeling position, they recited the verses and were about to bend forward once more when the Imam paused, momentarily distracted by a loud, high-pitched screech. The sound was unfamiliar to the residents of Cairo but one that enemies of the United States in Iraq, Afghanistan, Syria, and North Africa knew all too well. It was the sound of approaching death.

The first Hellfire missile partially penetrated the flat parapet-like roof of the mosque before it detonated, the explosive force sending a shockwave filled with shrapnel and chunks of concrete and rebar into the main hall. Terrified screams echoed throughout the building as those who weren't killed or seriously injured in the initial blast struggled to their feet. Dirt and debris floating in the air caked around the survivors' eyes, and they coughed and wheezed from inhaling smoke and dust wafting through the main hall. With the power knocked out and everything shrouded in darkness, many stumbled around like zombies with their arms outstretched, feeling their way through the destruction for a way out.

With the roof literally blown off the building, the Reaper's cameras gave the Russians a bird's eye view inside the mosque. From the devastation evident on the ground control station's high-definition monitors, it was obvious there was no need to fire the second missile. The pilot looked up to Zubkin hoping for a show of restraint. But Colonel Teplov had entered the room unnoticed, and restraint was not a word in the GRU officer's vocabulary. "Again," he ordered.

Against his better judgment, the pilot did as he was instructed. Along with everyone else in the room, he watched the monitor as the second missile dropped from the underwing pod, leaving a trail of exhaust as it sped toward the remnants of the mosque. The Hellfire passed through the gaping hole where the roof had been, breached the wooden floor, and crashed into the basement before exploding. The blast ruptured an underground gas line, setting off an even larger secondary explosion that ripped the mosque apart. Flying debris, some pieces the size of compact cars, shattered windows and damaged buildings within a two-block radius.

The intense heat generated by the fire caused the automatic shut-off valves to malfunction, and the gas line ignited. A white-hot flame, hissing and sizzling like a giant blowtorch, erupted from the mosque's basement. Racing up and down the pipes connecting the utility service to the rest of the neighborhood, the superheated accelerant reached reservoirs in the basements of adjacent buildings and set off a series of explosions. A demolitions expert daisy-chaining blocks of C-4 explosives could not have caused more damage. Three apartment buildings, a bank, and an Egyptian government building were engulfed in flames as an overwhelmed fire department fought a losing battle to contain the raging inferno.

Responsible for the pointless carnage, a sense of shame fell over the pilot and his sensor operator for what they had done. Zubkin stared in disbelief at the monitors, and even Colonel Teplov seemed somewhat taken aback by the extent of the damage. He turned to leave the room, reaching for his mobile phone as he stepped through the door. He needed to brief Moscow on this unexpected turn of events.

*

Everyone stood as President Andrews entered the Situation Room. He was in as foul a mood as Lawrence Sloan could remember. And for good reason. The drone strike in Cairo was the lead story on the front page of every paper, website, and news broadcast around the world. Initial reports had the death toll from the strike at close to a thousand, with nearly twice that number injured. The entire Arab world was laying the blame squarely at the feet of the United States, and as a result, the protests were transitioning from chanting and burning flags to outright violence.

The president took his seat at the head of the table and the rest of the group followed suit. "Claire, what's the status of our people in Cairo?"

The secretary of state said, "All accounted for, sir. Since the attack occurred after hours, most of the embassy staff were at home. They've been told to shelter in place until further notice. The compound itself is on lockdown but the situation is deteriorating."

"Meaning?"

"The contingent of Marine Security Guards shot three protestors who'd climbed the wall and entered the grounds carrying Molotov cocktails and an assortment of small arms. Two of the intruders were killed and a third was seriously wounded. The Marines are treating him in the consulate's medical bay, but I'm told he's probably not going to make it unless we get him to a hospital in the next couple of hours. The streets around the embassy are gridlocked, making it all but impossible for an ambulance to get through, so the ambassador is coordinating with the Egyptian military to bring in a helicopter to medevac the casualty and remove the two bodies."

President Andrews closed his eyes and pinched the bridge of his nose as he processed this new sequence of events. The situation was already bad enough, but he could only imagine the reaction when word hit the streets that three of their countrymen had been shot by the Americans. "Speaking of the Egyptian military, weren't they supposed to be protecting the exterior of the compound to prevent something like this from happening in the first place?"

Nichols exhaled in frustration with the lack of local support. "They were on duty, sir, but seemed to be turning a blind eye. It appears the soldiers guarding the embassy are more aligned with the protestors than with the foreigners they're tasked with protecting."

That's fucking great, Andrews thought, as he reached for a tumbler filled with ice water and took a sip, letting the cool liquid calm his thoughts. He swirled the glass, watching the ice cubes circulate in the filtered water before taking another sip. Giving himself a few seconds to get his emotions under control, Andrews set the glass back on the coaster and shifted the focus of the conversation to the heart of the problem. "Are we any closer to finding that goddamned drone?" He shifted his gaze to his left, leveling the question at the CIA director. "Lawrence?"

In a manner so calm that it seemed as if he were oblivious to the boiling cauldron erupting across the Middle East, Sloan said, "Sir, we've inserted a team into Syria. They're in place and have the site where we believe the Russians are operating the drone under observation."

"But no visual confirmation as of yet?"

"No, sir. But to be fair, they've been in place for less than twenty-four hours. The team was infiltrating to their designated observation post when the Cairo attack occurred and missed the opportunity to confirm if the Reaper returned to the location they are staking out."

Turning to his secretary of defense, Andrews asked, "And the AWACS, Hank?"

"Unfortunately, the plane developed a hydraulic issue and was grounded for repairs. By the time they were able to get the replacement bird airborne and on-station, we'd missed the chance to pick up the UAV taking off or landing."

No one else at the table had any good news to report, so why should the Pentagon be any different? *Unbelievable.* "Look," President Andrews said, his temper rising to the surface once again. "We have more resources to throw at a problem than practically any other nation in the world. And you're telling me we can't get a location on a piece of our own hardware that is killing people with impunity and turning a significant percentage of the planet's population against us? That is unacceptable."

Before he could continue, the door opened and a young woman in a naval officer's uniform entered the Situation Room. "I apologize for the interruption, Mr. President, but I have a message for Secretary Nichols. State's operations center said she needed it right away and that it was relevant to the subject matter of your meeting."

Since electronic devices, even those belonging to the members of the national security team, weren't allowed in the Situation Room, Andrews gave his approval and she walked around the table and handed a folded slip of paper to the secretary of state.

Nichols read the message but waited for the officer to leave and reseal the door before sharing its contents. "Ten of the twenty-two members of the Arab League have summoned our ambassadors, not to the foreign ministries, but to the presidential or royal palaces. It looks like they're going to start expelling our diplomatic personnel in response to the drone strikes. There's even talk of convening an emergency summit in Kuwait at some point to discuss the matter."

"Well, Lawrence," the president said, massaging his temples with his fingertips. "It appears your assessment of President Polovkin's motives for stealing the drone were spot on. At this rate we'll be lucky to have any remaining influence within spitting distance of the Middle East."

In that same calm tone, Sloan reassured his boss, "I'm sure their displeasure with us will subside once the truth of the matter comes to light, Mr. President." He paused for a moment as an idea began to crystalize in his mind. "And we may be able to use the Arab League's emergency summit to our advantage."

"How so?"

"I have a feeling that the congregation of the Arab world's leaders all in one place will be too enticing a target for your Russian counterpart to pass up. A strike on the summit in Kuwait would be the final brush stroke to President Polovkin's masterpiece, but it will also provide us with the general time and location of the next attack. Armed with that knowledge, we just might have an opportunity to interdict the Reaper before it can complete its mission."

One of the qualities President Andrews appreciated most about Lawrence Sloan was his ability to reassure him that even during a crisis of this magnitude, the light at the end of the tunnel might not be an oncoming train. With the beginnings of a plan starting to come together, his thoughts turned to how to make the Russians pay for the death and destruction they had wreaked across the region in the name of the United States.

CHAPTER 33

AN AVID OUTDOORSMAN, President Polovkin's favorite getaway from the grind of Moscow was a dacha on the banks of Lake Ladoga. Located northwest of St. Petersburg near the border with Finland, the lake was one of the largest in all of Europe. Since the regulation of the commercial fishing trade in the 1950s, the lake had made a remarkable comeback and was teeming with various species.

The dacha itself was not extravagant but did have all the comforts required of a head of state. Built on a high foundation with walls constructed from the processed logs of local trees, the elaborate trimmings around the windows, balconies, and roof gave the structure's exterior the appearance of a log cabin one might find in a fairy tale. But that was where the similarities to other nearby dachas ended. Since this one belonged to the president of Russia, it came with bullet-resistant windows and armored shutters, ballistic material built into the walls and roof, air quality sniffers to detect CBRN or chemical, biological, radiological and nuclear particles, and a fully operational command post for the SBP, the Presidential Security Service. A second building on the grounds served as a barracks for the protective agents, and a concrete helipad capable of accommodating four helicopters occupied a clearing one hundred meters from the main house. The entire perimeter of the property was wired with sensors and tripwires, and a platoon of soldiers patrolled the woods to supplement the protective detail.

The thump of rotors beating the air let Polovkin know his quiet spell of fishing had come to an end. He reeled in the line and slipped the hook through a small loop built into the rod's handle. With an SBP agent in tow, he turned and walked up the small dock to the main house, rod in one hand and the catch of the day in the other.

Entering the dacha, Polovkin handed off the fish to a member of the kitchen staff and went to wash up while the helicopter delivered his guests. He was waiting in the den, standing in front of a television watching a news broadcast on the aftermath of the Cairo attack, when there was a knock on the door. After receiving permission to enter, an agent opened it and led two men inside. The agent retreated and closed the door behind him, resuming his post in the foyer.

The taller of the two men, Vice Admiral Mishkin, the head of the GRU said, "Good afternoon, Mr. President."

Polovkin turned away from the screen to greet his visitors. "Please, Evgeny. We're in the countryside. Let us dispense with the formalities."

The minister of defense, Anton Shubovich, noticed the lead story on every news channel and smiled as he collapsed onto one end of a large, overstuffed sofa. Mishkin sat at the other end of the couch and straightened the crease in his trousers as he crossed his legs. Choosing a chair across the coffee table from the two men, Polovkin leaned forward and pulled a silver tray with a bottle of vodka and three glasses toward him. He filled the small glasses, offered a toast, then downed the clear liquid in one shot. Mishkin and Shubovich followed suit.

Replacing his glass on the tray, Polovkin asked, "So, what happened in Egypt?"

Mishkin replied, "Cairo is an old city. And even in the upscale areas like the one where the mosque was located, newer buildings were built on top of older, sub-standard utility lines. The missile's explosions ruptured one of those old natural gas lines and set off the chain reaction that destroyed much of the surrounding neighborhood. While it was an unforeseen consequence, it seems to have only intensified the anti-American sentiment in the region."

"Like throwing petrol on an open flame," Shubovich added.

The president leaned forward and refilled the glasses for another round. This would be the last one before dinner. He didn't want the collective minds in the room to be clouded by the alcohol. There was too much to discuss this evening, and he wanted everyone to be clear-headed. Once again, he offered a casual toast, and the three men downed the vodka in unison.

Mishkin grinned. "If anything, the images of Cairo burning and the large number of dead and injured have advanced the timeline of your plan."

"How so?" the president asked.

"Several countries have begun expelling American diplomats and their families. I believe it is only a matter of time before others follow suit. It is very possible that we could see a mass exodus of U.S. personnel from the region within the next thirty days."

"As a matter of fact," Shubovich offered, "my office has already begun fielding calls from my counterparts in the Middle East. They have been inquiring about our ability to step in and fill the void militarily if the Americans were no longer providing the support required to keep their regimes in power."

Pleasantly surprised, Polovkin said, "That didn't take long."

Shubovich continued. "For them, it is a matter of survival. Without the support and intervention of an external benefactor, many of the leaders of these countries fear they will be overthrown by a popular uprising. The video of Muammar Gaddafi being dragged through the streets of Sirte by an angry mob before being shot in the head is their worst nightmare come true. We should be able to negotiate very favorable terms if it means they can sleep well at night without the specter of a similar fate hanging over them."

Yaroslav Polovkin understood those fears more than the two men sitting across from him could ever know. Many countries had experienced revolutions or coups, his among them, and they usually did not end well for the ruling party. In 1991, a group of hardline Communists in the Soviet government and military attempted to overthrow President Mikahil Gorbachev in what came to be known as the August Coup. The uprising was organized by the head of the KGB, the minister of defense, and others who were opposed to Gorbachev's reforms and decentralization of Moscow's power over the republics that made up the Soviet Union. The coup ultimately failed, managing to put Gorbachev under house arrest for only three days. It was not lost on Polovkin that the heads of the defense ministry and the nation's top intelligence agency were involved in the coup, and that two men currently holding those positions were in his presence at this very moment.

Lost in his thoughts, the president noticed the room had gone quiet. Admiral Mishkin had asked a question and the men were awaiting an answer. "I'm sorry," Polovkin said. "I was just thinking about something."

Mishkin repeated the question. "With the operation moving forward so well, I was wondering if additional attacks were necessary? If we might not bring the UAV and its equipment back to Moscow for study?"

Looking to his defense minister, Polovkin asked, "What do you think Anton?"

"While studying the drone will advance our own UAV program exponentially, I believe one more attack might be the straw to break the proverbial camel's back. There are still a few regimes continuing to support the United States, and a spectacular finale could provide the spark that unites the entire Middle East against the Americans."

Polovkin weighed both arguments. Did the events they had set in motion with the drone strikes have enough momentum to carry his plan through to completion? If that was the case, then it would be reckless to risk losing the drone on a mission that provided only a marginal increase in the success of the outcome. However, if this last strike would in fact be the determining factor in driving the Americans out of the Middle East, then it was an acceptable risk. "And if we did fly one more mission, what might you have in mind for a target?"

Shubovich continued. "Evgeny and I were discussing this very subject on the flight here. It appears the Arab League will be convening an emergency summit in Kuwait to discuss the missile attacks and the ongoing American presence in the region."

"You're not suggesting we attack the summit?" Polovkin interrupted. "We need their leaders alive and well to be able to vote on the expulsion measure."

"We're not suggesting an attack on the summit itself, but on one or two of the member delegations. There are still a couple of countries, namely the Saudis and Jordanians, who are holding out against regional pressure. As you know, other than Israel, they are two of the Americans' staunchest allies in the Middle East."

Following their line of thinking, the president finished the thought. "If their delegations were attacked by an American drone, especially if members of the royal families were counted among the casualties, they would have no choice but to vote with the other states."

President Polovkin took a moment to weigh the risk but decided the reward was too great to pass up. With his decision made, he stood, signaling an end to the meeting. "Enough work for now," he said, and headed to the door. "Come, let us eat. My chef has prepared the fish I caught this afternoon."

CHAPTER 34

TIM SHANNON SCOPED the airfield from a window on the second floor of an uninhabited farmhouse nearly a kilometer from Bassel Al-Assad International Airport. The Nightforce NX8 scope mounted on his McMillan TAC-338 tactical rifle, easily provided a clear view of the airport from this distance.

Ron Foster had offered the use of the Ground Branch safehouse in the hills as their base of operations, but Joe needed the team to be closer to the airport. There was no way they could conduct the surveillance necessary to determine if the UAV and Tariq were onsite from such a distance. And the constant comings and goings of rotating shifts was bound to draw unwanted attention that would risk compromising the team.

As part of the reconnaissance of the area for their own mission, Ron had suggested the farmhouse as a viable option. It was uninhabited, as were many of the houses around it, abandoned when young men able to work the fields were conscripted into the military or fled to join one of the myriad rebel groups fighting the regime. Unable to tend to the fields, families moved away to live with relatives, hoping to be able to return at some point after one side or the other claimed victory in the civil war. So, under the cover of darkness, Joe and the guys had taken up residence, using camouflage netting and the stables behind the main house to hide their vehicles.

With a table set back from the window acting as a bench rest, and the fore-end of the sniper rifle stabilized on top of its soft-sided carrying case, Shannon was in his element. It was a position in which he had spent a good portion of his professional life. He was just thankful that the chair he brought up from the dining room had one of those seat cushions that tied onto the slats of the back rest. Tim had learned long ago to take advantage of any creature comforts on deployments. There were plenty of times when he had to be miserable, forced to embrace the suck, so he didn't think there was any harm in being comfortable when the opportunity presented itself.

Ten feet to his right was a similar setup where Kevin Chang used a spotter's scope to eye the airport through an adjacent window. The elevated position provided the operators with an unobstructed line of sight to the runways and the hangar complex on the east side of the grounds.

Unlike many larger airports with extensive maintenance facilities operated by each of the airlines, this one had only two small hangars on the northeast side of the property. Based on their map study of the overhead imagery prior to departing Amman, Joe and Scott agreed that if the Reaper was here, it would be kept out of sight in one of the hangars. And based on the significant armed presence around one and not the other, they felt confident about their assumption. They just hoped Tariq was being held there as well – assuming he was still alive.

The sun had finally dipped below the horizon, and as spectacular as the sunset had been, Shannon was happy he didn't have to stare into the fiery orb any longer. He and Kevin took turns attaching night vision devices to their scopes, ensuring one of them always had eyes on the airport. As darkness fell across the landscape Kevin glanced at his watch, noting the end of their shift was only ten minutes away. He was looking forward to the break, and the thought of handing his scope off to one of the other guys was sounding pretty good. His eyes were tired and bloodshot, and he was still seeing spots from staring in the direction of the sun for the last few hours. He stole a quick look over at Tim and shook his head. The guy looked perfectly comfortable, as if he could remain in that position all night.

The sound of footsteps climbing the stairs indicated it was, in fact, time for shift change. Mike entered the room and relieved Kevin behind the spotter's scope, ready to take his turn on the glass. Tim was just about to come off his rifle and let John take over when he noticed a slice of light split the center of the hangar doors. "Stand by. There's activity at the hangar."

The gap in the doors widened as they slid apart on their rollers. With them fully open, Tim had a clear line of sight into the interior of the hangar. He couldn't believe what he was seeing. "Quick. Get the camera up and running!"

A tripod with a DSLR camera and an 800-millimeter lens made even longer by the attached night optics was set up behind Tim's position. John turned on the camera, then looked through the viewfinder and brought the hangar's interior into focus. Switching the camera to video mode, he began recording. Confident the camera was getting the footage, he shouted down the stairwell, "Joe, you need to get up here."

They watched as a truck backed into the hangar and hooked up to a trailer. The driver hopped down to check the connection, then climbed back up into the cab, put the truck in gear, and eased out onto the tarmac. Then the massive doors slid back together, and darkness once again enveloped the ramp. The entire process took no more than ten minutes.

Joe and Scott retreated downstairs and inserted the camera's memory card into a laptop. Displayed on the screen before them, positioned prominently in the center of the hangar, sat the stolen MQ-9 Reaper. They watched with fascination as technicians moved casually around the UAV. The lack of urgency in the men's actions gave Joe the impression they were conducting routine maintenance rather than pre-mission preparations.

Scott motioned to a stack of containers to the right of the screen. "Those must be the Hellfires. Looks like they have four left."

Joe agreed while he continued scanning the video for signs of the ground control station. He saw two doors along the rear wall, one to the left and another to the right. The tinted glass cut into the upper portions of the doors made it impossible to see what lurked on the other side. "I don't see the GCS. Think it could be in one of those rooms in the back of the hangar?"

"Could be," Scott said. "Your guess is as good as mine."

Before they could speculate any further, two men entered from the left of the screen and stopped next to the Reaper. "Well, well," Joe said. "Who are these fine gents?"

Leaning in to get a better look, Scott said, "I'll be damned. I don't know about the guy in the lab coat, but the one in uniform looks a lot like Colonel Vadim Teplov. He's responsible for all GRU activity in the region."

The breath caught in Joe's throat as he watched the door to the room on the left open and a tall man in Russian ACUs, Army Combat Uniform, stepped out into the hangar.

"What is it?" Scott asked.

Joe hit the laptop's space bar to pause the video. He was silent for ten seconds as the memory of the firefight in Salkhad raced through his mind, propelling him back to the action. He felt the weight of Greg Jacobs as he dragged him to cover, remembered the eye contact with the Russian soldier tracking him with his rifle but who at the last second adjusted his aim and shot Jacobs instead. Joe paused the mental footage at the point where the Russian lowered his rifle, and with a big smile, gave Joe a respectful nod for his effort.

Scott nudged Joe with his knee. "You okay?"

"The guy in uniform," Joe said, as he mentally returned from the heat of the battle. "He was leading the Syrian forces we engaged on our mission in Salkhad." Joe paused a moment, feeling the anger build. "That's the Russian son of a bitch who killed Greg Jacobs."

"Holy shit!" Scott exclaimed.

"Yeah," Joe agreed. "I've got a serious score to settle with that guy."

"No, not that," Scott said, pointing to the screen. "That!"

Joe hit a couple of keys to zoom in on the spot where Scott was pointing. The soldier, having grown too comfortable in the secure environment, had made the mistake of leaving the door open. That slip gave the CIA men a clear view into the room. A man shackled to a table was clearly visible on the screen. He was hunched over and seemed to be resting his head on folded arms. At first, they couldn't tell if the man was unconscious or making the most of a break in what had all the appearances of being an interrogation. Joe hit the spacebar again to let the video roll and they watched in amazement as the man strained to lift his battered head. It was impossible to tell whether he was curious about what was going on in the hangar, or if he noticed the doors were open and hoped his American benefactors would be out there in the darkness looking for him. Regardless of the reason, the man used his last reserves of strength to hold his head up in full view of the camera, having no idea it was positioned nearly a kilometer away on the second floor of the farmhouse. His face was swollen and bruised from a severe beating, but even so, they recognized him immediately. It was Tariq Kabbani.

CHAPTER 35

EVEN THOUGH TARIQ knew the chances were slim that anyone was out there looking for him, he held his head up as long as he could, hoping beyond hope that someone had seen him. The door had been open for only a brief time, but he had made the most of the Russian's mistake and felt he had done his part. The rest was now up to the Americans.

Even though he was shackled to an eyebolt screwed into the metal table, the chain connecting the handcuffs was long enough that, with a little maneuvering, he could cross his arms and use them as a makeshift pillow to rest his battered head. He needed to take advantage of the respite while he had the chance.

Tariq's left eye was swollen shut and blood drained from a nose that may or may not be broken. Despite his injuries, he had the distinct feeling that the beating he'd received up to this point had just been the warm-up, an intimidation to make him feel helpless, and let him know he was no longer in control of his immediate future. Tariq knew the score. He had been on the opposite end of this equation more times than he could count, interrogating suspected traitors or captured rebels fighting to overthrow the Syrian regime.

What happened when the big Russian re-entered the room would give the intelligence officer an idea of how this drama was going to play out. If the incident was all a big misunderstanding, they could apologize for the mix-up and send him on his way with nothing more than the few bumps and bruises for his troubles. If, however, they had reason to believe his presence near the airport was more clandestine in nature, then what he had experienced up to this point had just been the preliminary round of questioning. The pain and suffering would be ratcheted up exponentially.

If that was to be his fate, Tariq understood he wouldn't be able to hold out indefinitely. No one could. Everyone had their breaking point. He couldn't count on a rescue from the Americans. They had no way of knowing where he was. Sure, they could track the GPS location of his phone when he made the call to Garrett, but that wouldn't help them identify his current location. And since he was routinely out of contact when he was operational, his own government wouldn't be looking for him yet either.

No, he wasn't going to hold out waiting on help from either of the governments he served. But he did have to endure whatever they had in store for him for at least three days. Years ago, when he had revealed his collaboration, as he called it, with the Americans, he and Rima had set up a contingency plan in the event he was ever compromised. If three days passed without any type of communication from him, she was to assume he had been found out by his government and was either on the run, being interrogated, or dead.

In any event, the plan called for her to take their son Nabil across to Cyprus via the ferry. Once there, she was to make her way to the Bank of Cyprus branch on Makarious Avenue in Larnaca. Inside was a safety deposit box containing new identities with passports, credit cards, cash, and a mobile phone. With the contents of the box in hand, she and Nabil would take a flight to the western European country of her choice and wait. If thirty days passed without hearing from him, she was to assume he was dead. If that eventuality came to pass, she was to call the one contact programmed into the mobile phone. The number had been set up by Greg Jacobs, Tariq's handler for all those years, in case this plan was ever put into action. The call would be routed through multiple switches around the world, but in the end, would be answered by someone in Langley, Virginia. With the Agency's help, Tariq's wife and son would be relocated to the United States where they could begin to rebuild their lives.

As he sat there resting his head on his arms, he was determined to endure whatever the big Russian had in store for him. He had to, for his family. Tariq wasn't sure how long he had been in custody, if the three days had passed, but he needed to give Rima and Nabil as much of a head start as possible. He heard the heavy footfalls of boots on the concrete floor and looked up to see the soldier called Kalugin enter the room. *Here we go again,* he thought.

*

Joe and Scott sat hip to hip on the old sofa, their knees rubbing against the edge of the coffee table. A blue ethernet cable ran from the laptop through the back door and connected to the portable satellite communications terminal providing a secure link for the video conference with headquarters. Moments later the screen came to life, and they were staring into the seventh-floor conference room. Director Sloan was flanked by the DDO, Katherine Clark, and Carl Douglas, the chief of the special activities division. Harold Lee, who ran the counterterrorism center was also in attendance.

Director Sloan kicked things off. "Before we begin, I want to commend you for locating both the Reaper and our asset. I'm heading to the White House to brief the president on your findings once we're finished here."

Scott dismissed the compliment and asked, "What's our next move, sir?"

"That's a good question, Scott. I would imagine a precision airstrike would be an option, but I'm not sure the president will be willing to approve what will be a very public attack on a known Russian facility."

"Sir, Tariq Kabbani is in that hangar. Give me a chance to get him out before we consider leveling the place."

Sloan said, "Your dedication to your asset is commendable, Scott. But I can't risk your safety, or that of Joe's team, in an assault on such a heavily guarded facility. This may be one of those situations where, as harsh as it sounds, he may have to be sacrificed if it means preventing that Reaper from getting back in the air."

The logical part of Scott's brain was telling him the director was right. Hell, he'd had to make plenty of tough calls himself over the span of his career, so he got it. But Tariq was not just some low-level informant to be discarded because it was convenient. He had done excellent work. Been loyal. Provided high-quality, actionable intelligence. He deserved better. "There has to be something we can do," Scott argued. "He's in there right now getting his faced bashed in, and the best we can do is to drop a bomb on his head? Pardon my bluntness, sir, but that's bullshit."

No one was more surprised than Joe at the outburst. It was one thing to have a disagreement behind closed doors, but calling out the director in front of everyone was unheard of. Joe was almost thankful for the distraction when Mike's voice came through his earpiece.

"I need you up here, boss."

Joe leaned away from the screen, out of view of the camera, and said, "Kinda busy right now. Can it wait?"

"Nope. There's something going on at the hangar."

Joe vaulted off the couch and took the stairs two at a time. Mike came off the spotter's scope and Joe slid into his position. Two SUVs, BMWs from the looks of the body style, were parked in front of the hangar with engines running. Once again, the doors slid open, but only a few feet this time, allowing just enough space for a couple of men to pass through. He saw Tariq, with his hands and feet shackled and a Russian soldier on each arm doing the prisoner shuffle toward the vehicles. When the trio reached the SUVs, the soldiers lifted Tariq off the ground and threw him into the back seat of the lead Beemer. One of them followed him into the back seat, while the other walked around the SUV and got in on the opposite side.

Without taking his eye off the scope, Joe switched channels on his radio and hailed the pilot of a U.S. Air Force AWACS patrolling the international air space above the Mediterranean Sea. Its crew was monitoring the comings and goings of Syrian and Russian military aircraft but were also on station to track the stolen Reaper the next time it took to the sky. "Major, am I correct in assuming you can track targets on the ground as well as in the air?"

The pilot's voice in his ear almost sounded offended. "If your target moves across this planet in the air, on the water, or on the ground, we can damn well track it."

Joe chuckled into his mic. "No offense, sir. Just checking." He then went on to describe what he needed.

After a short pause to confer with the radar operators in the rear of the plane, the pilot came back on the air. "The SUVs are locked into the system. We'll keep an eye on them for you."

Joe thanked the pilot and got up, allowing Mike to get back on the scope and resume his watch. He gave the big man an appreciative squeeze on the shoulder before heading back downstairs to brief the group on what had just occurred. Things were starting to get interesting.

CHAPTER 36

"IS EVERYTHING OKAY?" Director Sloan asked, as Joe's image reappeared on the screen.

"Sorry about that, sir," Joe said, before relaying the events of the last few minutes. "We'll see where the SUVs end up, but my hope is that they're taking Tariq someplace a little more secluded to continue the interrogation."

With concern for his asset's safety at the forefront of his priority list, Scott interjected, "Or they could be taking him to some out-of-the-way spot to put a bullet in his head and dump his body in a shallow grave. We need to hit those SUVs before they get to their destination."

"We're too far away at this point and have no idea where they're heading," Joe countered. "Racing headlong toward a heavily fortified military base or into a city we're not familiar with to conduct a spur of the moment hit on an Alpha team is a recipe for disaster." Joe paused a second, then softened his tone. "Look, I'm as concerned about Tariq's well-being as you are. But let's take a breath, find out where they're going, then come up with a plan to assault the place and extract him."

Director Sloan thought it over for a minute. "I agree with Joe. From Mr. Kabbani's appearance in the video, it doesn't seem as if the serious portion of the interrogation has begun. He's a professional intelligence officer and wouldn't have divulged any meaningful information after being slapped around a little. I think the real pressure has yet to be applied."

The voice of the AWACS pilot crackled in Joe's ear causing a slight grin as a plan began to form in his head.

Carl Douglas, the chief of SAD noticed the change in his demeanor. "What is it, Joe?"

"Do we have any rebel forces in the area?"

"Why? What have you got in mind?"

"The pilot of the AWACS just checked in. The SUVs stopped at a small compound near the southern end of the runway, about a mile and a half from the hangar. I need someone to create a distraction at the airport while we assault the compound and thought a group of highly-motivated rebels just might fit the bill."

Douglas withdrew his cellphone and fired off a text requesting the status of rebel positions in and around the airbase. His phone vibrated with the response thirty seconds later. "There's a small cell operating in the outskirts of Latakia. We can have them tasked to you within the hour. What else do you need?"

Joe thought for a second, then added, "We're going to have our hands full with the assault and I'd feel a whole lot better if there was someone I know and trust coordinating the rebel cell. Can I borrow Ron Foster and his Ground Branchers?"

Douglas looked to his boss, Katherine Clark, then to Director Sloan for their approval. Both nodded in agreement, so he said, "Done."

Director Sloan said, "I'll inform the president of our plans and see how he wants to handle the drone issue." He then went around the room asking if anyone had anything else to add.

"There's one last thing, sir," Joe said before the meeting wrapped. "When we assault the building to free Tariq, the soldiers holding him aren't going to be happy that we crashed their party. They're going to fight back, and when they do, we're going to kill them. I want everyone on this call to be aware of that fact before we commit to this raid. I don't want to come back and be grilled about why the other side took casualties or that I didn't understand the greater diplomatic sensitivities at play."

Sloan acknowledged Joe's concerns and did his best to put them to rest. "As you may know, President Andrews was a Marine infantry officer and combat veteran prior to entering politics. After the losses we sustained during the attack on the base in Jordan, I doubt he is going to lose any sleep over the deaths of a few Russian soldiers. Do what must be done to rescue Mr. Kabbani."

*

Having lost all track of time, Tariq had no idea how long he had been in the dimly lit house. When they had arrived at the triangular compound at the extreme southeastern end of the runway, he had been shoved into a back bedroom that would serve as his interrogation chamber. From the looks of the room, it was obvious that he wasn't the first guest at the inn. Dried blood, appearing black in the poor light, stained the thick wooden table and the smell of urine permeated the room. It was not a scene he was unfamiliar with, but he was usually the one conducting the interrogation, not the subject of one. With his hands chained to the center of the table and duct tape wrapped just above his ankles securing his legs to those of the chair, he knew he was not going anywhere without some help. If nothing else, he had to commend the Russians for their thoroughness.

The soldiers took turns working Tariq over, rotating in shifts so they didn't tire out or risk breaking a knuckle from repeated punches to his head. And there had been plenty. His face was so swollen, that he resembled a hideous black and blue jack-o-lantern. The left eye had closed the rest of the way. Its lid puffed out from the socket with a single line of eyelashes creasing the center. And it was official. His nose was broken. A constant stream of blood and mucus poured from his nostrils into his mouth causing him to gasp for air. Nauseated by the fluids running down his throat, Tariq had turned his head to the side and vomited onto the floor. But the relief to his stomach was only temporary as the bloody fluids continued to flow.

Sharp pain shot through his jaw, but he didn't think it was broken. Two teeth had been knocked out during the continuous beating, but as he felt around the inside of his mouth with his tongue, Tariq noticed a third gap. He was momentarily confused because he only remembered spitting out the two molars. Had he swallowed the other one? Curious, he glanced over at the puddle of what had been the contents of his stomach but didn't see the missing third tooth. *Oh, well,* he thought. *You've got more important things to worry about right now.*

One of the soldiers was winding up to throw another haymaker at Tariq's head when the door opened and Kalugin entered the room. He dismissed the two men, sending them to the kitchen to put some ice on their fists and get some coffee and a shot or two of vodka. Kalugin grabbed a chair from the corner and dragged it over to the table. He took a seat and reached into his left cargo pocket. Withdrawing a bottle of water, he unscrewed the cap, then slid it across the table.

Tariq accepted the offering, then turned his head to the right and spit out a large glob of blood. He took a sip, swirling the water around in his mouth, and spit it out, adding to the vile puddle on the floor. The water burned as it entered his split lip and the holes in his gums where his teeth had been, but he took another long swig from the bottle, relishing every drop of the cool liquid. Knowing he had to stay hydrated, he was determined to keep as much of the water down as his stomach would allow. He took another draw, then set the half-empty bottle on the table and turned his attention to the man sitting across from him. "Thank you for the water."

Kalugin remained polite, even though his patience was wearing thin. "It's nothing," he said, looking around the room, not bothered in the least by the disturbing sights and smells. "But there's so much more I could do to end all this unpleasantness if you would only answer my questions."

"I was under the impression I had been doing that ever since you detained me," Tariq countered, finding it more difficult to speak as the pain and swelling in his jaw and mouth grew more intense.

Without warning, Kalugin erupted upward, the force of his action sending the chair flying back away from the table. Standing at his full height he looked down on his captive, then balled his hand into a fist and drove his knuckles onto the top of Tariq's shackled hand. Three of the four metacarpal bones snapped as if they were toothpicks. Stunned by the suddenness of the action, the Syrian looked at his broken hand in disbelief. The pain registered in his brain a split second later and he howled in agony.

"Why were you at the airfield that night?" Kalugin demanded.

Still focused on the pain, Tariq did not answer right away, and his hesitance seemed to stoke an invisible fire inside the Russian. Furious and frustrated, Kalugin ground his knuckles into the top of Tariq's hand, feeling the bones shift under the thin layer of skin.

Tariq screamed for him to stop, and whimpered, "I've told you a hundred times. I had been investigating some dissidents in the area." He paused, trying to cradle his broken hand the best he could with it cuffed to the table. "It was late, I was tired, and I'd simply pulled over on the side of the road to make a phone call."

"And who was on the other end of the call?" Kalugin pressed.

Reciting the cover story he had concocted to hide his call to Scott Garrett, Tariq scoffed. "No one. Just a woman I happen to visit from time to time when I'm in town."

"That's unfortunate," Kalugin said, as he called one of his men into the room.

Confused, Tariq asked, "That I have a mistress?"

"No. That I don't believe you."

A steroid-enhanced soldier entered the room while another posted in the hallway closed the door behind him. Kalugin introduced the man. "This is Anton. I hope you don't mind, but he's going to join us for the next round of questioning."

Tariq's attention was initially drawn to the man's nose. It had obviously been badly broken and didn't appear as if it had been set. Anton grinned, revealing a set of shattered, jagged teeth that caused Tariq to recoil involuntarily.

Anton carried two items as he crossed the room to the table. The first was a pair of run-of-the-mill garden shears. Those, he handed to Kalugin. The other was a butane blow torch. As if the sight of Anton wasn't enough, seeing the two items made Tariq's blood run cold.

"You probably know this from personal experience," Kalugin offered, holding the shears up for inspection. "But I want you to be fully aware of the consequences for not answering my questions in a truthful manner. First, I'm going to start taking your fingers. One joint at a time. Then," gesturing to Anton, "he will use the torch to control the bleeding by cauterizing the wound. I can't have you passing out from blood loss."

Tariq had indeed witnessed the process used by members of the General Intelligence Directorate's interrogation teams. And while his mind knew there was no point in resisting, his body involuntarily struggled as Anton grabbed his hand. Kalugin began applying pressure and blood seeped around the shear's blades as they sliced through the skin of Tariq's pinkie finger about a half inch from the bottom of his fingernail.

"No! Don't do this!" Tariq screamed as the blades cut into his finger. Any second now, he knew the pain from the broken bones in his hand would be a distant memory.

CHAPTER 37

USING RON FOSTER's callsign, Joe whispered into his radio, "Texan, we're in position."

"Good copy, Spartan. Wait one," came Foster's reply.

As promised, Ron and his team had been made available to support the operation to free Tariq. The Syrian rebels had arrived on time and were split into three fireteams, each led by one of the Ground Branchers.

Ron had deployed the teams in a half-moon semicircle at varying intervals around the southern end of the runway. Using available structures for cover, the two Syrians assigned to each team unloaded a crate containing an M224 Lightweight Company Mortar System from the bed of their Toyota Hi-Lux pickups. After setting the baseplate and attaching the tube and bipod assembly, each team unloaded a second crate containing ten 60-millimeter high-explosive rounds. With the weapons assembled and ready to fire, Foster, Ivy, and Abrams checked to ensure the M64 sights on their respective mortars were set to the appropriate distances and elevations. The last thing they wanted to do was have one of the rounds come up short and land in the compound, killing the assault team or the man they were there to rescue.

Ivy and Abrams reported their status and were ready to fire, so Ron radioed the team. "We're good to go, Spartan. Stand by."

Foster counted down from three over the radio, and when he hit one, gave the order to fire. A rebel with each fireteam dropped a round into the tube and ducked away as it rocketed into the air with a familiar whoomp.

As soon as the round left the tube, the second rebel pulled another from the crate and handed it to his partner to repeat the firing process.

The first volley impacted the concrete runway one hundred and fifty meters from the compound's outer wall. Using the succession of ear-splitting booms to mask their entry, Joe ordered, "Execute! Execute! Execute!"

Chris initiated a small breaching charge that popped the gate's lock. The rusted metal door swung open, and the five operators flowed into the compound. Their night-vision devices locked down and suppressed HK416 rifles at the ready, Mike led the tactical train across the open expanse. He saw the BMWs parked near the front door and angled for them. The distance wasn't far. Less than fifty meters, but he was acutely aware that the team was totally exposed while they were in the open.

Advancing on their objective, Joe keyed his mic, "Texan, this is Spartan. We're in."

Foster acknowledged the call, "Roger that. Make your own luck, Spartan." With their diversionary role in the mission complete, Ron had each of the fireteams launch their remaining rounds. The impacts of the high-explosives tore craters in the smooth concrete that would render runway 35-Right inoperable for the foreseeable future. *Thirty rounds in roughly ninety seconds,* he thought. *Not as fast as an American infantry unit, but not bad for a bunch of kids fighting to free their country.*

Out of ammo, Foster instructed the teams to break down the mortars and evacuate the area. He wanted to be long gone before the Syrians and Russians mounted a response that he and his small band of men were unequipped to deal with. As the rebels packed the weapons and loaded the crates into the beds of the pickup trucks, the Ground Branch officers swept their respective firing positions for anything left behind that would identify them. Satisfied their areas were clean, Foster gave the order, and the small irregular fighting force disbanded. The rebels melted back into the cityscape while the three SAD men took their own routes back to the safe house in the hills.

*

Sweat dripped from the tip of Kalugin's nose as he listened to the first volley of mortars whistle overhead. Accustomed to the sound of battle, he could tell they were not aimed at his little hideaway. And while the first impacts were close enough for the explosions to rattle the windows, he knew he and his men weren't in any danger. Deciding this was as good a time as any for a break in the interrogation, he left one of his men to watch over Tariq, then headed to the kitchen for a strong coffee and a cigarette. He was about halfway there when the sound of the front door opening caught his attention. *Probably just one of the men going outside to watch the fireworks from the mortar barrage,* he thought. But the telltale clink, clink, clink that could only be a flashbang bouncing across the floor told him otherwise.

*

The team paused a beat, waiting for the blinding flash of light and disorienting bang to stun anyone in the room. Mike was the first through the door, and the image of a soldier sitting on a couch in the center of the room filled his holographic sight. Dazed but recovering quickly from the effects of the banger, the Russian reached for his AK. Mike pressed the trigger twice, sending two rounds into the man's chest. He continued left and moved along the wall, digging the corner.

Chris button-hooked through the door and went the opposite direction, clearing his own corner to make sure a bad guy wasn't getting ready to shoot his partner in the back. A ragged love seat was positioned midway along the wall, so Chris went up and over it to keep the guys behind him from getting jammed up in the door. Known as the fatal funnel, doors tended to draw a lot of fire, so as a rule of thumb, standing in an open doorway was frowned upon. The rest of the team flowed into the main room, alternating left and right, until everyone was inside.

The sound of the flashbang was unmistakable in the confines of the small building and drew the Russian soldiers to the front of the house like moths to a porch light. One man came out of a bathroom with his pistol drawn, but Joe put him down with two shots to the chest. A third press of the trigger sent a round through his forehead, its energy carrying him back into the bathroom. He collapsed on the floor with his upper body draped over the side of the tub.

Joe gave the command to advance, and the team had just begun to move forward when gunfire erupted from the kitchen, sending the operators scrambling for cover. The open floor plan offered a direct line of sight into the living room, and a Russian soldier taking cover behind the kitchen's island was using the design to his advantage. Rounds from his AK-74 tore through furniture and gouged divots in the plaster-covered walls, filling the air with dust and bits of drywall.

They had lost the momentum and were pinned down. Movement from the left caught Joe's eye, and he saw a second Russian emerge from a hallway and join his teammate in the kitchen. *Great! Now we've got two AKs behind the island throwing lead our way.* The area would be crawling with reinforcements any minute, and Joe knew they needed to get to Tariq then un-ass the area in a hurry.

He peeked around the corner of a sofa, trying to figure out a way to put the two Alpha men out of commission. Joe kept a sliver of his head exposed as long as he dared, taking in as much information as possible before sliding back out of sight. He took a moment to process what he had seen as the gunfight raged around him. Picturing the image of the kitchen, he saw the island, the pantry, shelves along the walls, counters, a sink…and a back door. *That's it!*

Keying his radio, Joe shared his plan with the team. The guys didn't seem to think it was a particularly good one and weren't shy about letting him know it. While he appreciated their feedback, the decision was not up for debate.

Joe got to his knees, took a couple of deep breaths to steel himself for what was about to happen, then said, "Moving!"

Chris replied, "Move!" and threw a flashbang into the kitchen while the rest of the team laid down covering fire.

Joe sprinted for the door and had just crossed the threshold when something hit him between the shoulder blades with the force of a sledgehammer. The impact knocked the wind out of him, and he pitched forward, sliding on his chest like a ballplayer stealing second base. He lay there in the dark for a second trying to catch his breath before realizing he was still in the fatal funnel. The pain in his back was excruciating and his lungs burned for oxygen, but he willed his body to roll to the left, out of the line of fire.

Joe managed to get on his hands and knees, then raised his body upright into a kneeling position. He sucked in two deep breaths and winced as the expansion of his rib cage aggravated the pain in his back. *Fuck!* he grimaced, hoping nothing was broken. Once his breathing was back to a semblance of normal, he got to his feet and began making his way around the perimeter of the house in search of the back door.

He had just turned the corner, thinking about how he was going to make entry, when he crashed headlong into something solid. He fell back on his ass and looked up, finding himself staring at a Russian soldier with a badly broken nose. The guy looked somehow familiar, and he seemed to recognize Joe as well. Then he grinned, showing off a mouthful of broken teeth.

"You ever been to Brussels?" Joe asked.

CHAPTER 38

AFTER THE INITIAL flashbang went off and the shooting started, Kalugin sprinted back down the hallway. He grabbed the soldier guarding the door by the arm and shoved him into the room. Pointing to Tariq, he said, "Watch him."

He then turned to Anton and directed him to circle around the house, come up behind the attackers, and ambush them through the front door. Having grown bored with torturing the Syrian, Anton was more than eager to get in on the action. He shrugged on his body armor and grabbed his rifle. Ready for battle, he climbed out a window and began his one-man assault. Throwing caution to the wind and not wanting the firefight to end before he had an opportunity to join the fray, Anton sprinted around the back of the house as fast as his thick legs could carry him.

He turned the corner and smashed into someone. The collision knocked the man onto his backside and sent Anton's rifle clattering across the packed dirt surface. He looked down at the individual sitting before him, and even in the darkness recognized him immediately.

In broken English Anton said, "You should have killed me when you had the chance."

Joe raised his rifle, "It looks like I have another one right now."

Before he could fire, the big Russian stepped forward and slapped the weapon to the side. With thick, meaty hands, he reached down and grabbed Joe by the shoulder straps of his plate carrier. Anton pulled him up to his feet, then reared his head back and brought it down to deliver a crushing head butt.

Joe saw the move coming and angled his head to the right to protect his face. The rock-hard bone of Anton's forehead connected with Joe's left eyebrow, splitting the recently healed wound he had sustained during their previous encounter. Blood flowed down the side of his face and into his eye.

Knowing it would be difficult for Joe to see an attack coming from his blind side, Anton caught him on the side of the head with a quick right hook. The blow stunned Joe, causing him to lose his balance and stumble back into the wall. Relishing the thought of killing the man who had caused him so much pain and embarrassment, Anton advanced, pinning his quarry against the house. He wrapped his hands around Joe's throat and began squeezing.

Joe grabbed Anton's wrists and attempted to break the hold on his neck. But he was weakened by the blow to the head, and the bastard was as strong as a bear. Joe threw a couple of ineffective punches that only seemed to amuse the Russian before tunnel vision started to set in. His right arm went limp and fell to the side.

Seeing this as a sign of his imminent victory, Anton's lips spread into a cruel smile, revealing the teeth Joe had shattered. But the look on his face changed the second he felt the barrel of Joe's Glock 19 pressing against the side of his head. Now it was Joe's turn to smile, and his smiling, bloody face was the last thing Anton saw before a pair of jacketed hollow-points passed through his brain.

Joe performed a tactical reload, swapping the partially spent magazine for a full one before holstering his pistol. Reaching to his right, he grabbed the rifle dangling from its sling, brought it up to the ready, and stepped over Anton's nearly headless body. He ducked under one of the kitchen windows, taking a quick peek into the house. If the angle was right, he could pop the two Russians in the back of the head and put an end to the standoff. But of course, that didn't turn out to be the case. *Figures,* he thought. Between getting shot in the back, and running face-first into Alpha man, why should anything start going his way at this point?

He continued forward and stopped at the edge of the back door. Since he was by himself, he would be the breacher and the assaulter. Joe reached up and used his sleeve to wipe the blood from his eye before keying his radio. "Cease fire. I'm coming in." When he heard only the distinct sound of the AKs cracking throughout the front of the house, he turned his back to the door and unleashed a powerful mule-kick. The sole of his boot splintered the door frame, and he spun around in time to see the two Russian soldiers turn toward him with shocked looks on their faces. Two quick double taps from his rifle ended the gunfight.

Blood continued to stream from the gash above Joe's left eye, but there was nothing to be done about it now. He entered the kitchen and was joined by the rest of the team as they formed up to resume clearing the house in search of Tariq.

Giving his dust-covered and bleeding team leader the once over, Chris said, "Told you it was a bad plan."

Joe used his sleeve to wipe the fresh blood from his eye. "Really? I thought it worked out rather well."

"You may change your mind once you see yourself in the mirror."

The team moved down the hall, clearing rooms as they advanced. So far, they had all been empty. Joe ended up on point and led the way toward the last remaining room. It was at the end of the hall on the right, and he hoped to God Tariq was in there.

The door was open, so four of the five CIA operators flowed into the bedroom turned interrogation chamber. Mike was in the trail position and stayed in the hall to pull security. Two men stood behind a table facing the business end of four suppressed rifles. The first was Tariq Kabbani. He looked like hell and appeared almost catatonic, his eyes glassy and unfocused. The second was a Russian soldier in desert pattern ACU pants and an olive-green wife-beater undershirt. He had pulled Tariq to his feet and was using the Syrian intelligence officer as a human shield while holding a Makarov pistol to his head.

The momentary impasse gave the team a chance to assess the scene, and what they saw sickened them. Tariq's face was badly swollen from the beating, and he cradled his right hand, or what remained of it against his chest. Inch-long sections of Tariq's fingers were piled next to a blood-covered set of pruning shears on the table separating the CIA operators from the Russian and his hostage. The aroma of charred meat from the use of the blowtorch to cauterize the wound each time a piece of finger was snipped off filled the air.

Time to end this, Joe thought, as his mind wandered back to a training session at the Farm. They had been working on this exact scenario in the shoot house – what to do when you encounter a bad guy with a gun to the hostage's head. He heard the voice of one of his instructors, a former SEAL and plank owner, an original member of SEAL Team Six, who spoke from personal experience. "As long as the shithead isn't pointing his gun at me, I take my time, get a good sight picture, and smoke the motherfucker."

The words had no sooner echoed through Joe's mind when he felt the rifle buck in his shoulder and saw the Russian soldier drop to the floor like a sack of meat. Too weak to support himself, Tariq collapsed on top of the dead man.

The sound of a vehicle's engine refocused Tariq's attention. In a voice barely above a whisper, he said, "It's the Russian. He went out the window."

"We met behind the house," Joe replied. "He's dead."

"No, the leader. Kalugin. He climbed out just before you entered the room."

"John, Kevin, check it out," Joe ordered.

The two men pointed their barrels toward the ceiling, then spun and headed for the door. John called, "Coming out!" and waited for Mike to respond, "Come out!" before exiting the room. He and Kevin sprinted down the hall and turned right, crossing through the living room where they had been pinned down. Kevin was the first to reach the front door just as one of the BMWs was pulling away from the house. Dirt and gravel shot from under the tires, and the SUV fishtailed as the driver accelerated toward the gate.

Kevin stepped through the door with John on his heels. In unison they shouldered their rifles and began pumping rounds into the SUV. Kalugin ducked low as the back window spiderwebbed before shattering into hundreds of tiny pieces. Paint chips flew as bullets punched holes in the tailgate and destroyed the red brake lights, but the Russian managed to maintain control of the BMW. The men lost sight of the SUV as it passed through the gate and turned right.

John said, "Sorry, boss. He got away. We'd better get the hell outta here before he comes back with a bunch of friends."

Joe couldn't agree more. They had overstayed their welcome and needed to move. He called Mike into the room and said, "Do me a favor and give Chris a hand with Tariq. It's time to go."

CHAPTER 39

LOCATED IN THE southwestern region of Germany near the border with France, the U.S. Army's Landstuhl Regional Medical Center is the first stop in the treatment process for injured military and diplomatic personnel operating in Iraq, Afghanistan, and throughout Africa. As the preeminent facility outside the U.S. for treating combat-related wounds, it was where the CIA had taken Tariq for medical care after his rescue and evacuation from Syria.

Joe strode down the hallway toward the room where two military policemen were posted outside the door. He presented his temporary ID to the female sergeant, and after a thorough inspection of his credential, she allowed him to enter.

Tariq looked like hell. A catheter was taped to the top of his left hand and another in the crook of his right elbow, pumped a steady stream of fluids, antibiotics, and pain meds into his system. His right hand was so heavily bandaged it resembled a club, and his face, covered in cuts and nasty multicolor bruises, was still swollen to the size of a basketball.

The Syrian intelligence officer was awake, staring blankly at a news program on the wall-mounted TV across the room. But from the look in his eyes, Joe could tell he wasn't paying attention to the talking heads on the screen. He was either out of it from the pain medication or his mind was a million miles away, thinking about something else. And who could blame him after what the Russians had put him through? Tariq had probably resigned himself to the fact that he was going to die a slow, excruciating death in the bleak bedroom of that dingy house south of the airport.

But now, twenty-four hours after being freed, he was in a state-of-the-art medical facility, being cared for by some of the most selfless medical professionals in the business. *Yeah,* Joe thought. *That could take some time to wrap your head around.*

Noticing the movement, Tariq turned his head to see who had entered the room. A weak smile spread across his battered face at the sight of the man who'd led the mission to rescue him. "Hello, my friend. It's good to see you."

"How's the hand?"

Tariq's bandaged right arm was resting on his chest. "Not too bad as long as they keep the pain meds flowing." Changing the subject, he asked, "And what of your men? Were any of them wounded during my rescue?"

Joe appreciated Tariq's concern for the guys who had put it on the line for him. "Everyone's fine. We managed to get a couple of rooms at the bachelors officers' quarters and they're catching up on some sleep."

Tariq was visibly relieved that no one had been injured on his behalf. Thankful for the good fortune, he asked, "And how about you? I heard you had a rougher time of it?"

"I caught a round in the back, but my trauma plate did its job. My ribs are a little tender but that's about it."

With his good hand Tariq pointed toward Joe's eyebrow, "And what of that?"

Joe winced as he reached up and touched the fresh stitches. The entire left side of his face was sore, swollen, and bruised. "Oh. That. I ran into an old acquaintance at the house. He caught me by surprise but won't be doing that again anytime soon."

Tariq understood his meaning, then turned serious, "Please tell me you got Kalugin in the assault."

Joe's shoulders drooped and the disappointment was evident in his voice. "I'm sorry, Tariq. He managed to get to one of the vehicles and was heading for the gate by the time the guys made it to the front door. They got some rounds into the SUV but not enough to disable it. And we couldn't pursue him because we needed to evac before he came back with reinforcements."

Tariq was disappointed as well, but it was a minor price to pay for being saved from certain death. "Maybe another time, then."

The door opened and their conversation was interrupted as a nurse came in to check Tariq's vitals. With the chart updated, she left the room, moving on to do the same for the next patient on her list.

Joe had come to check on Tariq's condition out of genuine concern for the man. But he was also there at the behest of the powers-that-be at Langley. "I'm assuming you had an exit strategy for your family in case you had to leave Syria in a hurry?"

Tariq went on to explain the plan, describing in detail the timeline, the route to Europe, and their communication protocol. When he finished, he reached out his left hand. "May I use your phone to contact her?"

Retrieving the device from his pocket, Joe tapped his eight-digit pin on the lock screen and placed it in Tariq's outstretched hand. "Would you like me to step outside?"

"That won't be necessary," he said, dialing the number of his wife's burner phone from memory. She answered on the first ring, and the combination of hearing his wife's voice and the knowledge that their plan had worked sent tears streaming down his face. Ten minutes later, he disconnected the call and handed the phone back to Joe.

"Good news?"

"Indeed. They were able to escape the country and are here in Europe as planned." Tariq pushed himself up with his good hand and attempted to swing his legs out of bed.

Joe stepped forward and grasped Tariq by the shoulders. "Where the hell do you think you're going?"

He struggled against Joe's strength for a moment before collapsing back against the pillows. "I must go to them, Joe. My wife and son need me. She thinks they got away clean, but elements of my government may have been tracking her. I don't have to tell you what they'll do if she's captured."

Tariq made another attempt to get out of bed, but once again, Joe's strong hands held him in place. Realizing his efforts were futile, he quit struggling. Exhausted, he reached up and used the sleeve of his hospital gown to wipe away the beads of sweat that had formed across his forehead.

The nurse who had been in earlier to check his vitals burst into the room as Tariq's elevated heartrate and blood pressure registered on her monitor. Joe assured her Tariq was fine, and after giving him the once-over, she left the room to resume her rounds.

When the door closed and their privacy was restored, Joe picked up the conversation where they had left off. "Look, you're in no condition to get up and go to the john, much less traipse around Europe in search of your family. And if they are in danger, what then? You can't even get out of bed without help."

The acceptance of his reality registered in Tariq's eyes, so Joe pushed ahead, "Let me take care of their extraction. Where are they?"

Resigned to the fact that he couldn't do this on his own, Tariq replied, "Munich."

The mention of the city caused Joe to smile. "Seriously?"

"Yes. Why?"

"Well, it just so happens that I know a very talented individual stationed there who'll be more than happy to help out with our little problem."

*

As it turned out, Meg Murphy was not at all happy when she received the call pulling her off her current assignment. She'd been tracking a Saudi arms dealer for the past six months and was convinced he was on the verge of a pivotal meeting with a client, a man she believed was in the final stages of planning a large-scale attack in Europe. But now, instead of throwing a hood over the arms dealer's head and rendering him to an interrogation facility, she was conducting surveillance on a Syrian woman and her child. The fact that her change of assignment came directly from the seventh floor at Langley was flattering, if not a little confusing, but it didn't soften the blow.

The tall, blond case officer employed by the CIA was a specialist when it came to running surveillance operations and possessed an uncanny ability to hide in plain sight, a skill that made her particularly effective at her job. Sitting at an outdoor café in Munich's historic Viktualienmarkt, a pedestrian shopping area with stalls selling everything from fruits and vegetables to meats, cheeses, flowers, and touristy souvenirs, she sipped an espresso and appeared to be flipping through a fashion magazine while keeping an eye on her new targets.

Meg's phone vibrated and she put on a show of being annoyed by the distraction that diverted her attention away from an engrossing article. Of course, it was all an act designed to make her look like every other customer stopping in for morning coffee in case anyone happened to be watching her. She touched the screen to accept the call, and after a short delay for the encryption to complete its handshake with the caller's device, Meg heard Joe Matthews' familiar voice over her Bluetooth ear buds. "How are things in Munich?"

Meg shook her head in disbelief. "Why am I not surprised? I should have known you'd have something to do with this."

"I'd take it as a compliment if I were you," Joe replied. "If you weren't so damn good at your job, I never would've held onto your number."

Meg had worked with Joe's team on an operation in Munich last year, and to a man, they had been impressed with her skills. Joe had even pitched the idea of recruiting her to the chiefs of SAD and the Protective Operations Division. Either the admin folks at headquarters hadn't gotten around to it yet or she had declined their offer, preferring to stick with her current job. Regardless of the reason, he was happy she was still in Munich.

"Do you have any idea what I was working on before you had me reassigned?" Meg vented.

"Yep. They filled me in when I made the request. Believe me when I tell you this is more important."

"More important than thwarting a major attack in Europe? Who made that boneheaded decision?"

Wanting to short-circuit the twenty questions routine, Joe said, "POTUS."

Not sure if she heard him correctly, Meg asked him to repeat that last part.

"I said, this op was authorized by POTUS. You know, the president of the United States. The commander in chief. Leader of the Free World. Any of those ring a bell?"

"Okay, smartass," she replied, resigned to the fact that her change in assignment had come from the highest possible level. Meg just hoped nothing dramatic happened with the Saudi arms dealer before she could wrap this up and get back on his trail. She took a sip of her espresso and performed another scan of the market as Joe brought her up to speed on the Kabbanis' escape from Syria.

"So, what can I do for you?"

"Have you located the woman and her son?"

"Yep. I have eyes-on as we speak. They're having breakfast at an out-door market in Old Town."

"That's great," Joe said, shaking his head. He was amazed she already had them under surveillance. Meg really was brilliant at her job. "We just landed. Do me a favor and don't let them out of your sight until we get there."

Meg casually observed the people moving through the pedestrian mall as the woman paid the bill and gathered up a couple of shopping bags at the foot of the table. The mother and her son held hands, looking nothing like a couple of fugitives who had escaped a brutal regime as they headed in the direction of the Airbnb she had rented for the month. At this moment, on this warm, sunny morning, Meg was hard-pressed to think of a more heartwarming sight. But she was immediately brought back to the harsh realities of the world when she saw two men emerge from a stall to her right and fall in behind the pair. She snapped a couple of photos of the men as they passed by and sent them to Joe's phone.

"How far out are you?" Meg asked, dropping enough Euros on the table to cover the espresso and a decent tip.

"About thirty minutes. Why?

"Because I'm not the only one keeping tabs on them."

CHAPTER 40

Joe's phone vibrated and he tapped the screen to open the message that contained the photos. His initial impression of the men was that they weren't intelligence officers conducting surveillance. No, these guys were muscle. And from the looks of them, they were either in Munich to do a snatch-and-grab with orders to return Rima and Nabil to Syria, or they were there to kill them at the first available opportunity. He cursed under his breath, knowing he was too far away to do anything about it.

Meg tapped her phone's screen as she walked, activating an encrypted beacon to allow Joe and his team to track her movement. She kept the two beefy Syrian hitters in sight, all the while searching the surrounding area to see if they had any additional support. If it was a rendition, they might have a third guy in a vehicle nearby, but that would probably be about it. These macho assholes would figure they could easily handle the woman and her young child. But what the men had no way of knowing was that the CIA had assigned one of their finest surveillance assets to watch the family. The hunters, oblivious of the fact that they were being stalked themselves, had become the hunted.

Fixated on his phone's screen, Joe cursed again. The distance between the blue dot indicating his position on the mapping app and the red dot representing Meg's was closing, but not nearly fast enough. Chris was doing his best to weave the minivan carrying the team of operators through traffic without drawing the attention of Munich's finest, but he was afraid they were going to be too late.

"What's your status, Meg?"

"Just exiting the market and heading toward the apartment building. I haven't picked up any additional hostiles or a vehicle. This is looking more and more like a hit. How far out are you?"

The app on his phone put their arrival at the market at fifteen minutes, but the way Chris was driving it would be more like ten. "Ten minutes, max," came his reply.

Meg took a deep breath, steeling herself for what was to come, and said, "Okay. We're going to need extraction, so here's what I need you to do. Park on Westeniederstrasse at the southeast corner of the apartment building and we'll meet you there."

Confused, Joe asked, "We who? What the hell are you talking about?"

"Rima and Nabil will be dead by the time you get here and I'm not going to stand by and watch it happen."

"C'mon, Meg," Joe countered. "You're not a field operative. You conduct the surveillance, then teams like ours come in and do the deed. If you go in there, you're just going to add to the body count."

"You have no idea," Meg said coolly as she watched Rima approach the building's front door with the two killers in tow.

*

The Syrians' orders had been simple – kill the woman and her child – and make it messy. Both men had taken plenty of lives during their careers and neither blanched at the tasking. Her husband was a traitor, and in their minds, it was as simple as that. Word of the gruesome murders would spread throughout the government's ranks and serve as a warning to others – betray the regime and this will be your fate.

They waited for the woman to unlock the door, then picked up their pace and closed the distance, ushering her and her son into the apartment building's foyer. The woman turned around and was about to scream at the sight of the men but was silenced as the one on the left put his hand over her mouth. He lowered his head next to her ear and whispered in Arabic, "Don't make a sound or my friend will kill your son in front of your eyes."

Rima submitted to the killer's request as tears began to stream down her face. The day had started so wonderfully and now, deep in her heart, she knew it was going to end in a most gruesome and painful manner. The man spun her around and pushed her toward the stairs. His partner did the same with the boy. From the looks in their eyes and the bloodlust on their faces, the men were going to enjoy their work today.

*

Meg slipped her foot in the door to keep it from closing and entered the foyer. With their backs to the door, the men had no idea she was in the building. *Sucks to be them,* she thought, deciding to take the man on the right first. Slipping her hand into the purse hanging diagonally across her chest, Meg used the bag to muffle the barely audible click of a blade seating in place. When she withdrew her hand, it held a matte black folding combat knife. Measuring each footfall, she closed in silently on her unsuspecting victim.

Crouching low, Meg rotated the knife in her hand, holding it in a reverse grip, and brought the blade across the back of the man's leg, slicing through his hamstring muscle. The Syrian thug let out a cry at the unexpected pain radiating up and down his leg. With the severed muscle unable to support this weight, the man released his grip on Nabil and dropped to a knee. Meg rose to her full height and grasped the man's forehead. Pulling it back, she hammered the knife down, driving the razor-sharp blade into the notch at the base of his exposed throat. The gruesome wound sent a geyser of blood spraying across the foyer. What didn't spill onto the floor poured into his open windpipe, drowning the man in his own blood. He collapsed face first into a red pool that was rapidly expanding across the white-tiled floor.

Rima screamed and clutched Nabil to her side, burying his face in her jacket in hopes of sparing him the nightmares that were bound to be brought on by the grisly sight.

Forgetting his primary mission, the second man spun, swinging a backhand strike at Meg's head. She managed to get both hands up to block the blow, but the force of the impact knocked her back against the wall. The man charged, infuriated by what this mere woman had done to his partner. Rage took over as he cocked his big right hand, preparing to deliver a blow that would surely crush this blond bitch's skull. He fired his fist toward her head, but Meg saw it coming and ducked under the punch. She spun the knife around in her hand and in a blur jabbed twice at his abdomen, each time sending the blade deep into the man's diaphragm. Confused as to what was happening, a questioning look spread across his face as the damaged muscle spasmed, making it impossible for him to breathe. With all thoughts of the mission forgotten, he was now more concerned with filling his lungs with air than avenging his partner's death. Taking advantage of the distraction, Meg's hand darted forward once again with blinding speed. Years of training with her instructor, a Vietnamese woman who was quite deadly despite her diminutive stature, ensured Meg's aim was true. The blade passed between the man's second and third intercostal ribs and entered his heart. The fight was over in a matter of seconds, the damage quick and catastrophic.

Rima looked at the tall blond woman, then down at the two dead men on the floor. She repeated the process several times as her mind tried to process what had just happened. Finally, her eyes settled on Meg with a combination of horror and admiration. It would be unheard of for a woman in her country to obtain the training and skills to do such a thing to two of the regime's hired killers. But here, standing before her, was a woman who had done just that. Unsure of what was going to happen next, Rima stepped in front of Nabil, placing herself between this femme fatale and her son.

The knife was still buried in the second man's chest, so Meg raised her empty hands to indicate she was unarmed and not a threat. She didn't speak Arabic, so she decided to give English a try. "Rima, I need you and Nabil to come with me. As you can see, it's not safe for you to remain here in Munich."

"You…you are American?" Rima asked in a shaky voice that held hope their ordeal was finally ending.

"I am."

"How…how did you know where to find us?"

With a smile, Meg said, "Tariq. He told us about your protocols. That's how we knew where to start looking."

"Where is he? May I see him?"

Meg reached into her pocket and checked her phone to see if the connection was still active. Seeing it was, she asked Joe, "Are you in place?"

"Yeah. Black Mercedes van,"

Returning her attention to Rima, Meg continued, "My colleagues are outside. They are the same men who rescued Tariq and got him out of Syria. They'll keep you safe and take you to your husband. Okay?"

Unable to think of a reason not to trust this woman, it didn't take Rima long to consider her offer. Desperately wanting to be reunited with Tariq, she said, "Okay."

Next, Meg asked, "Is there anything you need from the apartment before we go?"

Rima patted the oversized bag looped over her shoulder. "No. I kept everything important with me in case we were forced to run."

"Good girl," Meg said, appreciating Rima's thought process as she bent down to retrieve her knife. Grasping the handle, she pulled it out of the man's chest and wiped the blood on his pant leg before collapsing the blade and storing it in an interior pocket in her purse.

Meg stood and did a quick sweep of the area to make sure no incriminating evidence was left behind. Satisfied, she let Joe know they were coming out, then led the small family out onto the sidewalk, letting the door close on an unpleasant chapter of their lives, and the foyer that had come to resemble a slaughterhouse.

CHAPTER 41

"Roll the video please," Hank Coleman, the secretary of defense, said over the encrypted line linking him to the Pentagon's National Military Command Center. A lieutenant hit the Play button and the images came to life on the high-definition monitor mounted on the White House Situation Room's far wall.

"What are we watching?" President Andrews asked for the benefit of the other members of his national security team attending the Principal's Committee meeting.

"Sir, this is a recording of a video call from the aircraft commander of an AWACS, call sign Sentinel Five One, flying out of Sigonella Naval Air Station in Italy. The plane was on a routine patrol over the Med to keep an eye on Syrian and Russian military air activity."

The president nodded, then focused his full attention on the screen as the Air Force officer began speaking.

"Among the routine traffic we've been monitoring, we picked up an Antonov AN-12 taxiing away from the target hangar at Khmeimim Air Base outside Latakia, Syria."

Indicating he wanted the video paused, Andrews asked, "I'm assuming the hangar he mentioned is the same one where we think our stolen Reaper is being housed?"

"One and the same, sir," Coleman replied.

The video shook as the officer on the screen paused and grabbed a handle attached to the ceiling to steady himself. "Sorry, turbulence has been pretty rough tonight. There's a front moving into our area of operations."

Coleman continued. "Minutes before the Antonov left the hangar, two MiG-29s, at this point we're not sure if they were Russian or Syrian, not that it matters, launched from the base and took up harassing positions on either side of the AWACS. Nothing our crews haven't dealt with in the past, but the timing was a little coincidental."

The video shook again, then the screen went black. Sensing something catastrophic had occurred the president turned to Coleman. "What just happened, Hank?"

*

After a twenty-six-year career in the Air Force, with a lineage of military flying dating back to the Tuskegee Airmen, Lieutenant Colonel Margaret "Mags" Clement had experienced her fair share of nights like this. Flying the converted Boeing 707 through inclement weather while being hassled by a pair of enemy fighters was just another day at the office.

Looking at the MiG's anti-collision lights out the port side of the cockpit, she commented, "He's awfully close."

"Mine too," remarked her copilot, Major Rick Sanchez, as he kept an eye on the fighter off their starboard wing.

Not one to mince words, Staff Sergeant Jerry Wilkins, the flight engineer for the sortie joined the conversation. "Those guys better get their heads out of their collective asses and give us a wider berth. That front is almost on top of us and it's going to get bumpy from here on out."

Just as the words had left his mouth, the AWACS lurched upward, then dropped twenty feet, a roller coaster move that would have most people losing their lunch. Accustomed to flying in all kinds of weather, the experienced crew and the sixteen mission specialists in the rear of the plane monitoring the radar and communications systems took the turbulence in stride.

Each of the MiGs shadowing the American Boeing hit the same patch of rough air. The jolt was more dramatic for the smaller aircraft, but both pilots managed to maintain control of their jets.

Mags hoped the brief experience would encourage the fighter pilots to increase the distance between themselves and the converted airliner, but if anything, they seemed to be getting closer. *Fighter jocks were idiots!* she thought.

A communication link had been set up as a deconfliction tool to prevent air-to-air issues between the various countries operating in the skies over the conflict in Syria. Mags decided this was as good a time as any to make use of it. Pressing the transmit button on the yoke, she hailed the fighter pilots on the prearranged frequency. "Unidentified MiGs, this is Sentinel Five One of the United States Air Force. Move away from our aircraft. Your presence is creating an unsafe condition for all of us."

Before either of the fighter pilots could respond, a strong gust of horizontal wind shear hit the MiG on the Boeing's starboard side. Caught off-guard by the blast, the pilot was unable to maintain his direction of flight and his fighter was pushed into the path of American plane.

"Look out!" Sanchez screamed, but his voice was drowned out by the screech of metal on metal as the two fuselages came together and the MiG bounced off the nose of the larger plane.

The collision swung the back end of the fighter around and sent its twin vertical stabilizers crashing into the forward section of the AWACS. The impact shattered the MiG's tail section and gashed a hole in the Boeing's outer skin. Before the fighter disintegrated into the darkness, it struck a fatal blow to the converted airliner as broken bits of metal and composite material from the rear section of the fighter were sucked into the two turbofan engines mounted under the wing.

Warning lights lit up the cockpit as Sanchez reduced power to the two damaged engines and activated their fire-suppression systems. Sirens sounded throughout the plane at the loss of cabin pressure, and calmly, due to hours of training and preparation, everyone aboard the AWACS donned their oxygen masks and attempted to resume their duties.

Clement wrestled with the controls to maintain level flight but felt she was fighting a losing battle. "What's our closest airfield, Jerry?"

Consulting the charts on a tablet, the flight engineer displayed a remarkable cool and replied, "I'm assuming anywhere in Syria is a nonstarter?"

The quip brought a smile to her face. "Unless getting your head cut off by extremists or spending the rest of your life in a Syrian prison are two items you want to check off your bucket list, why don't you see if you can't find us someplace else to put this thing down?"

After a few seconds of map study, Wilkins said, "In that case, it looks like Larnaca, Cyprus, will be our best bet." He called out the heading.

"Rick, put out the Mayday and let Larnaca know we're declaring an emergency," Clement ordered.

Working the throttles in combination with the controls, she banked the big jet toward Cyprus, but would never make it to the safety of the island's runway. The collision with the fighter had weakened the airframe where the wing attached to the fuselage and everyone onboard felt the odd vibration as the lights of Cyprus beckoned through the cockpit's windshield.

Unable to support the damaged wing and its useless engines any longer, the last of the bolts popped from their moorings, and the sound of tearing metal filled the cabin. As the wing was ripped free, it took a section of the plane's outer wall with it. The mission specialist who had been on the video call wasn't buckled into his seat and was sucked out of the opening. He was the first American casualty in this midair mishap but would not be the last.

Without its starboard wing, the plane rolled to the right, despite the thrust Clement applied to the struggling port side engines. Not built to sustain such a violent maneuver, the thirty-foot rotating radar dish broke away from its support structure on the plane's roof and spun through the air like a giant frisbee. Hidden in the darkness, the enormous disk hit the remaining MiG behind the wing and sheared the plane in half before the pilot could take evasive action. Jet fuel gushed from broken storage tanks, and the remnants of the plane ignited in a fireball before the pilot had a chance to eject.

Mags Clement ignored the bright flash of the explosion just outside her cockpit window. She had her hands full with her own problems and didn't have time to worry about what was going on outside the confines of the Boeing's flight deck. Fighting valiantly to control the big aircraft as the nose pointed toward the dark waters of the Mediterranean, the realization that the situation was unrecoverable hit her like a ton of bricks.

Resigned to her fate, she broadcast, "Mayday. Mayday. This is Lieutenant Colonel Margaret Clement, pilot-in-charge of Sentinel Five One...."

The transmission cut out before she could finish the sentence as the plane broke apart and fell into the sea.

CHAPTER 42

IN THE SITUATION Room, Secretary of Defense Hank Coleman walked the president and the other members of the Principal's Committee through the last few minutes of Sentinel Five One's mission.

Infuriated, President Andrews said, "So we lost an aircraft and a crew of nineteen servicemen and women all because a couple of MiG pilots wanted to play chicken during a thunderstorm?"

"That about sums it up, sir," Coleman agreed. "We believe the Russians were repositioning the stolen Reaper after the mortar attack on the airfield and that the MiGs were sent up to harass and distract the AWACS. The sad part is that it wouldn't have mattered. Once the mission specialists had a lock on the Antonov, there was nothing the fighters could have done, short of shooting the plane down, to get them to lose contact. Turns out they did the next best thing."

President Andrews shook his head in disbelief. *What a waste,* he thought. *Such a senseless loss of life.* Thinking back to his days of writing letters to the families of the men he had lost in combat, he said, "Hank, could you have someone send over the contact information for the crews' next of kin? I want to call the families to let them know their sons and daughters didn't die in vain."

"Of course, Mr. President."

Refocusing his attention on the bigger picture, Andrews asked, "What about the Antonov? Do we have any idea where it went?"

"No, sir. When the AWACS went down all efforts were diverted to a search and rescue mission. After losing contact, all we have is the heading of its last known direction of travel."

Lawrence Sloan entered the conversation for the first time. "Sir, we have assets throughout the region scouring every known airfield for the Antonov or signs that the Reaper package is being reconstituted."

"They'd better hurry. Kuwait is only four days away," the president reminded the group, referring to the Arab League summit taking place in the tiny emirate. "Do we still believe the gathering is the most likely target?"

"We do, sir," Sloan agreed. "And with the window rapidly closing, I think it's about time we alert the summit's organizers to the threat."

"But will they believe us?" Andrews asked. "After all the havoc that's been inflicted across the region by our drone, I know I'd be hesitant if the roles were reversed."

Secretary of State Claire Nichols offered, "I don't think we have a choice, Mr. President. If we don't notify them because our evidence is circumstantial and the attack occurs, we'll only appear more guilty."

Sloan concurred. "Claire's right, sir. Besides, what's the worst that can happen? We share our concerns and the attack doesn't take place?"

Silence fell over the group as President Andrews considered the counsel of two of his most trusted advisors. Finally, he said, "Make the notifications. We're already getting crucified for the drone strikes. As public enemy number one over there, I don't want to make the situation any worse by having people think we had intelligence on an impending attack and didn't share it."

With his national security team in agreement, the president continued, "Claire, I'd like you to make a quick trip to brief the Saudis and Jordanians on what we know."

Saudi Arabia was the home of Wahhabism, the ultra-orthodox sect of Sunni Islam that teaches strict adherence to the Koran. Its followers included such radicals as Osama bin Laden and fifteen of the nineteen hijackers who attacked the United States on September 11, 2001, yet it was still one of America's most important allies in the Middle East.

Jordan, on the other hand, was an oasis of stability in the region, coexisting with its indigenous Christian population and providing sanctuary for Iraqi Christians who were at risk as ISIS rose to power. The Hashemite

Kingdom had long been a voice of moderation throughout the Middle East and a friend of the United States since the early nineteen-fifties.

Claire Nichols thought the president's request over for a minute, calculating flight times in her head. Finally, she said, "I don't think there's enough time for me to get to both countries, sir. Do you have a preference if I can visit only one?"

"Sir, if I may," Sloan interjected, "we could divide the responsibility. Might I suggest that Claire head to Riyadh to brief the Saudis while I travel to Amman and do the same for the Jordanians? That way we can brief both kingdoms before their representatives depart for the summit."

The president looked to Nichols, who agreed and said, "Sounds like a plan." He went around the room one last time to see if anyone had anything else to add. When they didn't, he said, "Thanks everyone."

As the national security team filed out of the Situation Room, Sloan spotted the head of his protective detail waiting patiently with the other agents in the small West Wing lobby. Doug Kelly alerted the detail, letting them know the meeting was over and fell in step with the director as they exited onto West Executive Drive.

While they waited for the black Chevy Suburbans to pull up, Sloan said, "Get the team ready, Doug. We're heading to Amman."

Holding the heavy, armored door open as his boss slid into the back seat, Doug asked, "When do we leave?"

"Six hours. We're wheels-up tonight."

Doug closed the door, securing Director Sloan inside the armored cocoon, and cringed. As he climbed into the right front seat, he knew his wife wasn't going to be happy with the short-notice trip.

*

President Yaroslav Polovkin was in a sour mood as he gazed out the bullet-resistant window of his Kremlin office at the tourists milling about Red Square. Some were queued to visit Lenin's tomb while others took selfies with the onion domes in the background or watched the guard of honor goose-stepping in front of the eternal flame and five-pointed star of Russia's Tomb of the Unknown Soldier. At times, he wondered what it would be like to be a normal person, with nothing better to do than travel around taking photos of historical landmarks. But regardless of how appealing that life might sound from time to time, he would never trade the power and influence he wielded for anything so frivolous.

A knock on the door drew him away from the window. He took a moment to compose his thoughts, then barked, "Enter!"

The door opened and Anton Shubovich and Vice Admiral Evgeny Mishkin entered the office, followed by an aide with a tea service for three. The aide set the tray on the rectangular conference table and closed the door as he left the room. President Polovkin poured three cups of tea but let each man add his own milk and sugar. Taking seats around the table, they stirred their tea, giving it a chance to cool, the only sound in the room the clinking of the silver spoons against the china cups.

Furious with the latest turn of events, President Polovkin broke the tense silence. "How the fuck did we manage to take down an American AWACS and lose two MiGs in the process?"

They had come so far, and up to this point, his elaborate plan to manipulate the removal of the Americans from the Middle East had gone about as well as could be expected. Now, when they were within sight of the finish line, having an incident where Russia was clearly at fault could prove to be a major setback.

"From everything we've been able to gather, the crash was purely accidental. Our pilots were following orders, harassing the American plane, when they hit some violent turbulence. As the planes were bounced around, one of our MiGs was pushed into the path of the AWACS. The midair collision initiated the chain reaction that led to the loss of all three planes," Shubovich explained.

Polovkin slammed his fist on the table, rattling the cups and saucers. "I don't give a shit why it happened, Anton," the president fumed. "We've come too far to have this operation derailed at the last minute by your pilots' incompetence.

Unaccustomed to being dressed down in front of someone else, especially a peer like Mishkin, the defense minister seemed to deflate and shrink back into his chair. It was as if he was hiding behind the shield formed by the rows of medals pinned to the front of his dress uniform.

With the cool demeanor of a professional intelligence officer, Evgeny Mishkin came to his friend's defense. "Actually, sir, downing the American plane was necessary in order for our operation to move forward." He paused and took a sip of tea to give his statement a chance to sink in and defuse some of the tension in the room.

Polovkin's head snapped to his intelligence chief, a look of confusion mixed with anger on his face. "Really, Evgeny? Explain yourself."

Even Shubovich was curious to hear Mishkin's line of thinking.

Setting his cup gently back on the saucer, Miskin continued. "It cannot be considered coincidental that the AWACS was in position at the exact time our Antonov transporting the Reaper to its new base of operations was preparing to take off. I have no doubt the Americans were tracking our plane with the intention of shooting it down or following it to its destination and calling in an airstrike to destroy the drone."

The president and Shubovich sat quietly as they contemplated the GRU man's rationale.

"The only way to keep the Americans from tracking our plane was to remove the AWACS from the equation. The midair mishap was fortuitous because it can be explained away as an unfortunate accident. It would have been much more difficult to deflect the blame had we been forced to shoot it down instead."

A fire crackled in the hearth as the three men went silent while President Polovkin ran scenarios through his head. Maybe Mishkin was right. If the crash had not occurred, there was a good chance the drone would have been destroyed, ending the operation before its final act.

With his demeanor softening but plenty of menace remaining in his voice, Polovkin said, "It looks like you've dodged a bullet, Anton. Figuratively and literally."

Shubovich breathed a sigh of relief, but realized he was on a very short leash. Any more mistakes on his part, or by men under his command, and he would not be able to dodge the next bullet, which would undoubtedly be aimed at the back of his head.

CHAPTER 43

Elijah Miller entered the outer lobby on the top floor of the building that resembled a black cube at Fort Meade and offered a tired greeting to the executive assistant. "Hey, Andy. Is she in?"

"Just got off a call and she has about thirty minutes before her next meeting. Your timing was perfect."

Miller walked past the first lieutenant's desk and knocked on the door twice before entering. He stepped into the office belonging to the director of the National Security Agency and closed the door behind him. While the assistant and security officer had clearances of the highest level, neither had the need to be privy to the conversation that was about to take place.

General Linda Meyer looked up from her desk, curious to see who had stopped by for a visit. Spread out behind her, a panoramic view of the base was visible through the double-paned, air-gapped windows. Not only were they bullet resistant, but the glass was treated to provide countermeasures to a multitude of eavesdropping and keystroke-logging techniques.

A warm smile crossed her face when she saw Elijah Miller. He was irreverent, bucked the system, and didn't fit the mold of the typical NSA employee. Those unusual qualities, when combined with his brilliant mind, endeared him to her. Her smile faded as she looked closer and noticed how utterly exhausted and worn out, he appeared.

"My God, Eli. When was the last time you slept?"

Collapsing into a leather upholstered chair across from her desk, he thought a moment. "Oh, I don't know," he replied, sarcastically. "Maybe it was the night before those idiots at General Atomics fell for a dumbass phishing scam that rendered my uncrackable encryption useless and allowed the Russians to use one of our most sophisticated UAVs to conduct attacks that everyone on the planet blames on us."

Linda Meyer was a career military intelligence officer, and as such, was accustomed to the unpredictable nature of the business. Sometime operations went your way. Sometimes they didn't. It was a lesson learned through experience, and although Miller was brilliant, real-world experience was something he had yet to gain.

"So, what's up?" she asked, in a casual manner that belied her position at the top of the intelligence agency's hierarchy.

"Ever since I got back from Belgium...," Miller's voice drifted off as images of the dead Russian's brain matter and the other man's broken, bleeding face flashed through his mind in vivid detail.

Seeing the distracted look on his face, Meyer said, "Go on," hoping to get him back on track.

"Oh, yeah, sorry. Like I was saying, ever since I got back from Belgium, I've been trying to figure out a way to hack the drone and track the satellite signal back to its origination point at the ground control station." The more Miller talked, the more energized and animated he became. Practically sitting on the edge of his chair, he continued, "And I...," he paused for a moment, seeming to run through the code in his head one last time before saying it aloud. "I think I've done it."

Meyer sat in quiet contemplation for a moment, liking the direction the conversation was heading, but at the same time, not wanting to get her hopes up as she digested what Miller had just said. "Okay, Eli. Why don't you walk me through it from the beginning?"

Fifteen minutes later they both leaned back in their chairs. Miller was visibly relieved to have had the conversation, running the idea past his boss to get a sanity check. Meyer, on the other hand, was busy mulling over the next steps.

With her decision made, she pressed the intercom button on her desk phone. "Andy, do me a favor and clear my schedule for the rest of the afternoon."

"Will do, ma'am. Anything else?"

"Call Lawrence Sloan's office and ask him to make some time for us." She paused a moment, then said, "Is Steve still out there?"

From across the lobby she heard the protective agent's voice answer that he was.

"Great. Have the detail fire up the cars. We're heading to Langley."

*

Lawrence Sloan rose to greet his counterpart, and the rest of the assembled group followed his lead. At the table were Katherine Clark and Bill Parker, the deputy director of science and technology. Parker had been promoted to the role after his predecessor, Paul Foley, was killed by a sniper's bullet in last year's attack by the Iranian hit squad in downtown D.C. Carl Douglas, the chief of the special activities division, was also in attendance.

There was one other person in the room who looked as out of place as Miller felt. While everyone else was in business attire, dark suits, and conservative ties, or in Clark's case, a charcoal gray skirt and white blouse with a matching cardigan, this guy wore jeans and a Star Wars t-shirt. His laptop was open, and he had an energy drink within arm's reach. Feeling as if he had found a kindred spirit, Miller naturally gravitated toward the outsider. The two of them looked like a couple of computer nerds who had inadvertently crashed a very formal party.

The man's name was Fred Jackson, and he was a technical operations officer in the directorate of science and technology. But the innocuous title belied the fact that he was probably the most skilled hacker in the CIA. Jackson was a wizard with a keyboard and a string of code who had conducted the most sophisticated cyberattack the world had seen. The only problem was that no one besides Director Sloan and Katherine Clark would ever know he did it. If word got out that he was the man who created the Stuxnet virus that crippled Iran's nuclear enrichment facility at Natanz, he would be a rock star among his peers. The only downside was that he would simultaneously vault to the top of an Iranian kill list. Weighing the pros and cons, he was perfectly content to keep the knowledge of his involvement in the operation limited to the nation's top two spooks.

Miller took the open seat next to Jackson, and Director Meyer sat across the table. After introductions were made, Jackson offered Miller a respectful fist bump. Having known the man by reputation only, he was happy to finally meet him in person.

Director Sloan said, "Mr. Miller, we're anxious to hear about what you've been working on, so why don't we get started."

Elijah opened his laptop and established a wireless connection to the large monitor on the wall. With a few keystrokes his presentation was mirrored on the big screen. He took a deep breath and dove into his presentation.

"Ever since the first drone strike, I've been searching for a way to regain control of the Reaper and track its signal back to the ground control station." He paused a couple of seconds. "Last night, I had a breakthrough. I think I did it."

Doing his best to keep from going too far into the weeds from a technical perspective, Eli explained the architecture of a UAV system. Like any computer, the drone ran on a base operating system that was connected to the various components that control the avionics, communication links, sensors, and weapons. Each of the individual components must be able to communicate with the others and, at times, the ground control station. As a result, the two most important connections that allow the drone to perform its functions were the flow of information between the drone and its ground control station, and its sensors and the environment. Much of that communication was done wirelessly and was therefore a challenge to secure. It was this weak link in the wireless communication that he believed he could exploit.

"You remember the RQ-170 the Iranians downed in their territory?" Eli asked. "Well, one of the theories on how they did it was by using a local transmitter so strong that it was able to overpower the signal the Sentinel's GPS was receiving from the satellite. The drone's navigation system locked onto the stronger transmission, and once the connection had been established, the Iranians fed the drone new coordinates and had it land at a location of their choosing. I think we can do something similar with the Reaper."

"Correct me if I'm wrong," Bill Parker interjected, "But didn't we patch that exploit after the incident?"

"We did," Eli confirmed. "But the code I've written will bypass the previous fix. The key will be getting close enough to the drone that we can transmit a signal capable of overriding the one it's receiving from the Russian satellite."

"And what exactly would your code do if you were able to connect to the Reaper?" Katherine Clark asked.

"For starters, I would transfer control of the drone back to one of our pilots."

Stunned, Clark said, "You can do that inflight?"

There was a slight shift in Miller's demeanor. It was the first time he didn't seem fully confident in his plan. "According to my calculations... probably. I doubt it's ever been attempted, but I've run multiple simulations, and it's usually successful."

"Can you put a number on 'usually'?" Parker asked.

"Sixty percent," Miller said. "I ran it ten times and six of the simulations were successful."

"And what happened the other four times?"

"On three of the simulations the injection of the code confused the drone's internal systems and it crashed."

"And the other sim?" Parker pressed. "What was its result?"

"Nothing. The code didn't work, and the Russians maintained control of the Reaper."

Feeling the tide begin to go against Miller, Fred Jackson spoke up for the first time. "Nine out of ten times we either regain control of the drone or destroy it in a crash. Either way, the Russians lose the ability to kill innocent people with our Reaper. That's a ninety percent success rate. I'll take those odds any day of the week."

"And as I mentioned," Miller continued, his confidence bolstered by Jackson's support. "My code will also track the signal back to the drone's point of origin at its ground control station. Then, once we have the location, you can do whatever you want to the evil bastards behind this scheme."

The room went quiet as the group considered their options and next steps. After a minute or two of silence, Director Sloan asked, "We anticipate the next and possibly final attack is going to take place in Kuwait in the next forty-eight hours. How do you propose we put your code to use, Mr. Miller?"

Eli was prepared for the question and moved to the next slide in his presentation. He laid out his plan and described how it could be implemented.

Sloan was impressed with the young man. Finally, he said, "It just so happens, Mr. Miller, that we're leaving for the Middle East this evening. If Director Meyer can spare you for a few days, I'd love for you to join us and see if we can put your plan into action."

Eli slumped in his chair. He had survived the Alpha Group men in Belgium by the skin of his teeth, thanks to the timely intervention of Joe Matthews and his operators. Now he was being asked to fly to the scene of an impending attack and do what he could to stop it. He was a computer guy, not a field operative. *How the hell do I keep getting myself into these situations?* he thought

CHAPTER 44

THE FLIGHT FROM Syria had been bumpy, cold, and uncomfortable in the cargo bay of the Antonov AN-12. But all things considered, uneventful. After the mortar attack on the runway and the armed assault of the compound on the grounds of Khmeimim Air Base to rescue Tariq Kabbani, the men calling the shots considered the threat of an American airstrike a distinct possibility. As a result, they had made the decision to move the drone. Vasily Zubkin didn't mind that the entire operation had been uprooted and relocated to this new site. The last place he wanted to be was inside the hangar when a two-thousand-pound, laser-guided bomb came crashing through the ceiling. Due to operational security concerns, Zubkin, his pilot, the sensor operator, and the ground crew had not been told where they were headed. It wasn't until the ramp at the rear of the Antonov was lowered and warm, moist air and bright sunshine filled the cargo bay that Colonel Teplov, who had come along to maintain operational control of the mission, announced that they had landed in Iran.

The port city of Bandar Bushehr lies directly across the Persian Gulf from Kuwait, less than two hundred miles as the crow, or in this case, a multi-million dollar, remotely piloted aircraft flies. The shorter distance to target the upcoming summit from the southwest coast of Iran would reduce the amount of time the Reaper was in the air. Theoretically, the tactic would minimize the chances that American and Kuwaiti forces would have to discover the drone. And without an idea of which direction it would be coming from, they would be forced to spend considerable time and resources monitoring thousands of square miles searching for the deadly needle in a haystack. The reduced flight time would also decrease the possibility for mechanical or weather issues to impact the mission. All in all, using Iran as a launch point seemed to fit the bill nicely.

Shying away from the busier Bushehr International Airport, a lesson learned from operating out of the base in Syria that shared runways with its commercial counterpart, the Russians had opted instead for the smaller Bahregan Airport, located southeast of the city's center. The Iranian population tended to mind their own business, especially when it came to the happenings in and around government and military facilities. That fact was particularly true when those facilities, like the airfield at Bahregan, belonged to the feared IRGC, Iran's Islamic Revolutionary Guard Corps. People who tended to be a little too curious could find themselves on the wrong end of a brutal interrogation, so privacy regarding what went on at the airfield was all but assured by the IRGC's fearsome reputation. The five-hundred-meter perimeter along the south and east sides of the small, triangular facility to discourage onlookers and prying eyes didn't hurt either.

Vasily Zubkin checked the connections and ran diagnostics on the ground control station and satcom unit. With everything in order, he exited the small room that would serve as the flight operations center and crossed the interior of the hangar. Before him, on the spotless floor, sat the MQ-9 Reaper, reassembled after having been unpacked from its transport crates. Zubkin ran his hands over every inch of the airframe, feeling for blemishes or other imperfections that might compromise the drone's structural integrity. As the aerospace engineer tasked with ensuring the Reaper could carry out its mission, he was keenly aware of the consequences should he fail in his assigned responsibilities.

Returning to the flight operations center, Zubkin found Colonel Teplov waiting for him.

"Everything is in order, I presume?" the GRU colonel asked.

"The drone and the equipment appear to have survived the trip, despite our hurried departure. But the diagnostic tests I plan to run over the next few hours will tell me for sure."

"Tick-tock," Teplov said, tapping his watch. "You'd better get to work. The launch time for our final mission is rapidly approaching."

*

Across the Persian Gulf, a small army of logistical and protocol officers were scrambling to put the finishing touches on the preparations for the Arab League's first emergency summit in years. Kuwait had last hosted the gathering in 2014, so it was not the first time the organizers had put together an event of this magnitude. Even so, workers swarmed over the emirate's Bayan Palace and its state-of-the-art conference center. With gleaming marble floors and rosewood and teak veneers accented with gold and bronze inlay, the stage was set in preparation for the arrival of the Arab world's most distinguished leaders.

In an interesting twist, the last time the summit was held in Kuwait, it was attended by Russia's deputy foreign minister, who addressed the forum and met with senior diplomats to discuss several topics. With Syria's membership in the body under suspension because of the ongoing civil war, the Russian minister spoke on the regime's behalf, lobbying for a political solution to the conflict and for the country's vacated seat at the table to be reinstated. His presence at the meeting in 2014 should have indicated Russia's opening move on the Middle East chessboard to enhance its reputation and standing throughout the region. But given President Polovkin's plans for this summit, it was unlikely any representative from the Russian government would be in attendance this time.

Security at the massive compound was already tight, since the palace served as the seat of the Kuwaiti government and was home to the tiny country's emir. But based on the events of the past few weeks, the security posture had been ratcheted up a couple of levels.

Members of the Emiri Guard, whose primary mission was safeguarding the country's emir and prime minister, walked the grounds with officers from the Army and Air Force, having pulled in military support to bolster their security plan. Armored vehicles with soldiers manning heavy machine guns ringed the compound, and members of an air-defense unit armed with shoulder-fired surface-to-air missiles mingled on the rooftops with the Emiri Guard's countersnipers in the event the rogue drone made an appearance in the vicinity of the palace.

Every vehicle entering the compound was subjected to a thorough inspection, searched for weapons, and swept by K-9 teams for explosives. Even though the primary threat from the drone would come from above, the last thing the Emiri Guard wanted was for a Vehicle Borne Improvised

Explosive Device, or VBIED, to slip inside the secure perimeter while everyone's focus was on the sky.

While all this activity was occurring on the ground, F/A-18 Super Hornets belonging to the Kuwaiti Air Force cut patterns through the cloudless blue skies above the emirate. With weapons hot and radar systems searching for violators of the country's airspace, the fighter pilots were determined to make short work of any threat to their homeland.

Ground crews set up landing zones on two large patches of emerald green grass next to the conference center to accommodate the pair of Airbus H225M Caracal helicopters outfitted for VIP transport use by the emir. The Caracals would be available to ferry individuals who chose the quick helicopter ride from the VIP terminal at Kuwait's International Airport to the palace instead of the fifteen-minute drive. For those who did prefer to drive, the National Police would shut down the sixteen-kilometer route from the airport, enabling the motorcades to make the trip without encountering another vehicle on the road.

The chief of the Emiri Guard returned to his office in the palace, savoring the chill provided by the building's industrial air-conditioning units. The temperature outside had hit the forecast high of one-hundred-twenty degrees, and after conducting the final walkthrough, he was drenched in sweat. He grabbed two bottles of water from a minifridge and quickly downed one. Sipping the second, he stood in front of a seventy-inch monitor mounted on the wall. Displayed before him was a map of the palace grounds with an overlay showing the positions of each of the units supporting the summit. A shower and a change of clothes were in order, but first, he wanted to review the placement of the postings while they were still fresh in his mind.

What am I missing? he thought, as he finished the second bottle of water and headed to the shower. He believed he had a good security plan in place, but with the summit only hours away, there was an annoying voice in the back of his head telling him that he could do more.

CHAPTER 45

THE VIP TERMINAL at Kuwait International Airport was a hive of activity as delegates from across the Middle East began arriving for the summit. A variety of luxury business jets and customized airliners filled the tarmac in front of the terminal, their size and opulence limited only by the wealth of the country whose leader they had delivered earlier in the day. Everything from Gulfstream G650s to Boeing 777s, and even one Airbus A380, the double-deck behemoth belonging to the king of Saudi Arabia, were parked wingtip to wingtip on the expansive apron.

A line of black Mercedes-Maybach S 650 sedans idled with air conditioners running, in the shade of a large hangar. A fleet of black Chevrolet Suburbans driven by agents from the Emiri Guard were nearby, waiting to be filled by the heavily armed men of the royal protective details. For some of the larger delegations, Sprinter vans, capable of transporting twenty passengers apiece, were available as well. The larger motorcades, some with up to ten vehicles, wound their way through the airport's grounds like giant black snakes until they cleared the final checkpoint and merged onto King Faisal Road. Devoid of traffic, thanks to the clearing operation by the Kuwaiti National Police, the drivers of the powerful Maybachs quickly reached speeds of eighty to one hundred miles an hour, easily making the drive to Bayan Palace in under twenty minutes.

One of the Caracal helicopters was lifting off from the helipad near the VIP terminal as its twin came to a hover and prepared to land. The pilots of the departing helicopter rotated the nose until it pointed northeast, then gained speed and altitude for the quick flight to the LZ at the palace. As it departed, the arriving Caracal settled on the white H painted on the concrete pad and shut down the engines, allowing the rotors to come to a stop before the next delegation was brought out. It would not do to have the rotor wash ruffle the thobes and keffiyehs or tailored Italian and Saville Row suits of the region's most wealthy monarchs. Once the next group was onboard and secured in their seats, only then would the rotor's five blades gently flexing in the warm breeze spin up to full power and lift the helicopter into the air. The well-orchestrated air shuttle and motorcade departures would continue until all the delegations were delivered to the summit.

Kuwait International Airport's VIP terminal was a world-class operation, and no expense had been spared to ensure a premium experience for its clientele. Those amenities extended to the pilots and air crews transporting the rich and famous as well. A gym, showers, twenty-four-hour food service, and an impressive pilots' lounge filled the second floor of the facility. On the roof was a large, enclosed and air-conditioned observation deck that provided a view of the tarmac and the expanse of desert beyond the airport's grounds. Facing west, the deck was a popular spot to watch the sun set as it fell below the horizon.

But the man wearing the generic uniform of corporate and charter pilots the world over, dark slacks and a white shirt with epaulets on his shoulders and gold wings pinned above his breast pocket, wasn't there to watch the sunset. No, he was awaiting the arrival of a specific airplane, an airliner bearing the gold crown of the Hashemite Kingdom of Jordan on its tail.

An Air Force officer from the Russian Embassy's military attaché's office, the man had been assigned the task of identifying the king's plane. He had no idea why and knew better than to ask. That decision was made way above his pay grade. All he knew was that he was supposed to send two text messages to a number he had been given by the shadowy head of the local GRU office. The first text was to be sent upon the arrival of the Jordanian plane. And the second was to alert the person to the king's departure from the airport, along with a description of the mode of transportation – helicopter or motorcade. So he sat, rather impatiently, waiting for the plane's arrival so he could finish up this spy business and get back to town. He had a date with a hot consular officer he'd been chatting up for weeks and didn't want to be late.

A gorgeous sunset, the sky a palette of pink and purple streaks across the Kuwaiti sky, provided a spectacular backdrop as the Royal Jordanian airliner lined up on final approach. The big jet continued descending until brief puffs of gray smoke that were barely visible in the fading light indicated the tires had touched down on the long concrete runway. After rolling to a stop, the pilots followed instructions from the control tower and taxied the big Boeing across the tarmac to the VIP terminal. But instead of parking near the other delegate's planes, it was directed toward the open doors of a hangar. The structure was not large enough to accommodate the entire plane, so the pilots brought it to a stop with only its nose and forward door inside the building.

Finally! the Russian in the pilot's uniform thought as he thumbed in the first text message. *Maybe I'll make that date on time after all.* He watched as a long motorcade pulled around the plane and came to a stop along its left side. With his view obscured by the hangar, he couldn't see who had deplaned and entered the Mercedes stretch limo. *But who else could it be?* he thought. With no way to confirm the luxury sedan's occupants, he assumed King Abdullah was inside. More concerned with being on time for his date than with positively identifying his target, he withdrew his mobile phone and typed in the second text. Considering his role in the operation complete, the man pocketed his phone and headed downstairs.

Across the Persian Gulf, Colonel Teplov was standing in the Reaper's flight operations center inside the IRGC hangar when his cellphone vibrated. He glanced at the screen before reading the second text message aloud. "The target is traveling by motorcade."

*

The lead advance agent, a member of the Royal Guard, the elite military unit responsible for protecting the King of Jordan and the royal family, watched the motorcade pull into the hangar. The first vehicle, a black Chevrolet Suburban, eased past him, allowing the limo, a fully armored stretch Mercedes Maybach to roll to a stop on his mark. Perfectly positioned, the car's back door was aligned with the bottom of the mobile air-stairs that had been brought up by the ground crew. A second, identical Maybach was parked inside the hangar and would join the motorcade for the drive to Bayan Palace. The Jordanians were hoping to play a shell game, making it difficult for any attacker to know which car was transporting their precious cargo.

Behind the limo was another Suburban that would be filled with Royal Guard agents. Two additional vehicles had been added to the motorcade to accommodate CIA Director Sloan and his protective detail. They were both Suburbans, an armored limo for Sloan and a follow car for the DPS agents. A member of the Royal Guard would ride along in the CIA follow car as a liaison officer and to assist with communication between the two teams.

The next vehicle in line behind the Americans was a Mercedes Sprinter. The twenty-passenger minibus would transport members of the traveling party, support staff, and a small medical team. Next in line was a Suburban occupied by a Counter Assault Team of six Royal Guard men kitted up in tactical gear. The CAT team was in place to repel any attack on the motorcade while the other agents of the detail covered and evacuated the king from the scene. When the motorcade departed the hangar, a couple of Kuwaiti National Police escorts would bookend the convoy. A total of ten vehicles would be making the trip to the conference center at Bayan Palace.

Happy with the formation of the motorcade, the lead advance agent made his way up the stairs accompanied by Special Agent Jeanne Emerson of the Director's Protective Staff. They entered the plane to brief their respective agents-in-charge. The Jordanian spoke with his AIC, while Jeanne gave Doug Kelly and Director Sloan a quick rundown of the sequence of events that would take place once they exited the plane and identified their vehicles' positions in the motorcade.

When Jeanne was finished with her brief, she and Doug walked toward the front of the main cabin. Standing just inside the door, he looked down on the motorcade and said, "The boss has accepted the king's invitation to ride with him to the summit."

Doug hated when Director Sloan agreed to ride in someone else's vehicle. It meant he would be the odd man out since there was no room for a second AIC in the king's limo. He would either be relegated to a seat in the Jordanian detail's follow car or end up riding in an empty limo that had been shoehorned into the motorcade. Neither situation was optimal, but the Jordanians had one thing going for them that gave Doug a small measure of comfort.

Because of the special relationship between the CIA and the Hashemite Kingdom, the Agency had spent a considerable amount of time and effort training various Jordanian units. The Royal Guard was always at the top of the list, not only as a priority but in their performance. Those training sessions were invaluable for a couple of reasons. First, it meant Doug and the other members of the DPS knew the Jordanians' playbook, because for all intents and purposes, it had been written by the CIA. Both details were pretty much on the same page when it came to protective philosophies and tactics. But more importantly, those training sessions gave the Agency a chance to build relationships with the members of the king's detail. And it was those relationships, that allowed Doug Kelly to trust the Royal Guard with protecting Director Sloan.

"Do me a favor," Doug said. "Have the Jord liaison ride with me in our limo. And while you're at it, why don't you jump in with us as well."

"You got it," Jeanne replied, then headed down the stairs to make the arrangements.

Doug turned back into the plane to rejoin Director Sloan. On the outside he portrayed the calm confidence of a professional protective agent. But on the inside, his guts were churning. He couldn't believe his ears when he had been presented with Elijah Miller's plan. Using the DCIA and the King of Jordan as bait to draw out the rogue drone was the dumbest idea he'd ever heard. And he shared that opinion with anyone who would listen, to include Director Sloan. But in the end, he had been overruled so Doug had done his duty and put together the security plan for the trip.

Whenever something off-the-wall occurred while on detail, an agent would say, "That's going to be a chapter in the book when I write my memoir." And another would counter with "You can't make this shit up," or "If this happened in a movie, no one would believe it." Doug knew this was one of those occasions. If they survived the trip to Kuwait, and he did decide to write a book one day, would anyone believe what they were about to attempt wasn't the brainchild of some screenwriter for a new Bond movie or the plot of the next Brad Taylor or Mark Greaney novel?

"This plan is about as fucked up as a football bat," he thought.

CHAPTER 46

THE RUSSIAN PILOT kept the Reaper low, no more than a hundred feet off the ground as he deftly maneuvered the drone through the hills of the uninhabited al-Jahra Governate to the west of the capital city to avoid Kuwaiti radar and the fighter aircraft searching for it.

"Are we ready to initiate the attack, sir?" he asked without taking his eyes off the ground control station's monitor.

Teplov told him to stand by while he contacted Moscow for approval.

The pilot had the sensor operator make use of the time by asking him to perform one last check of the systems. After a minute, the sensor operator confirmed, "All systems are in the green and functioning properly."

Now it was just a matter of waiting for the response from the suits in the Kremlin. No matter. He would continue to hone his skills at the controls until the powers that be gave the go-ahead to commence the mission.

*

Chuck Jamison loitered in the confined airspace over the tiny emirate in the left seat of the CIA-owned DHC-6 Twin Otter. Built by the de Havilland company, the high-winged, twin-engine plane was a mainstay of the Air Branch fleet, given its ability to operate in the harshest environments imaginable using remote, unimproved runways and dirt strips. The Agency's pilots loved the Twin Otter for its durability and short take-off and landing, or STOL, capability.

Joe Matthews sat next to Jamison in the right seat of the cockpit, his short-barreled HK416 securely tucked between his seat and the center console. In his lap was an aluminum device that looked like a miniature version of the old aerial antennas people used to have on the roofs of their homes before the invention of cable television. A cable ran from the grip of the directional antenna through the cockpit door and connected to a powerful transmitter strapped to the floor of the main cabin.

A blue ethernet cable ran from the transmitter to Elijah Miller's laptop. The NSA man was not thrilled with the trajectory his career had taken over the last couple of weeks. Between the attempted kidnapping in Brussels, and now being voluntold that he would be taking part in the mission personally, Eli had decided that he did not like being at the pointy tip of the spear one bit.

Fred Jackson, on the other hand, was having the time of his life. He absolutely loved his job as the CIA's top hacker, but he had always dreamed of getting out of the office and using his skills in the field. He'd jumped at the chance to join Eli on the trip to Kuwait and still couldn't believe he was really in the back of one of the Agency's special missions' aircraft on an operation to intercept and hack the rogue MQ-9 Reaper. Now all they had to do was find it.

The voice of the AWACS mission commander crackled through their headsets. "Sorry we're late to the party. Had a slight mechanical issue that delayed our takeoff. Give us a couple of minutes to get into our orbit and sort out all the traffic."

Jamison spoke into the boom mic attached to his headset. "No worries. Glad to have you on station."

*

Acknowledging his orders, Teplov disengaged the call and slid the phone back into his pocket. Getting the attention of the personnel in the flight ops center, he announced, "The mission is a go. Commence the attack."

Without a word, the pilot pointed the Reaper's nose in the direction of Kuwait International Airport and put the drone into a gentle climb to begin gaining altitude. The sunset was fading into darkness, but the lack of light would be of little consequence to the drone's all-seeing cameras. On the monitor, the pilot could easily make out the airport's runway lights on the horizon. He found the visual comforting even though the VIP terminal and the hangar's coordinates were locked into the Reaper's navigation system.

As the drone rose through the darkening sky, it was easier for the pilot to make out the airport's individual structures and characteristics. Using the futuristic-looking main terminal as a reference point, he eased the Reaper to the left and headed for the VIP area. Zooming in the cameras, the sensor operator let out a low whistle as the tarmac came into view. He had never seen so many business jets in one place. With the planes lined up in perfect rows, the VIP terminal resembled a luxury car dealership, or a high-end valet parking lot for the region's rich and famous.

The sensor operator manipulated the joystick on his console and the camera under the Reaper's nose panned left. The image of a Boeing 777 with its front end partially obscured inside a large maintenance hangar filled his monitor. Floodlights positioned around the tarmac illuminated the Boeing's fuselage and tail section. Another small adjustment of the joystick brought the purple background and gold crown of Jordan's royal family on the plane's vertical rudder into focus.

"There it is, sir," the sensor operator said, pointing to his monitor.

Teplov moved closer and leaned in to get a better view. With a hand on the top of each of the ground control station's seats, it was a position he had taken since the very first mission. From it he was able to see both monitors. The view gave him a front-row seat to the action, but more important, at least from the GRU colonel's standpoint, it reinforced his position of authority over the operation. The habit annoyed the pilot to no end. He hated Teplov, and his mind wandered occasionally, picturing the asshole in the crosshairs of one of the Hellfire missiles attached to the Reaper's underwing pods.

From the drone's approach angle they could see into the open end of the hangar. A long motorcade sat bumper-to-bumper alongside the plane as people scurried around the vehicles. The sense of urgency with which they moved gave the Russians the impression the convoy would be departing any minute.

"We should attack now," the pilot commented. "While they're stationary."

Teplov thought it over for a few seconds before responding. "Not yet.

We don't know if the king is still in the plane or if he's moved to the vehicle. Wait until they're on the open road and you have a clear shot."

With four Hellfires onboard, the pilot knew he had more than enough firepower to destroy the plane and the motorcade. But this was Teplov's operation, so he followed orders. "Yes, sir."

*

The mission commander hailed Jamison by his callsign. "Pegasus, we've got a possible bogey heading toward the airport from the west."

The small radar signature's relatively slow airspeed and the fact that the aircraft didn't respond to repeated radio calls led the crew to believe it was the missing Reaper. Jamison punched the coordinates into his nav system and set the Twin Otter on a course to intercept the contact. While he was doing his pilot thing, Joe adjusted the boom mic on his headset and asked Miller and Jackson to fire up the transmitter. He turned in his seat to look at the men, and the difference in their appearance made him chuckle. Fred Jackson was grinning from ear to ear, as if he were on the adventure of a lifetime. Elijah Miller, on the other hand, looked as though he would rather be anywhere except where he was at this very moment.

"Deep breaths, Eli. In through the nose and out through the mouth," Joe reassured him. Shifting his attention to Jackson he asked, "Everything good with the software?"

"Yep. Eli will work to gain control of the Reaper while I try to trace the satellite link back to its source."

"Any idea how long it'll take to get into the UAV's system?"

Eli looked up from his laptop and shook his head, "No one has done what we're about to attempt so there's no data to benchmark against. We're breaking new ground here tonight."

Turning back to the front, Joe thought, *That's great. People's lives are on the line and we're trying something that's never been done before. Maybe we would be better off just blowing this thing out of the sky after all.*

CHAPTER 47

THE SOUND OF vehicle doors slamming shut echoed through the cavernous hangar as security personnel and staff alike prepared for the departure. King Abdullah and CIA Director Sloan were the last to exit the plane.

As the two men descended the stairs to the waiting Maybach limo, the king asked, "Do you really believe we're at risk of being attacked, Lawrence?"

"I'm afraid it's a very real possibility, your Majesty," Sloan replied.

King Abdullah paused halfway down the stairs and looked at the American spy chief. "And yet you still chose to accept my offer to ride with me to the summit? Knowing full well that you might be putting yourself in harm's way?"

With a slight grin, Sloan said, "I didn't realize I had the option to decline an offer from the head of the royal family. Is it too late to change my mind?"

Abdullah laughed out loud and slapped Sloan on the back. "Come to think of it, you're quite right, Lawrence. I can't remember the last time someone turned down one of my invitations." He continued down the stairs and leaned into the open door of the limo. "Hop in. Let's get this show on the road."

The king's agent-in-charge closed the heavy armored door, then took a quick look at the motorcade before sliding into the limo's right front seat. With everyone in position, he pressed the transmit button on the microphone clipped to the sleeve of his suit jacket and gave the order for the precession to begin the slow roll out of the hangar.

*

The drone pilot temporarily lost sight of the motorcade as it weaved through the buildings and cargo facilities on the northern section of the airport's grounds. Gaining more altitude to get a better view, he reacquired his target. The red and blue flashing lights atop the Kuwaiti National Police cruisers that joined the motorcade as it merged onto King Faisal Road didn't hurt either. With a police escort, and the roads cleared of any traffic not affiliated with the summit, the vehicles accelerated and were cruising at a comfortable eighty-five miles an hour.

Teplov watched the monitors with anticipation. "You may fire when ready."

The pilot moved the Reaper into position.

*

From the main cabin of the AWACS flying fifteen thousand feet above him, Jamison heard the mission commander's voice through his headset. "Maintain this flight level and heading. The contact is about a mile ahead of you."

Jamison acknowledged the update and continued scanning the dark sky through the night vision goggles attached to the front of his flight helmet.

"By the way," the mission commander continued, "we've been sharing our tracking information with the Kuwaiti Air Force. There are two KAF F/A-18 Super Hornets tracking the contact as well. You'll want to get clear of the area if they decide to go off book and engage the target."

Jamison glanced over at Joe with a look of "I told you so." on his face. From the pre-mission briefing, they both knew the Kuwaiti Air Force was not thrilled with the CIA's plan to hack the drone inflight. Preposterous was the word Joe remembered the KAF chief of staff using. The flight leader who would be in the cockpit of his fighter patrolling the skies was more direct, saying their plan was "fucking reckless and foolhardy."

Joe found himself agreeing with both men. It would be much easier to shoot the drone down and find some other way to track the Russians. But that decision had been made way above his paygrade. And as if his plate wasn't full enough trying to intercept the Reaper before it killed King Abdullah and Director Sloan, he also had to worry about being caught in the Hornets' line of fire if the KAF decided to scrap this harebrained plan and destroy the drone.

Peering through the darkness, Jamison pointed. "There! Dead ahead at eleven o'clock." He applied the throttle and pulled alongside the drone, matching the Reaper's speed.

Joe had benefited from America's drone fleet on many occasions, but he had never seen one up close. Looking through the Twin Otter's window, he admired the simplicity of its design. But his eyes were immediately drawn to the items attached to the underside of the Reaper's wings. Four Hellfire missiles hung from the pods, waiting to streak toward whatever target the Russian pilot put in their crosshairs. And Joe knew it wouldn't be long before the motorcade below would be that target.

Jamison's voice boomed in his headset, "Anytime you're ready, sweetheart."

Joe unlatched the window and pushed it out and up, locking it into place. Cool air rushed into the cockpit as he extended the directional antennae through the opening and aimed it at the Reaper's bulbous nose.

"Alright," Joe called out to the guys in the back of the plane. "Work your nerd magic."

With nothing else to do while Miller and Jackson did their thing, Joe caught sight of the motorcade speeding along an empty King Faisal Road. Having done stints on the DPS off and on throughout his career, he thought about Doug Kelly and the other agents who were depending on him and the two tech wizards to keep them alive. The thought that things were about to go their way vanished when he saw the drone's position in relation to the motorcade. He felt a knot begin to form in the pit of his stomach as he realized the Reaper was getting in position to fire.

*

The video began to flicker as if there was some type of interference with the signal from the Reaper.

"What's wrong?" Teplov demanded, pointing at the image on the ground control station's monitors.

"I don't know," the pilot said, looking to the sensor operator who shrugged his shoulders, indicating he had no idea what was causing the issue. "The controls seem sluggish and the drone isn't responding as it should. We haven't experienced anything like this before."

"No! Not when we're this close," Teplov fumed. Needing answers, he yelled, "Zubkin! Get over here!"

The aerospace engineer dropped what he was doing and raced to the GRU colonel's side. Seeing the issue for himself, he said, "Give me a minute to run a diagnostic."

"Make it quick," Teplov snapped, realizing any failure in this mission would fall directly on his shoulders.

Zubkin moved to a workstation and shoved a technician out of the way. Taking the seat at the terminal, he began typing furiously. Sixty seconds later he looked up from the monitor with a confused look on his face. The satcom link and the ground control station were working normally. Whatever the problem was, it wasn't with the equipment in this room. He said, "The interference must be coming from elsewhere."

Pacing back and forth like a caged animal, Teplov racked his brain searching for a plausible explanation for the sudden malfunction. They hadn't experienced even the slightest glitch on any of the other flights. *Why now?* After another couple of laps through the flight operations center it dawned on him. And the realization stopped the GRU man dead in his tracks. *It must be the Americans! But how?*

He supposed it wasn't out of the realm of possibility that they had discovered a way to disrupt the satellite link or somehow interfere with the flight controls. After all, his hacker had accessed the drone's operating system and reprogrammed it for their use. Were the Americans trying something similar to regain control of it? Was it even possible while the drone was in the air? He had to know, so he reached for his phone and scrolled through the contacts until he found Anna Kovaleski's number.

As he waited for AK to pick up, Teplov felt the window for this mission's success rapidly shrinking. Turning to the pilot, he said, "You are weapons free. Take the shot at the first opportunity."

CHAPTER 48

Noticing what looked like a slight loss of stability in the Reaper's flight characteristics, Joe glanced over at Jamison. "You see that?"

"Yep. Looks like she's getting a little squirrely."

Over the Twin Otter's internal com system, Joe asked, "How's it coming back there, guys?"

Without looking up from his laptop's screen, Eli replied, "The program's working, but it's taking longer than I anticipated. I'll need a few more minutes."

"How many is a few?" Joe asked, knowing the Reaper could unleash one of its missiles any second.

"Did I mention something about no one ever having done this before? I'm working as fast as I can." Succumbing to the pressure of doing this outside the controlled environment of his office, he snapped, "It'll take as long as it takes."

Fuck! "How about you, Fred? Any luck?"

"I've managed to trace the drone's satcom link to the Russian satellite. But I'm going to need some time to navigate through the satellite and track the signal to its source on the ground."

Joe was about to come back with some smartass quip about typing faster, as if that would make a difference, when they hit a pocket of turbulence. Without warning the Twin Otter dropped about thirty feet.

The plane lost altitude so quickly that Eli's arms flew up over his head as if he were on a roller coaster. Without his hands on the keyboard to hold it down, the laptop seemed to float in midair. He realized what was happening a fraction of a second too late. In desperation he reached for the computer but missed and was sickened when it crashed into the cabin's ceiling. As it fell, it bounced off his seat's armrest, then ricocheted off the corner of the transmitter before landing in the aisle.

Joe heard Eli let out a scream. Thinking it had to do with the turbulence, he turned to look back into the cabin half expecting to see him puking into a barf bag. But Joe's eyes were immediately drawn to the fact that there was no longer a computer in his lap. The problem was much worse than Eli losing his lunch.

Unbuckling his seatbelt, Eli bent down and retrieved his laptop. He turned it around in his hands inspecting every inch of the aluminum frame. There was a nasty looking dent in the palm rest where it had collided with the corner of the transmitter's housing. But the bigger problem was the spiderweb of cracks that extended across the laptop's screen. It had gone dark from the impact and Miller held his breath as he gently pressed the Enter key. The screen blinked two or three times, then lit up, his program still running in the background.

"Yes!" he yelled, giving a fist pump before getting a high-five from Fred across the aisle. If he survived this ordeal, he was going to contact the CEO of the company that made the laptop and offer to buy him a steak dinner. With the banged-up computer up and running again, Eli resumed his work. There was only one problem. They had lost the connection to the drone.

With that mini-crisis averted, Joe returned his attention to the Reaper. But it wasn't there. He looked around frantically trying to find it, wondering where it had gone. It hadn't dropped in altitude along with the Twin Otter when they'd hit the turbulence. Instead, it had been thrown a similar distance upward. The change in altitudes broke the connection Joe had established with the directional antennae, and he saw the drone had leveled out and seemed to be in stable flight once again.

Before Jamison could get back in position alongside the Reaper, he and Joe watched in horror as one of the missiles' solid-fuel engines began to glow. The launch process had been initiated. Milliseconds later, Joe heard the high-pitched scream through his open window as the Hellfire left its underwing pod and streaked toward the motorcade below.

*

The Russian pilot noted the sudden change in altitude and was relieved to see the return of clear images on his monitors. Flight controls and responsiveness seemed normal and he updated Teplov and Zubkin. While Zubkin continued to study his diagnostic program, looking for something he might have missed that would explain the disruption, Teplov had moved to a corner of the flight ops center to take the call with Kovaleski.

After the attack on the airbase in Syria, she had returned to Moscow and was sitting at her workstation in APT28's office, sipping a venti Starbucks. Exasperated with the GRU jackass, she said, "Slow down. You're not making any sense. Start from the beginning and tell me exactly what you saw."

Teplov took a deep, calming breath, then explained what they had experienced, including Zubkin's diagnostic test that had come back negative. Setting the cup down, AK went to work on her keyboard, logging in to the software she had used to reprogram the Reaper. Reviewing the data being livestreamed from the drone, it took her only a couple of minutes to determine what was happening. And the realization took her breath away.

"The Americans are conducting a two-pronged attack on the drone's systems. They appear to be attempting to gain access to its flight controls." Stunned that they had the audacity to try something so complex while the drone was in the air, she paused to take a closer look at the code.

"What is it?" Teplov demanded, annoyed with the delay.

"Whoever wrote this code is a fucking genius. I've never seen anything so intricate. It's…beautiful," she added with an admiring tone in her voice. What she wouldn't give to have a couple of hours to sit down with this programmer and pick his or her brain.

"I don't give a shit if it's the digital equivalent of the fucking Mona Lisa!" Teplov fumed. "What do we do about it?"

AK thought it over for a minute before responding. "They must have a powerful transmitter nearby and that's what's causing the interference. My guess is that it's either on the ground and they're using a television or radio antennae, or they have a plane with a transmitter onboard shadowing the drone. I'm not an aerospace engineer like Zubkin, but at this point I'd say your best bet is to gain as much distance from the transmitter as possible."

Teplov reached up and massaged his temples with the thumb and middle finger of his left hand. "You mentioned this was a two-pronged attack. What's the second part?"

His question made AK smile, a fact she was sure would have infuriated him had they been in the same room. "The Americans have traced the communication link from the drone to the satellite. Now they're probably working their way through the satcom to follow the signal from the satellite to the ground control station." That last part made her thankful to be in her Moscow office, four thousand kilometers from the action.

"Meaning?"

"Meaning, that in a matter of minutes, the braniac who designed the code is going to pinpoint your location and know exactly where you are." She felt the smile on her face expand as she added, "If I were you, I'd get the hell out of there."

There was silence on the other end of the call as her words sank in. In a panicked voice, Anna heard Teplov shout, "Take the shot. Now!"

CHAPTER 49

WITH NO WAY to know which of the Maybach limousines King Abdullah was in, the Russian drone pilot was forced to make a choice. Following his gut, he chose the first one in line. After all, the Reaper had three more missiles onboard and he would just hit the other one if the motorcade continued to roll.

Placing the laser designator on the roof of the lead limo to guide the Hellfire to its target, he moved his thumb ever so slightly and pressed the fire button on the joystick. Seconds later the image of the missile appeared on his monitor as it rode the invisible laser toward the armored vehicle below. Once it was destroyed, the pilot decided he would hit the second Maybach for good measure. Better safe than sorry.

*

Doug Kelly hated not being in the limo with Director Sloan. Even though they were only two car lengths back, it seemed much farther. But having Shane Janzen, Sloan's driver, behind the wheel and Jeanne Emerson in the car with him provided a small measure of comfort. Still, he would be in a much better mood once he was reunited with the man he was charged with protecting.

The motorcade made the sweeping left and headed north toward the massive cloverleaf that would take them under Jassem Mohammed Al-Kharafi Road. Doug could see the outlines of the sprawling 360 Mall to his right and was about to say something about a restaurant where he had dinner the last time they were in Kuwait when Joe's voice came through his earpiece. What he heard made his blood run cold.

"Doug! The Reaper launched a Hellfire! Missile inbound!"

Before the words had a chance to register in his brain, Doug caught a streak of movement in the night sky and followed its trajectory with his eyes. Seconds later, he watched as the lead Maybach erupted in a fireball and the remnants of the armored vehicle blasted outward in every direction. A jagged piece of the limo's hood shattered the rear window of the Kuwaiti National Police car leading the motorcade and decapitated the two officers in the front seat. The driverless police cruiser veered to the right and shot across the shoulder. Deep sand between the highway and a frontage road slowed the vehicle, but not enough to keep it from slamming into the cinderblock wall surrounding a community center. The flaming remains of the Maybach's chassis drifted to a less spectacular stop in the left lane of the highway.

Years of training kicked in, and the Jordanian agent driving the king's vehicle didn't miss a beat. He swerved to avoid the wreckage, then mashed the gas pedal to the floor. The sedan's V12 engine roared as it accelerated up the highway, getting its occupants off the X as fast as it could. With the combined detail in full-on protective mode, the rest of the motorcade matched his speed.

Doug breathed a brief sigh of relief, knowing it was the decoy limo that had just been obliterated. But he realized it wouldn't be long before the drone pilot would have the car carrying the king and the director in his crosshairs. They were too damned exposed on the open road and had to get off the highway.

"The mall!" Jeanne suggested from the back seat while looking at the map application on her phone. "We can take cover in the parking garage. It'll keep us out of the drone's line of sight."

Doug agreed and told the Jordanian liaison agent to relay the message to the king's AIC.

*

"Direct hit. Target destroyed." the sensor operator confirmed for the group in the flight operations center.

"Again!" Teplov ordered. "Destroy the other one!"

The pilot was about to carry out the command when the distortion returned and the images broadcast from the Reaper began to jump all over his monitor. Try as he might, he could not get the targeting laser to settle on the roof of the remaining limo. And without the laser to guide it in, the pilot gave the missile a fifty-fifty chance of hitting its target. When he relayed that to Teplov, he received a stream of expletives in return. So he followed the order, even though he thought it was a waste of a perfectly good Hellfire, and once again pressed the button on the joystick.

*

"How much longer?" Joe demanded, knowing the Russian pilot was in the process of locking in on the second limo. With the directional antennae re-engaged, he just hoped the interference was severe enough to affect the accuracy of the shot.

Fred was the first to reply. "I've narrowed down the general location of the ground control station but need a few more minutes to determine the precise grid coordinates."

"What about you, Eli?"

Miller was so engrossed in the data on the screen of his laptop, that he didn't hear Joe's question. Fred leaned across the aisle and nudged Eli with his elbow. Annoyed at the interruption, he snapped, "What?"

Joe repeated his question. "How much longer?"

But before Miller could answer, a second Hellfire leapt from the Reaper's underwing pod.

"Fuck!" Joe screamed in frustration. "Doug, you've got another one headed your way!"

Doug cursed, then relayed the information to the Royal Guard officer riding with them. Keying his radio, the Jordanian rattled off something in Arabic to the rest of his detail.

Moments after the radio call, the roof hatch on the Jordanian Counter Assault Team vehicle slid open and the upper torso of one of the operators emerged. He reached down into the cabin of the Suburban and pulled a long, olive-green, cylindrical tube through the opening. Hoisting the thirty-three-pound Stinger antiaircraft missile onto his right shoulder, he began scanning the sky for the Reaper.

The unguided Hellfire bore down on the motorcade as it sped under the enormous interchange at Jassem Mohammed Al-Kharafi Road. A massive explosion rocked the vehicles as the missile struck one of the elevated roadways and detonated. Debris peppered the motorcade, battering the vehicles' armored shells and pockmarking their bullet-resistant windows, but the convoy continued along its route. No one was more surprised that they were still alive and moving than Doug Kelly

Seeing the surviving limo with the Jordanian follow car and the two CIA vehicles on its tail shoot under the crumbling overpass, Joe couldn't believe his eyes. The elevated roadway had intercepted the Hellfire, saving King Abdullah and Director Sloan, as well as those of their respective protective details. The rest of the motorcade wasn't so lucky.

Joe watched with a morbid fascination as the action unfolded below. Resembling a scene from a disaster movie, he looked on as huge chunks of concrete, twisted rebar, and mangled vehicles that had been crossing the overpass at the time of the explosion crashed down onto the highway. The horrified driver of the Mercedes Sprinter stood on his brakes, but his reaction was too slow, and the van collided with a particularly large section of the collapsed overpass. A long, exposed piece of rebar shattered the windshield and pierced the driver's chest, pinning his body to the seat.

The CAT vehicle swerved and came to a halt, narrowly avoiding crashing into the van. While the driver looked for a way around the destruction to rejoin the motorcade, the operator with the Stinger on his shoulder was still looking up, scanning the dark sky for the Reaper. He caught movement in his peripheral vision and interrupted his search for the briefest of moments, curious to find out what had drawn his attention away from the drone attacking them from above. It was the last thing he would ever see.

The enormous form of a truck hauling a tanker-trailer full of gasoline had not been able to stop in time and drove over the edge of the destroyed overpass. The rig crashed down onto the Sprinter and the counter assault team's Suburban, crushing them like a couple of empty beer cans. Gas flooded the area, pouring from gashes in the ruptured trailer. Mercifully, everyone in the vehicles was dead when the fumes ignited, sending an apocalyptic-looking fireball into the sky as flames engulfed the wrecked interchange.

Bringing up the rear of the motorcade, the Kuwaiti National Police car had been able to stop in time and back out of the kill zone. In a zombie-like daze, the police officers exited their vehicle and stood shoulder-to-shoulder, fixated on the inferno. Each man whispered a quiet prayer, thanking Allah for sparing their lives this day.

CHAPTER 50

JOE'S EYES DARTED back and forth between the Reaper and what was left of the motorcade, looking for signs it was about to fire another missile. Having been on a protective detail whose convoy had come under attack, he could imagine the conversations and actions taking place in the vehicles below. The members of the Director's Protective Staff were his friends and colleagues, and it tore at him that he was not down there in the mix with them. Then Jeanne Emerson's voice came through his headset, and she relayed their plan to take cover in the mall's parking garage. At this point, Joe thought it was as good an idea as any.

Having missed the exit for the mall back at the interchange, the motorcade slowed and then turned right, heading the wrong way up an entrance ramp. With lights flashing and sirens blaring, the Jordanian limo driver weaved in and out of oncoming traffic as if he were doing slalom drills on a closed track. The four-vehicle convoy rocketed up the ramp oblivious of the shouts and honking horns of infuriated drivers. Making a left off Jassem Mohammed Al-Kharafi, tires screeched as the motorcade looped around a traffic circle and exited onto the 360 Mall's perimeter road. All four drivers mashed their gas pedals to the floor, the perceived safety of the parking deck in sight a mere five-hundred meters away.

Even with the distortion created by the transmitter and the directional antennae, Joe saw the Reaper begin an unsteady turn, as if the pilot was lining up for another shot. With frustration evident in his voice he called out, "Fred?"

"Done. I've got the ground control station's coordinates."

About fucking time, he thought. "Eli?"

Miller was so close to breaking through and regaining control of the Reaper he could taste it. He just needed a few more seconds to complete something no one thought possible – hacking a remotely piloted aircraft during flight. Lost in the code scrolling across his screen, he replied, "Almost there."

"Not good enough," Joe said, aggravated with himself for going along with this crazy scheme in the first place. Good people had died tonight because someone wanted to test their proof-of-concept. Propping the antennae in his lap, Joe reached for his rifle. "I'm putting an end to this once and for all."

Looking up from his laptop, Eli said, "Wait! I'm almost there."

"You had your chance," Joe countered. "Now we're doing this my way."

Without realizing what he was doing, Eli reached out and grabbed Joe's arm in a feeble effort to prevent him from retrieving the weapon. Joe shifted in his seat so he could look the NSA man directly in the eyes. With a menace in his voice usually reserved for his nation's enemies, Joe growled, "If you want to be able to use that hand in the foreseeable future, you've got about three seconds to let go of my arm."

Legitimately fearing for his well-being, Eli released his grip on Joe's arm. "Sorry. I…I don't know what came over me."

"Joe, you may want to take a look at this," Jamison said from the cockpit's left seat.

The Reaper seemed to have resumed stable flight. *What the hell?* Joe thought, then looked down at his lap. *Shit!* When he had turned to face Miller, the antennae had shifted in his lap and lost line of sight with the drone. The break in the connection had once again given the Russian pilot full control of the UAV and its systems. And he was going to take full advantage of Joe's mistake.

Extending the rifle out the Twin Otter's open window, Joe seated the stock in his shoulder and thumbed the selector switch to Auto. But before he could pull the trigger and unload a full thirty-round magazine into the nose of the UAV, a third Hellfire missile erupted from its underwing pod and zoomed toward the motorcade below. "No!" Joe screamed, feeling the rifle buck in his shoulder over and over until the bolt locked back on an empty chamber. He watched the multi-million-dollar UAV spin out of control and disappear into the darkness, then refocused his attention on the motorcade below. Even though the Reaper was out of commission, Joe couldn't shake the sense that his actions had been too little, too late.

The Jordanian agents in the follow car scanned their sectors as the driver dodged shoppers and did his best to keep from rear-ending the limo.

The agent seated behind the driver yelled, "Missile inbound from the left!"

"Block left," the veteran shift leader ordered.

Without hesitation, the driver pulled up beside the Maybach limo carrying their king. When being selected for the prestigious positions on the royal family's protective detail, each man and woman had sworn to give their lives to protect the monarchy. Today it was these four men's duty to make the ultimate sacrifice.

Jeanne Emerson looked on with a combination of amazement and professional appreciation at the Jordanians' selfless actions. More than most in her position, she knew what it was like to put herself in harm's way to protect someone. But getting between your principal and a Hellfire missile took a level of commitment that was off the charts. She only hoped she would make the same decision if the roles were reversed.

The shift leader looked down to the right and made eye contact with the limo driver. Having been on the detail for over ten years, the men had become close friends. A wave of sadness came over the limo driver, knowing his friend and colleague had only seconds to live. But that sadness was quickly overwhelmed by a sense of pride in the man's dedication to his duty. Speeding toward the entrance to the parking deck, the shift leader gave his friend a smile from his seat in the Suburban as if to say, *"Everything's going to be okay."* Then the missile penetrated the left side of the follow car.

The four members of the Royal Guard died instantly as the Suburban was ripped apart by the Hellfire's explosion. Flinching from the shockwave's impact and bright flash of light, the limo driver jerked the steering wheel to the right to get away from the blast. Remnants of the follow car's chassis slammed into the Maybach as it approached the parking deck's ticket-taking machine and retractable arm. The heavy armored limo slid sideways, snapping the machine off its mount on the small island dividing the lanes. Furiously working the steering wheel and hitting the brakes, the driver attempted to regain control of the Maybach, but his efforts were futile. He had carried too much speed when entering the parking deck. But who could blame him when the alternative was to stay out in the open and eat a missile?

The squeal of the Goodyear run-flats struggling to gain traction echoed through the parking deck. Looking to his right, the Jordanian agent-in-charge's eyes went wide as the car slid toward a concrete support column. "Brace for impact!"

Doug Kelly had a front row seat to the action, and what he saw made him cringe. The Maybach seemed to be moving in slow motion as it headed for the support column. As to be expected, the concrete support didn't give. After bouncing off the column, time sped back up and the Maybach careened across the lane, the sound of crunching metal and screeching tires echoing through the garage as it smashed nose first into a row of parked cars.

Shoppers screamed and car alarms wailed, but Doug ignored the chaos swirling around him. Instead, he strained his eyes, looking for movement inside the crippled limo as Janzen eased to a stop next to the Maybach. Leaping from the Suburban, Doug ran to the left rear door of the Maybach. Cupping his hands around his eyes, he peered inside, scanning for signs of life. The Jordanian liaison officer sprinted around the other side of the car and frantically began tugging on the battered door handle. Desperate to rescue the king, he continued pulling, but the door wouldn't budge. The passenger side of the car had taken the brunt of the impact, bending the frame and wedging the door in place.

Doug wasn't having any luck with his door either, so he called out to his agents in the follow car, "Bring up the extractor!"

DPS agents Jim Haldeman and Brett LaCava appeared at Doug's side a minute later. Haldeman carried a big impact-resistant case and LaCava had what looked like large battery packs in each hand. Setting the case on the ground, Haldeman flipped the latches and opened the lid. Inside was a tool that resembled a miniature version of the jaws of life used by fire-fighters to pry open the doors of vehicles involved in traffic accidents. Due to space limitations in the back of the Suburban, this model was smaller, and battery operated, making it more portable and a fixture on the protec-tive detail's movements. Neither Haldeman nor LaCava ever imagined they would be using the device under these circumstances, but both men were happy it had been included in the loadout.

While Haldeman went to work on the Maybach's mangled back door, Erin O'Hearn and Rick Lauder exited the follow car to pull security. Their serious looks and the HK MP7s slung across their chests were enough to keep curious onlookers at bay.

After an agonizing minute or two, the door's locking mechanism finally popped. LaCava moved in and pulled the door open, holding it in place to create a clear avenue for Doug to enter the spacious cabin. Haldeman stepped around the back of the limo and put the extractor to work on the other door.

Fearing the worst, Doug crawled through the opening and sat on a jump seat facing Director Sloan. He was stunned by what he saw. Not only were both men alive, but they were fully conscious and having a conversation about the events of the last few minutes. Other than his silver hair being a bit disheveled and the knot of his tie pushed to one side, Sloan looked none the worse for the experience.

King Abdullah, on the other hand, was in some obvious pain and cradled his right arm. The bone between the elbow and the shoulder, appeared to be broken, probably from colliding with the door's armrest during the crash. Otherwise, he was in surprisingly good shape considering what he had just been through.

Doug stepped out of the destroyed limo, then bent down to help Sloan out of the car and ushered him into the back seat of the Suburban. He returned to the Maybach and offered a hand to help the king, but his assistance was politely refused. The former special forces commander was determined to leave the scene of the attack under his own power.

The crowd of onlookers that had gathered around the spectacle gasped once they recognized King Abdullah as the man exiting the car. A hushed reverence fell over the group, but a few teenagers in the crowd couldn't help themselves and pulled out their cell phones to snap a few pictures or record a video clip to upload to their social media accounts.

Doug escorted the king around the other side of the Suburban, and once he was settled in the plush leather seat, closed the heavy armored door. Haldeman and LaCava stowed the extractor, then helped the battered and bruised Jordanian driver and AIC into the back of the follow car.

Lauder and O'Hearn returned to the Suburban, and once everyone was buttoned up, LaCava asked over the radio, "Where to, Doug?"

"The embassy. And make sure they have a doctor standing by."

"No," King Abdullah interrupted. "We must go to the summit."

"Your Majesty," Doug pleaded turning in his seat to face the king, "You and your men need medical attention. And after everything we've been through this evening, we need to get to a place of safety. We have no idea if the Russians have set up some type of secondary attack in case the drone strike failed to complete its mission."

"I appreciate your concern, but I would venture to say there is not a more secure place in Kuwait than Bayan Palace at the moment. And as for my injury," he said, gesturing toward his broken arm, "I've had worse in my time, young man. We'll have it seen to once I've had a chance to address my counterparts."

Doug looked to Sloan for support, but the DCIA shrugged his shoulders, "You heard the man. Bayan Palace it is." Withdrawing his secure cell from his jacket, Sloan dialed the Operations Center at Langley to get an update on the situation, planning to use the drive time to brief the king on what they had discovered.

Exasperated, Doug keyed the radio. "Joe, tell me that goddamned drone isn't still up there hunting us."

Joe exhaled, thankful to hear his friend was still alive. "The Reaper's down. Sorry it took so long."

"You and me both, brother. But that's a conversation for another day. We're heading to the summit. Are we good to move?"

"There's a phalanx of first responders heading your way, but other than that, your route looks clear."

With Joe providing overwatch from above, Kelly gave the order, and what remained of the motorcade pulled slowly out of the parking garage, leaving the gathered crowd of onlookers with an experience they would not soon forget

CHAPTER 51

Two weeks had passed since the events in Kuwait, and the clamor against the United States for the drone attacks was a distant memory. King Abdullah's speech to the delegates at the Arab League's emergency summit had been one for the history books. His appearance as he stood before the group didn't hurt, either. Disheveled, with a line of dried blood running from his eyebrow to his jawline and his broken arm supported by a sling from the CIA protective detail's medical bag only enhanced his tale of survival on the way to the conference center. It was a tale that most if not all of the dignitaries in attendance would never experience or be able to fully appreciate. But ultimately, they had gotten the message. Russia, not America, had been the responsible party for the drone attacks across the region.

Backed by intelligence President Andrews had authorized Director Sloan to share with the Jordanian monarch, King Abdullah laid out a convincing case against not only the Russians, but the Syrians and the Iranians for their participation in facilitating the operation. Within hours of the king's speech, the full membership of the Arab League voted to pass a resolution urging Syria to expel all Russian personnel from the country and to cancel any leases of facilities in use by its military forces. Even though the resolution had no real teeth to it, the unanimous vote still sent a message to the Assad regime that they stood alone in this fiasco. The vote resonated twenty-five-hundred miles away in Moscow, where it signaled a halt to Russia's ambitions in the region and any future cooperation with the Arab League's members.

As quickly as the greater Middle East had turned against the United States, their anger was now directed at the three countries involved in the conspiracy to kill their citizens. Protests and demonstrations raged throughout the region, requiring host countries to increase security at the Syrian, Iranian, and Russian embassies. Many in the U.S. government took immense pleasure in watching the images on CNN International, Fox News, and the BBC of chanting mobs burning red, white, and blue flags. This time however, the red, white, and blue fabric embroiled in flames wasn't the stars and stripes of the American flag, but that of the Russian Federation.

*

The members of the Principal's Committee stood as President Andrews entered the Situation Room and walked to his seat at the head of the conference table. Sliding into the chair with the embroidered presidential seal, he motioned for everyone to sit and said, "Good afternoon, everyone. Let's get started."

Lawrence Sloan was relieved to see the president was back to his normal self. When he had briefed Andrews after his return from Kuwait, the president had nearly blown a gasket at being told the Iranians had once again been involved in an attack against the United States. Even though they hadn't pulled the trigger or fired a shot, they were equally complicit by allowing the Russians to launch the strike from their soil.

In response to last year's killing spree by a Quds Force hit team that had transformed downtown Washington into a war zone, the president had secretly authorized Sloan and the CIA to assassinate two of Iran's most senior generals. Amjad al-Massoud, the leader of the Quds Force, and Malek Ashkan, who commanded the Quds base in Ahvaz, were killed by a bomb, an explosively formed penetrator, or EFP, that had been attached to the door of their staff car. Andrews had hoped the deaths of two of Iran's most senior leaders would have made his point to the Ayatollah and his trusted circle of mullahs in Tehran. Apparently, that was not the case. This time, President Andrews was determined to send a message that would leave absolutely no room for misinterpretation.

Sloan reached for a remote and turned on one of the large monitors on the far wall. A young man with short brown hair and glasses appeared on the screen. "Sir, this is Mr. Charters. He is one of our most senior intelligence analysts in the Near East Division and spends the majority of his time working the Iran desk."

Andrews got straight to the point, his mindset in United States Marine Corps combat mode. "Nice to meet you, Charters. What do you have for me?"

Accustomed to briefing high-level officials, Charters was not put off by the president's abruptness. In fact, he preferred it. The senior intelligence analyst from Utah adjusted his glasses, then tapped a key on his laptop. A map of Iran filled the monitor, and Charters' image shrunk to a small picture-in-picture box in the bottom right corner. "Good afternoon, Mr. President. Per your request, I've compiled a list of Iranian military facilities." He hit another key and a group of pin icons appeared on the map. "Green indicates Army bases, the light blue, Air Force, and the dark blue are Navy."

"And the black pins?" the president asked.

"Those belong to the IRGC and Quds Force, sir." The airfield in Bandar Bushehr, launch point for the drone strike in Kuwait, and the base in Ahvaz, a key training and replenishment center used to plan last year's attack in Washington, D.C., were highlighted to make them stand out among the others. In all, Charters had plotted over fifty locations on the map

"And the star?"

"That icon represents the Beit-e Rahbari Presidential Palace. The home and office of the Supreme Leader, Ayatollah Ali Khamenei."

"Their version of the White House," Andrews commented, as he pushed back his plush chair and walked over to the monitor to get a closer look. Turning back to the group, he addressed Hank Compton, his secretary of defense. "Put together a target list, Hank. Make it painful, but don't weaken them to the point that their neighbors start having thoughts about invading. Let's start by taking out the facilities in the Strait of Hormuz like Bandar Abbas, Abu Musa, and Larak and Sirri Islands. Add Kharg Island to the list as well. I'm sick and tired of the IRGC naval units harassing international shipping in and out of the Persian Gulf. I'll leave it up to you and the joint chiefs to decide which of the army and air force bases to hit."

Compton acknowledged the presidential order, then asked, "What about the black pins, sir? Those belonging to the IRGC and Quds Force. How many of them would you like us to attack?"

President Andrews reviewed the map a moment before turning back to Compton. Looking him directly in the eyes so there was no mistaking his order, he said, "All of them."

CHAPTER 52

AN HOUR AND a half drive south of Kansas City lies Whiteman Air Force base, home of the 509th Bomb Wing and its B-2 Spirit stealth bombers. Looking like something out of the latest Batman movie, the matte black plane and its crew of two routinely launch missions to any point on the globe from rural Missouri. Accustomed to flying marathon sorties of twenty-four hours or longer, B-2 pilots and mission commanders schedule alternating naps to ensure they are fully alert when it comes time to release their payload on target. With tonight's mission clocking in at a distance of sixty-seven-hundred nautical miles, the crews were looking at a flight time of more than thirty hours to complete the round trip.

The Air Force had a total of twenty B-2s in its inventory and fifteen of the planes would be in the air for this mission. Due to the considerable number of sites in the target package, each crew was tasked with hitting more than one location. To avoid flying through Russian airspace, the over-all mission commander, Colonel Jose Avila, had chosen a more southerly route which would take the formation across the Mediterranean Sea. They would make landfall over Israel, then cross Jordan and Iraq before penetrating the Islamic Republic of Iran's borders. If all went according to plan, they would exfil into the international airspace of the Arabian Sea, then fly over the Indian Ocean before pointing the Spirits' noses west and heading for home across the African continent.

With the first leg of the mission pushing the boundaries of the B-2s operational range, they were going to need to refuel before making the run to their targets. Two KC-46A widebody tankers had rendezvoused with the ominous-looking formation over the dark waters of the Mediterranean Sea. Happy to see their flying gas stations, each of the B-2 crews took turns hooking up to the tankers' booms. When the last of the bombers had topped off its twenty-thousand-gallon tank, its pilot broke the connection and backed away from the aerial tanker. Refueled, the formation of batwings continued on their heading through the night sky unnoticed by friend or foe.

The flight was nearing the Israeli border when the B-2 crews began going through their pre-attack checklists, ensuring targeting coordinates were loaded and green lights were showing across the board on all weapons systems. Colonel Avila, the mission commander, was in the right seat of the lead Spirit designated Hammer Zero One. He and his pilot were working through their own checklist when a female voice came through his headset.

"Good evening Hammer Zero One. Athena Six at your service. I hope you don't mind, but I brought some friends along for the ride."

Avila looked out the starboard window as an F-35 Lightning glided into position alongside his plane. The interior cockpit lights came on just long enough for Avila to see the pilot snap off a crisp salute before they went dark again. The sight of the F-35, and the knowledge that there were twenty-nine more of the most advanced fighters on the planet out there in the darkness to protect his bombers gave him goosebumps. *So, this is what it must've been like.* he thought.

Taking a short break from the task at hand, Avila's thoughts wandered back to what his predecessors must have experienced in the cockpits of their B-17 Flying Fortresses on bombing raids over Nazi-occupied Europe during World War II. The massive bomber formations would be escorted by squadrons of P-51 Mustangs flying cover to protect them from the Luftwaffe's fighters sent up to do battle in the sky. Perhaps the most famous of those Mustang pilots were the Tuskegee Airmen of the 332nd Fighter Group, the first African American aviation unit in the United States military. To distinguish themselves, the pilots of the 332nd painted the tails of their P-51s red, earning them the nickname, The Red Tails.

Forcing himself back into the moment, Avila said, "Glad to have you along for the ride, Athena Six. Hopefully you won't be too busy tonight."

Due to their low-observable stealth capabilities, and the fact that most of their targets in recent years had been over countries without formidable air forces or air defense capabilities, the B-2s usually flew their missions without a fighter escort. But tonight's mission into heavily defended Iran was another matter altogether. While they could probably get in and out without being detected, the national command authority in the White House and Pentagon weren't willing to take any chances. Hence the F-35 support. And Avila didn't mind their company one bit.

Aside from being the most advanced supersonic fighter in the air, the F-35 performs well in an electronic warfare role. Combined with its stealth characteristics, the F-35's ability to suppress enemy radar gives it an unparalleled capacity to penetrate deep into hostile territory. And that was the plan for tonight's mission into Iran. To give the B-2s stealth capability a leg up on the competition, the F-35s would suppress Iranian radar installations either by electronic means or, if necessary, by destroying them with AGM-88 HARM, High-Speed Anti-Radiation missiles. Of course, they would also fulfill their primary dogfighting role and engage any of Iran's aging fighters if their pilots were delusional enough to take to the air during the raid.

Radio chatter was at a minimum as the aerial armada entered Iranian airspace. Colonel Avila gave the order and each bomber, with its dual F-35 escort broke off and headed for their respective targets. Some flew south along the coast dropping their payloads of GPS-guided two-thousand-pound bombs on Iranian naval bases at Kharg Island, Sirri Island, Abu Musa, and the IRGC Naval Command at Bandar Abbas. Buildings were reduced to rubble and fast-attack boats and vessels of all types were set ablaze before their shattered hulls sank below the waterline.

Two B-2s traveled to the northernmost point of the Persian Gulf to strike bases near the Iraqi and Kuwaiti borders while the remainder of the bombers penetrated deeper into the mainland. On the way in, one of the B-2s flew directly over Bahregan Airport, the location the Russians used to launch the drone strike in Kuwait and released eight of the sixteen GBU-31s it carried onboard. Thunderous explosions dug deep craters across the triangular airfield and the overpressure of the shockwaves ripped apart hangars and caused buildings to collapse in on themselves. Jagged bits of shrapnel ripped through the IRGC helicopters lined up on the ramp, the red-hot pieces of steel igniting the jet fuel in their tanks. Violent explosions blew the airframes apart and their rotor blades sagged to the ground as they were engulfed in flames. A bomb damage assessment would be conducted in the aftermath of the attack, but the crew of the B-2 knew it would be quite a while before operations would resume at this airfield.

While other crews hit targets around the country taking out infantry and armored divisions and a special forces brigade across Iran's provinces in Khorramabad, Dezful, Emamzedah and Qom, Colonel Avila's target package began with the Quds Force base in Ahvaz. The facility was a major training hub and logistical replenishment center for Quds operatives and other proxy organizations carrying out missions on the Islamic Republic's behalf. It also housed a detention and interrogation center specifically designed for torturing political prisoners and opponents of the regime in Tehran.

With the pair of F-35 Lightnings suppressing air defense radar, Avila's pilot lined up his bomb run. Approaching from the south, he opened the bomb-bay doors and released all but one of his JDAMs. The guidance packages on the GBU-31s worked perfectly and the bombs glided toward their targets. Barracks were demolished and deep craters occupied the ground where live-fire ranges and training facilities once stood. But the most spectacular sight of the run was the number of secondary explosions erupting from the logistics depot as ammunition and bomb-making materials ignited. The scene over the garrison rivaled the best fireworks show Avila had ever seen. With one bomb remaining, a special delivery of sorts, his pilot, along with Athena Six and her wingman in their F-35s, turned northeast on a heading for a special target in Tehran. Fifteen minutes later, with the coordinates locked into the guidance system, the bay doors opened one final time and the last bomb in the payload fell to earth.

In statements released to the media the next morning, the Ayatollah's press machine mocked the attackers for the errant bomb that missed the presidential palace and landed in a nearby courtyard. But everyone inside Beit-e Rahbari knew the truth. The bomb had not missed its intended target. No, it had been a warning shot, letting the mullahs know that the United States could have killed them all in their sleep, but had chosen not to. To some inside the building, the near-death experience began to sow seeds of doubt about the path the Ayatollah had chosen for their country. Perhaps it was time to start thinking about new leadership and an easing of tensions with the West.

CHAPTER 53

"RANGE...FOURTEEN HUNDRED THIRTY-SEVEN meters," Foster said as he looked through the spotting scope. Next, he directed his attention to the flags atop the terminal building. Seeing the red, white and black stripes of the Syrian standard fluttering lazily in the gentle breeze, he added, "Looks like the wind coming off the Med is negligible."

Perched in the same upstairs room of the farmhouse where they had spotted Tariq in the hangar, Tim Shannon reached up and made the subtle adjustment to the Nightforce optic without removing his eye from the glass. With his dope dialed in, all he could do now was get comfortable behind his McMillan TAC-338 tactical rifle chambered in .338 Lapua Magnum and wait for the target to present himself.

In the same meeting where the president had authorized the airstrike on Iran, he had approved an operation against the Russian presence in Syria. The first target, the man Shannon was waiting to put in his cross-hairs, was Colonel Vadim Teplov, the GRU officer who had led the drone mission from start to finish.

The second would be the Alpha Group team headquartered at the naval base in Tartus. Joe Matthews and his band of paramilitary operations officers were staged to exact some battlefield justice on the men who had killed Greg Jacobs and the entire compliment of Agency personnel at the drone base in Jordan.

With the help of the old groundskeeper who had provided Tariq with information regarding the mysterious happenings around the heavily guarded hangar at Bassel Al-Assad International Airport, the CIA had identified which office in the main terminal belonged to Teplov. It was that window that Shannon was eyeing through his optic from the farmhouse east of the airport.

*

Vadim Teplov strode down the long hallway toward his office with the arrogant air his subordinates had come to expect and despise. But the slight tremble of his hand, just enough to rattle the cup of tea and saucer he had retrieved from the officer's mess betrayed the fact that his nerves were shot.

The mission in Kuwait had been an abject disaster. He had failed to kill the king of Jordan on the final sortie of the operation and the Americans had shot down the Reaper, denying the aeronautical engineers in Moscow the opportunity to study and reverse engineer the drone for their own program. President Polovkin was furious, and with the ferocity of the subsequent backlash against any Russian presence in the Middle East, Teplov was shocked he hadn't been ordered home to answer for his failure.

Closing the office door behind him, Teplov set the cup and saucer on his desk then collapsed into the plush leather chair. His right hand reached for the drawer where he kept a bottle of vodka but the GRU colonel hesitated. *Not now, Vadim,* he told himself, knowing he would need to keep a clear head in the days to come.

The best way to keep his masters in the Kremlin from putting a bullet in his head was to redirect their anger. Place the blame on someone else. But who? Kalugin and his Alpha men would be a good place to start. They had cocked up the snatch and grab of the NSA analyst in Brussels, then, on the heels of that fiasco, been caught with their pants down right here in Latakia. Losing his team and the traitorous Syrian intelligence officer they were interrogating to the Americans' assault on the safe house had to have consequences. *Surely there would be a price to pay,* he thought. But would Kalugin's failures be enough to overshadow his own? That was the sixty-four-thousand-ruble question.

If not, his only other option was to run. For several years Teplov had been working on an early retirement plan in the event he got wind Moscow was looking to retire him permanently. His ill-gotten 401K had been funded by siphoning off operational funds and stashing the money in numbered accounts in Switzerland and the Cayman Islands. While the total dollar amount in the combined accounts was substantial, Teplov was still short of the number he had in mind that would allow him to live the rest of his days in relative comfort. But, if he managed the funds properly, and didn't live an extravagant life of luxury, what he had accumulated up to this point should be enough. It had to be. Because he knew he was as good as dead once set foot back on Russian soil.

Deciding now was the time to make his move, he pushed the chair back from the desk and crossed the room. Punching a sixteen-digit code into the keypad, he opened the safe and withdrew a laptop and a smart-phone. He closed the safe's door, then returned to his desk and took a sip of the piping-hot tea while he waited for the computer to boot up.

Yes, he thought. *Now is as good a time as any.* He logged into the laptop and connected to the Internet using the phone's mobile hotspot and a high-end commercial VPN to keep his online activities hidden from his own intelligence apparatus. Feeling good about his decision, the soon to be ex-GRU colonel began implementing his exit strategy.

*

The office door opened, and Tim Shannon's breathing slowed as his target came into view. With a teacup and saucer in one hand, he watched Teplov cross the room, set the cup on the desk, then crumple into the chair.

Having positively identified his target, Shannon radioed back to the operations center on the sixth floor of the headquarters building at Langley. Director Sloan was joined in one of the ops center's small conference rooms by Katherine Clark the deputy director of operations, Harold Lee, the chief of the counterterrorism center, and the chief of the special activities division, Carl Douglas.

"I've got PID on the target. Am I cleared to engage?"

Ending a life was not an act Lawrence Sloan took lightly. Especially when it was the life of an officer belonging to a rival service. Over the years, many of the civilized world's intelligence organizations had refrained from targeting each other's members for assassination. Fearing it would trigger an all-out war between the services, an open season on spies was not a scenario any of them desired. So, a gentleman's agreement of sorts had been put in place. Spies would be targeted for compromise or arrest, but the various organizations would go out of their way to avoid killing each other's officers. But in this case, Sloan felt the sanction was warranted and didn't think the Russians would retaliate. In fact, they may even thank him for saving them trouble of having to do it themselves.

Shannon, on the other hand, had no such qualms about ridding the world of people like Teplov. He had seen the footage of the carnage. The broken bodies of innocent people killed or maimed while worshiping at their local mosques. These weren't terrorists hellbent on attacking the West. Instead, they were your average moderate Muslims attending one of the five daily prayers as prescribed by their religion. No different than people back home going to church on Sundays. When Shannon was handed a target package on someone like the man in his crosshairs, he often thought of the quote attributed to the ruthless Soviet ruler, Joseph Stalin, "Death solves all problems. No man, no problem." In a matter of minutes, the world was going to have one less problem.

Realizing the magnitude of his decision, Director Sloan gave the order personally. "Approval granted. You are a go."

From their hide inside the Syrian farmhouse, Ron Foster checked the flags atop the building through his spotter's scope one last time. "No change in conditions. Send it when ready."

Placing the crosshairs of the scope's reticle on the back of Teplov's head, Shannon slowed his breathing even more and began taking slack out of the trigger. Just as it was about to break, the Russian suddenly pushed back from the desk and stood. Shannon released the pressure on the trigger and watched as Teplov crossed the room and opened a safe. He retrieved a couple of items before closing its door and returning to the desk.

With his target back in place, Shannon muttered under his breath, "Let's try this again," and began re-applying pressure to the trigger. He was so focused on his breathing and the other variables involved in long-distance precision shooting that the actual shot came as a surprise. Muscle memory took over, and in a move rehearsed thousands of times on the range and in real-world situations, Shannon worked the bolt to chamber a fresh round and regain his sight picture as the three hundred grain Sierra Match King bullet sped toward its target at twenty-eight-hundred feet per second.

Finished with his planning session, Teplov logged off and closed the laptop's lid. Thoughts of spending his days on a warm, sandy beach somewhere in the South Pacific or Caribbean ran through is head moments before the images were erased by the high-velocity round fired from Shannon's rifle. The Russian's brain matter and skull fragments covered the far wall, causing the sniper to almost feel sorry for the next unfortunate bastard to enter the office looking for their boss. What they would find would be the headless body of Vadim Teplov slumped forward into the growing pool of blood spreading across his desk.

"Target is down," Shannon transmitted as he sat up and stretched the tired muscles in his back. Then, without an ounce of regret, he unloaded the rifle and made it safe before going about the task of breaking down the site.

CHAPTER 54

COLONEL KONSTANTIN GUSAROV sucked on the filter of his cigarette until he felt the embers' heat begin to singe the skin on the inside of his fingers. Having inhaled everything it had to offer, he snuffed out the butt in an overflowing ashtray then immediately reached for the crumpled pack next to it and lit another.

Under the best of circumstances his mood could be described as surly. But with recent events, namely the lackluster performance of his men against the unknown American adversaries, he was even more volatile than usual. As the commander of all Alpha Group units in Syria he was unaccustomed to failures on the battlefield. Maybe his men had been in country for such an extended period that they were starting to perform down to the level of their competition. The phenomenon was a common occurrence in sports where a team with superior talent will take the victory for granted and lose to a lesser opponent. Perhaps the long stretches of combat against a horde of rag-tag rebels and religious fanatics had reduced his men's effectiveness when it came to encounters with highly trained counterparts like the Americans.

A knock at the door disturbed his quiet contemplation. The interruption, even though he had personally summoned the individual on the other side of the door, only exacerbated his already bad mood. Gusarov sucked the fresh cigarette to the halfway point before bellowing, "Enter!"

Captain Gennady Kalugin stepped through the door and closed it behind him before crossing the room to his boss's desk. He offered a crisp salute, then said, "You wished to see me, sir?"

"Sit," Gusarov growled, ignoring the salute.

Kalugin cringed inwardly at the old man's tone and did as he was told. Realizing that anything he said at this point would probably only make matters worse, he chose to remain silent and let the senior officer initiate the conversation.

Gusarov polished off the cigarette and reached for the pack once more as he exhaled the smoke into the low-hanging cloud that obscured the ceiling of his office. Leaning forward, he pushed a manila folder across the desk, then slouched back in his chair and thumbed his lighter while giving Kalugin a moment to look over the contents.

Finally, Gusarov broke the silence. "The signals section has intercepted communications between one of the rebel group's scout elements and their headquarters." Pointing to the folder with his nicotine stained fingers, he continued, "The transcript is on the third page."

Kalugin's demeanor became more energized as he read the printout of the conversation. One of the scouts had made the mistake of mentioning a meeting with a CIA team who had been training and arming the group. His first mistake was having the conversation over an unencrypted cellular network. Discussing the location of the CIA safe house was his second.

Looking up from the printout, he asked, "Do they think it's the same team that attacked the airport?" Kalugin would like nothing more than to have a chance to redeem himself against the Americans who killed his men in the operation to rescue Tariq Kabbani.

Gusarov waived his hand dismissively, "Does it really matter whether or not it's the same team, Gennady? Don't let your desire for revenge cloud your judgement. The key takeaway here is that in light of the Americans' involvement in thwarting Moscow's plans in the Middle East, we've been given the opportunity to start targeting their CIA and Special Forces outposts directly. The attacks will start small and be attributable to Assad's forces for plausible deniability, but make no mistake, we will be the driving force behind the attacks." He paused to take a long pull on his cigarette. Exhaling the blue cloud of smoke, he continued, "I'm giving you the chance to lead this initial assault…if you're up to the task."

Ever since the firefight in Salkhad, the Americans had gotten the best of him at every turn. Kalugin would do his job in a professional manner, but that didn't mean he wouldn't take some degree of pleasure in his work if he happened to come across those same men at some point in the future. Ignoring the not so subtle dig he flipped through the rest of the material in the folder. Impressed with what he saw, Kalugin had to admit the folks in the intel shop had put together a solid target package.

"Hand pick your team, then come back and see me this afternoon. I'll be expecting a briefing on your ops plan before you launch."

Taking his cue that the meeting was over, Kalugin stood and gathered the material, stuffing it back into the folder. He offered another crisp salute, then turned and headed for the door, anxious to get on with selecting his men and planning the mission. Going up against the Americans would be a challenge, but it was one he knew they were up for.

"Gennady..." Gusarov called as Kalugin reached for the doorknob.

He stopped and turned to face the colonel. "Sir?"

"If your entire team is wiped out again, you had better be counted among the dead. Run from a fight a second time and I'll put a bullet in you myself."

*

Looking down on the small house from the ridge north of the valley, Kalugin pressed the push-to-talk button attached to the front of his plate carrier. "Anything new?"

The helicopter crew had inserted the team far enough from the target that the sound of the rotors wouldn't alert the unsuspecting Americans. But there was always a trade off, and tonight's was an arduous march through the An-Nusayriyah Mountain range which lay approximately twenty miles to the north and east of the air base at Bassel al-Assad International Airport.

Touching down just after midnight, the men had been on the march for the last few hours before finally reaching their layup point. In a practiced routine, they set up a secure perimeter before taking a moment to grab a snack and suck down some water from the bladders incorporated into their rucks. It was from here that they would make their final checks of equipment, communications, and intelligence prior to advancing on their target.

Even though the temperature was in the low-forties, Kalugin had worked up a sweat humping the roughly seventy-five pounds of gear he carried for the mission. But now that they had stopped moving, the combination of a damp uniform and the cool night air sent a shiver through his body as he waited to hear from the crew of the Ilyushin Il-20 reconnaissance plane orbiting above.

"Looks quiet," came the reply from the flight crew. "Nothing out of the ordinary to report. Thermals do show the house is warm so I would assume it's inhabited."

"Good copy."

Thinking back to the overhead imagery he had reviewed during the mission planning, Kalugin was surprised the Americans had chosen this spot to set up their base of operations. There was only one way in or out of the valley, a poorly maintained dirt road by the looks of it. Not exactly a recipe for a quick getaway if the location was compromised. Perhaps the men from the CIA were counting on the remoteness and clandestine nature of the site for protection. *Not a terrible strategy,* he thought. But if he were the one picking the site, he would want more than one exfil option. Kalugin had already proven his ability to find and attack sites the CIA wanted to keep hidden. Just ask the personnel running the drone base in Jordan. Oh, that's right. You can't. Because he killed them all before making off with the Reaper.

He took one last swig of water from his drinking tube then gave the order to move out. The men appreciated the short break, but it was time to do what they came here for. The point man led the way off the ridgeline and each member of the eight-man team fell into a patrol column as they headed into what would soon become the valley of death.

CHAPTER 55

SURROUNDED BY TALL evergreens, the patrol fanned out and each man took a knee, scanning their individual sectors. The sounds of the branches rustling in the breeze masked any noise the squad made while moving to their objective. But the rustling cut both ways. It would also conceal the sound of anyone tracking the team or setting up an ambush, so the men were hypervigilant while pulling security.

If tonight's mission was simply to kill the Americans, it could have been completed easily enough by dropping a bomb through the roof of the safehouse, Kalugin knew. But this was about more than that. It was a test, a test of his leadership and continued ability to accomplish the missions assigned to Alpha Group. And he could not fail. The outcome of this operation would determine his fate, one way or another.

Reaching the edge of the wood line, Kalugin checked in with the crew of the Il-20 one last time while scanning the area through the night-vision device attached to his helmet. Confirming there were no changes at the target location, he gave the order, and once again the point man led the way as the Alpha assaulters emerged from the forest and advanced single file on the safe house. The men moved at a brisk pace, covering the distance quickly to minimize their exposure crossing the open ground.

As the point man closed to within fifty meters of the house, Kalugin was feeling more confident with each step that they had managed to maintain the element of surprise. Moments later, that confidence was shattered as he heard what sounded like the ignition of a rocket motor somewhere in the distance to his right. He turned his head just in time to see the glow of the solid-fuel engine break through the wooded canopy and streak into the sky. He was about to yell, "Incoming!" thinking they were coming under indirect fire, but he held off as his eyes followed the projectile's trajectory. "What the…," he muttered under his breath. Then it dawned on him. *The Ilyushin!* He was reaching for his radio to warn the aircrew but was interrupted by a brief flash that lit up the valley. It was immediately followed by an ear-splitting explosion that enveloped the operator leading the column. Blood and bits of what was once the point man blew backward, covering the next man in line with his remains.

*

Joe looked on through the green hue of the night-vision scope mounted atop his rifle, as one by one the Russians emerged from the woods north of the house. He counted eight, the same number of men he had with him. It would be a fair fight then. *Well…almost,* he thought. Joe wasn't really into fighting fair. No, he was more into winning. And in this game, winning meant killing the enemy before they had a chance to kill you.

Captain Gennady Kalugin, the man leading the patrol in the valley below, had inflicted irreparable damage on CIA operations of late. His list of transgressions was impressive and began with the trigger pull that killed Greg Jacobs during the attack in Salkhad, the same attack that had resulted in the grievous injuries to Mike McCredy and Kevin Chang. He personally ordered the execution of every man and woman on the drone base in Jordan and conducted the brutal interrogation and torture of Tariq Kabbani. And those were the only operations the Agency was aware of. There was no doubt in Joe's mind that Kalugin had done similar things to numerous people in the past, and if left unchecked, would do so again in the future. He was not going to let that happen. Kalugin would die tonight, and Joe was more than happy to be the one to do it.

Taking his eyes away from the patrol for a moment, Joe switched to the scope's thermal mode and traversed the ridgeline across the valley, looking for snipers or maybe a small fireteam left behind in an overwatch position. Seeing none, he keyed his mic, "Take the shot."

To his left, at a spot on the west ridgeline with an opening in the trees, Chris Ryan emerged from under an insulated tarp designed to hide the body's heat signature from thermal imaging. Standing to his full height, he hefted a five-foot-long, dark-green tube onto his right shoulder. Chris activated the battery pack and powered up the integral sight and IFF antenna, then aimed the FIM-92 Stinger surface-to-air missile at a point in the sky. Once the tracking system had acquired its target, he pressed the trigger on the pistol grip and launched the missile toward the unsuspecting Russian reconnaissance plane.

The Stinger's warhead struck the underside of the Il-20's starboard wing between the two turbo-prop engines and there was a bright flash as the explosives in the missile's nosecone detonated. The initial blast was followed immediately by a much larger explosion as the fuel stored in the plane's wing tanks ignited, ripping the wing apart and shearing the engines from their mounts. It wasn't long before the rest of the doomed plane followed the debris in a death spiral toward the earth.

Chris threw the spent launch tube to the side and went prone behind his HK416 rifle. Shrugging off their tarps, Ground Branchers Ron Foster and the Lurch-like Abrams were positioned to his left, each with their own rifles at the ready. Ivy, the thickly muscled former Green Beret and third member of Foster's team, was to Chris's right with the stock of an FN MK 48 MOD 1 light machine gun tucked into his shoulder. The titanium legs of the bipod were extended and a two-hundred round belt of 7.62x51-millimeter armor-piercing ammo in the box magazine was locked and loaded. He was ready to send some hate downrange.

With the Russians distracted by the missile launch, Joe set off the claymore to initiate the ambush. The point man was the closest to the mine when it detonated, and never knew what hit him. His body disintegrated as hundreds of steel ball bearings passed through flesh and bone. The second man in the patrol column was down as well, writhing on the ground in pain, screaming something in Russian Joe couldn't understand.

Mike McCredy leaned into the stock and opened up with his own MK 48, firing controlled bursts into the valley below. Through his NVGs, Joe watched the classic ambush unfold as tracers from the machine guns burned holes through the Alpha operators or skipped off rocks and ricocheted into the night. John Roberts, who never went on a mission without his trusty grenade launcher, lobbed a 40-millimeter high explosive round into the men's midst, sending deadly shrapnel flying in every direction.

And Kevin Chang was firing away with his rifle, calm and collected as if it was just another day on the range.

Hearing the same devastation emanating from Chris's fireteam echoing through the valley, Joe almost felt sorry for the Russians caught in the buzz saw of the ambush. Still on thermal mode, Joe angled his scope down into the valley. Men who were still alive registered white against a dark background. The glow of dead or dying men faded as their core temperatures dropped and their bodies cooled. There were a few Russians who appeared to be alive, but he couldn't imagine they were in any condition to fight, so Joe called for a cease-fire over the radio. The valley fell silent except for the sound of metal on metal as his men took advantage of the pause in the action to reload their weapons.

Leaving Ivy and Mike in place to provide overwatch, Joe gave the order, and the two fireteams left their positions and converged on the kill zone.

CHAPTER 56

KALUGIN LAY FLAT on his back in the cool grass, looking up at the brightly twinkling stars. He knew he was severely injured but was surprised by the lack of pain. Perhaps it was due to a heavy 7.62 round that had hit him in the stomach just below his body armor. Had it severed his spinal cord? Was that why he didn't feel anything from the chest down?

As he lay there waiting for death, Kalugin replayed the last few minutes in his mind. This whole mission had been nothing more than an elaborate trap set up by the CIA men he was sent there to kill. He appreciated the elegance of the plan, but his thoughts kept going back to Colonel Gusarov's last words as he left the office. *"If your entire team is wiped out again, you had better be counted among the dead. Run from a fight a second time and I'll put a bullet in you myself."* Had Gusarov suspected this was a trap all along and willingly sent him here to die? He would never know the answer to that question.

Movement to the left caught Kalugin's attention, and he groped around in the grass for his weapon. It had fallen just out of reach, the sling severed by the bullet as it passed through his torso. Instinctively, he reached for the pistol secured in the holster on his chest rig. But just as his fingers wrapped around its familiar grip, a booted foot pressed down on his hand, preventing him from drawing the weapon.

He heard an American voice say, "Don't even think about it, Ivan." Paralyzed and lacking the strength or energy to continue the fight, Kalugin relaxed and laid his head back on the cool grass. Standing above him like the Grim Reaper, the man called out, "Over here, boss." Moments later, a second man approached and knelt beside him. Locking his night-vision in the up position, the man removed his Ops-Core helmet and set it in the grass beside them. In the moonlight, Kalugin could see the man's dark red hair, and his thoughts went immediately to the firefight atop the citadel in Salkhad. With everything that had happened since, the engagement seemed as if it had taken place a lifetime ago.

Joe motioned toward the boot holding Kalugin's hand in place on the pistol grip. "Can I have him remove his foot from your chest or are you going to be a problem?"

Kalugin managed a weak nod of his head and the man released the pressure on his hand. Letting his arm flop to the side he said, "Our paths have crossed before, have they not?"

"You had me dead to rights on that hilltop in Salkhad but chose to shoot the man I was dragging instead."

A coughing spasm caused blood to erupt from Kalugin's mouth and he gasped for air. "In light of recent events, it would appear I made a mistake that day."

"I guess you did," Joe agreed. The conversation was interrupted when a third man approached.

Reporting on the Russian casualties, Chris said, "Five dead and two wounded." Motioning toward Kalugin, he added, "Correction, make that three wounded, counting this guy."

"How bad?" Joe asked.

Chris shook his head back and forth. "With the severity of their injuries and the remoteness of the location, there's not much we can do other than give them something for the pain so they don't suffer."

"Do it," Joe said, and Chris disappeared into the darkness.

"Thank you for taking care of my men," Kalugin managed in between another blood-tinged coughing fit. "I can't say I would have done the same had the roles been reversed."

"I guess compassion, even for one's adversaries, is one of the fundamental differences between our countries, and our cultures." Joe paused for a moment before asking, "How about you? Would you like something for the pain?"

Kalugin shook his head weakly. "Don't waste the meds on me. There's a good chance you may be needing them yourself before the night is over." Wetting his lips, he asked. "What time is it?"

Thinking the statement sounded ominous, Joe pushed up the sleeve of his jacket and checked his watch. "Zero three thirty-five. Why?"

Feeling he owed the American for showing empathy for his wounded men, Kalugin said, "I was supposed to check in five minutes ago. Missing my time hack automatically triggered the QRF."

Joe's stomach fell. His textbook ambush was about to turn into a mad scramble for survival. "How big is the element?"

The Russian didn't answer right away. He was beginning to fade in and out of consciousness, teetering precariously on that razor's edge between life and death. "A…a hundred men, give or take. Mostly Syrian army regulars, but they're being supplemented by twenty-five or thirty Wagner mercenaries."

"How much time do we have?"

"Ten minutes," Kalugin exhaled as his head lolled to the side. "Fifteen, if you're lucky."

Joe keyed his mic and raised the pilot of the Predator circling overhead. "I have an unconfirmed report of a large hostile force heading my direction. You seeing anything from up there?"

"Roger that, Spartan," came the pilot's reply. "We're estimating one hundred. Repeat, one-zero-zero hostiles. They're moving in a combination of troop transports and gun trucks with mounted Dishkas." He was referring to the Russian-made 12.7-millimeter DShK heavy machine gun, the same weapon that wreaked havoc on Joe's team and cost Mike his leg in Salkhad.

"How close are they?"

"No more than ten minutes out."

Son of a bitch! "Is your drone carrying anything that can slow them down a bit?"

"Negative, Spartan. This bird was re-tasked mid-flight to support your op. I'd already fired my ordnance on another target and didn't have time to return to base to rearm. The best I can do is keep an eye on them and give you constant updates on their position."

The reply wasn't what Joe was hoping to hear. He ordered the men to prepare for a hasty departure, and everyone except Kevin, who hung back to pull security for his team leader, sprinted for the vehicles pre-positioned in the woods.

Keying his MBITR multiband radio, Joe hailed the duty officer in the operations center on the sixth floor of the headquarters building at Langley. He waited as patiently as possible under the circumstances as he was patched through to the person he was looking for.

The soothing sound of Frank Copenhaver's voice came through his earpiece, "Hey, Joe. What can I do for you?" Copenhaver, a retired pilot who worked as a liaison between the CIA and the Air Force listened intently as Joe laid out the situation and what he needed. "Got it. Now move your ass. I'll call when I have something lined up."

Joe looked down and was about to say something to Kalugin but stopped himself when he saw the Russian's lifeless eyes staring up at the stars. Realizing there was nothing more to be done for his adversary, he turned his attention to his team's survival.

CHAPTER 57

THE TWO TOYOTA Hi-Lux pickups were tucked into the trees on the southern ridgeline. Foster and his men had their own vehicle stashed on the western ridge and would be executing their own evac plan at any moment. Joe did a quick headcount, ensuring his team was whole, then stole a glance back over his shoulder.

Headlights belonging to the vehicles carrying the Syrian and Russian quick reaction force illuminated the valley as the column made its way along the single dirt road. Roving spotlights swept over the safe house, then converged on a single area as their operators focused on the grizzly sight of wrecked bodies littering the ambush site.

Joe keyed his radio, "They found the bodies. It's time to go."

Before the mission, Chris had pulled the fuses that powered the trucks' lighting in the hopes that staying dark would help with their escape. But there was nothing he could do to minimize the noise of the engines, and he cringed inwardly as he and Mike turned the ignition keys.

While the QRF couldn't see the trucks in the darkness, all heads turned as the rumble of engines reverberated into the valley. On orders from their commander, soldiers atop two of the gun trucks swiveled their Dishkas in the direction of the sound and opened fire. The other soldiers let go with long bursts from their AK-47s, and a fusillade of lead flew toward the Toyotas like a swarm of killer bees.

Trees splintered and dark, rich soil kicked up all around the trucks as Chris put the pickup in gear and stomped the gas pedal to the floor. The all-terrain tires spun for a few rotations before gaining traction, and with Mike falling in behind him, the two trucks crested the ridgeline. With the mountain shielding them from the barrage, Chris eased up on the gas and navigated his way down a path that was little more than a single-track mountain bike trail. He wondered for the briefest of moments if anyone in Syria rode mountain bikes but quickly pushed the thought from his mind. Reaching the end of the trail, Chris brought the truck to a stop ten meters from where it intersected with a dirt road. Joe hailed the Predator pilot for an update while the trucks idled in the darkness. Again, the answer was not what he wanted to hear. This guy was just full of bad news.

"Looks like they split their forces, Spartan. A couple of the gun trucks are advancing from your left. They're roughly five hundred meters from your position."

Doing a quick calculation in his head, Joe figured they could pull out in front of the convoy and use the twists and turns of the dirt road to stay out of sight. Then they could lose their pursuers in the maze of streets and alleys that crisscrossed the nearby town that, for the life of him, he could not remember its name. So far, the darkness, combined with the lack of lights on the Hi-Luxes, seemed to be working in their favor. That ended when a roving spotlight on the convoy's lead vehicle flashed across the side of Chris's truck as he pulled out onto the dirt road. When the Syrian soldier realized what he had seen, he snapped the beam back and locked onto the Toyota.

"Five hundred meters, my ass," Joe growled. "Go! Go! Go!"

With a target illuminated, the Dishka gunner in the back let go with a burst from the big machine gun. Chris floored it and the truck shot out of the woods, its backend fishtailing back and forth on the dirt road before he gained control and increased speed to throw off the gunner's aim.

Mike matched the acceleration, and the move probably saved their lives as the Dishka's heavy rounds tore ragged holes in the rear quarter panels of the truck's bed instead of penetrating into the cab.

The gunner continued targeting the trucks with short bursts, but the combination of their speed and his own vehicle bouncing around on the unpaved dirt road made it nearly impossible to put accurate fire on the fleeing Toyotas. Fueled by anger and adrenaline, the convoy of Syrian soldiers and Russian mercenaries raced down the road, eager to exact a measure of revenge on the men who ambushed and killed their comrades. Errant rounds whizzed by the fleeing pickups as a fresh volley of automatic weapons fire erupted from the gun trucks. The Dishka gunner resumed firing, and the big gun's thundering booms drowned out the distinctive cracks of the AK-47s.

Joe glanced at the GPS unit suction cupped to the dash, searching for a turnoff that would get them out of the line of fire. His eyes flashed back and forth between the unit and the windshield as he compared what was being displayed on the small screen with the reality of the terrain outside the vehicle. Finally, he saw an opening and said, "Take the next left! It should lead us into town."

"Got it," Chris acknowledged. He slowed to make the turn onto the narrow track and was accelerating when a wooden fence filled the view through his night vision goggles. Keeping his foot on the gas, he yelled, "I'm assuming that wasn't showing up on the Garmin?"

Mike kept his truck tucked in behind Chris's, and the two Toyotas burst through the fence, sending splintered two-by-fours cartwheeling through the air. The front end of Chris's truck took the brunt of the damage and its right headlight was shattered by a section of fence post. *No biggie,* he thought. *We're not using the headlights anyway.*

In the passenger seat of the second truck, John heard a loud bang and felt the truck shudder. "What the...?"

Instead of accelerating as expected, the Toyota refused to respond, even though Mike had the gas pedal pressed to the floor. John wondered what had happened to their otherwise perfectly good truck. Had a piece of the fence or a good-sized rock kicked up into the undercarriage and broken something lose? Or had the engine block taken a direct hit from one of the Dishka's 12.7-millimeter rounds? Regardless of the cause, he knew their ride was done for as it continued to lose speed and coasted to a stop.

John keyed his radio, "Joe, our truck is down. We need to bail."

Without a word, Chris slammed on the brakes and brought his truck to a skidding halt. He threw it into reverse and headed back to retrieve his teammates.

Kevin and John were already out pulling security as Chris brought his Hi-Lux to a stop. Mike was lingering behind, and Kevin wondered what was taking him so long. "Come on, Mike. Shake a leg."

"So now we're making leg jokes, are we?" the big operator said, as he exited the truck's cab, then turned and threw something into the front seat.

"Too soon?" Kevin asked

Moments later the night was filled with a blinding, white-hot light as the thermite grenade began melting the bodywork. Realizing what was about to happen, John and Kevin turned and sprinted to Chris's truck. They piled into the back seat as Mike hopped over the tailgate and dove into the bed.

Chris took off just as the heat created by the grenade's aluminum and iron oxide mixture contacted the fuel in the stricken truck's gas tank. The explosion sent a ball of fire into the air, momentarily turning night into day.

Consulting the GPS on the dash, and with the help of the Predator pilot's voice in his ear giving turn-by-turn directions, Chris steered the truck into the town with the hopes of losing the soldiers and mercs in the warren of narrow streets and alleys. Feeling the building's walls on either side of them, he breathed a quick sigh of relief, but the respite was short-lived when headlights filled the rearview mirror. "Damn, these guys are determined."

He continued a hundred meters on his current heading, then made a left and zig-zagged through what looked to be a shopping district. Moments later, they exited onto a paved road that looped around the town. The good news about being on the improved roadway was that he could accelerate and use the Toyota's speed to their advantage. The bad news was that they were back in the open and exposed to the enemy fire.

Without any obstructions to block his view or his field of fire, the machine-gunner in the lead truck resumed the assault. Rounds screamed past the Toyota, and those that didn't pummel anything in their path, snapped and whistled as they ricocheted into the distance.

One of the rounds demolished the truck's side view mirror, sending shards of glass and plastic flying through the cab. Showered by the debris, Chris flinched and jerked the steering wheel, causing the truck to fishtail. The violent whipping motion caught Mike off-guard and sent him sliding across the bed. His right side took the brunt of the blow as he slammed against the inside of the rear quarter panel. Two more rounds penetrated the tailgate and exited through the opposite side of the bed, mere inches from where he'd been sitting a few seconds ago.

"Enough!" Mike screamed into the wind. Having his fill of being shot at, he braced his feet against the wheel wells protruding into the bed and pushed with his legs until he was sitting upright with his back against the cab. Shouldering his MK 48, Mike thumbed the selector switch to auto and dumped a long burst into the lead gun truck.

One of the headlights exploded and the patrol-car-like spotlight went out as well. Mike wasn't sure but thought he might have seen steam spewing out of the truck's grill. Feeling a little better about himself, he settled down and began firing one controlled burst after another into the truck's windshield.

The Syrian driver swerved back and forth across the road, trying to stay out of the stream of lead coming his way. While his tactic was somewhat effective at dodging Mike's rounds, it was also working to the Americans' advantage. The erratic driving was preventing the gunner from firing the Dishka. He was too busy hanging on for dear life to keep from being thrown out of the back of the truck.

Mike felt a tap on his shoulder and turned to see John's face in the sliding rear window.

"Here," John said, passing his grenade launcher through the opening. "There's an HE round in the chamber."

With the lull in Mike's fire, the gunner could resume his barrage. But the driver had no way of knowing about the grenade launcher, or that his attempt to get the gunner a clear shot was going to be a fatal mistake, for all of them.

Mike shouldered the weapon and pulled the trigger. The 40-millimeter round soared unseen in the darkness toward the oncoming truck. It punched through the windshield and exploded in the cab, ripping apart the driver and the rest of the truck's occupants. The violence of the explosion knocked the gunner off balance, and he lost his grip on the big machine gun. His fingers grasped desperately, reaching for anything to help him remain in the bed, but he tumbled into the darkness and fell under the wheels of the next vehicle in the convoy. Unable to avoid his comrade, the driver grimaced as his truck rolled over the gunner, grinding his mangled body into something resembling roadkill.

CHAPTER 58

STILL NAVIGATING, JOE said, "Take a right in a hundred meters. That'll get us back into town and we can try to lose them on the back streets."

Chris made the turn and sped through an alley barely wide enough for the pickup. He had already lost one mirror to the Dishka and was sure a wall was going to claim the other any minute. The alley was too narrow for the military vehicles, so they diverted to the right. The drivers seemed to know the town like the backs of their hands and stuck to a larger road that paralleled the alley.

Hidden from sight by the two and three story, flat-roofed buildings, Joe thought they might have lost the Syrians. But those hopes were dashed when the alley merged back onto the main road and they were greeted by the clattering sounds of multiple AK-47s.

Joe yelled back over his shoulder, "Mike, discourage them from getting too close." Mike complied and continued his harassing fire.

As the road widened, the smaller vehicles made way for one of the troop transports to move up the center of the road. In the bed stood two Wagner mercenaries. Both were veterans of Russia's Spetsnaz units who had made the jump into the world of private military contracting to cash in on their unique skillset. Each man had a rocket propelled grenade launcher on his shoulder and was taking aim at the Toyota Hi-Lux full of Americans.

From his position in the pickup's bed, facing back toward the vehicles, Mike had a front row seat to the action. At the sight of the twin RPG launchers, he yelled a warning to the other men in the truck, then found himself unconsciously inching lower and lower behind the tailgate as he continued the barrage with his light machine gun. With just his eyes and the top of his head peeking over the top of the tailgate, he resembled one of those Kilroy Was Here drawings made famous during World War II.

The mercenary on the left was the first to fire but his aim was off, and the high-explosive projectile whooshed over the top of the Toyota, leaving a trail of gray smoke in its wake. The warhead hit a tree and exploded with a thundering boom, showering the truck with shrapnel and splinters the size of number two pencils. The second rocketeer mocked his partner for the errant shot, letting him know he would be expecting the bottle of vodka they had wagered when they returned to base. When he was done with the good-natured ribbing, the second Wagner man adjusted his aiming point based on his colleague's miss and fired.

Once again, Mike screamed, "RPG!" vying to be heard over the wind noise and the constant cracks of enemy gunfire and his own MK 48.

Chris increased his speed and swerved to the left, using every inch of the road to make them a harder target. Getting precariously close to the shoulder, the tires ground into the gravel, searching for traction to keep the truck from sliding sideways into a drainage ditch. He was bringing it back to the right when the warhead skipped off the pavement and detonated under the rear end of the Toyota. Everyone felt the truck shudder as the explosion sheared off the right-rear wheel and sent its remains bouncing off into the darkness. The shockwave blew out all the windows, sending tiny bits of glass flying through the cab. Illuminated by the troop transport's headlights, they sparkled like fireflies.

The force of the blast and the loss of a wheel caused the Toyota's back end to lose traction. Chris worked the wheel for all he was worth, doing his best to regain control of the vehicle, but they were going too fast and his efforts only seemed to make the problem worse. The truck veered from ditch to ditch, whipping the men inside back and forth against one another.

The Toyota careened back into the right lane and left the road, giving the men inside a weightless sensation as the pickup soared through the air, a feeling that ended abruptly when it fell back to earth with a jarring crunch of metal. Try as he might, Mike lost his battle to remain in the bed as the truck bounced through a small plot of farmland and was sent flying through the air like a cowboy thrown from the back of an angry bull.

The Hi-Lux managed to travel about fifty meters on sheer momentum, digging a jagged groove in the plowed soil before it finally came to a halt. Except for the hiss of steam escaping from under the hood and the painful groaning of the engine, silence filled the cab. The lack of noise was almost deafening after the constant gunfire, revving engines, and the explosions from the RPGs.

Each man took a moment to check himself for injuries. Finding nothing major, they exited the destroyed truck. Joe scanned the surroundings through his NVGs and settled on a rocky outcropping seventy-five meters away as their destination. It was the only cover in sight and a place where his small team of operators could make a stand. He just hoped it wasn't a last stand like the men at the Alamo.

Realizing his best friend was no longer in the truck's bed, John keyed his radio. "Mike...where are you?"

There was no answer at first. But after repeated tries, Mike's voice finally sputtered, "Looking for my goddamned leg. It came off when I hit the ground and tumbled through the field like a fucking crash-test dummy." The comment made everyone on the team laugh, despite the dire nature of their situation.

John rushed over and helped Mike up. Throwing an arm over his friend's shoulder, Mike fumed, "That's two legs I've lost in this jacked-up country."

Joe wasn't sure if the force of soldiers and mercenaries had lost sight of them when the truck left the road or if they were dismounting to conduct a frontal assault on the field. Regardless, he took advantage of the lull in the action and directed the team to the rocks. With their backs to the hillside, each man took up a position, using the boulders for cover.

Joe moved from man to man, checking in with each member of the team. Other than Mike's missing prosthetic and the ammo he had expended on the convoy, they were in surprisingly decent shape, given the circumstances. Returning to the spot he'd chosen to command their defense of this tiny spit of rocky ground, he checked his own ammo and equipment, then settled in for the chaos of combat that was sure to begin at any moment.

CHAPTER 59

THE COMBINED FORCE of Syrian Arab Army regulars and Russian Wagner Group mercenaries advanced across the field. The chase had been long and hard, costing them friends and colleagues along the way. It was time to exact a measure of revenge and put this hunt to an end.

Seeing the ghostly images displayed in his night vision, Kevin's face twisted with concern. "I don't think we have enough bullets."

Joe had to admit that seeing this many men coming to kill his team was a bit unnerving. He felt the need to say something profound like, "Don't fire till you see the whites of their eyes," but nothing came to mind. Instead, he ordered, "Pick your targets and be disciplined with your fire. Help is on the way. We just have to hold out until it arrives."

He hadn't heard back from Copenhaver and wanted desperately to check in and get a status update. But he held off, knowing it would be a distraction that would only serve to take the air liaison officer away from organizing the support that would save their lives. Joe instinctively ducked behind the boulder he was using for cover as an AK round snapped past his head. All thoughts of calling headquarters were pushed aside, at least for the time being.

That one shot had the effect of a starter's gun at a track meet. Syrian soldiers charged the American position, some firing from the hip as they ran. As Joe instructed, the small team of operators controlled their fire, and he could hear the ones and twos of their aimed shots, supplemented by short bursts from Mike's machine gun, as he watched men fall on the field below.

Rounds from the advancing force pelted the rocks, spraying the men with fragments of lead and stone. Moments later, an RPG steaked overhead and slammed into a rocky overhang that directed the shrapnel down into the Americans' position. None of the men was seriously injured by the explosion, but none was spared, either. John bled from a nasty cut across his cheek, and Chris's left pant leg was dotted with blood spots where dozens of tiny metal slivers had entered his thigh. Mike, Kevin, and even Joe were all bleeding from one body part or another.

A flash of movement to Joe's right caught his eye as he was checking on his men's injuries. With their attention focused on the Syrian soldiers' frontal assault, three of the Wagner men had worked their way around the rocks and were sneaking up on the team's flank. One of the men fired a burst, raking the rocks mere inches from Joe's head. Dropping to a knee, Joe raised his rifle and put two rounds into the man's chest. The impact to his body armor knocked him off balance but didn't put him down. Joe remedied the situation by double-tapping two more through the bridge of the Russian's nose.

Sweeping to his left, Joe settled the optic's red dot on the second Wagner man's head and pressed the trigger. *Two down. Where'd the third guy go?* He tried to listen for sounds of movement, but the almost-constant automatic weapons fire and the ear-splitting blasts of RPG and grenade explosions made it next to impossible. Crouching to stay out of the main force's line of fire, Joe moved toward the spot where he had last seen the three men together. As he approached a large rectangular rock that looked as if it has been precision cut for a landscaping project, a three-round burst from the mercenary's AK-74 stitched across his chest. Joe's trauma plate caught the first two 5.45-millimter rounds, but the third passed through the meaty muscle just above his collarbone. The impact buckled Joe's knees and he stumbled like a drunk on the uneven ground before falling flat on his back.

Pleased with himself, the Russian left his position of cover and walked toward Joe with a triumphant grin spreading across his face. Surely, he would receive a special bonus for killing the American.

Joe's left shoulder was on fire. Feeling as if he'd been stuck with a hot poker, the pain radiated up the side of his neck and ran all the way down his arm to his fingertips. He took the fact that he could feel the pain as a good sign, even though he couldn't make his left arm or hand work. His brain was sending the signals, telling it what to do, but the arm would not respond.

Looking up, Joe saw the Russian approaching, and even through his night vision goggles could see the shit-eating grin on the guy's face. It reminded him of a trophy hunter walking up on his prey. Joe groped around with his good hand, determined to turn the tables on this scenario. *Keep coming, buddy,* Joe silently encouraged the Wagner man as his fingers brushed against the H&K. *I've got a little something in store for you.*

When the man closed to within five meters, clearly relishing the impending kill, the fingers of Joe's right hand wrapped tightly around his rifle's pistol grip, and he thumbed the selector switch from Semi to Auto. In one fluid motion, he raised the weapon and pressed the trigger, the recoil taking the muzzle up and to the right across the man's torso.

The Russian's eyes were as big as saucers at the sight of a steady stream of rounds erupting from the business end of Joe's rifle. He let out a guttural scream as the first bullets entered his groin. With his shattered pelvis unable to support his weight, the man began to drop as rounds continued to walk their way up the man's chest, peppering the spare magazines and other equipment attached to his plate carrier. Most were absorbed by his body armor, but as the muzzle continued its rise, two rounds tore through the left side of the mercenary's neck. The Wagner man collapsed on his side, gasping like a goldfish out of water while feebly attempting to halt the flow of bright arterial blood surging from the wound with every beat of his heart. Moments later, he stopped moving altogether. His fight over.

Joe wasted no time. Raising himself to a sitting position, he pressed the mag release to dump the empty magazine and grabbed a spare from his chest rig. Performing the reload one-handed took a couple of extra seconds, but it was a maneuver he had practiced countless times on the range. He was starting to regain feeling in the fingers of his damaged left arm and it reminded him of the pins and needles sensation when his arm had gone to sleep. Unsure if he would be able to use it any time soon and not wanting it to flop around, he slid his left hand into the front pocket of his cargo pants.

Satisfied with his makeshift sling, he grimaced as he got to his knees, then stood and moved in a crouch along the team's defensive line to check on his men. Rounds snapped overhead and cracked against the rocks, showering him with bits of stone and lead. Hundreds of spent shell casings littered the ground and crunched underfoot with each step. Realizing the team must be running low on ammo, Joe distributed his spare magazines as he went from man to man. Looking at his friends, it wasn't lost on him that every one of them was bleeding from multiple wounds. The injuries hadn't dampened their fighting spirit, but Joe was getting the sinking feeling that they might have pushed their luck one too many times with this most recent trip to Syria. He had promised himself prior to the mission that if there were any casualties, they would all be taken by the other side. But that wasn't turning out to be the case. His men were fighting valiantly, but there were just too many of the Syrian and Russian soldiers. Feeling very much like Custer at the Battle of Little Bighorn, Joe knelt next to Chris and offered him a thirty-round mag.

"Keep it," Chris yelled to be heard over the din of combat. "I've got one or two left."

Joe nodded and turned to move back to his fighting position when he felt his friend's hand on his shoulder.

With a look of concern that was unusual for the habitual smartass, Chris took on a serious tone. "If there was ever a time when you were going to pull a miracle out of your ass, it should be now."

Fuck! Frank! Joe thought, chastising himself for not checking in sooner. He pressed the transmit button on his MBITR and raised the operations center at Langley.

Copenhaver's voice betrayed the calm tone one comes to expect from a career pilot. "Jesus! Where the hell have you been? I've been trying to get you on the line for the last ten minutes."

"Yeah, I've, uh, been a little busy," Joe said, resting the fore-end of his rifle on a large rock for support. He centered the optic's reticle on a soldier's chest and pressed the trigger. Watching the man drop, he searched for another target. "Please tell me you have some good news. We're low on ammo and are about to be overrun. I don't know how much longer we can hold out."

"In that case, let me introduce you to a friend of mine. He's aware of your situation and is going to take good care of you. Stand by. I'm patching him in now."

A new voice came through Joe's earpiece. "Good evening, Spartan.

Dragon Three Four here. I'm orbiting over your current position. What can I do for you?"

"That depends. What are you flying?"

In a slightly sarcastic tone, the pilot replied, "I happen to have a Ghostrider strapped to my ass. Will that do?"

The AC-130J was a state-of-the-art gunship based on the time-tested airframe of the famed C-130 Hercules cargo plane. Modified with the Precision Strike Package, the J, or Ghostrider version, was designed as a direct-fire platform to support troops in contact, escort convoys, or generally kill anything and everything in its sights.

Joe's heart skipped a beat at hearing the news that an AC-130 was on station, preparing to deal death and destruction from the sky in support of his team. *We just might survive this thing after all,* he thought, as a slight grin spread across his face. "Yes, sir. That'll do nicely."

Next, he ordered everyone to activate the infra-red strobes secured to the tops of their helmets. Getting a thumbs up from each man, he said, "Dragon, please confirm IR strobes."

"Stand by," the pilot said as he checked with his sensor operator. "Spartan, we count five. Repeat, five strobes."

"Good copy. Now, you see all those other guys? The ones without strobes?"

"Yep. There's a bunch of them, alright. Looks like you kicked over an anthill down there."

"Do me a favor and kill 'em all."

"Can do, Spartan. That order fits nicely into our job description. Tell your boys to keep their heads down. This fire mission is gonna be the definition of danger close."

CHAPTER 60

ALL OF JOE'S men did their best to make themselves very small. They flattened out and tucked in tight next to the boulders they hoped would protect them from the steel rain about to fall from the sky. Even though they knew it was coming, the impact of the first artillery round shocked even the most battle-hardened members of the team.

Successive explosions drowned out the screams of the Syrian soldiers and Russian mercenaries eviscerated by shrapnel or blown apart by the concussive force of the shockwaves. The ear-splitting explosions seemed to merge into one giant rumble and the ground shook as if they were in the middle of a catastrophic earthquake. Syrian soldiers and Russian mercenaries ran in every direction, attempting to find someplace to hide from the savagery unleashed by the Ghostrider orbiting the field. But there was nowhere they could run, nowhere they could hide from the sensors directing the precision fire on their positions. When the shelling from the AC-130's canons finally stopped shaking the earth, the field that had been the scene of a raging battle fell silent. A layer of pale gray smoke drifted across the ground, adding an eerie quality to the silence.

Shrugging an inch or two of dirt and debris off his back, Joe reached up and lifted the Peltor hearing protection off his ear. He listened for thirty seconds or so, straining to pick up any sounds of movement, or life. Hearing none, he rose to his knees and eased his head around the boulder that had shielded him from enemy fire and the aerial bombardment. The only way he could describe the spectacle laid out before him was that the apocalypse had been visited upon the men who had occupied the field.

Craters pockmarked the landscape. Men and machines that weren't blown apart by the Ghostrider's 105-millimeter artillery rounds were shredded by its 30-millimeter canons. Body parts littered the ground, mixed among broken weapons and burning vehicles. Not a soul, except for the five CIA operatives, was left alive on the killing ground.

As Joe's hearing gradually returned, he heard the pilot's voice hailing him on the radio. "Go ahead, Dragon."

The pilot's relief at finally getting a response was evident over the transmission. "You guys okay down there?"

After taking a moment to check on his team, Joe said, "Yeah. We're good."

Relieved that he hadn't annihilated the good guys along with the bad, the pilot's voice returned to the mundane tone of a dad dropping the kids at school. "We're showing the area clear of any activity. You're free to begin your exfiltration. We'll remain on station as top cover until you're out of the AO, just to be on the safe side."

"Roger that." Joe paused, still fixated on the devastation displayed on the field below his position. "Thanks for the assist. There are five guys down here who their lives to you and your crew."

"No worries, Spartan. Just doin' what we do. Glad we were able to get here in time. Now get ready to move. Your exfil is inbound."

My exfil? Joe thought. *What exfil?* The plan had been to make their way to the coast where a team from the Agency's Maritime Branch would meet them with a boat for the quick run across the Med to Cyprus. But with both of their vehicles destroyed, Joe and his team were going nowhere fast.

That's when he heard Chuck Jamison's familiar voice over his radio. "I'll be wheels down in five. Be ready. We're gonna make this quick."

"What are you doing here?" Joe asked, confused but thankful to hear his friend's voice.

"When Frank ordered up your aerial support, he figured you might be needing a ride, so he called me."

As thankful as Joe was to have a way out of this hellhole, he was worried about his friend's safety. The Syrians and Russians weren't likely to let this go down without a response. "Are you sure about this? What if some fighters are scrambled to come after you?"

"Oh, I wouldn't worry about that too much," Jamison replied

nonchalantly. "Frank arranged a little escort for me. There's a pair of F-35s in the neighborhood, salivating at the thought of a couple of Syrian or Russian pilots taking to the sky to come after me. Truth be told, I think the fighter jocks will be a little disappointed if they have to return to base without firing a shot."

Joe couldn't do anything but stand there and shake his head. With the help of Frank Copenhaver, the full resources of the Central Intelligence Agency and the United States Air Force had been mobilized to rescue his tiny five-man team of operators. The act only served to reinforce what he already knew, that despite all its technology and expensive weapons systems, what America truly valued most were its people. They, the men and women serving the country in every capacity, were America's most valuable resource. A tear leaked out of the corner of his eye and ran down his cheek, carving a path through the dirt and dried blood caked on his face.

True to his word, Chuck Jamison brought the de Havilland DHC-6 Twin Otter in right on time. Using night-vision goggles attached to his flight helmet, he kept the landing lights off and touched down on the road as easily as if it were a smooth, nine-thousand-foot runway at a major airport. He flared the props to bring the plane to a stop, then spun it around for the ensuing takeoff.

Joe was the first man to reach the plane. The door opened and he was greeted by the smiling face of Adam Elliot. Elliot was a member of the CIA's Office of Medical Services who happened to be deployed to the forward operating base Jamison was resupplying when the call from Copenhaver came through. He knew Joe and the guys and volunteered to come along in case there were any injuries. As it turned out there were plenty, so he began triaging their severity as the men helped each other into the plane.

Making sure each member of the team was accounted for, Joe was the last to climb aboard. He moved up the aisle and stuck his head in the cockpit. "Thanks for coming to get us, Chuck."

"Pulling your ass out of sketchy situations is turning into a full-time gig. But I guess that's why I get paid the big bucks. Ready to get outta here?"

"You better believe it."

Joe was strapping himself into a seat when he heard Mike ask, "What do you say we don't come back to Syria anytime soon? Every time we set foot in this godforsaken country people start trying to kill us."

Amen, Joe thought, as a wave of utter exhaustion crashed over his body. Leaning his head against the seat, his mind drifted back to the trip he had taken to Cancun. Remembering the warmth of the sun and the sparkling blue waters of the Caribbean, he decided it was time for another vacation. With the thoughts of sun and sand running through his mind, the Twin Otter raced down the road and lifted into the air.

www.ingramcontent.com/pod-product-compliance
Lightning Source LLC
Chambersburg PA
CBHW031600240626